Winterman

Alex Walters

First published in 2019 by Bloodhound Books

www.bloodhoundbooks.com

Print ISBN 978-1-912986-15-6

Also By Alex Walters

DI Alec Mckay Series

Candle & Roses (Book 1)
Death Parts Us (Book 2)
Their Final Act (Book 3)

Praise For Alex Walters

"As soon as I finished the book I went and downloaded the first book in the series now as clearly I've been missing out on some excellent writing!! Definitely an author I'm going to be looking for in the future - a superb book!!!" **Donna's Book Blog**

"Death Parts Us is a highly entertaining and gripping read. Scotland's Black Isle is very much brought to life by the author and I felt like I was stood next to the characters absorbing everything that was around them. Great book and highly recommended." **Sarah Hardy – Goodreads**

"Another truly fascinating episode in the DI Alec McKay series of detective stories. Set amongst the glorious scenery of the Scottish Highlands, this crime thriller will keep the reader gripped from start to finish." **Amazon Reviewer**

"Alex Walters creates a very atmospheric feeling when youre reading,the descriptive writing makes you feel that you are 'right there' in the story." **Hammers – Amazon Reviewer**

February, 1947

The sound of the rain woke him again.

He lay for a long time, his eyes open, staring into the darkness, listening to the sounds. The rhythmic beating on the roof, the clattering of spray against the window, the roar of water along the gutters, spewing into the downspouts.

Endless noise, and his body held as if in chains.

He struggled towards full consciousness, a deep-water swimmer struggling towards the light.

Then he twisted in the large double bed, his mind suddenly free of constraint, his limbs tangled in the blankets and eiderdown. He felt the chill of the bedroom on his exposed face and hands.

There was silence. No sound of rain. No sound at all.

He pulled himself to a sitting position, conscious of the emptiness of the bed. The room was cold, and he shivered even in his thick flannel pyjamas. He put his bare feet to the hard wooden floor and reached for the dressing gown which, as always, he had left draped across one of the bedposts.

He could hear nothing but his own breathing and, as he rose, the soft pat of his footsteps on the polished floorboards. The room was pitch black, and he realised how well he knew it. He could find his way blindly through the maze of heavy wooden furniture – the bed itself, the wardrobe, the dressing table, the chest by the window. His old room.

He considered switching on the light but felt more comfortable in the darkness. Walking blind, he could pretend everything was the same, that nothing had changed.

He made his way to the window, his bare feet feeling the textures of the wood, the thick bedside rug, the thinner matting by the bedroom wall. Everything as he remembered.

For a moment, he was confused by the position of the wooden chest. He stumbled over its solid bulk, scraping his shin. Someone must have moved it, he thought. Then he recalled he had moved it himself, to prop open the door while airing the house.

He pulled back the heavy floor-length curtain, feeling a blast of icy air on his face. The window was clouded, and as he reached out to wipe the pane he saw it was coated inside with a thin film of ice.

He rubbed at the glass and peered into the night. Long past midnight.

Outside, the darkness was not quite complete. There was a sliver of moon riding above billowing dark clouds, a scattering of stars.

Below him, the landscape stretched away, flat fields and fenland as far as he could see. The bleak empty landscape of his boyhood.

But no rain. No sign of any rain.

Summer, 1940

When Mary opened her eyes, for a moment she was dazzled. Then she was lost in the air, as if poised to dive into the deepest, bluest sea she could imagine.

All she had was imagination. Tropical seas in far off corners of the globe. A dazzling blue, literally a world away from the grey-green of the flat North Sea on their day trips to Skegness and Mablethorpe.

On a day like this you could pretend. You could pretend you were somewhere other than here. With some life other than this one. Some future other than this.

She closed her eyes again, enjoying the soft radiance of the sun on her face, the mellow tapestry of birdsong, the brush of the breeze through the leaves. Somewhere further away, she could hear the boys' shouts, the splashing water. She had slept for a while earlier and could feel drowsiness creeping over her again.

'We should be thinking about getting back soon.'

A shadow blocked the sun, and for a moment she thought it was starting to rain. She opened her eyes. Paul was looming over her. Beyond him, the sky was as clear as ever.

'Get away,' she said. 'You're dripping all over me.'

'Sorry.' He obligingly took a step backwards, still towelling his hair. 'Glorious day, isn't it?'

'Beautiful. How's the water?'

'Freezing. But that's good. You should have come in.'

She touched her hair. 'Do you know how much this cost? Need to look my best for tomorrow.'

'Not setting your cap at the boss, I hope?'

She laughed. 'Hardly. I just want to make a good impression. It's a big opportunity.'

He finished drying his torso and threw himself onto the grass beside her. He lay on his back, still in his swimming trunks, and stared up at the cloudless sky. 'Just so long as you remember us lesser mortals when you've made it to the top.'

She closed her eyes again, taking a last chance to relax. 'I don't think that helping out the MD's secretary counts as making it to the top.'

'You wait. It'll be the first step to greatness.' He paused for a beat. 'Unless the MD's married already, of course.'

Without looking, she grasped the damp towel he'd dropped between them and flung it on to his bare chest. Still lying back, he caught it deftly, rolled it into a ball and tucked it beneath his head. 'Very comfortable. I could grow to like this.'

So could we all, she thought. It was the fantasy she occasionally allowed herself. That this glorious summer really could go on forever. Sunshine. Youth. Innocent pleasure. No threats, nothing to disturb it. Peace.

As if in mocking response to her thoughts, she could hear, away in the far distance, the monotonous hum of an aircraft. Paul had heard it too and he sat up, his hand held above his eyes, squinting at the sky. 'One of ours. Sounds out of formation. Wonder if he's in trouble.'

She followed his gaze, but there was nothing to be seen. Already, the drone of the aeroplane was fading. Little more than a half-heard echo, lost in the gentle sounds of summer. But that was the reality. This was just a respite, a brief pause before the real business of life resumed again. Tomorrow, and the days after that, everything would be different.

Mary looked about her. She could see the sparkling water of the clay pits through the trees, hear the splash of the swimming boys, the rhythmic shouts of some game they were playing. Their bicycles lay scattered randomly across the grass. A few feet away there was a tartan blanket with the remains of the picnic they'd brought for lunch.

She wondered what the next year – the next few months – would bring. Some of the boys were old enough to be called up before too long. If the war lasted that long. Since the retreat from France, nobody seemed to know what would happen next. They heard about the German bombers on the wireless, though they'd seen only limited evidence locally, apart from the occasional dumping of bombs by returning aircraft. The boys loved to watch for the dogfights, the Hurricanes and Spitfires dancing in the pale air, but this far north those were still few and far between.

Everyone spoke as if invasion was inevitable. They talked about what they would do when Jerry came, how they would resist, fight back. But that felt like a fantasy too. They prepared for the worst, but no one really believed it. Even though they knew what had happened across Europe, and for all Mr Churchill's rhetoric, it was difficult to imagine these green fields overrun by Nazi soldiers. It felt like some game they were playing.

One way or another, though, they were growing up. She still thought of them as children, a bunch from the village who had gone through school together. But most had left school. The older ones, like her, had been working for a year or two. Some of the younger ones had just finished school this summer. With the war effort, there was no shortage of vacancies. One or two, like Paul, were hoping to stay on at school and had applied for scholarships. But the shadow of the war loomed over all this. If the war continued, it would not be long till at least some of them were liable for call-up.

'When do you think we should be setting off back?'

Paul was fumbling in his rucksack. 'Soon really. We want to get back well before dark.'

Paul was the sensible one, she thought. Although not the eldest of the group, he was the one who organised outings like this, and he was the one who, more or less, kept them in order. She could see him going places. He had a natural authority – not bossy, just calm and in control.

She gazed at him unselfconsciously as he dressed, pulling on his trousers over his still-damp trunks, slipping his arms into his white cotton shirt. He was not yet fifteen, but his body was already growing into adulthood, a sheen of dark hair on his chest. He would be an attractive man, it occurred to her. She had never thought of him in those terms. To her, he was like a younger brother, he and Gary the siblings she'd never had.

Climbing to her feet, she pulled together her own clothes. She momentarily contemplated whether to change out of her swimsuit behind the awkward shelter of her towel, but decided it would be easier to pull on her slacks and shirt over the top. The sun was lower, and the return trip would be in the relative cool of the evening.

As she finished dressing, Paul went to gather the others. It took some time. Some of the younger ones – including, inevitably, Gary – were reluctant to leave the water, responding only to the threat of being left behind.

By the time they'd finished drying, dressing and collecting their various belongings, another half an hour had passed.

Paul was glancing, with mild anxiety, at his watch. 'Come on,' he said, for the third or fourth time. 'We don't want to end up cycling in the blackout. Let's get going.'

Eventually, he had them all mustered and, with a final look around to check nothing had been left, they set out, two or three abreast, along the track leading back to the main road.

It was a pleasant enough cycle ride. The lowering sun dappled them with golden light through dancing patterns of green leaves. The terrain in the woods was uneven, but the cycling would become easier once they reached the road. Paul and Mary were cycling at the head of the group, keeping a steady pace, chatting amiably. Mary was beginning to feel a touch of anxiety about the next day.

'Do you think I'll be all right? Tomorrow, I mean.'

Paul glanced across at her. 'Why wouldn't you be? It's not so different, is it?'

'I suppose not. But in the typing pool, you're just one of a group. You don't really have any contact with the bosses.'

'It won't be so different in the MD's office, I imagine,' Paul said, with the airy confidence of inexperience. 'You'll still be the junior.'

'I know, but I'll feel exposed. I won't be able to hide in the background.' Mary worked for a regional omnibus company. She had been offered a trial promotion to cover for one of the MD's assistants who had recently left to get married. 'I think some of the other girls aren't best pleased that I was chosen. I've only been there a year.'

'It's because you're so good. Why would they have considered anyone else?'

Mary laughed. 'Some of them reckon he might be interested in more than my typing skills.' Although she'd heard one or two catty whispers to that effect, the concern was really her own. She knew she was an attractive girl, well developed for her age. She just hoped this hadn't coloured the MD's decision to offer her the trial.

'Wouldn't surprise me.' Paul grinned. 'We'll see you marrying money one day.'

She had nothing to throw at him, so she contented herself with cycling harder, leaving him momentarily in her wake. She heard him ringing his bell defiantly behind her. Then she heard something else – a shouting from the back of the group.

She slowed and glanced over her shoulder. Paul was doing likewise, and it was clear that there was some consternation among the group. 'What is it?'

'We've lost Gary,' someone said.

She pulled to a halt and turned her bike around. Paul was making his way back into the knot of cycles. 'Who was with him?'

There was a murmur of confusion among the other cyclists. Finally one of Gary's classmates pushed himself forward. 'I was with him when we left. He was riding next to me.'

'Did you see where he went?'

Everyone had come to a stop. Mary looked around the group standing over their cycles. There was no sign of Gary.

The boy shook his head, looking as if he might burst into tears. 'No, he dropped back a bit. Messing about. You know. I assumed he was behind us.'

'Typical,' Paul said. 'Trust Gary to make things difficult. Why can't he just do what he's told?' It was Paul's perennial complaint.

Although the two brothers were as close as siblings could be, they were polar opposites. Where Paul was organised, Gary was chaos personified. Where Paul was considered, Gary invariably acted on impulse. Where Paul was calm, Gary was a fizzing firework, liable to explode at any moment. In part, this reflected their respective ages – Gary was two years Paul's junior – but Mary suspected that, at any age, their characters would remain markedly different.

Paul looked round at the others. 'I'll have to go back. You carry on. We'll catch you up.'

'I can come with you, Paul,' Mary said.

'You don't want to be late getting home.'

'We've plenty of time. And you know Gary. If he thinks it's just you looking for him, he'll carry on playing up. He'll be better behaved if I'm there.'

This was true enough. For all his faults, Gary was generally calmer in Mary's presence. He idolised his elder brother – even if this wasn't always evident in his behaviour – but he genuinely seemed to love his cousin. Perhaps it was because she'd been the first to realise quite how disturbed he was by his displacement. Gary was a city boy, lost in the country, bereft of his parents and all the comforts he'd come to associate with home. Paul had been the same but, Paul being Paul, had taken it calmly in his stride.

Gary had been anything but calm. His response to his new environment, from the first day they'd met him off the train, had been to create havoc. Within the first couple of weeks, he'd created more disruption than the village had known in years. After days of noise and bad behaviour, his teacher had finally run out of potential punishments – even the cane seemed only to worsen his disruptiveness – and had resorted to her last remaining sanction and suspended him from school. But that had simply given him freedom to make trouble during the day – stealing sweets from the village shop, leaving the farm gates open, throwing stones at the church windows. Mrs Griffiths, Mary's mother, had him immediately categorised as a city tearaway, wondering how her brother and sister could have raised such a creature. Wondering, for that matter, how he could be so different from his own polite and thoughtful older brother.

It had been Mary, one afternoon, who'd discovered the truth. Earlier that day, the local policeman had made a visit to their house, with a stern warning that any further misbehaviour on Gary's part would result in more severe punishment than a warning. This was, he'd announced sombrely, Gary's last chance.

An hour or so later, just home from work, Mary had found Gary loitering in the back garden of their cottage. It was obvious he'd been crying. She'd sat down with him, offered him a sweet, and persuaded him to talk, realising very quickly that no-one had been listening to Gary since he'd arrived. Even Paul had ignored him, embarrassed by his younger brother's behaviour.

He was lonely, scared, out of his depth. It wasn't that the Griffiths – Mary and her mother, with Mr Griffiths two years dead – hadn't been kind and generous. They'd done everything they reasonably could to accommodate the two unexpected evacuees, offering shelter within the family rather than as part of the formal programme. But whatever the countryside offered, it wasn't Gary's Nottingham home. He missed his friends, he missed the Trent-side hideaways where they played. He missed his mum and dad. Above all, he missed home.

It was obvious to Mary that Gary's behaviour was largely a reaction to all this. No one would listen to him, so he was making sure no one could ignore him. If that resulted in him being sent home, so much the better.

'You can't go home,' she'd pointed out. 'Your mam and dad want to keep you safe from the bombing.'

'What bombing? I seen no bombing.'

It was a fair point. They'd seen little sign of any bombing round here. From what she'd heard on the wireless, most of the German bombing to date had been concentrated on military and other strategic targets. But there were persistent rumours of a more general threat.

Eventually she'd talked him round, told him about all the good things to do in the village, promised she'd look after him. She was as good as her word, introducing him to children of a similar age, helping him become part of their small community. Paul, who was already becoming popular among his own peers, took the hint and helped his brother also.

Gary's behaviour had rapidly improved, though he remained a different and more volatile character from his elder brother. He'd spent the day at the gravel pits pushing the boundaries of what was permissible – diving from the trees, cannonballing his friends, constantly splashing those who were just drying out. Nothing too untoward, but enough to infuriate his brother.

'All right,' Paul said finally. 'We'll both go back.' He turned to the others. 'You might as well carry on. Don't want Gary ruining your night as well. We'll probably catch you up.'

There were two possibilities. Either Gary had decided that there was still time for one last swim before they headed back, or he was deliberately trying to antagonise Paul. Both were equally likely. Gary's lack of common sense was matched only by his desire for mischief.

As they cycled back through the woods, Mary appealed to Paul not to be too hard on his younger brother. 'He's just a kid. Wants some attention.'

'I'll give him attention. Wait till I catch the little so and so.'

The sun was low in the sky, and already the woods felt like a different place. The shadows of the trees were lengthening, and the shards of gold between the leaves were darkening. The heat of the day was passing too, and Mary could feel the chill of the evening breeze on her bare legs.

This had never been a favourite place for her. She would happily come here for a picnic and a swim with the rest of them, and on a fine summer's day the place was welcoming enough. But there was something about the flooded gravel pits, the dense woodland around, that made her uneasy. Now, as the afternoon waned, she felt that unease growing.

'Gary!' Paul shouted. 'Where are you?' He pulled up as they approached the gravel pits and looked around. 'Come on. Stop messing about. We need to get back.'

Mary came up behind him. 'Any sign?'

'Not yet. Little so and so must be hiding somewhere.' He climbed off the bike and wheeled it a few more yards towards the water. 'Gary! We haven't time for this. If we don't get back now, we'll be cycling in the blackout.'

No fun, as she'd discovered, trying to navigate the country lanes without lights.

There was silence, other than the rising whisper of the wind in the leaves.

'Gary! I'm warning you, if you don't come out in a minute, we'll set off without you.'

It was a hollow threat, Mary thought. Whatever his irritation, there was no chance of Paul leaving before finding Gary.

She peered about her, trying to spot some movement among the rippling trees. 'Gary,' she called, trying to sound less intimidating than Paul. 'Come on, love. We've really got to go now or we'll all be in trouble.'

No response. The wind was increasing, a chill easterly blowing from the coast as twilight thickened. She pulled her cardigan more tightly around her shoulders.

Paul was beginning to look worried. 'Where is he?'

'He's just messing about,' she said, but she was feeling anxious. Gary could be an idiot, but he must realise that night was coming.

'We probably missed him,' Paul said after a moment. 'He could have taken a short-cut through the woods.'

She nodded. 'He might not even have come back here. Might have just gone off the road for some reason. He's probably caught up with the others already.'

'Having a laugh at our expense.'

'Quite likely.'

Paul took a few more steps past the gravel pits. Beyond them were the ruined remains of an old farm building, scarcely more than a few low fragments of wall and some uneven stone slabs. It was the kind of place Gary would have chosen to hide.

'I don't know what's best to do,' Paul said. 'If we head back and he's not there…' He left the sentence unfinished, but Mary knew Paul wouldn't forgive himself if Gary were left alone there as night fell.

'I could cycle back and try to catch up with the others,' she said. 'But that wouldn't really help, would it?'

'Not really. And I'm not sure I like the idea of you cycling back on your own.'

She smiled, partly at his gallantry and partly at the notion that this fifteen-year-old boy could be her protector. The truth was, though, she'd have every confidence in him.

'What then?'

'I don't know. All I can think is we wait a bit longer, have another shot at trying to find him. If we can't, I suppose that means he probably has already made his way back.'

'I should think so.' She hoped her voice carried sufficient conviction.

Paul laid his bicycle carefully on the ground and made his way towards the ruin. On the far side of the old building there was an equally derelict farm track, uneven and overgrown with weeds, which had once led down to a long-abandoned farmhouse on the far side of the woods. Earlier on, while they had been swimming, they had seen an occasional passing hiker striding in that direction.

Mary watched as Paul approached the remains of the old building, his eyes scanning the surrounding trees for any sign of his brother. He climbed over the nearest broken wall into what once would have been the interior of the building. She saw him stop, and then his body stiffen.

'What is it?' she called.

He looked back at her. 'Mary, come and look at this.' He was staring into one corner of the ruined edifice, where two low pieces of walling, no more than eight or nine bricks high, still remained.

She hurried to join him, bruising her ankle as she climbed awkwardly over the wall. Her eyes followed where he was looking. Lying in the dark corner, as if thrown there, was a child's bicycle. She was not close enough to make out much detail, but she knew it was Gary's.

Paul bent over. As he straightened up, she saw that he was holding something in his hand. It took her a moment to recognise Gary's canvas rucksack, containing his swimming trunks, the remains of his sandwiches and a few other childish bits and pieces.

Without speaking, Paul looked around. The sun was low and the evening shadows were thick on the ground. Other than the bike and the bag, there was no sign of Gary.

'I think we'd better contact the police,' Paul said at last.

Part One

February 1947

CHAPTER ONE

'Hey, Reverend. Tell us your ghost story.'

Joseph Fisher raised his head wearily and lifted his bloodshot eyes from his pint glass. He stared at the young men by the bar, surrounded by half-hearted Christmas decorations, some homemade, most already faded. All reused from past years, Fisher thought. Make do and mend.

It was that one again. The son of the professor, or whatever the old bastard was supposed to be these days. The young one training to be a doctor, someone had said. Too young to have fought presumably. Set to make himself a packet, the way things were heading. Always a damn sight too familiar.

'Go on,' the young man said again. He was drunk, Fisher thought. Not as drunk as Fisher himself, perhaps, but that went without saying these days. 'It's a terrific story.' The young man – what was his name? William? – was appealing to his companions. They looked uninterested, embarrassed.

Fisher's eyes were fixed, unblinking, on the young man's florid face. Cheeky young bugger, he thought. What gives you the right? There was a time, not so long ago, when the young showed more respect. More respect to Fisher, certainly, though he could hardly complain about how things had turned out. Everything was changing. There were times when he was glad he wouldn't live to see where the changes might lead.

The young man had moved closer and was hovering over Fisher's table, looking penitent, but clearly reluctant to let the matter go.

'No offence, Reverend. But it is a terrific story. Perfect for this time of year.' He spoke with the exaggerated enunciation of the very drunk. 'You told me–'

Fisher stared up at the eager young man, who was swaying slightly over the table. Instinctively, Fisher's hand tightened protectively around his glass. 'Not now,' he said, struggling for some way to end the unwanted conversation, willing the young man to turn away.

Instead, the young man clumsily pulled across a chair from an adjoining table, turned it so the back was facing Fisher, and sat down, straddling the seat, peering over the back.

Like the cartoon of Chad, Fisher thought. Wot, no petrol? Another East Anglian, or so they said. The young man had a careworn look, his fair hair already thinning, his glazed eyes troubled.

'I'm sorry,' he said, his earlier enthusiasm apparently drained away. 'I've had too much to drink.'

Fisher raised his own glass and took a deep swallow. Mild and bitter. There was a time when Fisher would have made a joke as he ordered the drink. Mild and bitter. The story of his life. But that joke had ceased to be funny a long time before. 'You should probably go home,' he said, as calmly as he could.

'I'd like to hear you tell the story,' the young man said, his tone unexpectedly earnest.

Fisher shook his head. 'You wouldn't. Not that, or any other story.'

'Yes, but–'

'Just go. Your friends are waiting for you.'

The young man glanced over his shoulder. His companions were clustered around the bar, drinking and smoking, paying him no attention. Fisher could hear the boys talking enthusiastically about Bradman's innings in the First Test, about the hammering England had received. It didn't look as though the young man's presence was being missed.

'I just thought–'

'I know what you thought. Now please go.'

The young man looked bewildered, as though some carefully laid plan had gone awry. 'I don't–'

'Go.'

The young man nodded slowly, and pushed himself to his feet. He looked more drunk than ever, propped against the wooden chair. He opened his mouth as if to say something more, then seemed to think better of it. Staggering slightly, he stumbled back across to the bar and his companions.

Fisher could still hear the young men talking, perhaps about him, but he made no effort to listen. He had heard it all before, whatever it was. He looked down at his empty glass. Nearly last orders. He knew how to pace his drinking, stay sober enough so he didn't embarrass himself, still manage the long walk to the cottage. There was half a bottle of cheap whisky waiting for him there, which would furnish a nightcap or two.

He rose and stood for a moment, recovering his breath from the small exertion. He suddenly felt drunker than he had for years.

His ghost story.

He shuffled out from behind the table and made his way to the bar. The landlord glanced across with a raised eyebrow, the closest he usually came to acknowledging Fisher's presence. The crowd of young people parted as Fisher approached, moving back automatically. Someone was talking incoherently about Monty's departure from Palestine.

The professor's son was still blocking Fisher's path, his head wreathed in a cloud of smoke from a noxious-smelling cigar. Fisher gently tapped him on the shoulder. He turned and stared at Fisher as if he had never seen the old man before.

'You were wrong, you know,' Fisher said quietly.

'Wrong?' The young man gazed through him, his eyes unfocused.

'It's not a good story for this time of year. It's the worst story for this time of year.'

'I–'

But Fisher was already moving past him, heading towards the front doors. It was busy in there, he realised – he had barely noticed earlier – and there was a rising hubbub of noise from the lounge bar next door.

He stepped outside, the fresh air filling his lungs. The door swung closed behind him, and the silence took him by surprise, as if he had unexpectedly entered another world.

The clear sky was heavy with stars, giving some light even though the moon had not yet risen. The flat fields stretched out on all sides. It was surprisingly mild for December, despite the lack of cloud cover. There had been a cold spell a week or so back, but the temperature had risen again. Perhaps that was it for this winter, he thought. There would be the new year, then the spring. A new start for some.

His head still felt oddly fogged. He made his way along the high street, heading towards the north end of the village. His own cottage lay outside the village boundary, squatting in isolation. Not really his own cottage, of course. Another of the ties that helped ensure his silence.

His ghost story.

He walked slowly, conscious of his own unsteadiness and the roughness of the stones beneath his feet. It was perhaps a mile to the cottage – not a long walk, but long enough for Fisher.

The midwinter fields and fens looked ghostly enough. Miles of flat openness, bleak in full daylight, eerie by starlight. Other than the pub's small scattering of lights, there was no sign of human habitation. Saturday evening. Those not out would already be in their beds, sleeping, reading, listening to *Saturday Night Theatre* on the wireless. The habits of the blackout died hard – people hid behind their heavy drapes, doors locked. Many had removed their external lights during those dark years and never got around to replacing them. More ghosts.

He passed another cottage, its door firmly closed, its windows unlit. He couldn't recall whether anyone still lived there or whether, like so many, they had moved on or simply never returned.

There was no such question about the next cottage, the building that marked the northern edge of the village. The last cottage before his own. Fisher couldn't remember when the

Mortons had moved out. Just before the war, he thought. The father, George Morton, a heavily built, red-faced brute of a man, who had earned his living as a handyman – a jack of all trades who had turned his hand, with equal ineptitude, to bricklaying, plumbing, plastering, even electrics towards the end. He had lost a young daughter. Literally lost. She had disappeared one day on her way to school and was never found. A month after her disappearance, Morton had collapsed, dead instantly of a massive heart attack in his mid-forties.

The cottage had been another part of the estate owned by Lord Hamshaw, the local MP, and the bereaved Morton family – a harassed-looking wife and a second small girl – could no longer afford the tenancy. They moved away, back to the wife's family up near Wisbech. Since then the building had been empty, another minor product of wartime inertia. The children had thrown stones through the windows, dared one another to enter its dank interior, broken down its doors. After a while, stones and bricks and tiles had been surreptitiously removed by neighbours, in some cases contributing, with ironic justice, to repairing Morton's own botched-up work.

Now the place was a half-ruin, windows broken, roof half-collapsed, door gaping blankly open. Fisher hardly gave it a glance, his mired brain unfazed by its shadows and emptiness.

He was almost past the cottage when he realised his bladder was uncomfortably full. It was another half-mile or so home. He glanced back over his shoulder. The road was deserted, but he retained an incongruous sense of clerical decorum. The old proprieties died hard.

A rough path led past the side of the deserted cottage, providing access to the fields at the rear. Cursing mildly, he felt his way down the track, seeking privacy from the road.

The back of the house lay open to the track. By the dim starlight, Fisher could make out a stone yard, a gaping rear door, two blank broken windows, some scattered debris. He stumbled on to the stone flags, out of sight of the road, and fumbled with his fly buttons.

Afterward, when they were asking him what had happened, he realised he didn't know what had caught his attention. Some movement. Something skittering across his peripheral vision. A mouse or a rat, heading for the dark interior. Perhaps something else.

Whatever it was, it caused him to stop his fumbling and turn to peer at the open rear doorway. He straightened, holding his breath, straining to hear any sound.

There was nothing, not even a breeze. He stepped forward, squinting into the darkness.

At first, he could see nothing beyond the black rectangle of the doorway. To the left, there was a broken chunk of wood, jagged at the end – part of the original back door. To the right, there was another object – an old plant pot, earth scattered across the stone.

He took another step. He could see something, a shapeless mess of angles and curves. He felt a memory being stirred, somewhere deep in his mind.

Somehow, despite the darkness, it was clear to him. He could see the twisted legs, the neat shoes, the dishevelled little coat. He even thought – though this had to be a trick of memory – he could see a pale pink bonnet that lay, further inside, discarded on the dirty kitchen tiles.

He stood, frozen, his mind struggling to comprehend what his eyes were seeing. Unexpectedly, as if from another life, he heard distant voices. Singing, someone shouting. Chucking out time.

No, he thought. Not again.

Not his ghost story.

CHAPTER TWO

'The good news,' she said, preceding him up the narrow stairway, 'is that, as senior officer on site, you get an office to yourself.'

He followed her, a battered briefcase in his hand, awaiting the inevitable punchline. The sunlight caught his eyes as they reached the upper landing, dazzling him momentarily. Outside, the snow still lay thick on the ground, as it had for weeks.

'The bad news,' she went on, in what he assumed was a well-rehearsed monologue, 'is that this is the office.' She threw open the door and ushered him inside. As he crossed the threshold, he noticed the carefully hand-painted sign. DI Cross. What had happened to DI Cross, he wondered.

In fact, the office wasn't too bad. Smaller than most functioning broom cupboards, but that would at least discourage visitors. There was a heavy mahogany desk, too large for the room, a couple of battered-looking chairs, an old olive-green filing cabinet. A battered cork noticeboard with an old calendar pinned in the centre. 1945. Had that been left by DI Cross?

There was a view as well. The office looked out on to the yard at the rear, away from the town on to the snow-covered fields, the familiar flat fen land, the empty blue of the winter sky. She had already moved past him to the window and was fumbling with the catch. 'I'll let in some air,' she said. 'It's a little stuffy.'

He nodded, happy to let her get on with things. This was, he assumed, just her way of establishing her domain. He had no problem with that. As the new man, it was best to know where you stood.

'I hope you'll be happy here, Inspector.'

Winterman smiled. It wasn't necessarily the adjective he'd have chosen, but he recognised the sentiment was well meant. 'I'm sure I will be, Miss…?'

She smiled back at his transparent flattery. 'Mrs Sheringham.' There was a momentary hesitation, as if she were about to offer her Christian name.

'You're the…' He paused, unsure of the correct terminology. 'Office Manager?'

She laughed, an attractively musical sound. 'That sounds terribly important. I'm just a secretary, really.'

'But the place would fall apart without you, I'm sure.' Winterman joined in with her laughter, but he knew enough about the likes of Mrs Sheringham to be confident he spoke the truth. For all her bouncing blonde curls and pneumatic figure, she would run this place with an iron discipline. In any case, he noted she didn't bother to contradict him.

He moved across to join her at the window. 'Decent view,' he said.

She followed his gaze. 'I suppose so, if you like that kind of thing.'

It wasn't entirely clear to Winterman what kind of thing she had in mind. 'It's been a cold winter though,' he offered.

'Very. And turning even colder, they say.' There was a faint suggestion of an undertone to her words. Perhaps he would need to be careful.

He stepped away and dropped his briefcase on to the desk top, hoping to convey a business-like air. 'So how many are we here?'

'They didn't tell you?' Her tone suggested this was hardly surprising, though it wasn't clear whether the implied criticism was directed at him, or at those who had failed to provide the information.

'Not really. Everything was a bit rushed. It's a small unit though, I understand?'

'You could say that. There's you and two DCs. A part-time clerk. And me of course.'

'It sounds plenty.' He immediately wondered whether his words were tactless. 'Unusual though. A separate unit like this. I'm surprised we've not been swallowed up by headquarters.'

Her eyes narrowed, as though she was applying some kind of test. 'It will happen,' she said, with untroubled certainty. 'It's all about money these days, isn't it? We're really just an accident of history.'

'Are we?' Winterman thought he might as well try the desk out for size. He sat down carefully, gazing at Mrs Sheringham as she stood silhouetted against the window.

'The unit. There was some dispute about where we belonged. Then, when the war came along, I suppose they had bigger fish to fry.'

Winterman opened his briefcase, wondering whether there was anything he could put out on the desk. Apart from a small pocket diary, he could see nothing. 'It's the same story everywhere. Whatever else it was, the war was a great excuse. No doubt the Act will sort it all out in due course.'

'No doubt,' she said, without obvious conviction. The Police Act, passed the previous year, had been intended to rationalise the structure of local Constabularies. No one really believed its impact would be more than cosmetic. 'Though I imagine for the moment they're pleased to have us here.'

There was nothing untoward in her tone, but Winterman took her words as a mild rebuke. Enough small talk. 'I suppose I should meet people,' he said. 'The others, that is.' He had seen the two DCs downstairs as Mrs Sheringham had led him through the building, both sitting upright behind their desks. Trying to look busy, he thought, though with no conspicuous success. He had nodded to them, but Mrs Sheringham, determined to make her own presence felt, had given him no opportunity to stop and talk.

She moved away from the window and stood by the door. 'Would you like to see them up here?'

Winterman looked around at the limited floor space, the single chair facing him. 'I think we'll risk a little informality downstairs, don't you?' He was careful to smile as he spoke, but there was no reciprocal expression from Mrs Sheringham.

'As you wish, Inspector.'

CHAPTER THREE

Mrs Griffiths sat up suddenly, her eyes wide but still unfocused. It took her a moment to realise what had happened. She had fallen asleep, sitting there in the armchair. Her library book – a new Georgette Heyer that had not yet caught her interest – had slipped from her lap to the rug.

It's age, she thought. *I never used to fall asleep in the daytime.*

She glanced at the old carriage clock on the mantelpiece. How long had she been sleeping? Not long. Perhaps a quarter of an hour. The power restrictions meant the electricity was out till mid-afternoon, and she had dropped off as it became too dark to read easily. Now, it was nearly four.

But something had changed, even in that short time. She sat back in her chair, trying to work out what it was.

The children. She had the children here today, of course, while Mary was at work. Before, she had been able to hear them playing in the kitchen, a low-level persistent squabble between them like a babble of running water.

Now, the house was silent.

A twinge of anxiety fluttered through her mind. What could happen in fifteen minutes? *Any manner of things*, she thought. Any manner of things.

She pulled herself slowly to her feet, feeling the ache in her joints, and made her way to the kitchen. The door was ajar and, with relief, she saw Ann sitting in the far corner by the cooker, her head down, engaged in some complicated game with her dolls. Mrs Griffiths pushed the door fully open.

'Where's Graham?' she asked.

There was no sign of the boy. Ann continued playing with the dolls, oblivious to the question.

'Ann, where's Graham?'

Finally, the girl looked up at her grandmother. She still gave no response, but glanced across towards the door leading out to the rear of the bungalow. That too was ajar, an icy breeze spilling in from the garden.

Outside, the snow lay thick across the small well-tended garden – across the neat lawn, the straight path her late husband had constructed from old stone inkwells from the school, the bare flower beds, the hedge and the wooden gate that led to the lane beyond.

No sign of Graham.

She peered out across the garden, though there was no place where Graham could be concealed.

'Graham!' she called. There was no response.

She looked down at her carpet slippers, feeling the chill of the air through her thin blouse. She hesitated, wondering whether to go back for her coat. Finally she plunged out into the cold afternoon.

She strode as quickly as she could along the inkwell path, conscious of the snow beneath her feet, the polished stone. It would help no one if she were to slip and injure herself.

She saw that, like the back door, the rear gate was slightly open. She gazed out into the lane beyond.

It was a moment before she spotted him. Across the lane, a dyke separated the road from the snowy fields beyond. Some yards away, a row of wooden planks had been set across the dyke to provide access from the lane into the field. Graham was sitting on the edge of the planks, staring down into the frozen mud below the improvised bridge.

'Graham!' she shouted. 'What are you doing? Come back in at once.' She glanced down the deserted road, suddenly feeling as if they were being observed. 'It's too cold to be out here. And you shouldn't leave the house without asking–'

She stopped, aware that the boy was looking up at her. His expression was puzzled, the face of a child about to ask some unanswerable question.

He looked back down at the darkness beneath the planks. 'Nan, there's something here. What do you think it is?'

CHAPTER FOUR

Winterman followed her slowly down the narrow stairs, with the awkward air of a visiting dignitary on a desultory guided tour.

The offices had clearly once been a domestic residence. The rooms on the upper floor – his own new office, two meeting rooms, a small storeroom, a basic WC – had been converted from bedrooms. On the ground floor, the two DCs were accommodated in what had presumably been the main living room. Mrs Sheringham and the part-time clerk – who seemed to be absent today – shared a smaller, second room, which Winterman assumed had once been the parlour or drawing room. At the rear of the house, they had retained the old kitchen, with a gas ring and a kettle for making tea.

Mrs Sheringham ushered Winterman into the larger office, where the two DCs were still sitting, one ostentatiously perusing an open file, the other with his fingers resting on the keyboard of a large upright typewriter, earnestly scrutinising the text of the report projecting from its carriage. Winterman wondered how long the two men had been sitting in these positions.

Both DCs looked up expectantly, as if they had not noticed his entry until that point. Then, with unexpected co-ordination, they half-rose simultaneously, each hovering behind his desk in an awkward crouch, unsure how to acknowledge Winterman's presence.

This must be how the king feels, Winterman thought. He should have had some suitable banalities prepared to put them at their ease. Instead, he stuck out his hand to the bobbing figure on his left. 'DI Winterman. Good to meet you at last.'

For a second, the DC looked unsure how to respond. Finally, he extended his own hand to shake Winterman's, his expression suggesting this was a wholly unfamiliar social gesture.

'DC Hoxton,' Mrs Sheringham said from behind, with only a faint emphasis on the policeman's rank. 'And this is DC Marsh.'

Winterman turned his attention to Marsh, who returned his handshake with more straightforward enthusiasm. 'Good to meet you, sir. We look forward to working with you.'

The two men could not have been more different. Hoxton was tall, slightly overweight and ineffably lugubrious, his dark eyes regarding Winterman with a mixture of anxiety and suspicion. The resemblance to a bloodhound seemed clichéd, given his profession, but it was undeniable, somehow intensified by a black drooping moustache that he had presumably cultivated deliberately.

Marsh, on the other hand, looked a bundle of uncontrolled nervous energy. Slightly shorter than Hoxton – though still towering substantially above Winterman – he was almost hopping on the spot, constantly brushing back a lank fringe of Brylcreemed black hair that immediately fell down again into his blinking eyes. In contrast to his colleague, he looked genuinely pleased to see Winterman.

Winterman gestured the two men to sit. He pulled up one of the office's numerous hard-backed chairs and lowered himself on to it, careful to position the chair equidistant between the two desks. He glanced back over his shoulder. 'Mrs Sheringham, I wonder whether you'd mind getting us all a cup of tea?'

She opened her mouth as if to challenge his request, then nodded, a smile fixed on her neatly made-up face. 'Of course, Inspector. How do you take yours?'

'Just milk. I'll donate my sugar coupons to the office, if you like.'

She nodded again. 'Sweet enough, Inspector.' She turned on her high heels and vanished into the kitchen.

Winterman turned back to the two DCs. Marsh had a hand to his mouth, apparently suppressing a smirk. Hoxton looked genuinely astonished. It occurred to Winterman that perhaps no one had ever dared make a direct request of Mrs Sheringham before.

'It's good to see you here, sir,' Marsh said again. He sounded unexpectedly sincere.

'What happened to DI Cross?' Winterman looked from Marsh to Hoxton and then back again, smiling blandly.

'Promoted, sir,' Hoxton said. His voice was deep and ponderous, his accent rich with a cockney twang. The overall effect did little to dissipate the impression of a morose canine. 'DCI somewhere in Lincolnshire, I believe. Couple of years ago now.'

'A couple of years ago?' Winterman repeated. 'How long have you been here?'

'Eight years,' Hoxton said, in a tone which suggested this was a matter of infinite regret. Eight long years, he might well have added. 'Came out here just before the war.'

'Only a year for me, sir, ' Marsh added brightly.

'There's been no DI here since Cross left?'

'No, sir,' Marsh said. 'You can see why we're glad to see you. Particularly in the circumstances.'

Winterman could see all too easily. He could even, he supposed, see why they might have chosen him. No one else would want to risk his career in this benighted backwater. 'So who have you reported to?'

'We've notionally been based out of Ely,' Marsh said. 'Reporting to one of the DIs there.'

'He did come down here once,' Hoxton acknowledged.

'Twice,' Marsh corrected. 'You were off sick the second time.'

'Aye. Twice then.'

Winterman observed this exchange, his neck twisting like a spectator's at a tennis match. *A variety act*, he thought. They had this routine off pat.

Behind him, the kitchen door opened and Mrs Sheringham reappeared bearing a tin tray holding a teapot, milk jug, sugar bowl and – he noted – four teacups. She had judged him worthy of the best china. He wondered how long that would last.

She placed the tray carefully on Hoxton's desk and poured cups for them all. She poured her own last, and then stood looking down over Winterman. 'Do you need anything else for the moment, Inspector?'

He gazed back at her impassively. 'Not for the moment, Mrs Sheringham, thank you. Please don't let me interrupt your work any further.' Winterman bit his lower lip, conscious that at any moment he might start laughing.

'Not at all, Inspector.' Her own expression was equally unwavering. 'I'm here if you need me.'

She walked silently back into her own office. After a moment, the door closed behind her with a gentle but firm click.

'An impressive lady.' Winterman turned back to the DCs. 'Keeps the place ticking over, I'm sure.'

'She scares the hell out of me, anyway,' Marsh said.

Hoxton shot him a look of what Winterman initially took to be disapproval. Then, unexpectedly, both men burst out laughing.

'She keeps us on our toes all right,' Hoxton said. 'Don't need no DI when she's around.' He suddenly seemed to have relaxed, his posture changing, as he slumped forward across the desk. He still resembled a bloodhound, but now perhaps one about to be taken for a walk.

Winterman was slightly taken aback by the sudden release of tension. But it was not so surprising. The men had been living for days with a substantial responsibility and the prospect of his own impending arrival. Winterman wasn't quite sure what he'd done in these first few minutes, but it appeared it was something right. They obviously thought that, if he could handle Mrs Sheringham, he could handle anything. Perhaps they were right.

'You've seen the file, sir?' Marsh said.

'I've read nothing else for the past two days,' Winterman said. 'Since they decided I was coming here. Not that it leaves me much the wiser.' This was partly, he didn't add, because the quality of the statements left something to be desired. 'Let me make sure I've got it clear. You've got an unidentified body?'

Marsh nodded, as though he might be about to produce the object in question.

'The body of a child,' Winterman went on. 'Aged – what? – between about eight and nine years?'

Hoxton nodded, his former lugubrious manner returned. 'That's what the doctor chap reckoned.'

'A body that's been dead for at least five years?'

'Doctor reckoned he didn't know for sure, but something like that, he said. Body'd been *preserved.*' He spoke the last word with relish. 'Skin was like leather. Doctor reckoned the fens can do that.'

'They didn't know how old the body was at first,' Marsh elucidated. 'Apparently you sometimes find bodies like that in the fens that have been there for decades, centuries even. But the clothes were fairly modern, so they reckon probably between five and ten years.' By contrast with his colleague, Marsh's tone was one of barely suppressed horror.

'So the body's been preserved in the fens, and then it turns up in some deserted cottage in this village – Framley? It couldn't have been there all along?'

'Seems unlikely,' Marsh said. 'Cottage had been empty since before the war. But it's a small village. Folks had been in there. You know, taking stuff that wasn't wanted–'

'Anything as wasn't nailed down,' Hoxton annotated. 'And some stuff as was, I shouldn't wonder.'

'If they were in there helping themselves,' Winterman pointed out, 'they might not have wanted to report anything to us.'

Marsh shrugged. 'If someone had found a child's body, they'd have found some way to let us know, surely. Even anonymously.'

'Aye,' Hoxton agreed, 'and there was kids always in and out of that place. You know, daring each other. If one of them had found a body, they'd have screamed the bloody place down.'

'It was found in the kitchen?'

'Not even just in the kitchen,' Marsh said. 'Half out into the back yard. Not hidden at all.'

Winterman sat back in his chair. 'Maybe some animal dragged it in.'

'Maybe,' Marsh said, sounding unconvinced.

'What about the chap who found the body? Do we see him as a suspect?'

'Possible, I suppose.' Something in Marsh's tone suggested he had more to tell.

'Who is he?' Winterman prompted. 'This Fisher?'

'Fisher,' Hoxton said. 'The Reverend Joseph Fisher.' There was something in Hoxton's tone too, something in the emphasis he placed on Fisher's title. Something a long way from reverence.

'Fisher's a clergyman?' Winterman said in surprise. As far as he could recall, the fact hadn't been noted in his statement or any of the reports.

'Was,' Hoxton said. 'Retired.'

'Tell me about him,' he said. 'Fisher.'

Hoxton glanced across at Marsh, who coughed gently. 'He has a bit of a reputation,' Marsh said.

'What kind of reputation?' In Winterman's experience, retired clergymen always had a bit of a reputation, one way or the other.

Marsh made a drinking gesture with his hand. 'That for one thing. Bit of a lush.'

'And for another thing?'

Another meaningful glance passed between Marsh and Hoxton. Finally, Marsh shrugged. 'There are all kinds of stories,' he said. 'He's not a popular man locally.'

'No?' Winterman nodded. 'What do they say about him?' He had a sense that Hoxton, at least, was not finished yet.

Marsh sat in silence. Hoxton looked across at him, but received no answering glance this time. 'It's not for me to say,' he began finally, with the air of one about to say as much as he wanted. 'But they says he treated his wife badly. And his daughter. And they says more than that.'

'They say a lot of things,' Marsh interposed. 'The way I read it, Fisher never made himself popular. A cold fish, fire and brimstone preacher. Plenty of enemies in the parish. And because of all that, they say–'

Hoxton leaned forward, his eyes fixed on Winterman. 'They says,' he interrupted, 'as how he killed his wife.' He paused, apparently for dramatic effect. 'And as how he killed his young daughter.'

CHAPTER FIVE

Afterwards, she had felt proud of her response, though she was unsure whether that was an appropriate emotion in the circumstances. She had managed to prevent herself from screaming, or even from letting the child see how terrified she was.

'Graham,' she had said quietly. 'Come here. Come here at once.'

The boy was still sitting on the snow-covered planks, legs swinging gently. He was wearing his black wellington boots, she noticed irrelevantly, and he'd put on his green duffle coat and even the bright blue balaclava she had knitted for him. *A good boy*, she thought, who usually did what he was told. He looked up at her.

'Nan. What is it? What is that thing?'

'Come here, Graham. As a quick as you can, love.' She moved a step closer, her eyes fixed on the dyke, the darkness under the rows of planks. She didn't want to look, but she needed to be sure she wasn't just being a hysterical old woman.

The snow-covered lane was still empty, her cottage gate standing open. In the distance, she could see the rest of the village – the church, the pub, the rows of cottages, the land designated to build the new council houses. But no sign of human life, other than herself and the boy.

It suddenly struck her that Ann was alone in the cottage. 'Graham, we need to get back into the house. I think it's going to snow some more.'

He looked up at the empty sky, the scattering of grey clouds to the east. 'Do you think so, Nan?'

'I think so, love. You can't be too careful. Come here.'

Reluctantly, the boy climbed to his feet and stepped carefully across the snowy planks. His grandmother took his hand, her eyes flickering towards the shadows beneath his feet.

'Nan, what's–?'

'Let's get inside, love. Then we can talk.' She felt his tiny fingers between hers, the warmth of his hand. Her mind was racing ahead, wondering what she would say to him. Wondering how she might get to a telephone. How she could let someone know.

'Come on, Graham. Hurry up, love.' She was almost pulling his hand, her steps quickening as she reached the garden gate.

She glanced back towards the dyke. She could still see it in her mind, as vividly as if it were burned into her retina. The tiny fist of bone, skeletal fingers slightly unclenched, raised upwards as though reaching into the air. As though seeking help.

CHAPTER SIX

'Look what the cat's dragged in.'

For once, there was no real venom in Professor Callaghan's voice. His tone suggested he was past all that, that all he felt was weariness, an endless impossible burden.

William stopped in the doorway and regarded the old man. 'Do I look as bad as I feel then?'

'Only if you feel like a recently exhumed corpse.'

'That just about sums it up. With your characteristic precision.'

'You were back late.' It wasn't a question.

'I was back early,' William corrected. 'The wee small hours.'

Callaghan had commenced the endless ritual that would conclude with the lighting of his pipe. 'I know exactly when. You made enough noise about it.'

William slumped in the armchair opposite his father. 'Sorry if I woke you.' His tone was devoid of any conspicuous regret.

'I was awake.'

'And why wouldn't you be? Do you ever sleep?'

The old man was still fumbling with his pipe, tapping the bowl into a metal bin by his armchair, blowing down the stem, selecting an appropriate measure of tobacco. 'How long do I have to put up with this?'

'With what?' William had climbed restlessly to his feet again, and was prowling up and down by the mahogany drinks cabinet, inspecting the contents through the leaded glass.

'With this. With you,' his father said. 'How long are you planning to stay this time?'

'Is there any hurry?'

Callaghan looked up at him, then pointed with the pipe stem. 'You're supposed to be at medical school. Making something of yourself.'

'It's the Christmas vac.'

'Christmas has been and gone,' the old man said. 'I'd be grateful if you'd consider doing the same.'

'The paternal spirit.' William had pulled open the drinks cabinet and lifted out an expensive-looking malt. It was unclear whether his words were addressed to his father or the bottle.

'I don't want you here,' Callaghan said. 'Is that clear enough?'

'Perfectly.' William had found a glass in the bottom of the cabinet and was in the process of pouring himself a generous measure of the whisky. 'As clear as this delightful liquid. Can I get you one?'

'For God's sake, William. It's three o'clock in the afternoon. You've only just managed to drag yourself out of bed.'

'I know.' William slumped back down into the armchair, spilling some of the whisky across his white shirt. 'Ain't life grand.'

'Look at you. You can barely hold that glass steady. And you're training to be a surgeon.'

'Makes it more of a challenge. Can't have things too easy, can we? You've always made that principle very clear.'

'I don't recall you ever taking much notice of anything I might have to say.'

'You'd be surprised.'

'I think the only surprises you've ever given me have been unpleasant ones.' Callaghan had struck a match and was holding the flame to the bowl of the pipe. 'Though there have been plenty of those.'

William looked at the old man over the top of the nearly drained whisky glass. 'You really hate me, don't you?' he said, as if the thought had only just occurred to him.

Callaghan laughed suddenly. 'Do they teach you some psychology on that course of yours then?' He puffed on the pipe, clouds of noxious smoke drifting in William's direction. 'Freud and all that.'

William shook his head. 'I don't think Freud got it right. He'd say I should want to kill you.' He paused, and swallowed the last of the whisky.

'You don't agree?' The old man was wreathed in smoke, his bald head shining in the afternoon sunset.

'No,' William said, rising from his chair. 'No, I don't. Funnily enough, it's always seemed to me that quite the opposite is true.'

CHAPTER SEVEN

It was turning even colder, Winterman thought. A chill wind was sweeping across the flat fields, low grey clouds scurrying across the sky. 'We could get more snow,' he shouted to Marsh, who was driving. 'Wouldn't surprise me.'

As far as Winterman could remember, before the war hardly anyone knew how to drive. Now everybody seemed to have learnt – in the forces or the Home Guard or whatever they'd been doing. Marsh seemed a capable enough driver, but Winterman hadn't asked him where he'd picked up the skills. It was better to be cautious about enquiring into others' backgrounds. Those who'd had a bad war didn't want to talk about it, and those who'd had a good one were often even more reticent.

'How much further?' he asked.

It was late afternoon, and already growing dark outside. The snow-bound fields were eerie under the pale, heavy sky – the contrasting black lines of dykes, the drifts against the low hedgerows, an occasional angular scarecrow dispassionately observing their passing. The main road had been cleared for the moment, but, apart from an agricultural truck that had sped past shortly after leaving the town, they had seen no other traffic.

'Couple of miles,' Marsh said. He was driving more cautiously than Winterman might have expected, given his excitable manner back in the office.

'This is Framley again?' Winterman looked over his shoulder at Hoxton, who was hunched in the rear seat.

'Just outside anyway,' Hoxton said. It was clear, not least from Marsh's good-natured but recurrent jibes about inbreeding, that Hoxton, though not a native, had lived in the area for some years.

Marsh was a definite incomer – born in one of the rougher parts of Nottingham, he had said, though he'd given no reason for his move eastwards.

'And the same story,' Winterman mused, as if to himself.

Marsh shrugged. 'We'll see.'

'Bloody coincidence though, ain't it?' Hoxton said. 'Our Mary, I mean. Of all people.'

'Suppose so,' Marsh said. 'But it's a small world.' He peered through the front screen at the empty landscape. He had turned on the headlights, and it was as if their existence had been reduced to the narrow yellow cones of light. 'Anyway, somebody had to find it.'

The call had interrupted their meeting, and Winterman had never discovered quite why or how the Reverend Fisher was said to have to killed his young daughter. He had assumed from Marsh's demeanour that the truth would be less startling than had been suggested by Hoxton's melodramatic pronouncement.

In any case, the call had been startling enough. It had come from the local police station that covered Framley and the surrounding villages – a shocked-sounding village PC reporting that a body had been found in one of the nearby dykes. Winterman had taken the call, transferred from Mrs Sheringham, and had at first assumed the man was talking about the victim of some farming accident.

'Do you have any reason to suspect foul play?' Winterman had enquired, as gently as he could. 'I mean, do you think this is a case for CID?'

'CID?' the policeman said, as if the concept was unfamiliar.

'Yes,' Winterman said patiently. 'You know, detectives. Plain clothes.' It was conceivable that the man had never had reason to deal with the sister branch of the force.

'Don't know about that. It was Mrs Griffith asked me to phone you.'

'Mrs Griffiths?' Perhaps this was some kind of local celebrity. Winterman felt he had a lot to learn.

'Yes, Mrs Griffiths,' the man went on patiently. 'Mary's mam.'

'Mary's mam?' It was possible that the man was mad. Or drunk. Most likely drunk.

'Mrs Griffiths said she might well be there.'

Winterman lifted his head, placing his hand across the Bakelite mouthpiece. 'Does anyone know a Mrs Griffiths?'

Hoxton nodded. 'Aye. Mary's mam.'

'So I understand,' Winterman said. 'Who's Mary?'

'Mary,' Hoxton repeated. 'Works here.'

Winterman glanced across at Mrs Sheringham. 'You're not–?'

She shook her head, perhaps more vehemently than strictly necessary. 'Mary's my assistant. Works part-time.'

Winterman nodded, finally beginning to make sense of the telephone conversation. He spoke back into the mouthpiece. 'I'm afraid Mary's not in today. Is she the reason you called here, Constable–?' He realised that the PC had not so far revealed his identity.

'Brain. Bryan Brain. That's Bryan with a y,' Brain had added, apparently for the avoidance of any doubt.

Winterman found he was chewing on the inside of his cheek. 'Well, PC Brain. I think your best bet is probably to call Divisional HQ and report it to them. I take it you've already called an ambulance–'

'Bit late for that.' Brain's tone had become more clipped, as though suspecting that Winterman was not taking his call seriously.

'You can't be too–'

'Years too late, I'd say.'

There was a moment's silence. 'You mean this isn't a recent fatality?' Winterman said at last.

'Could put it like that,' Brain said. 'What with it being a skeleton and all.'

'I see. So do you have any idea how long–?'

'Poor little thing. Shocking to see.'

'Poor little thing?' Winterman had a sudden startled suspicion that perhaps they were talking about the body of some domestic animal, rather than a human being.

'Aye. I'm no expert, but not more than nine or ten, I'd say. Just a child.'

Winterman looked up at the others in the office. Marsh was watching him eagerly, as if trying to learn something from Winterman's example. Hoxton was slumped back in his chair, discreetly picking his nose. Mrs Sheringham was hovering nearby, determined not to be excluded from whatever might result from the telephone call.

'You think these are the remains of a child?' Winterman said slowly. 'Is that what you're telling me?'

'Isn't that what I've been saying?' It was Brain's voice that now took on a note of condescension. 'We've found the skeleton of a child.'

That had been an hour earlier. Slightly to Winterman's surprise, Hoxton had revealed that the unit had the use of a police car, an unmarked black Wolseley, garaged at the rear of the building. The information had been volunteered readily enough, but Winterman was left with the suspicion that, prior to his own arrival, the two constables had effectively commandeered the vehicle for their own use, along with the even more valuable petrol ration that accompanied it.

As they had climbed into the stately vehicle, he had wondered how often the car had previously been used for official business.

Whatever its history, the car had been maintained in perfect condition, and Winterman had been glad of its relative comfort as they travelled through the darkening afternoon. They had sat in silence for much of the journey, watching the white landscape, each of them lost in his own thoughts.

'Tell me about Mary,' Winterman said at last. 'Mary Griffiths?'

'Mary Ford,' Marsh corrected. 'Widow.'

'Her husband–?'

'Killed in the war.'

'Not even a bloody hero,' Hoxton said morosely from the back of the car.

Winterman glanced at him in surprise. Another part of the unspoken etiquette. Everyone – especially those who had been called up – had been a hero unless there was good reason to say otherwise.

'Don't get me wrong,' Hoxton went on. 'No disrespect intended. He was one of us before the war – on the force, I mean. Decent bloke and a good copper. Just an unlucky bugger.'

'Unlucky how?'

'Mary doesn't talk about it much,' Marsh said, with an odd edge to his voice. 'He was one of those evacuated at Dunkirk. Was on a fishing boat, got turned over. Not through any enemy action. Just blind panic, I imagine.'

'He died at Dunkirk?' Everyone had their stories, Winterman thought. All different. All the same.

'No,' Hoxton said from the back seat. 'That's just it. That's why he was an unlucky bugger. Nearly drowned at Dunkirk, but was picked up by some Naval launch.'

'Doesn't sound unlucky,' Winterman said. 'Sounds bloody lucky. In the middle of that mêlée.'

'Ah, well. Got picked up – nearly dead from the cold. Touch and go. But he gets shipped back to England and pulls through. That's when he meets Mary, ain't that right, Marshy? Falls in love, gets married. Seized the moment like we all did in them days. Then he's back into training, ready to be shipped out somewhere else. And the poor old sod only goes and gets himself shot.'

Winterman looked back, his eyebrows raised. In his mind, he had already designated Hoxton as the raconteur of the unit, though that was perhaps a generous term. He clearly revelled in local gossip, even when it concerned one of his own colleagues. 'Okay,' Winterman said. 'I'll bite. Shot by whom?'

'By whom?' Hoxton echoed, with only the faintest trace of mockery. 'I don't think even Mary ever found out. It was all hushed up. Some mess up in training, apparently. Shot by one of his own team. One of his mates probably.'

It was hardly a unique story. Not even that unusual, Winterman suspected. Plenty of servicemen had been killed in training accidents, often through their own or someone else's ineptitude. It wasn't even that surprising. Soldiers were, by definition, dispensable, though nobody ever expressed it like that. In this war most of them had been inexperienced, thrown into situations they could never had imagined. Mistakes had inevitably been made, many of them much more serious than this one.

'Poor old Mary was left in the family way,' Hoxton went on. 'He'd been back just long enough for that.'

'Twins too,' Marsh added. 'A boy and a girl.'

'Sounds as if she was the unlucky one,' Winterman said. 'Left on her own.'

'You're right enough there,' Hoxton said. 'She's not had an easy time of it.'

'She works part-time for us?' Winterman asked, vaguely wondering whether there might be scope to extend this arrangement.

'Only through the goodness of Mrs Sheringham's heart,' Marsh said. 'Which shows you how deserving a case she must be. There isn't really the workload to justify it, but Mrs Sheringham pulled a few strings.'

Marsh took his hand momentarily off the steering wheel and gestured in front of them. For the first time, Winterman could make out a line of pale lights in the distance. 'Framley in all its glory. Forty houses and a pub.'

'And a church,' Hoxton said. 'Don't forget the church.'

Winterman nodded. 'I'll try not to.' He had the feeling that, by the end of all this, he might be in need of a little succour. But he was probably more likely to find it in the pub than the church. 'I always try not to.'

CHAPTER EIGHT

PC Brain sometimes worried he was more of a nuisance than a help, but Mrs Griffiths seemed pleased to have had him there, at least until Mary had returned.

'I'd never say no to another nice cup of tea,' he said, though he wasn't entirely sure Mrs Griffiths had actually offered him one.

'I'll go and put the kettle on,' she said. 'You'll be wanting one, Mary?'

Mary looked at her blankly. She seemed even more disturbed by the discovery than her mother had been. 'What?'

'Tea, Mary. You'd like another cup of tea? I'm making some for Bryan.'

'Yes. That would be good, Mam. Thanks.' Mary's eyes were fixed on the twins who were playing together, apparently good-naturedly, in front of the open fire, their heads silhouetted against the nimbus of flames. She looked across at the PC. 'How long are they going to be? Your colleagues, I mean.'

'My coll–?' PC Brain had almost been caught out by the question. He had tried hard earlier to convey the impression that he was accustomed to working alongside his plain-clothed counterparts. 'Not long, I imagine. Probably not easy driving in these conditions.'

'I hope we're not wasting their time.' Her tone suggested she meant the opposite. 'I mean, we don't know for sure what it is.'

PC Brain nodded solemnly. 'Better safe than sorry. Always better to call about something like this, even if it turns out to be nothing.' He had been rehearsing these lines in his head, in case he had to use them in his own justification. He was already beginning to worry he might have been precipitate in calling in CID.

What if there was some innocent explanation? If the bones were not those of a child, but just some animal? Earlier he had been in no doubt, but he had been reluctant to approach the skeleton too closely.

Perhaps he had been over excitable, his judgment clouded by that other body they had found. That had turned up on his day off, and by the time he started his next shift, the team from headquarters had already taken over. Wasn't that typical? The first dramatic case on his beat in years – even the war hadn't brought too much excitement to this neck of the woods – and he hadn't been here to witness it. Perhaps, in his eagerness to get involved, he was about to make a fool of himself.

'I thought they'd be here by now.' Mrs Griffiths re-entered the room bearing a tray containing a pot of tea, three cups and a jug containing as much milk as she felt able to spare.

'Any time now, Mrs Griffiths,' Brain said confidently.

That was his real job, he thought. To reassure, inspire confidence that all was well. It was what he spent most of his time doing, pedalling his burly frame from village to village, dealing with the occasional errant schoolboy or over-inebriated reveller. There was no real crime out here, just the odd misdemeanour for him to dismiss with a sharp word. When Mrs Griffiths had waved him down from her front gate, he had assumed she wanted to chat. Even her anguished expression had raised thoughts only of lost cats or minor vandalism.

Mrs Griffiths busied herself pouring the tea, while her daughter still stared blankly into the crackling coal fire. Finally, Mary looked up. 'Do you really think it is?' she asked.

For a moment, Brain contemplated pretending he didn't know what she meant. But he knew this young woman – the girl he still thought of as Mary Griffiths – well enough to know she was no fool. He lowered his voice, throwing a warning glance towards the youngsters by the fire.

'Another body? I honestly don't know. If it is, I don't know what that might mean.'

'Have they found out anything about the other one?' Her voice was only a notch above a whisper.

In truth, he knew little more than she did. He had tried to call a couple of acquaintances at headquarters, in the hope they might be able to update him on the case. But either they had not known, or they were not saying. The DCI from headquarters had promised to keep him updated, but no one had made any effort to contact him. Any knowledge Brain had was drawn from the regional evening newspaper.

'I don't believe so,' he said finally. 'They've got no reports of anyone missing, as far as I know. But it goes back to the war, so the records aren't always what they might be.'

Mary's eyes were still fixed on the fireplace. 'Poor little thing though. Whoever it is.'

Brain gazed at her, wondering what to say. It wasn't one of his strengths, this side of the job. Bluff, hale and hearty. Those were the kind of adjectives people used to describe him. He could deal authoritatively with the local menfolk – the cynical farmers, the labourers, the returning servicemen, the increasingly disaffected youths. He could chat amiably with the older residents – those who'd known and respected his own parents. He could act tough when he needed to – breaking up a petty brawl outside The Angel on a Friday night, or moving on the gippos who'd camped outside the back of the church.

But the sensitive stuff – he was never comfortable with all that. Once in a while, he had to be the bearer of genuinely bad news – a labourer who'd been trapped in some farm machinery, a child who drowned one summer late in the war somehow trapped head down in a dyke. He wasn't good at it. He delivered the news ineptly, insensitively, often even more distraught than the relatives he was supposedly comforting. Fortunately, they barely seemed to notice, caught up in their own misfortune.

He sat, twisting his hands. 'We don't know yet. Might be no one. Might just be some animal.'

She looked up at him, her expression giving nothing away. 'You know. I know. We both know.'

He opened his mouth, without knowing how he was going to respond. But before he could speak, there was a fierce rapping on the cottage's front door. The sound, Brain thought, of someone more confident in his authority than he would ever be.

'Well,' he said with relief, 'it looks as if we'll find out soon enough.'

CHAPTER NINE

Fisher stepped cautiously out into the darkness of the garden. He had been drinking heavily all evening. That wasn't a problem in itself. He was accustomed to drinking heavily, night after night, and to looking after himself, finding his own way home. Avoiding disaster.

Tonight, there was no need to find his way home. He was already home. Perhaps that was the problem. He had his familiar corner at the pub. He preferred to be there, even though he shunned the other customers. He felt more comfortable with the noise and the conviviality, though he wanted no part of it himself. If nothing else, it legitimised his own drinking.

But for the last few weeks he had not wanted to go out. He told himself it was the weather, that the snow had made the journey impossible. But the truth was that, even if there had been no snow, he did not want to face the long walk past the deserted cottage. Did not want to think about what he had found there. Did not want to think about what it might mean.

He stepped warily on the frozen snow. It was another cold night, though slightly milder than earlier in the evening when the sky had been clear and empty. The chill air sobered him momentarily.

He remembered finding the body, of course. How could he forget that, for all his inebriation? The poor little twisted thing, shrouded in those shabby fragments of clothes, the shreds of strange dark leathery skin. But he remembered things he could not have seen. A child's body, uncorrupted, no sign of decomposition, cold and dead on those hard kitchen tiles. A child's bonnet, tossed across that floor.

He took some more steps towards the bottom of the lawn, among the twisted trunks of the old apple trees, the long-abandoned child's swing. For a moment, for all his caution, he slipped, almost losing his footing on the icy ground. He grasped the wooden frame of the swing, felt the slimy woodwork beneath his fingers. Breathing heavily, he straightened, gazing over the back fence to the white fields beyond.

Suddenly, he felt something on his cheek, delicate and cold. The fingers of a ghost child, a lifeless hand reaching out for human warmth.

Then the sensation was repeated, again and again, with increasing frequency, and he was tempted to laugh at his own fanciful poetics. A man of God who had long ago lost touch with his own faith, overwhelmed by nonsensical superstition.

More snow. That was all. They had predicted it on the wireless earlier in the afternoon. Further heavy snowfalls, up the Eastern coast, spreading across the country.

He looked into the heavy winter sky. He could see it now, the dark swirling mass of snowflakes. It was already settling on the grass around him, a pale sheen thickening on the boughs of the trees, the angular wooden crosspieces of the rotting swing.

Snow. Falling fast and heavy. Covering everything.

CHAPTER TEN

'This is far from ideal,' Pyke said.

'You're telling me. At least you're under shelter.' Winterman was crouched on the slippery wooden planks, holding an umbrella at an angle. The police doctor, clad in wellington boots and an ex-services sou'wester, was hunched below him, a cumbersome electric torch in his hand, peering into its ineffectual light.

The snow had been falling for some time, deepening on the road beside them. Winterman could feel it melting on his neck, the water dripping from his hat and shoulders. If he stood like this for long enough, he would turn into a snowman.

'I'm hoping to get home tonight.' Pyke raised his moon-like face towards Winterman. The torchlight glinted blankly across his spectacles. 'Don't want to hang around in this.'

'You and me both. So let's be as quick as we can.'

Winterman had had to persuade Pyke to come out in the first place, given the predicted further snowfalls. That was the trouble with these academics, he thought, life's too cosy for them. But he knew that was unfair. He'd come across Pyke before and judged him to be decent and reliable. Anyone would have thought twice about being dragged out on a night like this.

Pyke grunted an acknowledgement and continued scuffling about in the shadows, the torchlight flickering back and forth below the makeshift bridge.

Winterman looked back along the lane. He'd left Hoxton and Marsh in the cottage with Mary and her mother. The children had been sent to bed, though Winterman assumed their noses were pressed against the windows observing his movements outside. They'd tried to persuade Brain his presence was no longer required, but he was still there, drinking his umpteenth cup of tea, supposedly looking after the old lady. Winterman could hardly blame him. As a young copper, Winterman would have given anything to be involved in a case like this.

He was growing conscious of the melting snow permeating his clothing, the ache in the hand holding the umbrella steady. 'What do you think?' he shouted, peering down at Pyke's hunched body.

Pyke straightened slightly. He aimed the torch beam under the planks and gestured towards the scattering of pale bones. 'Definitely dead.'

'Thanks for that, Pyke. Always pays to ask the expert.'

Pyke smiled faintly. 'And human. Definitely human.'

'Ah.' Winterman lowered the umbrella, and eased himself down the edge of the dyke, keeping well back to avoid disrupting the area around the body. He could make out the tiny skeleton, the angled bones draped in scraps that Winterman didn't want to think too closely about. 'How old?'

'Young. Nine or ten maybe. Female.'

'Cause of death?'

'You know, my psychic powers must be waning. I've been peering at those bones for several minutes and I still don't know.'

'Sorry. I just meant anything obvious.'

'You can rule out decapitation, if that's any help.'

'Sorry,' Winterman said again, wondering why he was apologising. 'How long do you think it's been there?'

'There?' Pyke waved the torchlight towards the hollow space. 'Not long, I'd say. Maybe a day or two.'

'But how long since death?'

'Now that's a different question.' Pyke pressed his hands into the small of his back and arched his body, with the air of a tenor about to burst into song. 'I don't know. Years though. Five, six. Maybe more. Looks as if the body was buried in the Fens. Some of the flesh is well preserved.'

'So how did she get here?'

'Forgive me, Inspector, but I'd rather assumed that was your job.'

'Any advice gratefully received, as always. You know it's not the first.'

'I was called out to that one as well.' Pyke spoke as if Winterman had been personally responsible. 'So yes, I know.'

'Similar?' Winterman had read Pyke's report in the file, though the content had been only partly comprehensible to him. 'From your perspective, I mean?'

'The worm's eye view?' Pyke nodded thoughtfully. 'More or less. Similar age. Broadly similar time of death, give or take a year or so. Also female.'

'Cause of death in that case?'

Pyke gazed at him impassively, the drifting snow gathering on his eyebrows and spectacles. 'You'll have read the file, Inspector.' It wasn't a question.

Winterman nodded. 'No evident signs of trauma. Difficult to give a definite view after so long. But most likely asphyxiation. That's what you think?'

'It's what I wrote. So it's what I think. Probably suffocation. Perhaps strangulation.' He looked up at the pale night sky, the thickening swirling snowflakes. 'I'd like to be getting back, if that's all right with you.'

'Of course. You see anything else down there?'

'Clues, you mean? A dropped cufflink. A book of matches with the name of an exclusive cocktail bar printed on it. The footprints of a gigantic hound.' Pyke shook his head. 'No. Just bones and flesh.'

Winterman took the torch and shone its yellow beam under the planks, steeling himself for the sight of the remains. They were less fearsome than he had expected – a loose assemblage of stripped bones, some lingering ochre strips of what might have been either flesh or fabric, resting on the rich black ooze characteristic of the flatlands. He moved the torchlight around the recesses beneath the planks, but, as Pyke had said, there was no sign of anything else. Nevertheless, it would have to be treated as a crime scene and would, in due course, be thoroughly searched.

Winterman straightened. *No likelihood of that tonight*, he thought. The snow was falling thicker than ever, slowly transforming the landscape into a uniform white. Pyke was already scrambling up on to the roadside. The site was unlikely to be disturbed, and he could get Brain to keep an eye on it until it could be cleared and searched properly in the morning. Brain, he felt sure, would appreciate being asked.

Winterman dragged himself up on to the road beside Pyke. 'I'll get the remains to you as quickly as I can.'

'You're too kind, Inspector. I'll treat it as a priority. It's not a good one, this, is it?'

'Few of them are. But this is looking worse than most.'

CHAPTER ELEVEN

'You boys ought to be heading home,' Brain said. He was standing at the living room window, holding back the curtain, peering into the night. 'Coming thick and fast now.' He spoke with some relish, as though introducing city folk to country conditions they might not have previously encountered.

Winterman was at the kitchen door. 'He's right. If we don't make a move soon, we're going to get stranded.'

Mrs Griffiths and her daughter were sitting on either side of a roaring coal fire. The older woman looked pale and slightly shocked, Mary concerned and attentive. For a moment, Winterman regarded the young woman.

She looked in her mid-twenties, but with a maturity of manner that suggested someone older. Her face was pale and drawn, her hair pulled tightly back, her clothes plain and anonymous – a white blouse, a grey skirt, neat black patent-leather shoes. She looked strained. Not surprising, given the day's events. But there was something in her expression that made him wonder.

Mrs Griffiths looked up suddenly. 'You're not going to leave us here. With that.' She looked towards the back of the house, her subject unmistakable.

'We don't have much choice, Mrs Griffiths. There's nothing more we can do till morning.' Winterman paused, wondering how much more to say. 'We need to ensure everything's looked after properly out there. We'll need a team from headquarters. I don't think we can do that tonight, in this weather, but we'll get someone out first thing.' He glanced across at Mary. 'Is there nowhere else you can stay?'

She shook her head. 'Not really. I mean, the neighbours might… But we wouldn't want to impose. I'm sure we'll be fine, really.' She looked across at her mother. 'I'm sure we will.'

Winterman gestured towards Brain. 'PC Brain will look after you. You're in safe hands.'

Brain frowned, unsure whether he was being complimented or patronised. 'Of course. I'll take care of things.'

Winterman nodded his thanks, then let his gaze flicker meaningfully towards the kitchen and the back door. 'And I'd be grateful if you could ensure that nothing is disturbed.'

Brain nodded with some enthusiasm. 'Of course, sir. You can rely on me.'

'Sir,' Marsh said. He was looking past Brain, through the uncurtained window, into the snow-filled night.

'I know,' Winterman said. 'We need to go. Before we get trapped.' He looked at Mrs Griffiths, wishing he had bitten back the last word. 'Let's go,' he said again.

CHAPTER TWELVE

Madness, Pyke thought, lowering his head.

He was struggling to see even a few yards in front of him. A frozen wind was sweeping in from the east, off the fens, driving the snow across the road and almost toppling him as he rode.

In fact, the wind was his only salvation. It came and went, buffeting his exposed body, rendering his progress unstable. But the blizzard at least drove the snow across the road, piling up drifts against the hedgerows to his left. The surface itself was for the moment relatively clear, apart from the odd treacherous patch of black ice. As long as he stuck to the right-hand side, he could make some progress.

But it was madness to be travelling at all on a night like this. More than madness to be doing so on a motorcycle.

Pyke was a skilled cyclist. He had learnt before the war and then had the chance to hone his skills in the army. The bike was an ex-military Enfield he'd picked up for a song from an old contact. It was a terrific machine – fast, tough, reliable.

But bloody suicidal on a night like this.

He should have left earlier. He should, for that matter, have refused to bloody well come out in the first place. Poor little kiddie, whoever she was, but she'd been dead long enough. She could have waited another day.

He travelled a further mile or so before it happened. He had been travelling as slowly as the bike would allow, and that probably saved his life. But suddenly he lost control, the machine skidding from under him, a blur of white and black as he was thrown backwards. Somewhere he saw an arc of golden sparks as the bike careered into the field beyond, and the impact of the road crushed all breath from his body.

He lay, the falling snow kaleidoscoping across his vision, wondering how badly injured he might be. It finally occurred to him that, perhaps, he was almost untouched. The combination of the drifted snow, his heavy leathers and the relatively slow speed had been sufficient to allow him to escape unscathed. His shoulder felt sore, bruised, and there was an ache in his left leg, but nothing that felt serious.

His medical training had taught him it would be unwise to take this diagnosis at face value, but it was good enough to be going on with. He also knew enough not to underestimate the possible effects of shock. He felt unexpectedly calm, but that might not be a good sign.

He pushed himself up to a sitting position. So far, so good. Peering through the blizzard, he finally spotted the black shape of the bike on the snow-covered field. He stood up, realising his body was still shaking. It took him a moment to calm himself, then he walked slowly to the edge of the field. There was no dyke or hedgerow, so he was able to step cautiously across to where the bike lay. The black trail left by its progress was already disappearing under the steadily falling snow.

He raised the motorbike slowly from the ground. The rear mudguard was bent against the tyre, but otherwise the bike seemed undamaged. He tugged hard on the twisted metal, pulling it back from the rubber. Assuming the engine was okay, the bike looked rideable.

What now though? It was another fifteen or so miles home, and the snow was unremitting. The aches in his shoulder and leg were growing more pronounced – still not serious, probably, but likely to cause severe discomfort over a long journey.

There was one obvious answer, though he had resisted the thought until now. He looked at his watch. To his slight surprise, it was only just after eight. It felt much later, as if he had been travelling for hours. Not really too late then. He couldn't use that excuse. Though, of course, the time of night would be the least of the issues.

He slowly wheeled the bike back to the road. Where was he? He had a rough idea – only a couple of miles from Framley. Certainly, still at a point where going back would be much easier than going forward. For all his hesitation, he wasn't sure he had much choice.

He climbed on to the bike and slammed his foot down to start the engine. To his relief, it caught immediately. He hesitated only for a moment longer, then turned the bike back towards Framley.

The worsening state of the road, combined with his own anxiety, rendered the return even more nerve-racking than the outward journey. Twice he almost lost control again, but each time managed to slow, steering skilfully into the skid, finding a grip on the road surface before he lost equilibrium.

Finally, he glimpsed lights ahead, a faint glimmer in the pale darkness. He would soon be at the turning.

He slowed as much as he dared, peering into the night. Even so, he overshot the junction, spotting it only in his peripheral vision after he had passed. This landscape couldn't have been more familiar. He had made this journey dozens of times, could trace it without thinking in the light of day. Tonight, he could scarcely recognise it.

It had never occurred to him to wonder whether Howard would be at home. He knew Howard's habits well enough – or at least he had known them, not so very long ago. It was unlikely that he would be out on a night like this. And if he was – well, the cottage's outbuildings would offer some shelter until the snow lessened.

He spotted the cottage a few hundred yards from the main road, a blank white-painted edifice almost invisible against the swirling snow. The sudden familiarity of it was like a physical shock – unexpected and, he told himself, unwanted. He tried not to think about the last time he had been in this place, but he could not dispel the unarticulated memory of the summer's heat, the scent of wild flowers.

The cottage looked to be in darkness, and for a moment Pyke half hoped that Howard really was away. But he knew well enough that Howard's heavy curtains and drapes were sufficient to prevent any chink of light escaping those narrow windows. Even in the blackout, the cottage had needed no additional concealment.

He pushed the motorbike into the lee of the cottage, a small area largely sheltered from the gathering snow. Then he made his way to the imposing front door.

He hesitated only momentarily before raising the heavy wrought-iron knocker. It fell back against the door with a solid thump.

There was a long silence, and with each second that passed, Pyke grew more convinced the cottage was empty. He was reaching out to try the knocker one final time when the door was pulled open.

Howard stood there, his plump body arched back as he squinted short-sightedly into the night. His face wore a baffled slightly aggressive expression. Pyke's recollection was that he wore the same expression whenever anyone knocked unexpectedly on his door, whatever the time of day or year.

'Howard–'

'Goodness me. Look what the snow's swept in.'

'Look, I'm sorry…'

There was something else in Howard's expression, some other emotion Pyke could not pin down. His own voice trailed off as he struggled to find any suitable words.

Unexpectedly, Howard took a step back, pulling the door wide open. A small flurry of snow blew into the hallway, scattering across the polished tiles.

'You'd better come in.'

CHAPTER THIRTEEN

Winterman stood at his open back door, staring out into the night. It was after midnight, and the snow was still falling, wave upon wave blown in on the east wind. His garden was thickly covered, its untended chaos temporarily civilised by the undulations of white. There was no sign of the snow lessening. This was set in at least for the night.

That was bad news in every way. He had seen it already that evening – finding themselves almost stranded in bloody Framley as the snow had continued to fall. They had made it back to town in the end, largely thanks to Marsh's driving skills. As it turned out, Hoxton lived, presumably alone, in a rented cottage only a mile or so outside Framley, and they had dropped him on the way. Many of the roads across the county would be impassable and it would be some time before they were cleared.

Winterman could feel the cold emptiness of the house behind him. It had always felt too big, this place, though as a child he had loved the sense of space, the hidden corners. Its vastness – its high Edwardian ceilings, silent unused bedrooms, the over-formal parlour still as his parents had left it – only mocked his isolation. He should sell up, buy himself a neat little flat somewhere, stash away a few quid. Give himself some choices.

The snow continued to come down, whipped by the frozen easterly wind, drifting against the walls, piling deep against the French windows. If this continued, he wouldn't even be able to get out of the house the next day.

He stood for a few more moments, his eyes fixed blankly on the eddying snow, his mind a decade away, wondering how it had come to this. Then, with a sense of desolation as great as if he were literally closing off a route into that past, he pushed the door firmly shut and locked up for the night.

CHAPTER FOURTEEN

That was it, William thought. His usual exquisite sense of timing.

He had been planning to return to medical school. He'd checked the trains were running, and had even been out to buy his railway ticket the previous day, seeing it as a tangible demonstration of his intentions. A third-class ticket to Nottingham, knowing that his father would happily have shelled out for first class if it guaranteed William's departure. A single, not a return, even knowing that he would inevitably come back and that the cost would be greater. But, as he had counted out the money at the station, it had felt as if he was making a clear statement.

A worthless statement, as it had turned out, like virtually every one he made. He had not gone, had been seduced by another night with his friends, another night in the pub. Come on, they had said. We can't let you go without a celebration. A farewell party. What's one more night?

A pretty deadly night, as it had turned out. The pub had been empty, its interior reeking of stale beer and smoke, already redolent of the morning after. The friends who had urged him to stay had, for the most part, not bothered to turn up. The few who were there seemed morose, already bored at the evening's start. More snow had come down, just as forecast, and everybody was keen to get home before it really set in. William was stranded here until the snow cleared.

Ten o'clock had found William tramping home alone, his gait unsteady from the beer and chasers, the road treacherous underfoot, his feet cold and soaking inside his thin shoes, his body numbed by the knife-like wind. Deeply miserable, deeply fed up.

The snow was falling much more thickly than he had realised. Although it was drifting in the bitter wind, it was beginning to cover the road again. He pulled his coat more closely around him, tightening his college scarf around his neck.

At the end of the main street, he lost his footing momentarily, his legs skidding from under him. He reached out to steady himself against a low cottage wall, but missed and tumbled over, falling clumsily into the snow.

He rolled over and lay on his back, staring up into the falling snow. He had a sudden vision of himself not bothering to rise again, succumbing to his warm alcoholic stupor, relaxing into unconsciousness as the snow covered him with its frozen blanket.

This was how people died, he thought, his embryonic medical training nagging at his mind. Hypothermia, overcome by the siren lure of the drink, relaxing into oblivion. He could imagine his body lying here undiscovered, to be found only in the thaw, when the snow would slowly melt to expose his lifeless features.

He laughed suddenly, overcome by the absurd melodrama of the image. Recovering his strength and equilibrium, he dragged himself upright, resting for a moment on his hands and knees.

He was soaked, his trouser legs dripping and cold, gloved hands frozen. If he wasn't careful, his melodramatic vision might end up being realised after all. He needed to keep moving.

He wondered whether he should return to the relative shelter of the pub. But it was already past closing time, and there was no chance the landlord would welcome after-hours visitors tonight. In any case, the prospect of a return to those bleak rooms – the smell of smoke and stale beer, the stained table tops, the lingering air of forced joviality – was hardly enticing.

William trudged on, struggling to maintain his balance, pounding heavily through the dense drifts, making slow but steady progress out of the village. The flurrying flakes stung his eyes, and he kept his head down, peering under the brim of his hat, walking with the rhythmic gait of an automaton.

A quarter of a mile out of the village, he was surprised by a sudden lessening of the icy east wind against his damp cheeks. He glanced up to gain his bearings.

He was passing the ruined cottage – the place where the reverend, old Fisher, had supposedly stumbled across that child's body a few weeks before. In the snow, the place had gained an unexpectedly benign air, its crumbling framework softened by the growing drifts, its rotting timbers camouflaged a uniform white. He glanced at the old building, thinking again of the poor child's body, and shuddered.

He pulled his coat more tightly around him and trudged on. This was insane. He wouldn't make it. He would collapse out here in the night, too cold and exhausted to continue. It would be an absurd but fitting death – a young life lost because he had been unable to resist one more night in the pub.

Home was another mile or more away – a suitably sobering walk even on a fine evening. Tonight, it was looking increasingly impossible.

The reverend. The thought came to William suddenly, and he wondered why he hadn't thought of it before. Fisher's was the next cottage along the road – still another quarter mile or so, but surely reachable. If Fisher was capable of making this journey, at his age and usual state of inebriation, then it couldn't be beyond William's powers even on a night like this.

Emboldened by the prospect, he paced on with renewed energy. The reverend wouldn't be pleased to see him, of course. He had never encouraged visitors to his cottage. On the contrary, he had always refused any bloody visitors – never let anyone near the place.

But he was – had been – a clergyman. Whatever the state of his faith now, he surely wouldn't refuse William sanctuary in this kind of weather.

William stumbled on, feeling the melting snow dripping down his neck, the sweat soaking his hair beneath his hat. He slipped again, almost falling, and felt the despair overwhelming him. It was impossible. It was too far. It was too cold and wet. He was too drunk.

Then he saw it – the square dark silhouette of Fisher's cottage, squat against the shifting, whirling sky.

There were no lights in the cottage, no sign of life. But there was nowhere else Fisher would be on a night like this. The only excursions he ever made were to the pub, and he had not been in there earlier in the evening. Probably he had already gone to bed. If so, William would have no qualms about waking him up.

He forced his way up the path to the cottage's front door. The place was pretty run down. The paint peeling, the roof tiles sagging in the porch, one window cracked. William raised the rusty iron knocker, its hinge creaking from disuse, and slammed it hard against the wooden door. The thud echoed internally, the sound deadened by the endless miles of snow.

William strained his ears for any sound of movement. The old man surely wouldn't just ignore his presence. William would just keep hammering away at the door until he had to take notice. He raised the knocker again and dropped it, as heavily as he could.

Despair was creeping back. What if the old man was sound asleep? What if he couldn't hear the knocking, no matter how loudly William banged this bloody piece of metal?

He banged it once more, savagely. Then, with no idea what else to do, he reached down and twisted the door handle, expecting nothing other than to make more noise.

To his surprise, the handle turned and the door opened.

He stared into the hallway beyond. It was in darkness. William could just discern the flowery wallpaper, the dark-stained wooden flooring. There was a faint scent of mould, mildew, mild putrefaction, almost welcome after the freezing freshness of the snowy night.

'Reverend! It's William. William Callaghan.' His voice echoed through the empty hallway, but there was no response. At the end of the dark hall, he could see a glimmer of light from behind a half-closed door. 'Reverend!'

The house was cold. Not as cold as the night behind him, but colder than he had expected. He walked a few more steps down the hallway, towards the light.

He had a sudden sense of unease. It was the cold. Perhaps the old man had no fire, no other heating, but even so the house was chillier than it should be. The chill of a place that had been abandoned, that was no longer inhabited.

He reached the internal door and pushed it fully open. The cold hit him again, more intense. And something else. A draught of air, rushing through the house, slamming shut the front door.

William looked around. A living room – sparsely furnished, but chaotic with scattered books and papers. The embers of a dying fire glowed faintly in the grate. An easy chair, a table with a glass and an empty bottle of gin.

The draught was coming from beyond the living room. Another door led into a kitchen. William crossed the room quickly, his discomfort growing.

The kitchen was in darkness, but William could make out a table and chairs, a gas stove, an old-style stone sink. The remains of a meal sat by the sink, an unwashed teacup, a half-empty tin of luncheon meat.

And the back door of the cottage, standing open to the snow-filled night.

CHAPTER FIFTEEN

After the three detectives had left, Mrs Griffiths closed the living room curtains very firmly, as if the flimsy material would be proof against whatever ghosts might have been summoned that evening.

PC Brain lingered, apparently reluctant to tear himself away from the warmth of the room. 'Don't you worry, Mrs Griffiths,' he said. 'I'll be around to keep an eye on everything.'

Mrs Griffiths regarded him as if he offered slightly less protection than the curtains she had just drawn. 'We're very grateful for all your help.' There was an undeniable undertone of dismissal in her words, but Brain seemed not to notice.

'It's bound to be a shock,' he went on. 'Just stumbling across it like that. And with the children too.'

This time it was Mary's turn to intervene. 'We really shouldn't keep you, Bryan. You've been a tremendous support. But you've a job to do and–'

'My job's to make sure you and your mother–'

'I know, Bryan. But we're fine now. You ought to be making sure that all the evidence is undisturbed.'

'You've got a point there, Mary. Those chaps…' He gestured towards the door through which Winterman and his colleagues had recently departed. 'They're dependent on me.' With a sigh of evident regret, he placed his empty teacup on the sideboard. 'I'd better be off.'

He was well-intentioned, Mary thought, and no fool. But he was too young to be wasting his life in this backwater, desperately seeking excitement where none was to be found.

Or was she simply projecting her own emotions on to the eager-looking young man? He had been sweet on her once, back at school, she remembered. She had thought he was a bit wet, though nice enough. Perhaps they should throw their lot in together and make a break for somewhere that would fulfil both their ambitions.

'You're sure you'll be all right?'

'We'll be fine. Really.' She was growing accustomed to the imaginary life developing inside her head, an alternative to the bleak tawdry reality. Most of her fantasies involved flight, leaving everything behind, finding a new life. In those dreams, she was prepared to consider almost any potential partner. Even dear old Bryan Brain. 'It's not as if there's any kind of real threat, is it?'

'I suppose not,' Brain conceded. 'But I'll pop in tomorrow just to make sure.'

He finally made his departure after what seemed an endless routine of gathering his overcoat, putting on his helmet, collecting his notebook and other paraphernalia, and bidding yet another round of farewells to Mary and her mother.

Finally, Mary closed the front door behind him, briefly watching him trudging disconsolately away through the falling snow before returning to the comparative warmth of the living room.

Mrs Griffiths was sitting by the dying fire, her head in her hands.

'You okay, Mam?'

Her mother looked up, as if momentarily surprised by Mary's return. 'Just a bit tired. You know.'

'You should get up to bed.'

'I will. And so should you. It's getting late.'

Mary nodded. 'And I'm supposed to be at work again tomorrow.' She caught the look in her mother's eye. 'In theory.' She waved her hand towards the curtained window. 'They'll understand if I take a day off. In any case, unless this snow lets up, I can't see much chance of getting in anyway.'

Mrs Griffiths smiled. 'You mustn't let them down, but I'd be glad if you were here tomorrow.'

Mary sat down heavily in the chair opposite her mother. 'They'll have the team from HQ out here tomorrow to sort out the evidence.' She stopped abruptly, embarrassed at having brought up the subject again.

'Who do you think it is, love?' Mrs Griffiths said unexpectedly. 'Out there, I mean.'

Mary's eyes were fixed on the glowing coals in the fire. 'Who are they, you mean? There are two of them. Two little girls.' Despite herself, she found she was moving into territory she would rather have left unexplored. 'Two little children.'

'Poor things.' Mrs Griffiths spoke without obvious emotion, her words automatic, a routine incantation to ward off harm.

'But who *are* they, Mam?' Mary spoke with sudden vehemence, as though the question had only just occurred to her. She rose and, with a restless air, strode across to the window. As she tugged the curtain back, she could almost feel her mother's anxious wince behind her. 'Nobody's missing. Nobody's been missed.' She paused. 'Not since Gary.'

She felt, rather than heard, her mother coming up close behind her, and she turned to see Mrs Griffiths staring past her into the night, her eyes wide with what might easily have been fear. 'It was the war, love. You know that. Things happened. People weren't missed.'

Mary stood watching her mother, conscious of the movement of the snow, ceaseless in her peripheral vision. 'No, Mam,' she said at last. 'People were missed. People *are* missed.' Ignoring her mother's presence at the window, she abruptly closed the curtains and returned to her seat by the dying fire.

'People *are* missed,' she said again.

CHAPTER SIXTEEN

Winterman woke earlier than he had expected. Opening his eyes, he had the sense that he had been disturbed in the middle of a dream, but for once the details had already faded. He knew better than to try to chase down the fragmented memories.

The sun was not yet up, but there was a bleached quality to the darkness that told him the snow still lay thickly outside. He rolled over, feeling the weight of the bedclothes – the tightly tucked sheets, the blankets, the quilt – as an unacceptable burden. He reached out his hand to push himself upright, and felt the shocking graveyard cold of the empty half of the bed.

Why had he come back?

He knew that the question was hardly worth asking. He had come, after his mother had died, simply because the house was there. Then Spooner had presented him with the transfer, and it had felt destined, though he had no idea whether for good or ill. He still assumed that, before long, he would sell the house and find a place of his own. Until then, here he was. It was better than returning to the flat he and his wife Gwyneth had rented in Cambridge.

He climbed slowly to his bare feet, conscious of the chill of the bedroom, shivering despite his thick flannel pyjamas. Bloody cold. It took him a moment more to find his dressing gown and slippers. Bloody, bloody cold.

He dragged back the curtains and peered out. It was still dark, though he could discern a paler band in the clouds to the east. Even by that faint glimmer, he could see that the snow was thick across the flat fields, white as far as he could see.

It had stopped snowing, but there was an ominous heaviness to the sky that suggested more was on the way. A bloody nuisance, for him and for everyone. As if people didn't have enough to deal with.

He fumbled his way to the bedroom door, finally finding the light switch. The bedroom looked bare and rather bleak, in need of decorating. Not surprising, after all these years. He imagined that decorating materials would be hard to come by, though he couldn't see himself making much effort in the near future.

His work suit was hanging up on the front of the wardrobe, and for a moment he contemplated getting dressed before going downstairs. But he needed to boil some water for a shave, get washed. It would be easier to brave the cold.

He shuffled through the kitchen, feeling increasingly sorry for himself. The stone floor tiles were icy underfoot, and he could see the traceries of ice on the insides of the kitchen window. It was growing light outside, revealing the thick drifts of snow piled across the back garden. He filled the old tin kettle and stuck it on the gas stove, and began the ritual of preparing the teapot.

Getting into work would be an interesting challenge, even putting aside the question of what he might be able to do once he got there. On a normal day, the house was only a twenty or so minute walk from his new workplace – one of the practical reasons he'd decided he might as well move back in. At the time, so soon after his mother's death, it had seemed only sensible. Now it felt more like inertia, the path of least resistance.

Thirty minutes later, after a cup of tea and a lukewarm wash and shave, he emerged from the house, clad in his heavy suit and thick winter overcoat, his hat pulled low over his forehead. He had found an old pair of wellington boots in the scullery – his father's or perhaps even his own from way back, though he had no recollection of them. He had tucked his polished black brogues in his briefcase for wearing at the office. He couldn't imagine that

Mrs Sheringham would accept wet boots inside, and he imagined she would be even less tolerant of stockinged feet.

The journey was less arduous than he had feared. The pavement was thick with snow, but the wind had blown large drifts against the line of front walls and fences, leaving the edge of the pavement relatively navigable.

He glanced at his watch. Just gone eight, but the street was deserted. The rows of Edwardian villas were blank faced, curtains closed, with no sign of habitation. At that time, there would normally be a few pedestrians beginning their journeys to work – on foot or heading for buses or the railway station. It was eerily quiet, with no passing traffic and the deadening thickness of the snow. He might be the last man alive.

He trudged on, beginning to enjoy the solitude despite himself. As he neared the market square, he glimpsed one or two more pedestrians, doggedly matching his own slow progress, heads down, eyes fixed on the treacherous ground in front of them.

He was already thinking pessimistically about the day ahead. They had nothing to go on, no information. He could imagine the endless hours of door-to-door questioning, the hope that someone, somewhere had an inking of who these little girls might be. It was an unenticing prospect given the size of the investigation team available to him. He could seek more resources from HQ, but he knew how long it had taken even to finalise his own transfer. Manpower was limited, and bureaucracy was apparently infinite. The snow would add a whole new set of challenges.

Almost without realising, he had reached the anonymous building that housed the outposted CID team. He stared up at the blank windows. Another Edwardian villa, a larger version of his parents' home. His own home, he corrected himself. At least for the moment.

Mrs Sheringham had provided him with a key the previous day, and he expected he would have to use it. But the front door was unlocked. He stepped inside, struck immediately by the relative warmth of the interior. 'Hello,' he called.

'Good morning, sir.' Mrs Sheringham emerged from her office, immaculate in a neat black dress, her painted lips opened in an apparently genuine smile. 'Bright and early.'

Winterman nodded. Perhaps she slept here. Perhaps she didn't sleep at all. 'Good morning, Mrs Sheringham.' He found himself inescapably drawn into the formality of her speech patterns. 'Nasty weather.'

'Very nasty,' she agreed. Then her smile disappeared so rapidly that Winterman was left thinking that he had mistaken its sincerity. 'And not only the weather. I've just taken a message. I think you'd better have a look at it.'

CHAPTER SEVENTEEN

Pyke woke suddenly, as if something – some unexpected noise or impact – had disturbed his sleep. For several seconds, he couldn't work out where he was. Nothing felt right – the angle of the morning light from the window, the colour of the ceiling, the feel of the bed. But everything was eerily familiar – not home, but tantalisingly close to home. Somewhere he once called home, he told himself, not even sure what he meant.

Then he woke fully and realised where he was, his mind slowly reconstructing the events of the previous evening.

It had been a mistake, he realised that now. Probably all of it, in retrospect. But certainly coming back had been a mistake. He had seen it in Howard's eyes as soon as he opened the door. He could see what Howard was thinking. Though Pyke had tried to make things clear, Howard had believed what he wanted to believe. As Howard always did.

Another fine mess.

But what else could he have done? It wasn't as if he'd come here on a whim. The previous night, he hadn't had much choice.

At least he was in the guest room. At least he'd managed, for once, to resist Howard's distinctive form of moral blackmail. That was something, even if the signal hadn't been sufficiently unequivocal for Howard.

This was also, he realised, why the room had seemed so familiar and yet so strange. It was like coming home, but he was only a guest.

He sat up and looked around. It was daylight – he could see the pale corona around the lemon-coloured curtains – but he had no idea what time. He didn't really even know when they'd finally retired for the night, after Howard had broken out the whisky. After midnight, certainly.

Pyke pulled back the bedclothes and sat on the edge of the bed. He was wearing a pair of pyjamas he had borrowed from Howard. Probably another mistake.

He hated this room, he realised. He was slightly taken aback by the strength of his emotion. He had never felt like that while he lived here – not so strongly anyway. Perhaps because then this room had been peripheral to his existence. It had been Howard's friends who stayed in here, and most of them probably loved everything about it. The brightly coloured décor. The endless photographs of Howard and his theatrical associates – each shot posed while straining every sinew to appear natural. Those phoney smiles, over-slick grins.

Now here he was again. The last place he should have been. Sighing, Pyke rose slowly to his feet and fumbled his way across to the window, pulling back the lemon curtains.

The snow was still there, thick and unsullied across the fields and, more importantly, across the road in front of the house. The snow was still here, and so was Pyke, and there was little sign he would be able to leave any time soon.

CHAPTER EIGHTEEN

PC Brain was rapidly drifting out of his depth. He knew this all too well, but didn't have the faintest idea what to do about it. He should probably call a halt, wait till someone most senior, more experienced, was here to assist. But then what? They couldn't just sit in silence or try to generate some small talk – not in the circumstances.

Perhaps he should take William back to the station, make this formal. That would be the smart thing to do, though he couldn't imagine William's father would take kindly to his son being arrested – or even helping police with their enquiries, that infamous euphemism.

'Let me make sure I've got this straight,' he said, though it was the third time he had asked the question in slightly different words. 'You found the body last night, but you didn't report it till this morning?'

'Bloody early this morning.' William's reddened eyes carried the expression of one who didn't want to be reminded quite how early it had been.

Brain couldn't argue with that. It had been before seven when William had turned up on the doorstep of the police house, banging on the door and shouting up to the windows. Before that William had presumably had a half hour's walk back into the village.

But even so.

He looked past William, out through the still-open French windows, to where the body lay spread on the snow-covered lawn, its limbs distorted like a huge broken-backed crow.

'Can't we sit down now?' William asked. 'I'm dog tired.'

He looked it, Brain thought, and not just tired. It was definitely the morning after the night before. There was a manic quality to William that made Brain increasingly nervous. He looked around. 'We shouldn't really. This could be a crime scene. We don't want to disturb it.'

'It can't all be a crime scene,' William argued. 'Anyway, I've already disturbed it.'

That was rather the point, Brain thought, realising he had already lost control of the situation. 'I suppose we could sit in the kitchen. If we're careful.' He had no real idea how such care ought to be exercised.

He led William back into the kitchen, trying not to look too closely at the congealing remains of what had presumably been Fisher's last meal. In these circumstances, everything took on an unexpected poignancy. Fisher's ration book on the table, a thin tablet of allowances that would never be used.

William sat at the table and dropped his head into his hands. 'What a bloody mess.' It wasn't clear whether he was referring to Fisher's position or his own.

'Take me through it again,' Brain said, still unsure if he was doing the right thing.

William looked up and stared at him, catching a hint of Brain's uncertainty. 'What is this? Am I being questioned?'

'Just making conversation. Though no doubt the CID will want to interview you when they get here.' Which Brain profoundly hoped would not be much longer.

'No doubt,' William agreed. 'Better get my story straight then, hadn't I?' He smiled faintly. 'I suppose it doesn't sound too good, now I think about it? I find a dead body and then decide to stay the night. But it wasn't really like that.'

'But that is what happened?' Brain said. It was a genuine question. William had been making little sense when he'd arrived at the police house that morning.

'Yes. Sort of. But you saw what the snow was like last night. I came in here looking for shelter, and what I found was that…'

He gestured out towards the garden where Fisher's body still lay. 'Poor old bugger.'

'So you decided to stay the night?' Brain was genuinely baffled.

'No – well, yes. I was bloody sozzled. Not thinking straight. Not thinking at all. I don't know what I else I could have done. The snow was still coming down. It was real brass-monkey weather. I was all sheets to the wind. If I'd tried to get back to the village, you'd have ended up with two corpses on your hands.'

'Where did you sleep?' Brain had a sudden unwanted image of William drunkenly crawling into the old man's unused bed.

'On the couch in there,' William said. 'Suddenly all became too much. Didn't even close the bloody windows properly. Hope I didn't mess up the crime scene.' He paused, as if he'd only then registered the significance of what he'd said. 'Though crime scene would imply a crime.'

'Just routine.' Brain hoped his bluff wouldn't be called. 'If there's a dead body, we have to protect the scene until we know the cause.'

He got most of this stuff from Edgar Wallace thrillers on the Home Service. He was acutely conscious he hadn't actually been out to examine the body for himself. It was better to leave it until the experts arrived.

William frowned, as if some thought had just struck him. 'That's…' He shook his head as though trying to clear it. 'I'm sure you're right. Don't want to speak ill of the dead, and we all know old man Fisher liked a drink or two. ' He hesitated again. 'It's just–'

'What is it?' Brain wondered whether he should find William a glass of water. It looked as if the hangover was finally beginning to strike in earnest.

William lowered his head into his hands, then peered at Brain through his spread fingers. 'I'd swear off the bottle for good, if there was any chance I meant it. I'm trying to think…' He rubbed his fingers against his temples as though hoping literally to stimulate his brain cells. 'I remember coming in. I remember the cold and finding the windows open. Then it's all a bit hazy. But there's something…'

William stumbled to his feet, looking as if his inebriation had returned. His face was ashen and for a moment Brain thought the young man might be about to vomit. Instead, he pushed past Brain and staggered back into the sitting room.

By the time Brain reached the living room, William was already stumbling through the half-open French windows out into the freezing morning. Brain leapt across the room, but it was too late. William had crouched down by Fisher's prone body and was struggling to turn it over.

'You can't–' Brain's thoughts were already racing ahead to what Winterman and his colleagues would have to say. Then he stopped dead.

'Look at it.' William's voice was hoarse. 'I saw it last night. I must have seen it last night. I checked whether he was breathing. I'm sure I checked…' He forced the corpse over on to its back.

Brain had stopped at the windows, transfixed by what he was seeing, trying to make sense of it.

The ground underneath the body was clear of snow, and the grass was stained black – a small pool of congealed blood that had spread, tainting the whiteness around it.

'I saw it,' William repeated. 'I must have blanked it out. It was the drink and the shock. But I must have seen it…'

Protruding from the body's abdomen, jutting at a low angle below the rib cage, was the black bone handle of a kitchen knife. Before Brain could stop him, William touched the knife handle, apparently intent on pulling it from the flesh. Reacting a moment too late, Brain knocked William's hand away. 'Don't be daft. That's evidence. Just leave it.'

William looked up at Brain for a moment, his expression blank. Then he slumped on to the frozen snow beside Fisher's body, his face pressed into his hands. 'I must have seen it.'

Brain stood, unable to move, wondering what the hell he was going to do next.

There was no doubt about it. He really was seriously out of his depth.

CHAPTER NINETEEN

Winterman was beginning to see himself as the angel of death.

He had been here only two days, and already he'd tripled the body count. Quite impressive, even though he was assuming the old man would turn out to be natural causes. Hoxton had already told him Fisher was something of a drinker.

Frustrated by inactivity, Winterman strode to the rear of the building, unlocking and unbolting the back door, and made his way out into a small courtyard. It was a place where they stored the rubbish bins and, it seemed, any other junk discarded from the offices. He assumed Mrs Sheringham had chosen not to extend her domain out here. It had a chaotic untidy air not evident in the interior of the building, although the worst of the mess was concealed beneath the drifted snow.

Winterman had told Mrs Sheringham he needed a breath of air. In truth, he needed a cigarette. He wasn't sure whether she allowed smoking in the building, but no one else appeared to have had the courage to light up.

His earlier foreboding about the weather had proved correct. The snow was falling again, as heavily as before. He tucked himself into a corner by the door and lit a cigarette, sheltering the flame from the chill east wind. Even the cigarettes were shoddy these days, the tobacco adulterated with something even less palatable. He had heard on the wireless some government spokesman recommending that you should smoke it down to the last drag. 'It might even be good for your health!' the man had added in that over-bright voice politicians used to patronise the man in the street. As if, Winterman thought, any of us cared about living longer.

God, this country was in a mess. Not at all what most people had envisaged, a year or so ago. Winterman barely remembered VE night. He'd still been in London, charged with tidying up the endless array of loose ends his superiors couldn't be bothered with. He'd been in no state to enjoy the celebrations taking place around him. He recalled walking through the West End late in the evening, impelled by a sense of duty and vague curiosity. People were gathered in Trafalgar Square, milling about as if they couldn't remember what they were doing there. Some idiot playing endlessly on a trumpet, a jazz tune. A few amiable drunks.

Even then – and even allowing for Winterman's own jaundiced outlook – it felt like an anticlimax. As if all the energy, the tension, of those extraordinary six years had been dissipated, and no one quite knew what to do next.

Election night had been something else again. He was regaining some equilibrium by then, getting his life back in order. He was weeks away from formal demobilisation – not that it was clear he'd ever been formally mobilised in the first place – and was stuck in a dusty Holborn office working out his last days, not much to do, finally beginning to think about what might be coming next. At a loose end, he'd accepted a request from a friend to help out with the election campaign for one of the London Labour candidates, an enthusiastic youngster with no serious expectation of success.

The candidate had invited his campaign workers to a post-poll party in a down-at-heel pub off Fitzroy Street. Somehow – Winterman couldn't recall the details – they'd moved on from there to the party at Transport House, realising by then that, not only were they going to win, but that it would be a landslide. It was more than they had ever envisaged, more than they dared dream of. He had a memory of seeing Attlee in the middle of that mêlée, blank-faced and bemused, the expression of an understudy drafted at the last minute into the leading role.

At dawn, hung over, exhausted, he had returned to his shabby flat, half-believing he had dreamed the victory. Hours later, having slept through the day, he woke wondering why it had mattered to him so much. He was no political animal. He had no real faith in politicians of any persuasion. He had no conviction this was a new socialist dawn. It was just another government. They'd bumble along, perhaps take some positive steps, certainly make mistakes. In the end they'd betray anyone who had any real faith in them.

And this bunch, whatever their good intentions, had nothing going for them. The country was on its last legs, bankrupt, already having to go cap in hand to the unsympathetic Americans. No food in the shops. No coal in the furnaces. No thanks for whatever we might have done over the last six years. And now this – even the elements themselves conspiring to squeeze out whatever last shred of resource and energy might remain.

'Penny for them.'

Winterman turned. Hoxton, hands in pockets, was slouched against the doorframe.

'I don't think they're worth that much. I was just watching the snow.'

'It's a bugger right enough. Last thing we need.'

'I'm surprised to see you in,' Winterman said. 'Don't imagine any of the roads are clear yet.'

Hoxton shrugged. 'Committed, that's me. Wouldn't catch me risking a day's pay for a bit of snow. Got on my bike – bit treacherous, but not too bad in the end. Don't think we'll see Marshy today though.'

Winterman smiled. 'Lives further away, does he?'

'Five minutes' walk. But always glad of a lie in, Marshy.' Hoxton moved to stand next to Winterman at the door. Winterman pulled out the packet of cigarettes and Hoxton plucked one out, looking grateful. 'Thanks. I was about out. Didn't fancy a trip to the shop.' He peered out at the swirling snow. 'Staying locally yourself then?'

'Not far,' Winterman agreed.

'But then you're something of a local man.' Hoxton fumbled with a box of matches, lighting the cigarette.

Winterman raised an eyebrow. 'Why do you say that?'

Hoxton took a deep drag on the cigarette, his eyes fixed on the snow-filled sky. 'I'm not necessarily the fastest runner in the field. But I usually get there in the end.'

'That doesn't surprise me.'

'Thought I recognised your face. Seen you around here, before the war. Someone told me your mam and dad lived round these parts. So I did a bit of checking. Asked around at HQ. You've got a reputation.'

'I imagine so.' Winterman had lit another cigarette. 'I take it you didn't speak to the chief constable.'

'Not directly, no. I was told he thought you were the bee's knees.'

'Once, maybe. Not now, I don't think.'

Hoxton looked as if he was about to say something, but then he moved silently to stand next to Winterman.

Both men stood for some minutes, unspeaking, gazing out at the panorama of grey and white, the imperceptible accretions of snow on the piled drifts.

'Bleedin' cold,' Hoxton said at last. 'Has been for weeks.'

'They reckon there'll be fuel shortages. Factory closures. More powercuts. That's what they said on the wireless this morning.'

'Just as well we're living in the land of bleeding plenty then, isn't it?' Hoxton sounded more jovial than bitter. 'They had some stories about you, I'll tell you that for nothing.'

'Largely apocryphal, I imagine.' Winterman blew a perfect smoke ring. It was immediately whipped away by the bitter east wind.

'I'll take your word for it. Given as I've no idea what that means. But then they said you were educated.'

''Fraid so,' Winterman acknowledged. 'For what it's worth.'

'Bugger all, in my experience. With all due respect, sir.'

Winterman laughed. 'I'll have to earn your respect in other ways then, Hoxton.' He took a step forward, his polished shoes crunching into the snow, flakes gathering on his shoulders.

'I've no doubt you will, sir,' Hoxton said, sounding sincere enough. 'They seemed to hold you in pretty high regard at HQ. Some of them anyway.'

Winterman turned and looked at him, his expression one of genuine surprise. 'You think so? There's a turn up for the books.'

'Yeah. Bright boy. Hard working. Committed to the cause. Never gives up. All that.' Hoxton tossed his cigarette stub casually out into the snow.

'So what went wrong? That's what you're going to ask.'

'You mean, how did you end up in a deadbeat dump like this, working with the likes of me? None of my business. But, anyway, they told me.'

'Did they? What did they tell you?'

'Breakdown,' Hoxton said. 'Nerves, I suppose. All got a bit too much for you. These things happen. Nothing to be ashamed of.'

'No. Nothing to be ashamed of.' Winterman laughed, then flicked his own cigarette end elegantly out into the gathering snow. 'They tell you much about this breakdown?'

'Like I say, none of my business.'

'Who knows?' Winterman was smiling, apparently good naturedly. 'You ought to be forewarned. So you can keep an eye out for any odd behaviour.'

Hoxton stepped out beside him into the snow. A white dusting had already gathered on Winterman's hair and shoulders. 'You're a local man, guv. I'd say odd behaviour goes with the territory.'

'You reckon so?'

'I reckon so. Mad as bloody hatters. It's what comes from living in the back of beyond.' Hoxton shook his head. 'Look at this lot. Dead kiddies' bodies appearing out of nowhere. A pissed old padre casting himself out in the snow. What a place.'

'So that's what you think it is then? Madness. The children, I mean. Not the pissed old padre. Given some of the things we've seen in the last year or two, that's probably the only sane response for a man of god.'

Hoxton regarded him for a moment, as if about to take issue with Winterman's words. 'It makes no sense to me,' he said at last, and for a moment Winterman wondered whether Hoxton was about to engage in a theological debate. 'I mean, who are these kiddies? In a place like this, people notice if a cat goes missing, let alone a child.'

'Maybe they did,' Winterman pointed out. 'Those deaths go back a few years. We'll need to track through all the missing persons.'

'Not local though.'

'Maybe not. It depends what you mean by local. It's not like it was. Even round here, people are a lot more mobile.'

'Aye, and there are a lot more strangers. People coming and going. Bloody incomers. Even the bloody Yanks. Those kiddies could have come from anywhere.'

Winterman looked up at the heavy grey sky, still thick with swirling snow. 'What's the forecast?'

'More of the same.'

'And how long before they get the roads cleared?'

'Weeks, I should think. The only good news is there aren't many roads out here. Once the snow ploughs get going, they should get the main routes cleared pretty quickly.'

'Including the road to Framley?'

'Including the road to Framley.'

'Can we get them to give that one some priority? Can someone speak to the council?'

Hoxton smiled. 'I think you'll find Mrs Sheringham is already onto that one.'

'That's something then. We can get a team out there to recover that second body, and find out what happened to your pissed old padre. When do you reckon? Sometime today?'

'With a bit of luck. Though we haven't had too much of that so far.' Hoxton shook the gathering snow from his shoulders. 'I'm going in, guv. You can stay out here to build a snowman if you like.'

'Maybe I will. We could all do with a bit of cheering up. Find a scarf, a carrot, couple of bits of coal.'

'You'll be lucky to find any coal.' Hoxton stopped and glanced over his shoulder. 'You know what I reckon?'

'What?'

'I reckon a week or two of this place will really drive you doolally. If I were you, I'd forget this place and bugger off back to whatever you were up to in London.'

Winterman brushed the snow from his hair, gazing impassively at Hoxton. 'You're quite right,' he said finally. 'You may not be fast, but you do get there in the end.'

CHAPTER TWENTY

Mary had woken early, around six. Sometimes, even at this time, her mother was already up and about, clattering through the washing up in the kitchen. But the house was silent – the distinctive deadening of a landscape thick with snow.

Mary lay staring at the ceiling, aware of how fitfully she had slept. She had never seen herself as the nervous type but those human remains, those tiny bones, had haunted her dreams. The dreams themselves had vanished, shredded by the pale morning light, but she was left with half-memories, fading imprints on her mind's eye. A child's eyes, blue and shining. A child's hand reaching out in the expectation of comfort. Dredging up memories Mary would rather have left buried.

She dragged herself from the double bed, pushing back the heavy quilt and eiderdown. It was still freezing cold in the room. It seemed to have been freezing cold for weeks.

She dressed hurriedly, pausing briefly to consider whether she should put on her office clothes. But she knew she would be staying home. Her mother needed her. Nobody would be expecting her at work and the buses were unlikely to be running. In the end, she dressed in some old slacks and a heavy jumper, utility clothing she had kept for years.

Downstairs, the cold was even more intense. There was no sign of her mother or the children. All still in bed, the most sensible place to be. She busied herself lighting a fire in the sitting room grate, trying to get some warmth into the place. The stock of coal – the thin dusty stuff that had become the norm since the war – was getting low. There was already talk of coal shortages.

She finally got the fire going, and pushed herself to her feet, feeling a weariness in her bones. Years of this. Years more trying to make ends meet. Years of trying to cope. For her and everyone.

She strode through to the kitchen, trying to shake off the feelings weighing down her body and her mind. *Pull yourself together. Grit your teeth.* She filled the kettle and set it on the gas ring. A nice cup of tea.

While the kettle boiled, she unlocked the back door, feeling the sudden gust of frozen air. The snow was still falling, the sky grey and heavy. The garden fence and the gate were almost invisible beneath the drifts.

Behind her, the kettle began its stuttering whistle, the pitch rising as the water reached boiling point until the shrill incessant noise filled the house, unignorable.

CHAPTER TWENTY-ONE

Winterman spent the morning flitting around the office with the air of a bird trapped in a particularly unattractive cage. He had started with good intentions, sitting himself down in his box-like office, determined to review the case files, make productive use of the time.

After half an hour of flicking through endless typewritten pages, he had slammed closed the cardboard folder, acknowledging he was taking nothing in. He walked over to the window, staring out at the snow-covered fields. The previous day, he had been pleased by the view. Now, he already felt trapped by the featureless landscape.

Why had he come back here? Because he had little choice, he told himself. But even that wasn't really true. He hadn't needed to return to the force at all. He'd built up some good Whitehall connections from the war. He could probably have found himself a nice little billet in the Civil Service, stayed in London pushing paper.

But he'd have hated that even more. He'd got himself out of the backroom job as soon as he decently could, managed to land a secondment to the Met. He'd had a good year there, still backroom but at least doing something useful, helping to collate intelligence on organised crime. He'd almost concluded that the powers-that-be had overlooked him when he'd been summoned by his commanding officer, DCI Renton. Renton had been brandishing a letter.

'Just got this.' He squinted at the signature. 'From one Detective Superintendent Spooner of the Cambridgeshire Constabulary. Know him?'

'Vaguely. Don't think our paths really crossed.' Winterman had had an image of a stocky, overweight figure. Spooner had been a DCI in Winterman's time, a career copper who had progressed mainly just by keeping his nose clean. The opposite of himself, Winterman acknowledged ruefully.

'He's written to remind me that, whatever we might think, you still belong to them. I've checked and, unfortunately, it seems he's right. Officially, you've been on secondment all along. Now they want you back.'

He could probably have resisted and Renton, who knew talent when he saw it, would have supported him. But it struck him that, after everything that had happened, he had been half looking for an excuse to get out of London, to leave behind this part of his life and responsibilities. A week or two later, Winterman's mother had fallen ill and that had brought him back here anyway. When she had died unexpectedly and the family house had become his, it had seemed only to confirm the inevitability of his return.

Spooner's original letter had referred to a supposed shortage of experienced officers, but that had turned out to be largely eyewash. Winterman assumed the request for his return must have emanated from some bean-counter keen to balance the books. Whatever staffing shortages there might be, no one had much enthusiasm for getting too close to Winterman and his history. After a few weeks, Spooner had announced he was transferring Winterman out to Erringford. Erringford was the market town in which Winterman had been born and brought up, and in which his parents had lived and died. More destiny.

'I thought you were short of manpower,' he had said to Spooner at the time.

'We are,' Spooner replied. 'Especially in Erringford.'

Winterman had assumed this was simply the force's obscure way of punishing him for his past indiscretions. When, a day or two later, Spooner had handed him the file on the child's corpse, that assumption had seemed to be confirmed.

Now, after another five minutes staring at the blank panorama, he made his way downstairs. Mrs Sheringham was standing at the bottom, as though she had been waiting for him.

'I was about to offer you a cup of tea.' Her tone suggested he had somehow spoiled the gesture. 'There's no milk though.'

He shook his head. 'Thanks for the thought. I was going to ask you to show me the filing system.'

'I'm happy to give you the tour. But it's really very straightforward. And very dull.'

He briefly considered disputing the point, but guessed she was right. 'And I was going to ask you to put a call through to HQ.' He should formally report Fisher's as yet uninvestigated death in the half-hearted hope he might be offered more resources. Or, failing that, at least ensure his own back was covered.

Mrs Sheringham was shaking her head. 'I've been trying. No luck in that direction, I'm afraid. The lines must be down.'

'The telephone's dead?'

'Not ours. I can call out to the exchange, but they can't connect me to Cambridge. Local calls seem all right.' She paused. 'I called the council to find out about the roads. They're doing their best to get them opened.'

'What about the road to Framley? We've got this old chap Fisher to find out about now as well.'

'The reverend,' she said. It wasn't clear whether she was supplementing or correcting his description. 'They've said they'll give it priority.' She turned on her elegant high heels and disappeared with an unexpected abruptness back into her office, leaving Winterman wondering whether he had managed once again to offend her.

He pushed open the door into the main office. Hoxton was sitting with his feet up on the desk reading the previous day's copy of the Daily Mirror. He made no obvious move to alter his posture as Winterman entered. Marsh's desk was still empty.

'Snowman finished?' Hoxton said.

'You were right about the coal.' Winterman lowered himself into Marsh's chair and swung his feet up on the desk to match Hoxton's. 'Tell me about Fisher.'

'*De mortuis nihil nisi bonum*,' Hoxton said surprisingly. 'That's what I always say.'

'I imagine so. But you could start by finishing your story from yesterday. You know, about how he killed his wife and daughter. How did he manage that? Without being hanged, I mean.'

'During the war.' Hoxton spoke as if that explained everything. Which, to be fair, Winterman thought, it often did. 'Wife left him, taking the kiddie. Ran off with another bugger.' Hoxton shook his head, his expression suggesting one who had grown inured to the iniquities of his fellow man. 'Can't really say I blamed her though. Even without the drink, he was a violent angry bugger. Pick a fight with anyone.'

'Including his wife?'

'Especially her, by all accounts. But that was a bit odd anyway. She was a lot younger than him. A widow.'

'War widow?'

Hoxton nodded. 'Husband bought it in North Africa somewhere, I think. Left her with a young child – five, six years old. Vicar comes round to offer comfort. You know the deal.'

'It's hard to imagine,' Winterman said. But it wasn't really. He knew only too well. However unattractive a character Fisher might have been, it wasn't usually difficult to charm the vulnerable.

'Well, that's how it was.'

'And he was violent with her?'

Hoxton's face betrayed nothing. 'Aye, I'd say so. No real evidence, mind you. But everybody knew.'

'And the child?'

'I honestly don't know. Maybe.' Hoxton looked as if he was about to say something more, but then shook his head.

'So she left him.'

'Don't know the whole story, but he just woke up one morning to find them gone. Wife and kiddie. The war was a bloody nightmare, but it did some good. Don't think a vicar's wife would have dared up sticks like that ten years ago, do you?'

Winterman raised an eyebrow. 'Do you think that's a good thing then?'

'In this case.'

'So where'd she go? It can't have been easy. Even in this day and age.'

'She must have planned her departure pretty carefully. She and the kiddie slipped away overnight. The reverend woke up to find them gone, apparently. Not even a note. I don't know how much of it was planned but she ended up moving in with a don from the university. He told everyone he'd offered her shelter, but no-one believed it was just a noble act. He was a widower, and she was an attractive woman. Passed herself off as his housekeeper.

'So what's all this about Fisher killing them?' Winterman said finally, when it became clear that Hoxton was waiting for some dramatic prompt.

'No one seems to know exactly what happened Well, I don't, any road. But the wife had some bust up with the don, and she turns up one day back on Fisher's doorstep.'

'She must have been desperate.'

'I'd have thought so. I imagine she thought she could throw herself on Fisher's mercy, what with him being a vicar and everything. Hoped for some Christian charity.'

'But she didn't find it?'

'Fisher was a mess by then. He'd been drinking more and more since she left. Increasingly eccentric on the job. He'd already been relieved of his duties in the church – you can imagine what it must have taken for the authorities to do that. Don't think there was much evidence of Christian anything, let alone charity. He just threw her out, with the kiddie.'

'What happened?'

'I don't know exactly. I don't think anyone really wanted to know. It was the middle of winter. Nothing like as cold as this bloody one, but cold enough. Late at night.' He stopped and for a moment his expression changed.

There was something different there, Winterman thought, as if briefly some genuine emotion had emerged from behind Hoxton's usual bluff cynicism.

'Someone would have taken them in,' Hoxton went on. 'If she'd asked. It's that sort of place. But instead she just went off, out into the fens. They walked a long way, apparently. Away from the village. Into the darkness …' His voice trailed off. He was staring at nothing, his expression suggesting that he still couldn't believe it had happened. 'It was a couple of days before anyone found them. It was one of the farmers, spotted something in the middle of one of his fields. Turned out to be them. Hypothermia, they reckoned.'

'She allowed her own child to die like that?'

'Not of sound mind, that was the judgment. You're bloody telling me. Farmer who found the bodies recognised them, so the coppers were soon back at Fisher's.'

'Awkward questions for him then?'

'I should think so. Certainly enough to destroy any lingering standing that Fisher might have had in the community. Maybe that was her final revenge.'

Winterman leaned back in the seat and stared at the ceiling. It needed painting, he noticed. But then everything in this bloody country needed a coat of bloody paint. He was about to offer some similar thought to Hoxton when the office door opened and Marsh peered in.

'Just got in, sir. Mrs Sheringham says to tell you there's a message. From that chap Brain. Sounded a bit panicked. He wants us to try to get out there as quickly as we can.' Marsh paused, sounding out of breath, then went on. 'That chap, the vicar. Says he told you they found the body.'

'He told us that earlier,' Winterman pointed out. 'We'll get out there as quickly as we can.'

'Doesn't he know there's a war on?' Hoxton intoned hollowly. 'Can we still use that one?'

Marsh shook his head. 'No. This was a new message. It's not just that the vicar's dead.' He stopped, this time apparently mainly for dramatic effect. 'Brain reckons he'd been murdered. Stabbed.'

Silence followed the last word. Winterman glanced across at Hoxton, his mind replaying the horror story he had just heard.

'It goes to show,' Hoxton said, his eyes avoiding Winterman's. 'There's always room for one more revenge.'

CHAPTER TWENTY-TWO

Pyke hesitated momentarily on the stairs. He had dressed fully before coming down, wanting to risk no further misunderstandings. Now he felt absurdly formal in his heavy dark grey suit, his college tie and his sturdy polished shoes. Howard, he had no doubt, would be lounging in some ornate dressing gown. Pyke wondered whether all actors took the concept of "resting" quite as literally as Howard.

He pushed open the door into the small but beautifully furnished living room. The smell of bacon assailed his nostrils. How the hell did Howard get hold of bacon? But that was always the way with Howard. As far as Pyke could recall, the imposition of rationing had had no discernible impact on Howard's standard or style of living. Howard knew people, and people – the right people – knew Howard. That had always been one of his attractions.

As Pyke had expected, Howard was looking relaxed, apparently unaffected either by the previous night's intake of alcohol or Pyke's presence. He had taken Pyke's presence for granted, right up until the moment it had ceased. Even then, as last night's drink-fuelled conversation had confirmed, he had seen Pyke's absence as merely a temporary deviation from the normal state of affairs.

For the moment, despite all Pyke's protests to the contrary, he had been proved right. To Howard, it was the same as always. He got what he wanted, usually without appearing to lift a finger.

'Good morning!' Howard said brightly. He was lounging on the leather sofa, a half-eaten bacon sandwich and a cup of tea on the occasional table beside him. He was dressed in a blue and gold silk dressing gown, garish even by Howard's unique standards. 'Can I get you some bacon, dear boy?'

It was a style modelled loosely on Noel Coward or perhaps Ivor Novello, and it no doubt had gone down a storm with Howard's actor friends, but Pyke had grown weary of its repetition. He shook his head.

'Tea and toast is fine. I'll get it.' Howard had, in any case, made no move to rise from the sofa.

Pyke busied himself in the tiny kitchen, pouring tea, lighting the grill, slicing bread – even the bread seemed better than the stuff everyone else was forced to eat.

'You can stay, you know?'

Pyke was crouched over the grill, manoeuvring the bread so it would toast evenly. He looked over his shoulder. Howard was leaning against the doorway, a faint smile playing across his face.

'I know,' Pyke said. 'You said so last night. Several times. But I can't. Won't.'

'But you're here.'

'An accident. I told you.'

'You were passing. Yes, I know.'

'It's true. I didn't have a lot of choice. Even so, it was a mistake.'

'Don't say so, dear boy,' Howard exclaimed in mock dismay. 'It's always lovely to see you.' He sounded as sincere as Howard ever did.

'And it's good to see you, Howard. That's not the point.'

'So what exactly is the point? What people will think?'

The toast was beginning to burn. Pyke flipped it over and looked up at Howard. 'We've been through this. Repeatedly.'

'Have we?' Howard nodded. 'Your job, your profession, your career. All of that? Yes, I suppose we have.'

'We've said everything there is to say.'

'I suppose so, dear boy. If you say so.'

Pyke felt nervous when Howard conceded the argument so easily. It meant only that Howard was re-grouping to approach the topic from some other, more devious direction.

'What is this work you're engaged in anyway?'

Pyke pulled the toast from under the grill, swearing as the hot bread burnt his fingertips. Howard obligingly handed him a plate.

'Language,' he chided. 'But you never did tell me why you were out here in the first place. What the job was, I mean.'

This was new. Howard had never previously expressed much interest in Pyke's admittedly rather off-putting line of work. Then Pyke realised where the queries were heading. Howard assumed the case was nothing more than an excuse, that the visit had been pre-planned.

'I told you,' Pyke said, though he knew he hadn't. 'It was a body they found.'

'A body?' Howard spoke as though Pyke had referred to some local tourist attraction.

'Two bodies, actually.' Pyke decided there was little point in pulling any punches. 'Children.'

Howard turned from the window with unaccustomed rapidity. 'Children? Dead children?'

'Little girls. Maybe nine or ten years old. The bodies have been there some time. Years.'

Howard drifted past Pyke back into the living room, as though he'd lost interest in what was being said. Not an unusual outcome to their conversations. Pyke followed him, plate of toast in one hand, mug of tea in the other.

Howard was once again slumped on the sofa, but he looked unexpectedly interested. 'This was in Framley? These bodies, I mean?'

'Yes, of course.'

'And that's all you know? No explanation. No reason for them to be there.'

Pyke frowned. 'Not as far as I know. What are you getting at?'

Howard smiled, suddenly reverting to his familiar relaxed self. 'Still, they'll blame us, you know.'

'Blame who? '

'The queers.'

'I don't think–'

'It's children. Who kills children? It's the queers. We'll get the blame.'

Pyke sighed and lowered himself on to the sofa next to Howard, munching on the toast. 'That's your trouble, you know, Howard. Whatever I talk about, whatever I do, whatever happens in the world, somehow you always make it about you.'

Howard was lying back on the sofa, his eyes closed. 'It's a gift, dear boy. Or perhaps it's a curse.'

CHAPTER TWENTY-THREE

'He's in there.'

Brain looked exhausted. Mentally and physically. Winterman's respect for the young man was increasing all the time. At first, he had dismissed Brain as the usual fumbling yokel flatfoot. There were plenty of them about, particularly the ones who'd kept their heads down and their noses clean during the war, hiding behind their "reserved occupation" status. The good ones had generally taken the opportunity – the increased demands, the shortages of manpower – to make something of themselves. The others, especially the little Hitlers who'd taken full advantage of their temporarily enhanced powers, didn't generally have much else going for them.

But Winterman had quickly decided that Brain was a lot smarter than he'd originally appeared. And the young man was also much more resilient than anyone had any right to expect. Certainly, his ordeal had been enough even for the most experienced officer.

'How is he?' Winterman asked.

'Difficult to say.' Brain glanced nervously towards the cell door. 'He really broke down at first. Crying and wailing. He seemed as shocked by it as I was. Claimed he'd seen nothing last night. That he hadn't noticed the blood or the knife.'

'Did you think he was telling the truth?'

'I don't know. If the knife was already in the body when he first found it, I don't really see how he could have missed it.'

'It was dark in the garden, presumably, and he was drunk.'

'He was very drunk, by his own account. But then we've only his own account.'

Smart boy, Winterman thought. 'But he had been drinking? When he first came and found you this morning, I mean.'

'I suppose so. He smelled of drink. Stale drink.'

'How did you persuade him to come back here?'

'It wasn't easy.' Brain suddenly looked anxious. 'Did I do the right thing? I wasn't sure what to do. It didn't seem right to leave him there.'

'At the crime scene? No, I don't think that would have been right. It's important to protect the evidence. If he's a suspect, or even if he isn't, you handled it well.'

'It wasn't easy to get him back here.' Brain spoke with more confidence. 'He wasn't in a state to do much at all, to be honest. I virtually had to carry him. I just kept saying it would be better for everyone if we tried to leave things undisturbed. He didn't argue.'

'I don't know how you got him back through this snow.' It had been hard enough for Winterman and his team. After they'd received the message from Brain, he'd immediately asked Mrs Sheringham to put a call into the local council to get the road to Framley cleared. He'd spent fifteen minutes being fobbed off by officious jobsworths before Mrs Sheringham had finally taken the telephone from him.

'Let me,' she said. 'They know me.'

She was, of course, quite right.

Five minutes later, she had poked her head back into the main office where Winterman was sitting with Hoxton and Marsh. 'All done. They say to give them half an hour or so, and they'll have the road open.'

It had taken slightly longer than that, but not much.

Eventually, with Marsh navigating the Wolseley along the still-treacherous road, they had arrived here back at the village. They dropped Hoxton at Fisher's cottage with instructions to ensure the crime scene was sealed off until they could get the experts in from HQ. Back at the office, Mrs Sheringham had been busy trying to track down Pyke who seemed – like half the world in the face of this snowstorm – to have gone to ground.

'He didn't mind you putting him in the cell?' Winterman asked.

'I don't think he really even realised,' Brain said. 'I didn't make a big deal of it. Just implied that it was the official place for him to wait until you arrived.'

Winterman snorted with amusement. 'We ought to get you on the Bench. You'd have them all behind bars before they even realised it.' He smiled to show his approval. 'But well done. You've handled everything just right.'

Brain beamed. 'Do you want to see him now?'

'In a minute.' Winterman looked up at Marsh who was sitting at the far end of the room, reading carefully through the detailed case notes that Brain had prepared while waiting for them to arrive. 'Are you ready?'

'Ready as I'll ever be.' Marsh stacked up the notes and smiled at Brain. 'I think you've told me everything I need to know.' It was difficult to tell whether there was any undertone of irony to his words, but Brain seemed happy to take them at face value.

'How do you want to play this?' Marsh asked.

Winterman shrugged. 'Gently, I think. To start with anyway. He sounds as if he's in a bit of a state, though we shouldn't jump to any conclusions about why that should be.'

'But we should take advantage of it?'

'If you like. But gently.'

'As a lamb,' Marsh agreed.

Winterman glanced at Brain. 'How well do you know him? Before yesterday, I mean?'

'I knew him a bit. I had to deal with him and his friends once or twice when they were the worse for wear.'

'He caused trouble?'

'Not really. A little boisterous.'

'Stole your helmet?' Marsh chipped in, his face deadpan.

'No–' Brain said, then blushed. 'Well, once. Just high spirits. I thought they were good lads, on the whole.'

'Varsity types?' Winterman asked.

'No, not really.' Brain frowned. 'I mean, William himself is, of course. Medical student. But his friends round here are a pretty mixed bunch. Just the local youths. Farm workers. Office types. You name it.'

'Spends a lot of time here still, does he?' Winterman said. 'If he's an undergraduate, term's started by now.'

'Don't know about that,' Brain said. 'I'm told there's some bad blood between him and his father, so it won't be that that keeps him hanging around.'

Winterman nodded, looking interested. 'What about the father? Who is he? Local gentry?'

'Not really. He really is a varsity type. Retired. Widower.'

'Oh.' Winterman's passing interest seemed to have faded. 'Maybe someone for us to interview in due course, depending on how this goes. Perhaps it's a girlfriend that keeps young William here.'

Brain shrugged. 'I've seen no signs of one. There are some girls who tag along to his crowd, but I don't know that any of them's sweet on William particularly.'

'And what about Fisher?' Winterman said. 'How did William come to know him in the first place?'

'Everyone knew the reverend. But in William's case…'

Winterman sensed some discomfort in Brain's tone. 'Yes?'

'They reckon Fisher's wife left him for William's father. The professor.'

'Ah.' So this was the Cambridge don Hoxton had referred to. Local gossip had clearly given little credence to the suggestion that Fisher's late wife had been only the professor's housekeeper. 'What did William think about that?'

'I don't rightly know.' Brain looked slightly embarrassed. 'Professor had a bit of a reputation as a womaniser already, if you get my drift. Never seen any sign of bad feeling between William and the reverend though – not that the reverend was exactly sweetness and light with anyone. William would sometimes exchange words with him in the pub, seemed to want to make the effort, even if the reverend didn't always return it.'

'So what made William go there last night?'

'Just shelter from the storm.' Marsh brandished Brain's report. 'That's what you reckoned?'

'It's the only house out there,' Brain pointed out. 'Between the village and the prof's house. William was drunk, snow was coming down. He was just looking for somewhere out of the weather. That's what he said.'

'And a clergyman should be obliged to provide refuge,' Marsh added.

'That's his explanation?' Winterman sounded like a teacher challenging a bright pupil's hypothesis, but with no real expectation that he would refute it. 'And no motive for murder?'

'Can't see it,' Brain responded. 'I mean, William was drunk, so he might not have been in control of his actions…'

'Does he strike you as the violent type?' Marsh said. 'When you've dealt with him and his chums before?'

'I wouldn't say so. One or two of his mates are a bit on the rough side – might get into a scrap at chucking-out time. But even they're not really what I'd call violent. Couldn't see any of them attacking an old man.'

'What about robbery?' Marsh offered. 'Maybe old Fisher had a nest egg tucked away?'

Brain's expression suggested that, while it might be acceptable to accuse a middle-class undergraduate of murder, robbery was quite another matter. 'I wouldn't have thought William was short of money.'

'Who knows?' Winterman said. 'I've seen less likely candidates seduced by the prospect of some easy money. And undergraduates are always skint. But it doesn't seem likely. Why was the body in the garden? Why did William hang around? If there was money, what's happened to it?'

'Maybe he's still got it,' Marsh said. 'I don't imagine anyone's searched him yet.'

Brain coughed. 'I have actually. Pretty much.'

Winterman raised his eyebrows. 'How did you manage that without attracting his attention?'

Brain smiled smugly. 'It was easy actually. His clothes were sodden when we got back here – not to mention slept in. I offered him a change. He's more or less my size. His clothes are drying out over there. But I took the opportunity to check the pockets. Nothing of significance.'

'Smart boy,' Winterman said. 'I suppose it's still conceivable that he might have hidden something somewhere – in the garden at Fisher's maybe, or on his way back here when he first came to find you. But again if he was sufficiently compos mentis to do that, why come and find you at all? Why not just make himself scarce? But we'll need to have Fisher's house checked. See if there's any sign of anything missing. Does Fisher have any relatives?'

'Not as far as I know,' Brain said.

Winterman glanced across at Marsh. 'Something for us to check up on. Okay, let's go and talk to young William. You'd better sit in,' Winterman said to Brain. 'You might spot something. Some inconsistency with what he told you before.'

Brain nodded enthusiastically, and for a moment he reminded Winterman of an enthusiastic spaniel. 'Only too pleased to help, sir.'

CHAPTER TWENTY-FOUR

The police cell was not what Winterman had expected.

It was an intrinsic part of the house, the whole building combining a part-time local police station – a sub-branch of the main station in a larger adjoining village – with domestic accommodation for the incumbent officer. Winterman imagined the holding cell had rarely been used in recent years. Erringford was hardly a hotbed of crime. The cell had probably been maintained during wartime as a precautionary measure in readiness for that legendary creature, the parachuting German airman.

Brain had effectively annexed the cell as part of his own living accommodation. Although the room's décor remained spartan, it was furnished with a battered old leather sofa and a pair of matching armchairs, complete with neat antimacassars. There was a small cabinet with a wireless on top of it, and even a couple of cheap-looking framed prints on the grey walls.

William was slumped face down on the sofa, his head buried under his arms. At first, Winterman assumed William was asleep but then the young man raised his head, staring in some bafflement at his new visitors. His face was drawn and pale, his eyes bloodshot.

'Am I under arrest?'

Winterman lowered himself into the armchair opposite William. Marsh took the other seat, leaving Brain hovering awkwardly by the door.

'Is there any reason why you should be?' Winterman settled back and felt in his pocket for his cigarettes.

'I don't know,' William said. 'I don't know what's happening.'

Winterman held out the cigarette packet. William accepted one with an expression of gratitude, and took a light from

Winterman's proffered lighter. The young man's hands were shaking badly, though it was unclear whether this was the result of nerves or the previous night's alcohol. 'No, we're not sure either,' Winterman said finally. 'But you're not under arrest. We just want to talk to you as a witness.'

William pushed himself upright. 'I'm not an idiot. You must have me in the frame for that–' He stopped. 'And I don't even know–'

Winterman held up his hand. 'We just want to hear what you've got to tell us.' He nodded towards Marsh. 'DC Marsh will be taking notes. You know PC Brain. I'm DI Winterman. We're CID officers. Detectives. All we want you to do is tell us, as fully and accurately as you can, everything you remember from last night and this morning. We don't want speculation or guesses. Just the facts, as best you can recall them.'

The lengthy speech appeared to have had the desired effect of calming William. He nodded.

'First, your full name and address, for the record.' Winterman's experience was that, in dealing with nervous witnesses, it was helpful to start with the basics. It might be difficult to start them talking, but once started it was often equally hard to get them to stop.

'William Nigel Callaghan,' William began. 'Westland House, near Framley, Cambridgeshire.'

'That's your permanent address?'

'I'm a student. In Nottingham. The City Hospital.'

'A doctor?'

'One day. If the police or booze don't get me first.' It was obviously a well-used line, but suddenly rendered inappropriate. 'But that's my father's house, so I suppose that's my permanent address. Permanent for the time being anyway.'

'So, Mr Callaghan, talk us through everything you remember from last night. Start from when you left the pub. What time was that?'

'Ten thirty or so. Didn't even stay for last orders.'

'Then what?'

William slowly described the events of the previous night – leaving the pub, the slow trudge home through the thickening snow, the decision to seek shelter at Fisher's. The unlocked front door, the ice-cold interior of the cottage, the open rear door. Fisher's body lying prone in the snow.

'He was dead when you found him?'

William hesitated. 'I think so. I must have checked. I'm a medical student, for goodness' sake.'

Winterman eyes were fixed on the young man. Eventually, William went on. 'I don't know. I was drunk – I'm struggling to piece it together now. I remember looking out of the windows, seeing his body out there on the snow.'

'You didn't have any doubt who it was?'

'I didn't really think about it. It never occurred to me it was anyone but the reverend. Everyone knew he lived on his own.'

'So you went outside?'

'Of course. I thought he must have had some sort of accident or collapsed.' He stopped, as though catching his breath. 'So I must have gone out to see if he was – well, whether he was all right.'

'But he wasn't.'

'I don't think it took me long to realise that.'

'You checked his pulse? His breathing?'

'It's all a bit of a blur after that. I don't know. Maybe it was the shock of finding him. I've been trying to get it clear in my mind, but I can't. It's just a series of disconnected images. But it was clear that he was dead.'

'What about the blood?' Winterman's tone was casual.

There was another longer pause. 'I don't know.' For the first time, William sounded genuinely anxious. 'I didn't see it. I'm sure I didn't. Not last night. I just assumed he'd had a heart attack or a stroke or something. It never occurred to me that–'

'That he'd been stabbed? You're a medical student.'

'I wasn't trying to pass a bloody examination.' William's voice was cracking. 'I was drunk. I was incapable. I'd just stumbled across a dead body. But I'd no reason to imagine–'

'Of course. I'm just trying to get the facts straight.'

'If you think I killed him, bloody arrest me, so we can deal with this properly.'

'Did you kill him, Mr Callaghan?' Winterman spoke calmly, as though inquiring about the weather.

'Of course I didn't kill him. Why would I want to kill him?'

'People kill for a lot of different reasons. You'd be surprised.'

'I hardly knew him.'

'You knew him well enough to enter his house uninvited.'

'I've told you–' William stopped. 'Is that what you're thinking? That – what? – that I broke into his house and killed him? What for? To rob an old man?'

'I'm not thinking anything. I just want the facts. I understand the Reverend Fisher wasn't on the best of terms with your father.'

William was clearly surprised by the apparent non sequitur. 'They weren't on any terms, as far as I'm aware. You've obviously heard the story. How my father stole Fisher's wife. It's pretty much true. From what I know now, she'd have left Fisher anyway. But my father was only too happy to greet her with open arms. As long as it suited him anyway.'

'How did you feel about all that?'

'It was nearly ten years ago. I was a boy. She wasn't the first of my father's floozies. She was just one of the older ones.' There was a note of bitterness in his voice. 'To be honest, I liked Christina more than most of them. I largely kept out of their way, but she was kind to me. Showed a bit of interest, which is more than most of them did. I was sorry when she went, but that was always going to happen in the end. Sorrier still about what happened...' His voice trailed off.

'Did you blame Fisher for what happened?'

'You think this was some sort of revenge for Christina's death? Hardly. I was sorry about what happened to her. Sorrier still about

Amy, her little girl. Poor little thing had done nothing to deserve that fate. But it wasn't as if Christina was my mother or anything. She was just another of my father's unfortunate conquests. As it turned out, more unfortunate than the rest of them.' He stopped, as if worried that he might have said too much. 'As for Fisher, yes, he was responsible, along with my father. But my father had no excuse for what he did. Fisher was hardly responsible for his own actions.'

'Not everyone would be so forgiving.'

'It's not my place to offer him forgiveness,' William said. 'I suppose that was a matter for his own faith. Not that he had much of that left by the end, poor bugger.'

'Why do you say that?'

'If ever there was a lost soul, it was Fisher. The only spirit he believed in came in a bottle.'

Winterman pushed himself to his feet, hovering momentarily over the young man. 'And how about you?'

'Me?'

'What do you believe in?'

'Apart from the booze as well, you mean. I don't know. Life. Justice. Freedom. All that stuff, I suppose. The stuff we fought a war for, so they tell me.'

'So we did,' Winterman agreed. 'What are your plans now?'

'Plans?'

'For the next few days. Were you planning to return to college?'

'I suppose so. I'd intended to go back yesterday in fact, but the trains weren't running.'

'Simpler for you if they had been. We don't want to keep you from your studies for any longer than we need to, but I'd appreciate if you'd stay around here for the moment. And I'd be grateful if you could provide DC Marsh with your contact details, here and at medical school.'

'I'm free to go now?'

'You're free to go now, Mr Callaghan. We can give you a lift to your father's house, if that's where you're heading.'

‘I hadn’t really thought about it. I suppose so. Thank you.’

Winterman nodded, his eyes fixed on William. ‘No place like home, eh?’

William nodded, his expression suggesting his mind was elsewhere. ‘No place at all,’ he said finally.

CHAPTER TWENTY-FIVE

Winterman hesitated then pressed the doorbell. Somewhere deep inside the house he heard the faint chime but there was no sign of life in the blank windows.

He was beginning to curse himself for embarking on a fool's errand. The sky was darkening again, threatening more snow. The ever-present east wind was blowing harder across the fens, and even in his heavy overcoat, hat and scarf he was starting to feel bloody cold.

He had detected no movement from inside, but the door opened unexpectedly, a face peering through the narrow gap.

'Bloody cold!' Winterman said, breezily, then immediately regretted the words.

If it was Mrs Griffiths answering the door, she would almost certainly not approve of bad language. Even if it was the daughter, she might be shocked.

Half expecting the door to be slammed in his face, he leaned forward. 'It's me. DI Winterman.'

The door opened a few more inches. It was the daughter, Mary. She regarded him for a moment, expressionless. Then she smiled. 'Bloody cold,' she agreed, with an amiable vehemence that surprised him. 'Bloody, bloody cold.'

'Sorry to disturb you…' He hesitated, suddenly unsure whether he should address her as Mrs or Miss.

'Mary.'

'Mary,' he repeated. After all, she was a member of his own team, he told himself.

She nodded as if in approval that he had succeeded in repeating her name correctly. 'Would you like to come in…?'

She hesitated to indicate she was waiting for him to give his own name. When he didn't immediately respond, she added: 'Or should I call you sir?'

'No, of course–' He was already on the back foot. Perhaps she had been well trained by Mrs Sheringham. 'Ivan,' he said finally.

Her smile widened, but avoided turning into a laugh.

'I know,' he said. 'My parents were big admirers of the Bolsheviks. I was born at the wrong time.'

'Weren't we all.' The smile hadn't wavered. 'You'd better come in, Ivan.'

He followed her into the gloomy hallway, then through into the kitchen. 'Come in here. It's the warmest room. Though that's not saying much.'

The kitchen was as neat as he remembered from their visit the previous day. Some newly washed crockery was stacked tidily by the sink. 'How's your mother?'

'Bearing up. She's in the back room with the children. Likes to keep busy. I hope you didn't mind me not coming in today. What with the snow and everything.'

'I don't think anyone really expected you. Even without the snow.'

'That's good of you. Would you like a cup of tea?'

'I'd love one. If only to warm my fingers on.'

She gestured for him to sit down at the kitchen table and busied herself with the kettle. 'What can we do for you?'

It was a good question. Winterman had given Marsh some guff about pastoral care – Mary being a colleague. 'I'd better just check how she and her mother are, after yesterday.' He wasn't sure Marsh had bought it. He wasn't sure Mary was going to buy it either.

'I just wanted to see how you were,' he said, speaking perhaps slightly more honestly than he'd intended.

'Me?'

'And your mother,' he added. 'After yesterday. It must have been a shock.'

'For Mother, yes. I didn't see much.'

'No, I suppose not.' He was already running out of things to say. Infanticide wasn't conducive to intimate small talk.

She carried the teapot over to the table and took some cups from the cupboard above the sink. 'I'm afraid we're out of milk. And sugar, for that matter. I think we do still have some tea though.'

'I don't take sugar. I should let you have my ration.'

She laughed gently, pouring the tea. 'I'll take you up on that. We never have enough.'

'The least I can do.'

'In return for what?' She frowned, though her eyes were still playful.

'Just for a colleague.'

'Well, thank you.' She nodded towards the back door. 'When do you think they'll be coming to deal with it? The body, I mean.'

'I'd hoped later today. Depends on the weather. Whether they can get out from HQ.'

'And whether they can be bothered. I know HQ.'

'In fairness, it won't be their top priority anymore. We have another body. A little more recent.' He briefly recounted the finding of Fisher's body.

'Reverend Fisher? Old Joe? Goodness.'

'Not necessarily the most appropriate word, from what I understand.'

'Perhaps not. He wasn't much liked round here.'

'Enough for someone to kill him?'

'I wouldn't have said so. But then who dislikes someone enough to kill them?'

'Plenty of people, in my experience. But it's not easy to understand.'

'But you think he *was* murdered?'

'We've not had the doc look at him yet. But it seems an unlikely accident or suicide.'

'You don't seriously suspect William Callaghan?'

'You know him?' This wasn't quite the conversation Winterman had had in mind, but he supposed it would do.

'A bit. I mean, a place like this, you know everyone a bit. I've seen him around. Enough to say hello to.'

'You don't think he's a killer?'

'I can't imagine many people as killers. But not really. Not William.' She paused. 'I probably shouldn't say this in the circumstances, but I do think he's a bit – well, nervy is probably the word.'

'Nervy?'

'I don't quite know how to put it. I don't want you to misunderstand. It's just that, from what I've heard, he's someone who gets very wound up about things. I think it's why he drinks. That's the only time he seems relaxed.'

'What kind of things?'

'Most of this is second hand. But things to do with his father, mainly. They don't get on. They've been known to have blazing rows in the street.'

'I understand there was some bad blood between the father and Fisher.'

'On Fisher's side, mainly, from what I've heard. William's father was one of those responsible for getting Fisher relieved of his clerical duties – but that was understandable enough. Then of course there was the wife. You'll have heard about all that.'

'How she left the reverend to take up duties as the father's housekeeper.'

She laughed. 'Something like that. The old man had a few housekeepers over the years.'

'Must have kept a tidy house,' Winterman agreed, straight-faced.

'Spotless,' she smiled. 'How's the tea?'

He regarded the pale brown liquid in his cup. 'Bracing. I think that's the word.'

'Like Skegness. But warmer, I hope.'

'Definitely warmer. I could take you there. Skegness, I mean. In the summer.' The words had slipped out before he could stop them, buoyed on the back of their banter. But he knew from experience it was best to trust his instincts. The alternative was to wait too long, miss the moment.

Her mouth was slightly open. The look in her eyes, he was relieved to note, remained playful. Perhaps he hadn't misjudged. 'That's very kind of you, Ivan.' She placed a faint emphasis on his name. 'But I hardly know you yet.' The tone was gently mocking.

He nodded, giving full consideration to this point. 'But then we're still a long way from summer.'

'You're not backwards in coming forward, I'll say that.'

'Life's too short.' This time he did immediately regret the words, recalling her widowhood.

But she showed no reaction. 'As you say, we're a long way from summer. Let's see, shall we? Plenty of time to get to know one another.'

He felt more relaxed, with the sense that some first hurdle had been cleared. He heard the distant toot of a car horn outside and glanced at his watch. 'I'll need to go. Marsh is picking me up.'

'Paul.' It took him a moment to realise this must be Marsh's first name. It hadn't occurred to Winterman to ask.

'Paul.' He repeated the word with the air of one learning a foreign language by rote. It also hadn't occurred to him, he realised, to wonder whether there might be any other man in Mary's life. Paul Marsh, for example. But he didn't think so. Another area in which he'd learnt to trust his instincts.

She followed him through into the hallway. There was no natural light other than the pale illumination from a stained-glass fanlight over the front door. It was a narrow space, gloomy with dark heavily patterned wallpaper.

'Do you want to see Mother before you go?'

Winterman remembered his ostensible for visiting and hoped his faint blush was invisible in the dim light. 'I don't want to disturb her if she's with the children.'

There was an unreadable twinkle in Mary's eye as she turned to open the front door. 'I'll tell her you were asking after her.'

Marsh was outside, leaning casually against the gate. He gazed at Mary and then beyond her to Winterman with undisguised curiosity.

Winterman eased his way past Mary, out into the icy air. The sky was heavier than ever, definitely threatening more snow.

'Doesn't look promising,' he said to Marsh. 'Let's hope we can get back okay.' He glanced back at Mary. 'Don't feel you need to come in tomorrow.'

'I might not be able to if there's more snow. I'll do my best.'

'What's happening at Fisher's?' Winterman asked Marsh.

'HQ team are there now. I've asked them to make sure they come here next. You know, to deal with–'

'We know.' Winterman turned to Mary. 'I don't imagine we'll need to disturb you or your mother again on that. We've got your statements.'

'I'll tell Mother. And I hope I'll see you tomorrow – Inspector.'

The momentary pause before the last word told him she was teasing. He had wondered whether she might use his forename despite Marsh's presence. It was probably only a sense of mischief rather than propriety that had prevented her. He hoped so anyway.

He turned back to find Marsh still gazing at him, his curiosity clearly undiminished.

'Nice girl,' Winterman said tonelessly.

'Very nice,' Marsh agreed. 'Everyone says so.'

'Any word of Pyke yet? We need to get the gen on Fisher's body.' A consummate gear change, he thought ironically. Masterful double declutching.

'Funny you should say that.' Marsh jerked his thumb towards the black Wolseley parked by the front gate. Pyke was in the back seat, his homburg pulled forward over his eyes. He looked as if he might well be asleep.

Winterman raised an eyebrow. 'Where'd you find him?'

'He turned up at Brain's on his motorbike. Looking for a telephone so he could call into the office.'

'So where's he been all night? Not,' Winterman added, 'that it's any of our business.'

'Staying with a friend apparently. Got stranded out here. Couldn't risk his bike in the snow. Found someone to give him shelter.'

'Lucky man then.'

'Or plenty of friends.' Marsh was already trudging back through the snow towards the car. 'I thought we should take him up to Fisher's. Let him have a gander at the body *in situ* so they can get it back to the mortuary.'

Winterman followed him to the car. As Winterman climbed into the back seat, Pyke tipped back his head, peering from under the brim of his hat. 'We must stop meeting like this.'

'People will talk.' Winterman eased himself back into the firm leather seat as Marsh executed a neat U-turn.

'People already are talking,' Pyke pointed out. 'We seem to be collecting dead bodies. Now you've killed the vicar?'

'Ex-vicar. And not personally, you understand.' Winterman was watching the empty snow-bound fields. Marsh's driving was as cautious as ever. 'But yes, it looks like murder.'

'Seems an extraordinary coincidence. Three murdered bodies in the space of a couple of weeks.'

'Though only one of them new, of course.'

'That just makes it odder.'

'Or more of a coincidence.'

Marsh pulled up in front of Fisher's cottage, remaining seated as Pyke and Winterman climbed out. Hoxton was leaning against the front wall, a cigarette dangling from the corner of his mouth. He nodded an acknowledgement at their arrival and gestured over his shoulder. 'Experts in there.' He imbued the first word with an impressive disdain. 'Didn't want me under their feet.'

'How are they doing?' Winterman asked.

'Nearly finished, I reckon. Just waiting on the good doctor here with his bag of tricks.'

'At your command.' Pyke stepped past Hoxton into the gloom of Fisher's hallway.

'So what's the story?' Winterman asked.

'Nothing new.' Hoxton proffered his cigarette packet. 'Definitely murder, unless the doc surprises all of us. He didn't fall on the knife by accident.'

'And it would be an impressive way to commit suicide.' Winterman cupped his hand to light his cigarette.

'More impressive than you think.' Hoxton blew a steady stream of smoke into the grey air. 'They're waiting on the doc's view, but there's a bit of a mystery about the stabbing.'

'What sort of mystery?'

'When and why, for a start. They reckon he was already dead when the knife entered his chest. That's why there wasn't much blood. They say the poor bugger was probably suffocated.'

'Suffocated? So why stick a knife in him?'

'Beats me, guv. They were waiting on the doc to be sure, but that's the way they've pieced it together. Looks like the poor bugger had gone out into the garden for some reason when someone waylaid him, grabbed him from behind and thrust something across his mouth. Held it there till he stopped breathing.'

'Suggests some strength.'

'Fisher was hardly Charles Atlas. Don't reckon it would have taken that much.'

'So why stab him?'

'As I say, beats me. To make sure he was dead?'

'It might explain why young Callaghan didn't see the knife last night though. If it wasn't there when he first went out.' Winterman paused, thinking. 'Brain reckoned Callaghan touched the knife when he turned the body over, so his fingerprints will be on it. But maybe they were on it already. If the knife was put there when Callaghan was asleep on the sofa, maybe the killer had already pressed it into his hand. Perhaps the killer was attempting to frame Callaghan for the murder.'

Hoxton snorted. 'You been reading too much Agatha Christie, guv? Though, of course, if Callaghan is the killer, he knew his prints would be on the knife so he made sure that Brain saw him touch it.'

'Rather than just wiping the handle, you mean?'

'You started it, guv. But if we're playing Sherlock Holmes, perhaps he was too drunk to think about it the night before, but was quick-witted enough to cover himself in the morning.' Hoxton tossed his cigarette butt out into the heaped snow. Winterman automatically offered him one of his own, which Hoxton took with a nod of thanks. 'But it's a bit far fetched.'

'What about footprints around the body? Any clues there? This snow must be good for something.'

'There are some. But through all the layers of snow it's difficult to be sure what might belong to Fisher and what might belong to Callaghan. Or anyone else. They've taken dozens of photographs, but I can't honestly see them telling us much.' He stepped back, with the air of one who had just received a telepathic signal, as Fisher's front door opened and Pyke's head peered out.

'Hope you chaps aren't getting overheated out here. I'm just about done.'

'Anything to report?' Winterman said.

'Oh, plenty. I'll have it on your desk tomorrow.'

'I'll try to contain my anticipation. Anything interesting, I meant?'

'A very different question, dear boy.' Pyke moved out to join them on the doorstep, unceremoniously holding his hand out for one of Winterman's cigarettes. 'Certainly a bit fresher out here. And I don't just mean the sobering scent of decay. Fisher's housekeeping left something to be desired.'

'Cause of death?' Winterman asked.

'Your chaps guessed right. It turns out that, against all the odds, it wasn't actually that bloody great knife sticking out of his chest that killed him. He was already dead by then. Some sort of chemical was used on him. Chloroform at a guess, but we can confirm that back at the shop.'

'Somebody who knew what they were doing?'

'Probably. Certainly wasn't just opportunist.'

'And he was stabbed after death. So why would someone do that?'

'I just deal with the what, when and how,' Pyke said. 'I'll leave you to deal with the why. Not to mention the who.' He squinted up at the lowering sky. 'I've told them to get their magic boxes over to that little kiddie's body. Before the snow comes down again. Someone'll need to go with them.'

Winterman glanced at Hoxton. 'I'll go. They can always give me a lift back afterwards, and you and Marsh can be getting home.'

'Won't argue, guv,' Hoxton said. 'I'll be glad to get out of this bloody cold. Looks like more snow though. Don't get caught.'

'I'll survive.'

'I don't doubt it.' Hoxton glanced from Winterman to Pyke, his expression blank. 'It always helps if you've got friends to call on though, eh, doc?' His face broke into an unexpected smile. 'Give you a lift back to your bike?'

CHAPTER TWENTY-SIX

He stepped out into the rain, staring up at the black sky. He had never seen rainfall like it. Incessant, pounding, the air thick with water, visibility down to a few feet. Walking out into it was like throwing yourself into the ocean. Within seconds, despite the raincoat he had hurriedly thrown on, he was soaked to the skin, freezing cold, the icy water trickling down his neck, into his shoes. He could feel the chill eating into his body. The temperature had risen a degree or two as the rain fell, but this was still a winter storm, precipitation on the verge of turning into sleet.

It had to be nearly dawn but he could see nothing. The wind had picked up again and was buffeting the house behind him, rattling the loose sash windows, whipping through the overgrown garden, roaring down the passageway by the back door.

How could he have heard a voice in this cacophony?

But he had. He was sure of it. He could hear it, echoing in his head. The strained voice of a child, caught momentarily on the gusting wind. Calling out. A voice in need. Perhaps in pain.

Reason told him he had imagined it, that it had been a trick of the keening wind and his own imagination. Reason told him he should return indoors, warm himself up, go back to bed. Forget all this. Forget everything.

But something else kept him out here, wondering whether he should venture further into the darkness.

Then he thought he saw something in the thick undergrowth. A movement, two glinting eyes.

The pale face of a child, staring.

'Sam!' he called before he could stop himself. And he wondered why, what that name had meant to him. It belonged to a story he had once heard, somewhere in another life, but which he had long forgotten.

With hope fading, he realised there was no alternative. He stumbled forward, pushing against the rising wind and the driving rain.

The drenched undergrowth was thickening beneath his feet, around his ankles, as he forced himself forward, and he realised he had lost his bearings. He turned, looking for a glimmer of light from the house he expected still to be behind him, but there was only darkness. Working by instinct, he cautiously moved forward.

It took him a moment to realise the ground was falling away beneath him. He was on a slope, the gradient dropping away unexpectedly. He took another step, doubting his reason, unable to recall any such slope in the proximity of the house.

The riverbank. But that had been somewhere else. Somewhere far away.

Then he was falling, the oozing ground striking his face, his shoulders, his back, as he tumbled headlong through the rain and the wind.

He came to an abrupt halt, his body striking jarringly against a solid object. Brickwork, part of a wall. And beyond that a yawning hole, and somewhere the acrid smell of burning…

In front of him, despite the ebbing darkness, he could see the face again, the child's staring eyes.

'Sam!' he called once more, desperate, still not knowing why.

CHAPTER TWENTY-SEVEN

Winterman was in early, despite the snow. It took him a few minutes of rooting about in the kitchen to find a tea caddy. He lit the small gas hob, boiled a kettle and succeeded in making himself a pot of tea. There was no milk, but the fragrant warm liquid felt like an achievement in the cold unfamiliar environment.

Winterman poured himself a cup and, after a brief look around the main office, made his way upstairs to his own room. He sat down at the desk and looked around. An ugly and loudly ticking clock above the door told him it was still only 6.30am.

The dream had rattled him. It wasn't so much that it had been a nightmare – he was accustomed to those. It had been the content. Like all his dreams, however vivid, it had melted away rapidly on waking, and he had been left with little more than impressions, emotions, fading images. Pouring rain, yet again, and the wind. The familiar devastating sense of loss.

Winterman rose and stepped over to the office window. He needed to know more about Framley. Hoxton had called him a local, but he wasn't really. He knew well enough that in these parts a visitor even from the next village was likely to be treated as an incomer. Winterman was a city boy, even if the city was barely more than a large town.

He turned back from the window, tensing as he heard the slamming of a door from somewhere downstairs. He glanced at the clock. Still not yet seven. Mrs Sheringham presumably. He had no idea what time she normally started work, but was hardly surprised to discover she was an early bird.

He opened his office door noisily and called her name, keen to ensure she shouldn't be startled by his presence. There was silence from down below. He descended the stairs, his empty teacup clutched in his hand, calling out her name again.

Mrs Sheringham's office was ahead of him, the door closed. He stepped forward and twisted the handle, but the door was locked. She had not, he had noted, included a key to her office in the set she had given to him. Feeling irrationally jittery, he pushed open the door of the main office. Mary was sitting behind Marsh's desk, a copy of the previous day's newspaper spread in front of her. She looked up as he entered. 'Oh! You frightened the life out of me.'

Winterman stood in the doorway, mildly embarrassed by his previous anxieties. 'I'm sorry. I thought you were Mrs Sheringham.'

'I'll need to decide how to take that.'

'You're in early. To be honest, I didn't really expect you in at all.'

'I couldn't sleep. Thought I might as well try to do something useful.'

'Any help welcome. But don't do too much.' A thought struck him. 'How did you get here?'

'I cycled. I sometimes do. You can't rely on the buses out our way even at the best of times.'

'But it's pitch black out there.' He looked past her towards the office windows. He was exaggerating slightly, but the leaden skies were far from welcoming.

'That's winter for you.' She spoke as if alerting him to a hitherto unnoticed phenomenon. 'I'm used to leaving home in the dark this time of year.'

'But the roads must be lethal.' He realised that he did genuinely care about the risks she must have taken.

'Not as bad as you'd think. And I was very careful.'

'I'm glad to hear it.' He suspected that his tone was giving away more than he intended. 'We can't afford to lose any manpower at the moment.'

She smiled at him, her eyes mischievous. 'Manpower?'

'You'll want a cup of tea. You must be freezing.'

'You sound like my mother. But yes, thanks. That would be nice.'

He wandered back through into the poky kitchen, wondering precisely what kind of emotions he was wrestling with. Something more serious than he'd intended, certainly.

'Still no milk then?' He turned to see she had followed him into the small room. Involuntarily, he took a step back. 'I'll pop out later. See if I can track some down.'

'That would be good.' He busied himself boiling the kettle, spooning out the tea, pouring on the water. She watched him with what he assumed was mild amusement. He decided there was no point in putting off the moment much longer. 'Mind you, you can have too much tea. Why don't you let me buy you a proper drink? After work.'

She said nothing for a moment, but her sense of amusement grew more evident. 'That's very kind of you. Thank you for the invitation, Ivan.'

He handed her the steaming cup of tea. 'Does that mean you accept?'

'I'll have to think about it.'

He had been expecting this, but was untroubled. It as, after all, just the first move in a much longer game. 'You–'

'The thing is, Ivan,' she spoke his name with an unexpected emphasis, 'that you come with something of a reputation.'

'A reputation?' He wondered what gossip had been shared amongst the team. 'Nothing bad, I hope?' He spoke lightly, but could sense that he was not fooling her.

'I suppose that depends. On what one's looking for.'

'I'm not sure I really understand,' he said, though he understood all too well.

'You have a bit of a reputation as a – well, I think womaniser is perhaps the word.'

'Oh. I see. And where did you hear this?'

'I have my sources.'

'You don't want to believe everything Hoxton tells you.'

The smile momentarily turned into a laugh. 'George? I don't believe *anything* he tells me.'

George, Winterman thought. So Hoxton had a Christian name too. 'Who then?'

'As I say, I have my sources. Are you saying they're wrong?'

'I–' He stopped, not even sure what the honest answer might be. He wondered what rumours had been circulating about him. No wonder Mrs Sheringham had seemed so frosty. 'I think it's a bit of an overstatement.'

'But then you're a man.'

'I can't argue with you there. So what have they been saying about me?'

'Oh, you know…' She turned and made her way, her teacup balanced in her hand, back into the main office. She sat down behind her desk, tucked unobtrusively in a corner of the room behind a row of filing cabinets. He followed her, pulling across the chair from Marsh's desk, and sat down opposite her.

'I don't really know,' he said. 'What they're saying, I mean. But I imagine it's worse than the truth.'

'So what is the truth?'

'The truth is…' He hesitated again. 'The truth's nothing. Nothing much at all. I mean, when I was younger, when I was an undergraduate–'

'You were one for the ladies?'

'That's a long time ago.'

'You're a changed man?' Her tone still conveyed amusement rather than scepticism.

'Yes.'

'Now that you're married?'

He said nothing for a moment. 'Who told you that?'

'Isn't it true?'

He took a long slow sip of his scalding tea. 'Sort of.'

'You're sort of married?'

'I think that sums it up.'

'I'm an old-fashioned girl. I tend to believe you're either married or you're not.'

'You'd think so, wouldn't you? But it's a long story.'

'It usually is. And no doubt you'd like the opportunity to tell it to me.'

It wasn't going quite the way Winterman had hoped, and for a moment he was tempted to throw in the towel. 'I'd prefer you knew the truth.'

She nodded, as though she had just made up her mind. 'So would I. Okay. You're on. You can buy me a drink.'

'Really?' He blinked, startled by the unexpected turn in the conversation.

'Assuming you still want to. I'll call Mam and tell her I'll be a bit late back. Not too late, mind. Just the one.'

'One drink it is then. And I'll give you and your bike a lift home. You'll probably get home earlier than usual.'

'Don't get ahead of yourself. We'll see.'

'We'll see,' he agreed.

Well, he thought, it was at least a start. But to what, he wasn't sure.

CHAPTER TWENTY-EIGHT

Mrs Sheringham arrived just after eight, and showed no surprise that two of her colleagues were already in the office. It occurred to Winterman that this in itself might be enough to set tongues wagging, but there was nothing much he could do about that.

By eight thirty, the whole small team had assembled in the main office. The snow was still thick on the ground, but no more had fallen in the night and most of the local main roads had been at least partially cleared.

'It's not the end of it though,' Hoxton predicted. He was lying slouched in his chair, his feet propped on a metal waste-paper bin. 'There's more to come.'

'Feel it in your water, do you?' Marsh was aimlessly flicking through one of the morning's newspapers, waiting for Winterman to call the meeting, such as it was, to order.

'Feel it in the air, more like,' Hoxton said. 'Never known it so cold.'

'If you're right,' Winterman observed, placing himself in the centre of the group and striving to exert some authority, 'it's all the more reason why we should move quickly. Make the best of things while the roads are clear.'

'All ears, guv.' Hoxton leant back and gazed at Winterman with apparent rapt attention.

'I'm open to any better suggestions,' Winterman said, glancing back at Hoxton's blank visage, 'particularly from those who've got the most local knowledge, but I think we need to get down to some legwork. We've got two – maybe even three – potential cases here, and almost nothing in the way of evidence.'

'So where do we start?' Hoxton made the question sound like an initiative test.

'We've got almost nothing on the children,' Winterman said. 'We'll get the forensic reports which might give us some clues – for example, about precisely where in the fens the bodies might have been all this time – but I'm not building my hopes up.' He turned to Mrs Sheringham. She was sitting beside Mary's desk, her posture implying she had some important copy typing waiting in her office. 'We don't even seem to have any reports of missing children that might relate to these bodies. Mrs Sheringham, can you speak to HQ, see what regional records they've got on missing persons?'

'I've already put in a request, Inspector,' she said predictably. 'Asked them to pull out records of any missing children. I said to go back to the start of the war.'

'What did they say?'

'They didn't sound very optimistic. The wartime records are a mess. They moved offices four or five times, to my knowledge, and they were bombed once. Records were destroyed or lost. And I don't know how much effort was really put into keeping them in the first place.' She spoke as if barely able to conceive of such negligence.

'I imagine they had other priorities,' Winterman offered.

'I imagine they had to make do with a skeleton staff of wastrels and incompetents,' Mrs Sheringham corrected. 'Most of whom certainly had other priorities.'

'Meanwhile,' Winterman said, 'we need to get back out to Framley. I want to have a chat with Callaghan's father, this academic.'

'The prof,' Hoxton said. 'Reckon he'll be able to tell us much?'

'He can give us a view on his son, if nothing else. And we can perhaps get him to corroborate Callaghan's movements.'

'Unless Callaghan's primed him already,' Marsh said. 'A father's testimony won't be worth much.'

'That depends on the father,' Hoxton said. 'No great love lost between Callaghan and the prof.'

'Anyway, it's a route we need to explore,' Winterman said. He turned to Hoxton. 'So who else should we speak to? We can do a door to door in the village, but we'll be pushed if there's more snow coming.'

'No chance of any backup resource?' Marsh asked.

'I can't see them rushing to push manpower in our direction. We need to make best use of what we've got.'

'We should start with the pub,' Hoxton said. 'If the local landlord doesn't know it, it's not worth knowing. Especially that nosy beggar. Excuse my French, ladies. '

'Not a bad thought,' Winterman said. 'Who else?'

Hoxton shrugged. 'Everyone and no one, really. Fisher had no close friends, as far as I'm aware. No real neighbours either, for that matter.'

Marsh leaned forward. 'What about Hamshaw?'

'Hamshaw?'

'Lord Hamshaw, that would be, since his elevation,' Hoxton said.

'The MP?'

'Former MP,' Hoxton corrected. 'Sir Thomas Hamshaw.'

Winterman had a vague memory of the man in question, a red-faced slightly pugnacious figure who had risen to some junior ministerial role in the dying days of the war. Winterman assumed Hamshaw had lost his seat in the '45 election. 'Why him?'

'Something Mrs Griffiths – Mary's mam – said yesterday, just in passing. She said it was a coincidence that both bodies had been found on Hamshaw's land. That old cottage, where Fisher found the first body – that had been one of Hamshaw's tenancies apparently. The farmland opposite Mary's house belongs to Hamshaw. Wouldn't be surprised to find Fisher's cottage belonged to Hamshaw as well. He was turfed out of the vicarage when they relieved him of his duties. Can't see he'd have been able to afford anything of his own, so perhaps Hamshaw stepped in to smooth things over. Another coincidence, if so.'

'Not that much of a coincidence,' Hoxton observed. 'He's the nearest there is to local gentry in that part of the world. Family's ruled the roost there for generations. Owns half the land in them parts.'

'Now he's been ousted by a Labour man,' Winterman mused ironically. 'Makes you think.'

'There's maybe more than one farmhand got tired of tugging his forelock. But I think it was a shock to him. Subservience runs deep in these parts.' Hoxton shook his head. 'Like as not, Hamshaw'll have nothing useful to tell us. But he'd have known Fisher well in his vicaring days, and there's not much of importance happens around here without Hamshaw knowing about it.'

'Worth a try, anyway,' Winterman said. 'We should think about using young Brain on some of the door-to-door stuff. He's got his own job to do, but I don't imagine his duties are too onerous, so we can probably co-opt unofficially to give us a hand. He seems enthusiastic enough.'

'He's that all right,' Marsh said. 'I'll have a word with him.'

Winterman turned to the others. 'Let's go to it. Before the snow comes down again.'

CHAPTER TWENTY-NINE

'I can't pretend your presence is welcome,' Professor Callaghan said, 'but it's hardly a surprise either.' He was standing at the open front door, regarding Winterman and Hoxton with a mix of suspicion and contempt.

And a good morning to you, Professor, Winterman thought. Clearly not a man for the conventional courtesies. 'I'm sure you appreciate why we're here, sir.'

'I'd expected you earlier.' Callaghan's tone managed to imply that inefficiency could be added to the list of their manifest failings.

'You'll appreciate that we're very busy, sir.'

'No doubt. Though not too busy to detain my son overnight. I've already lodged a complaint with the chief constable.'

'I'm sure he'll give it his full attention, sir,' Winterman said. This kind of pomposity seemed, oddly, to have become even more prevalent since the war. Perhaps it was because the likes of Callaghan felt less secure about their social position. 'Though your son wasn't detained. He spent the night at Reverend Fisher's house and then volunteered himself at Framley Police Station. He's been extremely co-operative in assisting us with our enquiries.' Winterman smiled faintly. 'Speaking of which, I wonder if we might come in. It is rather cold out here.' He glanced up at the house, a sizable Victorian villa situated at what was clearly the more socially aspirational end of the village. These houses would have been built in proximity to the railway for the prosperous middle-classes moving out of the city.

Callaghan stared at him for a moment, as though considering rejecting his request. 'Please come in, gentlemen. Unfortunately, my housekeeper is a little unwell, so I'm unable to offer you any refreshments.'

Winterman presumed that refreshments would not have been forthcoming in any circumstances. 'Of course, sir. We're on duty in any case.' As if the old boy might have been about to ply them with a whisky and soda.

They followed the professor through into an immaculately furnished reception room. Winterman glanced around. Parlour would hardly do it justice. It was definitely a drawing room. Most of the furniture looked, to Winterman's inexpert eye, antique and probably valuable. But there was something unnatural about the room, as if it were furnished for effect rather than comfort. The cliché would be that it lacked a woman's touch. That might well have been the case – there was nothing overtly feminine visible, and the hunting prints that lined the walls had a masculine air – but it wasn't the whole truth. This wasn't a room for living in.

Callaghan gestured for them to take a seat. Winterman found himself perched awkwardly on the edge of the pristine sofa, aware of the contrast with his battered raincoat. Hoxton had no such scruples, and lounged back comfortably, his face unreadable.

'You're an academic?' Winterman said.

'Microbiology,' Callaghan snapped. 'Is this relevant?'

'Just making conversation, sir.'

'You might have all day, Inspector. I don't. Please get to the point.'

Winterman's smile broadened. The professor had clearly taken note of the rank shown on his warrant card. Perhaps there would be another call to the chief constable after their departure. 'You appreciate, sir, that we are conducting a murder enquiry?'

'I do, not being completely in my dotage. But I fail to see why you are conducting it in my house.'

'How well did you know Reverend Fisher?'

Winterman fancied that something flickered momentarily in Callaghan's eyes, but his expression remained blank.

'Not particularly well. I had some dealings with him on church matters from time to time.'

'Dealings?'

Callaghan lowered himself into an armchair and gazed at them with barely disguised impatience. 'Fisher and I didn't see eye to eye.'

'Can I ask in what respects?'

'I'm sure you know that he drank. And that his behaviour could be erratic. I was delegated to express the concerns of a number of parishioners. We had a number of meetings.'

Winterman had no difficulty in imagining the pomposity with which Callaghan would have undertaken this role. 'And did he accept your concerns?'

'What do you think, Inspector? But I felt we should give him the opportunity to address the issues before we elevated our concerns to a higher authority.'

For a moment, Winterman wondered whether Callaghan had perhaps sought an audience with God. 'And you did that? Took your concerns to a higher authority?'

'Something had to be done. The congregation was shrinking by the week. So I spoke to the bishop.'

'I see. How did Reverend Fisher take that?'

'I've no idea. But I believe the bishop engineered Fisher's retirement at the earliest opportunity. So we achieved our aim.'

'Those were your only dealings with Reverend Fisher?'

There was an almost imperceptible hesitation. 'I take it you've been made aware of the gossip, Inspector. I'd advise you to disregard it.'

Winterman allowed himself the luxury of a similar pause, noting that, for the first time, Callaghan was not entirely at ease. 'I'm aware Reverend Fisher's wife left him, sir. And that she and her daughter lived here for a period.'

'I'm sure the grapevine has implied more than that. I'm not a fool. I know what has been said. None of it, of course, has any substance. Fisher's wife left him because he drank and he beat her. I believe strongly in the sanctity of marriage, but felt, reluctantly, that she had taken the only course open to her. She had nowhere to go, and I had no option but to offer her shelter. I knew it would provoke gossip, but I've long since ceased to concern myself about that.' He glared defiantly at Winterman, as if challenging him to question this account.

'I understand she eventually tried to return to Reverend Fisher.'

'Apparently, it's not so unusual, Inspector. Men like Fisher can exert, if you'll forgive me, an unholy influence over the impressionable. She persuaded herself it was the right thing to do. I did my utmost to dissuade her, but there was nothing I could do. The result was a tragedy.'

'You had no other contacts with Fisher?'

'Other than those I've described, no. Is that all, Inspector?'

There was a finality to the closing words that suggested Callaghan was about to terminate the interview. 'Thank you, sir. That's extremely helpful. Do you know if Reverend Fisher had any other, closer acquaintances? Is there anyone else we should be speaking to?'

'I'm not aware of any. Even as our clergyman, he tried to have as little contact with his parishioners as possible. In the last few years the sentiment was mutual. By the end, Fisher cut a very lonely figure. He had no visitors I'm aware of.'

'Other than your son?' Winterman said.

'I'm not aware that my son was in the habit of visiting Fisher.'

'Yet he did so on the night that Fisher died.'

'You've spoken to my son. He's told you exactly what happened.'

'He gave us his account, yes, sir. I'm assuming he gave you the same account.' Winterman left his words hanging in the air, an implied question.

'He was caught by the snow. He went to Fisher's to seek shelter.'

'A prudent move, I'm sure. Particularly given his state of inebriation.'

'You sound very moralistic, Inspector. Do you disapprove of drinking?'

'I have no strong opinion, sir. I've been known to take the occasional glass of beer myself. I'm more concerned with confirming the sequence of events that evening. Were you not surprised or worried when your son failed to return home?'

'I'm long past being surprised by anything my son might do. I was tired and went to bed relatively early. I rarely stay up to await William in any case. It was the next morning before I realised he had not returned. Even then, I simply assumed that he had stayed overnight with one of his acquaintances. It would not have been the first time.'

'To the best of your knowledge, your son had no prior contact with Fisher?'

'To the best of my knowledge,' the professor concurred. 'I can see no good reason why he should have.'

'Indeed, sir. Which raises the question then, of who else might have been at Fisher's house that night.'

'I think that's rather your territory. I'm afraid I can't help you.' He shifted forward in his chair, clearly intending to rise and show them off the premises.

Winterman sat back in the sofa, determined not to move until explicitly asked to do so. 'You and William live here all alone?'

'Our housekeeper lives in. But yes. I'm a widower. Will that be all?'

'I think so, sir. I hope we won't need to trouble you again.'

'I imagine that will rather depend on whether you consider my son a serious suspect for Fisher's murder.'

Winterman recognised there was little point in prolonging the discussion. Anyone who could coolly discuss his own son as a potential murder suspect was unlikely to be intimidated or cajoled into an incautious response. 'Do you think we should, sir?'

'I've really no idea. I don't see him as a murderer. I'm not sure he has the courage.'

'Courage?'

'It's not an easy thing, killing someone, Inspector. I survived the First War, so I speak with some experience.'

'No doubt, sir.' Winterman reached for his hat and coat, and nodded to Hoxton.

Callaghan escorted them to the front door, as if to ensure that they really did leave the premises. 'I think we're due for more snow. I hope it doesn't inconvenience your work too much.'

'It doesn't help,' Winterman acknowledged. He pulled his coat around him as he stepped back out into the chill air, and turned back to look at Callaghan. 'What are your thoughts on the children, sir?'

'Inspector?'

'The children's bodies? You're aware that Reverend Fisher discovered a child's body in the village?'

'Another nasty bit of business. But you said "bodies"?'

'I'm sorry. I thought you'd have heard. A second body was found, down in the village. Another girl, apparently, a similar age to the first. And again well preserved, but dead for some time. Several years. As you say, nasty business. And very puzzling.'

'You haven't discovered their identities?'

'Not definitively, sir, no. You'll appreciate that I'm not in a position to say any more at the moment.'

'I imagine that, as the deaths occurred some time ago, they inevitably carry a lower priority than poor Fisher's death.'

'For the moment.' Winterman paused. 'We'll be in touch if we need to trouble you again.' He turned and made his way back towards the car, his feet crunching into the frozen drifts of snow.

Behind him he heard the echoing crunch of Hoxton's steps, and then Callaghan's voice, quieter and sounding, to Winterman's ears, a little less confident. 'Good day, Inspector, and good luck.'

CHAPTER THIRTY

'"Not definitively,"' Hoxton echoed. 'What was all that about?'

'What?' Winterman sat tensely in the passenger seat. Hoxton was a noticeably less cautious driver than Marsh, and Winterman was convinced they were driving too fast. He had been expecting for the last ten minutes or so that they would hit a patch of black ice and lose control. So far though, Hoxton had managed to maintain both speed and equilibrium.

'"Not definitively". "I'm not in a position to say anything more." All that guff. sir.'

'He was lying,' Winterman said. 'He was hiding something.'

'The prof? Oh, definitely. But what?'

'No idea. But none of it quite rang true.'

'As true as a cracked pisspot,' Hoxton agreed graphically. 'You shook him with the kiddies.'

'I seemed to, didn't I.' Winterman paused, as Hoxton took a tight left bend. 'That was odd.'

'Thought you knew something,' Hoxton glanced across, apparently taking his eyes fully off the road. 'Being a clever bugger and all.'

'I'm always most clever when I haven't a clue what I'm doing. It was just a random prod. Trying to get a reaction from the chilly old sod.'

'You did that all right. Only question is what it meant.' Hoxton slowed the car momentarily and took one hand off the wheel to point through the windscreen. 'That's the place.'

Winterman peered through the murky glass. He could make out a squat grey building, stretching forbiddingly along the flat horizon. 'Not what I expected.'

'Not the ancestral pile, you mean. They were never ones to fritter money on decoration, the Hamshaws. And the family fortune isn't quite what it was, by all accounts.'

Winterman glanced at him inquisitively. 'Money troubles?'

'Wouldn't say that. Hamshaws' is old money. Landowning, farming. But it was the last two or three generations really built it up. Started taking the farming seriously as a commercial business, sullied their hands by dealing with tradesfolk. Hamshaws went from being wealthy to being extremely wealthy.'

'Now things are declining again?' They were approaching the Hamshaw residence – a grey shingled building, impressively sized, but with the air of a working farmhouse.

Hoxton pulled the car as close into the roadside as the frozen snow drifts would allow. 'Not quite clogs to clogs in three generations, but they've suffered like everyone else.

'Thought farmers usually had a good war.'

'Some did,' Hoxton agreed. 'Even some round here. Hamshaw did all right from the farming, but he made a few unwise investments. You know, wine, woman and song, and then he frittered the rest.'

'You seem to know a lot about him?'

Hoxton glanced curiously at Winterman. 'Only what everyone knows. Hamshaw knows everyone, and everyone knows Hamshaw. Everyone who's anyone. I wouldn't underestimate him. You'll think he's a pussycat – certainly compared with Callaghan – but he turns it on when he wants to. A wheeler dealer, as they say.'

Hoxton turned off the engine and squinted through the foggy windows. 'We'll have to walk the rest of the way. Don't reckon I'd fancy the Wolseley on that terrain.' He gestured towards the rutted track that led to the farm buildings.

They stepped out into the frozen air. Winterman turned up his collar and thrust his hat firmly on his hand. 'You reckon it's too cold to snow again?'

Hoxton was wrapping a thick woollen scarf around his neck. 'No. I reckon it's just bloody cold enough to snow again.'

Close up, Hamshaw's property looked even less prepossessing. It was a rambling two-storey building, dark windows peering blankly, paint peeling, rendering cracked in several places. 'Doesn't look as if he spends a lot on maintenance either.'

'It's a working building,' Hoxton said. 'Not the ancestral home. That went long ago.'

They reached what appeared to be the front entrance – a large black painted door with an ornate but tarnished brass knocker, topped by a rickety porch. 'He's expecting us?' He lifted the knocker and rapped firmly.

'Mrs Sheringham said she'd call. But it won't be a problem. Hamshaw's always keen to do his civic duty. Big supporter of the local constabulary.'

Winterman had been surprised that Callaghan had answered his own front door. He was even more surprised when the battered door in front of them was opened by a man he recognised instantly as Lord Hamshaw. Whatever had happened in the last election, Winterman thought, the class structure was as pervasive as ever. As soon as he found himself facing someone designated a Lord, the old deference kicked in. He reminded himself that Hamshaw, however much he might be old money, wasn't a real Lord. This was the first Lord Hamshaw, not the umpteenth. He'd been granted his peerage, supposedly in recognition of his loyal Government service, but probably just as a sop for the loss of his seat. Winterman had recognised him from wartime photographs – a junior minister exhorting the public to support the military effort. He had a feeling he might even have met Hamshaw once, when a cluster of MPs had passed through his office in London.

'Lord Hamshaw?' He was conscious he didn't even know how a peer of the realm should be addressed.

Hamshaw looked younger than he'd expected – younger than his wartime photographs had suggested. Perhaps that was the effect of losing power. Winterman had expected someone in late middle age, an elder statesman. The man in front of him was probably no more than forty-five. He looked fit, well built, his ruddy face suggesting time spent in the open air. He looked anything other than the stereotype of a politician.

Hamshaw regarded the two men standing in front of him. 'Inspector Winterman.' He nodded to Hoxton. 'Constable Hoxton. We've met before, I believe.'

The politician's training, Winterman thought. Remembering names, and making sure you used them. 'We're very grateful to you for sparing us a few minutes.'

'Not at all, Inspector. Though I don't know that I can really help you.' He took a step back. 'Please come in.'

They followed Hamshaw into a gloomy passageway. From somewhere there was a smell of cooking vegetables. The passage was lined with piles of unidentifiable clutter. Whatever Hamshaw's status or wealth, this house was the opposite of Callaghan's. 'In here, gentlemen.'

Hamshaw led them into a reception room even more gloomy than the entrance hall. He stepped across the room and threw back the heavy curtains from a set of French windows, allowing pale grey light to percolate through the shadows. The additional illumination did little to improve the appearance of the room. There were two over-stuffed sofas, a couple of battered occasional tables, and a set of bookshelves apparently overflowing with ancient-looking volumes.

Hamshaw gestured them to take a seat on one of the sofas. 'Can I organise you gentlemen a cup of tea?' The question sounded genuine, rather than rhetorical.

Winterman shook his head. 'Don't worry, sir. One of the perils of conducting these interviews is that we find ourselves awash with tea.'

Hamshaw smiled, his face suggesting that Winterman's response had lifted a substantial burden, and he lowered himself onto the other sofa.

'You're aware of why we're here, sir?'

Hamshaw considered for a moment. 'The lady who called me said something about Reverend Fisher. I hadn't been aware…'

'No, sir. It's not common knowledge yet. We found his body yesterday morning.'

'Given your presence here, gentlemen, I assume there are circumstances that need to be investigated.'

'We believe so,' Winterman said. 'It appears that Reverend Fisher was murdered.'

'Good Lord.' Hamshaw's exclamation sounded far from heartfelt. 'That's a bit of a shock.'

'I'm sorry, sir. Did you know Reverend Fisher well?'

'Not really, not at a personal level. Of course we had some contact when he was the incumbent reverend. Not the easiest man to deal with, as I'm sure you've heard.'

'In what way, sir?'

Hamshaw hesitated, as though surprised by the direct question. 'In almost every way, to be frank. He was stubborn, opinionated, rude, disdainful of other people – especially his own parishioners. And I'm sure you know that he drank heavily. He could be very aggressive.'

'You had some confrontations with him?'

'Not me, not really. He tended to behave differently with me. The usual characteristics of a bully. Rude and aggressive to his inferiors, but deferential to those above.'

Winterman noted the terminology. 'He considered the parishioners his inferiors?'

'That was my impression. Not just socially – though there was something of that. Fisher came from a decent background – a good school, Oxford. He felt that he'd fallen among the *hoi polloi* here. '

'That's surely the lot of a clergyman?'

Hamshaw shrugged. 'I've no idea why Fisher took orders. He didn't strike me as the spiritual type. If I were cynical, I'd say it was because it gave him a platform to express his disapproval of lesser mortals.'

'It sounds as if you didn't like him very much, sir.'

'Does that make me a suspect, Inspector? If so, I think there might be dozens more people you'll need to interview.'

'Reverend Fisher wasn't popular?'

'That would be an understatement. The man had a chip on his shoulder a mile wide. Disappointed expectations perhaps. I imagine we all think we could have done better with our lives.'

'I imagine so, sir.' Winterman resisted the urge to glance around the shabby room. 'Other than his general unpopularity, can you think of any other reasons why Reverend Fisher might have been killed?'

'If you mean,' Hamshaw responded carefully, 'can I think of anyone with a motive for killing him – no, not really. Not a serious motive. Though I can imagine some would have hated him for what happened to his wife.'

'I'm aware of the story, sir.' Winterman glanced at Hoxton. 'Do you know if his wife had any relatives or friends?'

'Who might have avenged her death by killing her uncaring husband? I'm not aware of any, Inspector. And why would they wait so long?'

'Revenge is a dish best served cold, and all that,' Hoxton suggested unexpectedly. 'Or perhaps this was the first chance they had.'

Hamshaw nodded respectfully. 'I suppose. But I'm not aware of any. Fisher had little contact with anyone. Just drank himself into a stupor.'

'Was he a wealthy man?' Winterman asked.

'I assume you're looking into that yourselves, but I'd be surprised. As far as I'm aware, he lived on his stipend. You've probably discovered that his cottage is part of my estate – a small gesture of charity on my part for which he never showed the slightest gratitude. I suppose he might have had some other source of income – family money, perhaps – but he showed no sign of it. I can't imagine that anyone would have thought it worth trying to rob him.'

'Someone might have,' Winterman said. 'These things happen. Do you know William Callaghan?'

Hamshaw blinked, clearly thrown by the non sequitur. 'This would be Professor Callaghan's son?'

'That's right, sir.'

'I've met him once or twice, with his father. I can't say I know him.'

'You know his father?'

'I've known his father for years. We were at university together. Or, at least, we were at university at the same time. I didn't really know him then. We've developed an acquaintance since, as our paths have crossed.'

'He's a friend of yours?'

Hamshaw looked uncomfortable, as if he had been challenged about some unsavoury peccadillo. 'I wouldn't say "friend". We have little in common. But we've got on well enough when we've been thrown together.'

'You were both involved in church matters?'

For the first time, Hamshaw's equanimity seemed to crack slightly. 'I'm sorry, Inspector, this does begin to sound like some kind of interrogation.'

'My apologies, sir,' Winterman said smoothly. 'That wasn't my intention. I'm just trying to build a picture of the various relationships surrounding Reverend Fisher.'

'Of course, Inspector. I realise that you have a job to do. I'm very happy to give you any support I can. But there's little more I can tell you. Yes, Professor Callaghan and I were both involved in church matters, but only because we were pillars of the local community, I suppose.' He paused. 'And towards the end of Fisher's tenure in the role, we both had some difficult conversations with him.'

'About his drinking?'

'His drinking and his general behaviour. His sermons were often – inappropriate would be the most generous description. His treatment of parishioners also left something to be desired.'

'In what way, sir?'

'You name it. He got bees in his bonnet. Made wild accusations. He was rude to people. He made it very clear he didn't suffer fools gladly and that most of his parishioners fell into that category. If anyone went to him seeking help or succor–' He stopped. 'All in all, inappropriate behaviour for a clergyman.'

'This was after his wife left him?' Winterman asked the question casually, leaning back on the uncomfortable sofa.

Again, Hamshaw appeared momentarily thrown, as if Winterman had displayed unexpected knowledge. 'I don't really know, Inspector. The unpleasant business with Fisher's wife was some years ago. My recollection is that Fisher was always a rather erratic character. But yes, matters took a considerable turn for the worst after his wife left him. That was the point at which he began drinking excessively. After that, things deteriorated.'

'I understand Fisher's wife lodged with Professor Callaghan?'

'Professor Callaghan did his Christian duty,' Hamshaw responded piously. 'Sadly, some chose to misinterpret his actions.'

'And I understand that Professor Callaghan eventually made an approach to the bishop about Fisher's behaviour?'

'It was a collective decision. We decided we had no other option.'

'You said that Reverend Fisher was unpopular with parishioners, sir. Would you say that he made any real enemies?'

'Among our parishioners? I don't think we're talking about potential murderers here.'

'You'll appreciate we have to consider every possibility.' Winterman paused. 'It's even possible that there's a link between Fisher's death and the children's bodies.'

Hamshaw blinked, though his expression suggested simple puzzlement, rather than the apparent surprise that had crossed Callaghan's face at the same reference. 'I'm aware that Fisher found a body. Your colleagues spoke to me at the time because it was found on my land. A strange business. I'd assumed it had no connection with Fisher's death.'

'We can't ignore any possibility, sir.'

'You said "bodies". You've found another young girl?'

'That's right. Apparently a similar age. Funnily enough, sir, I believe this was also on your land.' He described the farmland opposite Mary's house.

Hamshaw nodded. 'Yes, that's mine. But, as you'll have discovered, Inspector, much of the land in these parts belongs to the Hamshaw estate. Is this a more recent body?'

'Not significantly. We're still waiting for the detailed report, but our assumption is that both bodies date from the same period, give or take a few months. Probably six or seven years.'

'Baffling. But it wouldn't be the first wartime oddity we've stumbled across and I don't imagine it'll be the last.'

'Oddity, sir?'

'People applied different standards.' Hamshaw's eyes were fixed unwaveringly on Winterman's face. 'We were all a little too close to death. We took it for granted.'

'Even the deaths of children, sir?' Winterman's face was mask-like, his tone emotionless.

'Plenty of people lost their children, Inspector. My own brother was killed in action. As for these children, who knows? I don't imagine that your investigations into their deaths are likely to progress very far after all this time.'

'We'll do our best, sir. The pertinent question is perhaps not who they were or why they were killed, but why their bodies have appeared now. That's why we can't write off a possible link with Fisher's death.'

'I wish you luck, Inspector. With both investigations. Do please let me know if I can be of any further assistance.' He pushed himself to his feet, signalling unmistakeably that the interview was at an end.

Callaghan had tried the same strategy, and Winterman had taken a mild delight in resisting his leaden hint. But when Hamshaw rose and ushered them politely but inexorably towards the front door, Winterman found himself unable to resist Hamshaw's air of patrician entitlement.

Outside, the chill air struck them full in the face. 'Well, Inspector,' Hamshaw said. 'I really do wish you luck. None of us likes the idea of there being a killer out there. Do let me know if I can be of any further assistance. Good day.'

'I'm quite sure we will, sir,' Winterman murmured to the closing door. A few more flakes of snow were beginning to fall.

'What do you think?' Winterman asked, as they made their way down the snow-bound path towards the car.

Hoxton turned up his collar against the thin but drifting snow. 'I think we'd better get back before this bloody weather gets any worse.' He trudged a foot or so behind Winterman. 'About Hamshaw? I'm not sure. Superior old bugger, I know that for certain. But I felt there was something he wasn't telling us.'

Winterman nodded, as if some hypothesis of his own had just been confirmed. 'Something significant?'

'Who knows? Maybe. Or perhaps just something sensitive he didn't want to share with the *hoi polloi*.'

Winterman waited while Hoxton fumbled with the icy locks of the car. 'Yes. That's pretty much what I thought.'

CHAPTER THIRTY-ONE

They had dropped Marsh in the village on the way out, and had arranged to meet him at Mary's house at the end of the day. Mrs Griffiths needed to be interviewed, alongside all the other villagers. Marsh had suggested Mrs Griffiths might be more relaxed in her daughter's presence, and so Mary had travelled back out with them.

By the time they arrived, the snow was coming down heavily again, endless white flakes roiling in the darkening air. Mary was peering out from behind the lace curtains apparently awaiting their approach, and had opened the front door by the time they had climbed out of the car. 'Get in here. We were beginning to wonder what had happened to you.'

Hoxton stamped cautiously along the path to the front door, his expression suggesting he might be about to lose his footing. 'Bloody weather happened to us. 'Scuse the French, lass.'

Winterman walked a few steps behind him, his hat tipped forward to keep the snow from his face. 'Weather's closing in. We'd best be getting back to town before it really comes down.'

Mary peered out into the swirling darkness. 'I think you're too late. You can't drive back in this.'

Hoxton had stopped at the doorway and was banging his heavy boots against the step to shake off the snow. 'Lass's right. The road was lethal even getting here. We'll end up in the dyke. Or worse.'

Winterman followed him into the house, scrubbing his feet on the doormat. 'So what do you suggest? It's already after four. We can't stay here all night.'

Mary was watching them from the doorway to the living room. 'We were just discussing that. We could put you up. Between us, I mean. We've got a spare room here. And Bryan's got a spare twin room over at the station.' She gestured behind her to where PC Brain was sitting, slouched in an armchair with the inevitable cup of tea balanced beside him. Opposite him, Marsh and Mrs Griffiths were sitting on the sofa. 'We could cope with the three of you for the night.'

Winterman stood in the doorway for a moment, feeling an unexpected awkwardness. 'That's very kind.' He addressed his words as much to Brain and to Mrs Griffiths as to Mary. 'I don't want us to take advantage. But we might not have much choice.' He glanced past Brain towards the still-uncurtained window. A constant barrage of white flakes beat against the glass, seething out of the darkness behind. 'We can wait a while though. See if things improve.'

'Come in and sit down,' Mrs Griffiths said. 'You look frozen.'

For the first time, Winterman realised that he really was cold and wet, icy water dripping from the hat he held in his hands. With numb fingers, he unbuttoned his heavy coat. Even in the short distance from the car to the front door, it had gathered a sodden weight. Mary took it from him and spread it out over the back of a kitchen chair. Hoxton had already removed his and was hanging it alongside.

'Don't lose the heat.' Winterman gestured towards the roaring open fire. 'You shouldn't waste coal drying my coat. You need to keep the house warm.'

In fact, the room was cosy enough, even allowing for the chill he and Hoxton had brought through the front door. The two children, Graham and Ann, were playing quietly in the far corner, furthest from the fire, a pile of battered die-cast metal vehicles spread between them. Everyone else was clustered around the crackling flames, warmed by the fire and by their collective body heat. Suddenly, Winterman felt less inclined to brave the frozen world outside, even if the snow were to lessen over the evening.

'How did it go?' Marsh leaned forward and held his hands out towards the fire. 'Anything useful?'

'Difficult to say, really,' Winterman said. 'We saw Callaghan's father and we saw Hamshaw.'

Mrs Griffiths glanced up. 'Lord Hamshaw,' she said, in a tone of the mildest reproof. Her tone implied that traditional niceties should be respected, regardless of what one might think of the individuals involved. It was probably what many people had fought the war for, Winterman thought.

'Lord Hamshaw,' Winterman corrected himself. 'Useful background, I suppose, but not much of substance. How'd you get on here?'

'Lots of elimination, to look on the bright side.' Marsh nodded towards Mary's mother. 'Mrs Griffiths has been very helpful. Gave us the names of all the best people to speak to in the village.'

Mrs Griffiths' warm smile demonstrated the pleasure she felt in the accolades. 'I didn't do much. I was just thinking of who might have known Mr Fisher. There aren't that many, I'm afraid. I don't like to speak ill of the dead, but he wasn't a popular man.'

'Too right,' Hoxton said.

'There were a few people who knew him through the church, of course,' Mrs Griffiths went on. 'And a few who'd had disagreements with him.'

Winterman lowered himself on to the edge of the sofa, stretching out his damp shoes towards the roaring fire. He was a little unsure of the etiquette, wondering whether he should have removed the shoes before entering the room. 'Disagreements?'

Mrs Griffiths shook her head. 'I don't want to give you the wrong idea. I said that to young Paul here.'

It took Winterman a moment to recall that Paul was DC Marsh. He had already noted Marsh's apparent easy familiarity in the house, and he wondered about its significance. 'What sort of wrong idea?'

She looked momentarily flustered. 'Quite a few people were at loggerheads with him. But I wouldn't want you to think–'

'That they were responsible for his death?'

'Well, yes.'

'No, of course,' Winterman said. 'It takes more than dislike to lead to murder. But *someone* was responsible for his death.'

'But not someone from the village,' Mrs Griffiths persisted. 'Surely.'

'We don't know, Mrs Griffiths. That's the truth. Stranger things have happened.' He turned to Marsh. 'You managed to speak to some of the neighbours?'

'Most of them,' Marsh said. 'Bryan gave me a hand on the note-taking. We managed to cover most of the key villagers. There were only a dozen or so. There were a couple we couldn't find.'

'Probably away,' Brain added helpfully. 'I know one was visiting relatives in Lincoln. Probably can't get back with the weather.'

'I've got notes on the ones we haven't seen,' Marsh said. 'We can pick them up later.'

'Anything worthwhile in the rest?'

'Nothing very surprising. Plenty of anecdotes about Fisher. Sounds like someone who could start an argument in an empty room. But all trivial stuff.'

'Did Fisher have any other friends or acquaintances?'

'If he did, nobody seems to have been aware of them. A bit of a loner would be the polite description.' Marsh smiled. 'And there were plenty of less polite descriptions.'

'But no motive for his murder?'

'Not that I could see. I know you never can tell, but I can't really see any of the people we interviewed as potential murderers. Apart from anything else, I don't think their motives are strong enough. Most of them didn't seem that interested in Fisher. They just saw him as a sad old eccentric, stuck out there in his shabby old cottage. No one saw him much, except in his cups in the pub. And most of them stayed out of his way there.'

'What about the landlord? He must have a view about Fisher. Did you speak to him?'

'Not yet. Pub was all shut up when we went down there, and we couldn't get an answer at the door. Neighbours reckon the landlord usually gets forty winks before he reopens at six.'

'Sleep of the just,' Winterman said.

'Sleep of the just knocked back three large brandies, by all accounts.' Marsh started to laugh then fell silent at a disapproving glance from Mrs Griffiths. 'I thought we could perhaps go and have a chat with him later if the snow lets up. I don't imagine he's all that busy in this weather.'

'Any excuse.' Winterman smiled. 'But yes, why not? Once my feet have dried out I'll be only too keen to get them wet again. Okay, so that's the village largely accounted for. What about other possibilities? Dubious local characters? Outsiders?'

'Not much,' Marsh admitted. 'One or two had stories about delinquents – always from other villages or even coming in from the bigger towns – but we couldn't pin them down to actual names. And there were a few stories about outsiders in the area. But nothing that sounded useful.'

'As you say, elimination. It had to be done, and you've got a lot further with it than I expected.' Winterman nodded to Brain. 'Thanks for all your help, Constable.'

The epithet sounded unduly formal, but Brain didn't seem to mind. 'Not at all, sir. My pleasure to help. Makes a change from the usual run of things round here.'

Mrs Griffiths pushed herself to her feet. 'You'll all be wanting some supper.'

'We shouldn't impose...' Winterman began, in automatic politeness. But the truth was that there were few options open to them, assuming they couldn't get back to town. He opened his mouth to offer some form of financial contribution, but realised any such offer was likely to be insulting. In any case, while Mrs Griffiths might not be wealthy, the real issue was likely to be simply a shortage of foodstuffs – the need to eke out their rations to feed so many people. 'That's very kind of you, Mrs Griffiths,' he said. 'Very kind indeed. Are you sure you've enough though?'

Mrs Griffiths looked at Winterman appraisingly, as though trying to calculate what sort of man he might be under the surface. 'I think we can cope.'

I'm sure you can, Winterman thought, as she turned and made her way slowly through into the kitchen. Her steady gaze had left him feeling uncomfortable. *I'm sure you can.*

CHAPTER THIRTY-TWO

Supper was a convivial affair. Mrs Griffiths had produced a mutton stew which Winterman suspected had been intended to last several days, and which was more than ample to feed the assembled group. The mutton itself had little more than a token presence, enough to flavour the root vegetables that formed the bulk of the dish, but the meal was hearty and tasty.

'Lovely bit of grub.' Hoxton scooped up the last few dregs from his plate. 'You've done wonders, Mrs G. Surprised you can get veggies like that on the ration. Nice bit of mutton too.'

Mrs Griffiths glanced across the table to her daughter. 'We grew the vegetables ourselves, mainly. And we've a decent butcher in the village. He does what he can.'

Winterman took this to mean that at least some of the produce had been acquired under the counter. Well, so what? Everyone was doing it. It was what kept a lot of them going. Even the police. Especially the police, because they had some power.

Marsh rose and peered through the kitchen window. 'Still snowing. Who fancies a trip down to interview the landlord of the local?'

'Who's staying with me tonight?' Brain said. 'We'll have to brave the walk back to the village in any case.'

'Reckon the governor should have the privilege of staying here,' Hoxton said. 'Me and Marshy can share your room.'

'Fine by me,' Marsh said.

Winterman was unsure whether a glance passed between Marsh and Mary.

'Which means, boss, that if you want to go to the pub – sorry, interview the landlord…' Hoxton nodded mischievously towards Marsh. 'Then you'll have to brave the walk both ways.'

'I'm happy to give it a go.' Winterman recognised a challenge when he heard one.

'Gents only, is it?' Mary asked.

'Up to you, lass,' Hoxton said. 'You feel up to the walk, you're most welcome. And you, Mrs G,' he added gallantly.

'Someone's got to stay and look after the kiddies,' Mrs Griffith said. 'And you wouldn't get me out on a night like this.'

'You all right if I go, Mam?' Mary asked.

'If you feel up to it,' Mrs Griffiths said. 'It's a nasty old night out there.'

'I'm sure the inspector will take care of me. Won't you, Ivan?'

Winterman caught the twinkle in Hoxton's eye at the mention of his Christian name. He looked at Marsh, but the young man was merely smiling back amiably. 'I'll do my best,' Winterman said.

The five of them set off a few minutes later, wrapped in heavy overcoats, scarves and hats. There was an almost juvenile spirit in the air as if the incessant snow demanded the casting off of adult responsibilities. Even the ever-present cold seemed almost bearable, accompanied by these smooth icy landscapes. It was an illusion but welcome nonetheless.

Hoxton, true to form, was already making snowballs, throwing the hard-packed snow at the dark shapes of trees. The snow was coming down as heavily as ever. The Wolseley was already buried into a thick drift, its black contours almost invisible. Progress along the road was difficult, their booted feet ploughing slowly through the packed banks of snow.

Winterman peered across at Mary. 'Are you all right? We can turn back if it's too much for you.'

'I'll pretend I didn't hear that.' She reached down and picked up her own snowball, throwing it half-heartedly in Winterman's direction. 'It's wonderful. Cold, but wonderful.'

'Lovely for the children.'

'They love it,' she agreed. 'But then so do I.'

It took them thirty minutes to cover the half-mile to the pub. The centre of the village was deserted, and Winterman had wondered whether the pub would even be open. But the glow of its lights indicated the landlord had not allowed the extreme weather to disrupt his usual routine. They pushed open the door of the lounge bar and stumbled into the warmth and light, scattering snow and water across the floor.

The lounge was deserted, though they could hear the sound of voices from the public bar next door.

After a few minutes, the landlord appeared. He was a large, cheerful-looking figure – almost a caricature of the traditional pub landlord, his overweight face reddened from the heat and, most likely, a generous imbibing of his own products.

'Blimey. Didn't expect much of anyone in here tonight, let alone a party.' He peered short-sightedly at the group, eventually recognising everyone except Winterman. 'Evening, Constable. Evening, Mrs Ford, Paul. And, strike me down, George Hoxton? Not seen you in a while.' Not a local man, Winterman thought. Probably a Londoner.

'It's since you started watering down the beer, Norman,' Hoxton said morosely. 'Gives me no reason to come back here. And it's Detective Constable Hoxton to you.'

'If you say so, George. And what brings you a-detecting down here?'

'We're here to try your watery beer, Norman. I've already warned my friends not to expect much.'

'You're too kind, George. That was always your trouble. Four pints for you gents then. Mrs Ford?'

'Tonic water for me, Norman.' She was shrugging off her heavy coat, draping her scarf over the back of a chair. The landlord slowly pulled the pints.

'Actually, Norman,' Hoxton said, 'this isn't just a social call.'

'Never is with you lot.' The landlord glanced at Winterman. 'You a copper as well?'

'DI Winterman.'

'An Inspector. I'm honoured.'

'People usually are,' Winterman said. 'We just wanted to ask you a few questions about Reverend Fisher.'

'Thought you might. Terrible business.' The landlord finished pouring the first two pints and handed them past Winterman to Hoxton and Brain.

'You know about it then,' Winterman said.

'Word travels like lightning in a place like this. We don't get too many murders.'

'I imagine not. What did you think of Fisher?'

'Cantankerous old bugger. Pardon my language. Good customer though.'

'Drank in here a lot, did he?'

'He drank in here a lot, and he drank a lot when he was in here. Just how I like it.'

'In here every night?'

'Pretty much. Put it this way, people commented when he wasn't.'

'Popular man, was he?'

'Not so's you'd notice. People generally steered clear of him. He used to sit over there.' The landlord paused momentarily from pulling the remaining pints and gestured towards a table in the corner.

'In the lounge?'

'Always sat in the lounge. Bit too raucous in the public. Just sat there quietly and sank his pints. And his Scotches.'

'Any trouble?'

The landlord shrugged. 'Not really. Sometimes he had too much even by his standards, and I'd politely point that out. And he'd respond less politely. Had to throw him out once or twice when he got a bit obstreperous. Usually when his language became a bit ripe for the ladies.' The landlord glanced around self-consciously, nodding in Mary's direction. 'Not that we get many ladies in here, present company excepted. But it's the principle. No, old Joe wasn't really any trouble. He usually went quietly in the end.'

'We don't know how he went,' Winterman pointed out. 'In the end. What about before his death? Was he in here the night he was killed? Or the night before?'

'Hadn't seen him for a while. In fact, I'd remarked on it. It was beginning to hit my takings.' The landlord laughed, with no obvious sign of mirth. 'There was the weather, of course. Not easy for someone of Fisher's age to get in here. Not that it had usually stopped him before. Don't know if it was just that though. Don't think we'd seen him in here since the business with that poor kiddie.'

'The body, you mean.'

'Aye. Since Fisher found the body. Must have been a shock. You lot any nearer to sorting that one out?'

Winterman shook his head. 'So Fisher hadn't been in since then.'

'Don't think so.' The landlord paused, his expression suggesting he was reflecting on the matter. 'Maybe it was that business with young Callaghan. That must have been the same night, as well.'

Winterman exchanged a glance with Marsh. 'Young Callaghan? William Callaghan?'

'Young William,' the landlord confirmed. 'I remembered it because not many people spoke to Fisher.'

'What was the business with Callaghan?'

'Usual story with young William. He'd had a pint or two too many and took it into his head to engage Fisher in conversation. Don't really know what he was on about – don't think Callaghan did either – but Fisher clearly didn't like it.'

'What *was* he on about? I mean, what did you hear?'

'Something about a ghost story. Callaghan wanted Fisher to tell them a ghost story.'

'A ghost story?'

'You did ask. But yes, something like that.' With a practised movement, he picked up a tumbler, pressed it to the whisky optic and poured himself a measure. 'Brain juice.' He took a mouthful and, as if benefiting from its effects, said, '*His* ghost story. That's what he said.'

'Whose ghost story?' Winterman wondered how much the landlord had already knocked back that evening.

'Fisher's. That was what it was all about. Callaghan wanted Fisher to tell them his ghost story.'

'What ghost story?'

The landlord swallowed the remainder of the whisky. 'Haven't a clue. It seemed to mean something to Fisher. He looked shaken.'

'What did he say?'

'Not much. Just told Callaghan to leave him alone.'

'But you think Fisher knew what Callaghan was talking about?'

'He was pretty far gone by that time in the evening, so it's difficult to be sure. But I'd say so, yes.'

'And this was the evening Fisher found the body? The same evening?'

The landlord frowned and then glanced over his shoulder, perhaps considering the potential benefits of another shot of "brain juice". 'I'm pretty sure so. Don't think we saw Fisher in here after that.'

'That so? Maybe we'll need to have another chat with Mr Callaghan.' He gestured towards the drinks. 'What's the damage?'

The landlord smiled. 'On the house, just this once. Goes against the grain, but it's not often we get a Detective Inspector in here.'

CHAPTER THIRTY-THREE

'It's stopped,' Mary said, peering through the doors into the darkness.

'Perhaps.' Winterman craned his neck to look past her. 'For the moment.'

'Always the optimist.'

'I thought you liked the snow.'

'I do, but you don't.'

'I've no problem with it if I can just build snowmen. It's when I have to work that it gets in the way.'

'Not the only one getting in the way,' Hoxton grumbled from behind them. 'Are you two going out there or not?'

Winterman stepped forward, his feet crunching into the thick snow. It had been falling heavily while they were in the pub, and the white drifts were unblemished around them. The night was silent, even the sound of their voices muffled. The cottages across the street were in darkness and the village looked deserted. A large portion of the sky had cleared of cloud, and the sky was thick with stars. A biting wind swept in from the fens.

Mary emerged from the pub doorway, closely followed by Hoxton, Marsh and Brain. They had stayed for only one more round – Winterman had felt obliged to reciprocate the landlord's generosity – but Brain was already looking the worse for wear, his feet unsteady on the frozen snow.

'You two ready to get back?' Hoxton said to Winterman and Mary. 'We can walk with you, if you like.'

'It's hardly any distance,' Mary said. 'And it's stopped snowing. We'll be fine.'

'Anyway,' Winterman added, 'I have my trusty police-issue torch.' He brandished the heavy rubber-covered flashlight as though about to use it as a weapon.

'Watch out for the mad axe-man,' Brain said, his words marginally slurred.

'Thanks, Bryan,' Mary said. 'That's done wonders for my confidence.'

'Sorry. Just a joke.'

'And very funny too.' Hoxton slapped Brain heartily on the back. 'Come on, lad. Show us the way to go home. We're tired and we want to go to bed.'

Winterman stood with Mary, watching the three men set off in the direction of the police station. Caught in the pale lights of the pub, they resembled a staged tableau – perhaps some kind of religious image. Three unwise men.

'It's a good question though,' Mary said from behind him.

They trudged through the frozen snow. 'What is?' He used the torch sparingly, flashing its beam on to highlight the path whenever the darkness grew too dense.

'Whether it's safe for me to walk back like this.'

'I imagine so. What sort of mad axe-man would come out on a night like this?'

'The sort who killed Fisher perhaps. But that wasn't what I meant.'

'I know it wasn't. You meant is it safe to walk home with a well-known womaniser.'

'Something like that.' With an unselfconscious movement, she linked her arm in his.

Winterman glanced down. 'You're living dangerously.'

'I can look after myself. As you'll discover if you try anything.'

'I don't doubt it. But that's not my style.'

'I don't doubt it,' she echoed, mocking. 'So what is your style?'

'I'm much misunderstood.'

'I don't doubt it,' she said again.

'You're making fun of me.' Winterman didn't feel too troubled by the prospect.

'I am.' She had her head down, plodding steadily through the snow. 'But I don't imagine you mind. Anyway, you said you'd tell me the truth. I'm still waiting.'

'You said you'd let me buy you a drink.'

'I did let you.'

'I suppose so. But I'd assumed you meant just you, rather than Curly, Larry and Moe as well.'

'Then you need to be more precise in your requests. Or you'll continue to be disappointed.'

'Fair enough. And you want to know the truth?'

She stopped, drawing him to a halt beside her, and gazed up at him from beneath her scarf and woollen hat. He could barely make out her face, but her eyes were bright and searching. 'I think so. I want to know how you can be sort of married.'

He gazed back at her. 'My wife's ill. Very ill.'

Her hand moved to her mouth, an involuntary gesture. 'Oh – I'm sorry. I didn't know.'

'Very ill. Incurable. But sadly not terminal.' His voice was toneless, giving no clue to his feelings.

She seized his arm. 'That's a terrible thing to say–'

His face was as inscrutable as his voice. 'No, it isn't. You don't understand.'

'You said you'd tell me the truth. You're just playing games.'

'I'm telling you the truth. My wife, Gwyneth, was hit by a bomb, a doodlebug, in the last days of the war. She survived but was severely brain damaged. She has the mental age of a child.' He paused. 'And, as far as they can tell, the life expectancy of a healthy adult.'

Mary's mouth had dropped open. 'Dear Lord. I'm sorry.'

'It's how it is.' He was staring past her into the cold blackness. 'It's awful. But it's not the most awful thing.'

'What do you mean?'

'When the bomb hit Gwyneth, it also hit my son. My little boy.'

'Oh my goodness,' Mary whispered.

His expression suggested he had almost forgotten she was there. 'He was only six years old. Killed instantly. They told me that as if I was supposed to be grateful.'

'I'm so sorry. I'm really so sorry.'

Above them, the sky had grown heavier, and the first fresh flakes of snow swirled between them. 'I'm not even sure that's the worst thing.'

'What do you mean?'

His eyes had filled with tears, snowflakes settling on his face. 'I loved him. I loved Sam, my little boy. But I didn't love her. I didn't love Gwyneth.' His eyes were fixed on hers. 'I didn't love her then. And I don't love her now.'

CHAPTER THIRTY-FOUR

The church was dark above, a sprawling patch of nothing in the star-freighted sky. The snow was still swirling between them, not yet falling heavily, but threatening more to come.

'We need to get back,' she said. 'Before it really comes down.'

'I know. I'll be all right in a moment.' He was leaning across the snow-topped stone wall, his eyes fixed on the regiments of gravestones.

'You can tell me,' she said. 'If you want to.'

He said nothing more for a moment. 'Yes. I think I do want to.' He pushed open the iron gates of the churchyard, and took a step along the path. 'You were right.'

'Right?' Mary looked anxiously over her shoulder. It was not far back to her mother's house. They should still be all right if the snow were to come down more heavily.

'I did have a reputation as a womaniser. A deserved reputation probably. I had a few… relationships. Probably didn't behave well.' He paused, then laughed slightly. 'I had a relationship with the chief constable's daughter.'

She had moved closer behind him. 'It sounds like the first line of a song. It also doesn't sound very wise. Your wife?'

'Yes, my wife. She… we–' He stopped. 'We discovered she was expecting. It was a shock. We thought we'd been careful.'

'Not careful enough.'

'No, well – we didn't have a lot of choice after that. We announced we were getting married. Kept it quiet, though I don't imagine we fooled anyone. Not anyone capable of using a calendar anyway. I'd been the chief's blue-eyed boy – his high-flyer. He never said anything, but he didn't need to.'

'When was this?'

''Thirty-nine. Start of the war. I'd been wondering what to do. Felt I was too young to hide in a reserved occupation.' He paused, thinking about what he'd said. 'I'm sorry.'

'Don't be. My husband felt the same. He'd already resigned from the force so he could join up.'

'I didn't,' Winterman said. 'They didn't allow it, not officially. And I thought I should stay with Gwyneth. Though even then we both knew it wasn't ideal. If it hadn't been for Sam, we wouldn't have married.'

'Your son?'

'He was a lovely baby.' Winterman's voice was steady. 'A lovely little boy. We both loved him. Even if we didn't love each other.'

'You're not the first,' she said. 'It's not a unique story.'

'Oh, I know. But that doesn't make it any easier. And I had another problem.'

'What problem?'

'Gwyneth's father. The chief. I'd been pursuing a case. A big deal, by local standards. Trafficking in stolen goods – flooding the black market. We knew who they all were, but hadn't been able to get near them. Then I got a lucky lead. I was nearly there, and I was told to back off.'

'By the chief constable?' There was a note of disbelief in her voice.

'One of the senior officers. There were good reasons. One of the people I'd been looking at was an informer. They wanted him protected. Another was being watched as part of a bigger case so we shouldn't tread on their toes. Usual story. Don't step out of line, son, or you'll make it difficult for all of us.'

'Perhaps they were right.'

'I'd already heard things. They were being bought off. A long way up. Maybe all the way to the top.'

'You can't know that,' Mary protested.

'I knew it. I even made a half-hearted attempt to do something about it. I don't think I expected to succeed. I just wanted to bring things to a head.' He laughed, humourlessly. 'I did that, all right.'

'I heard–'

'You heard I had a breakdown? I suppose I did, in a way. I certainly didn't handle things very cleverly. It suited the chief perfectly. He wanted me out of the picture. I was an embarrassment to him, personally and professionally. He pulled a few strings. There I was with a smart university degree, so I got called up for some confidential work in London.'

'Intelligence work?'

'I'm not at liberty to divulge the nature or content of my activities,' he intoned, in what was presumably a parody of some official pronouncement. 'But you can imagine.'

'And your wife went with you?'

'Not at first. We thought it would be too dangerous to take Sam to London once the bombing started.'

Mary took another look at the sky. 'We really ought to get back.'

He made no response. 'But she wanted to give it another go. Things were getting desperate for her. She was lonely. She wanted to try.'

'We need to get back,' she repeated. The snow was swirling more thickly around them.

'So she came. It was that weekend. That weekend it happened.'

'Ivan,' Mary said. 'We need to move.'

He was staring into the darkness, his eyes fixed on one of the rows of gravestones.

'What is it?'

'There,' he said. 'Can you see it?'

She peered towards where his finger was pointing. 'I can't see anything.'

'I thought I saw something move, but that's not possible. But there's definitely something there.'

'There's more than enough snow. I know that much. We really need to get home.'

'Wait. There is something.' He switched on the torch and aimed the beam out across the churchyard. The light was dazzling for a moment, catching the endlessly turning snow.

Mary's eyes followed the cone of light. The trunk of a twisted elm. The angular blocks of worn gravestones, diagonal shadows across the white-coated earth. A shape.

'What is it?'

Winterman glanced at her, unsure whether to ask to stay where she was or to accompany him further into the churchyard. 'Come on.' He walked forward, his gloved hand still clutched in hers. The torchlight glanced across the blank snow-coated stones, emphasising the thick shadows behind.

Winterman shone the beam high in the air. Twenty feet away, there was a small clearing among the clustered graves. Beyond that was a larger raised grave – a rectangular stone box, the last resting place of some local notable. Something was resting on the tomb. Something out of place. Something black and formless.

'It's another body.' Mary's voice was barely audible in the night. 'Another child.' Winterman felt her hand close more tightly around his.

He took one more step forward, the torch-beam unwavering. Then, suddenly, he lowered the light, as if he had seen enough. 'Stay there. Don't move.' He raised the torchlight again and shone it across the blank surface of the tomb.

It was a child's body, sure enough. A pale shrivelled scrap of a thing, not yet bone but scarcely flesh, clothed in a few shreds of disintegrating cloth. Not fit clothing for a night like this. He moved the torch-beam over the body, the light glittering once, shockingly, on a pair of sightless eyes. The body was on its back, its leathery face twisted towards him, limbs spread like a sacrificial offering. He flashed the light briefly around the tomb, but in the dim light the snow looked untouched.

'What do we do?' Mary spoke from just behind him, her voice breaking unexpectedly into his thoughts. Her face in the torchlight was calm – the look of a mourner who has grown all too accustomed to death.

The snow was still coming down heavily, the rising wind blowing it into a toiling blizzard. It was already thick on their hats and shoulders. For the first time, Winterman was conscious of how cold he felt.

'You were right. We have to get back.' He glanced at the body. 'We can't do anything now. I can't even move the poor thing without risking disturbing the scene. We'll have to leave it till the morning. Nobody else is likely to come here before morning.'

She looked past him towards where the body lay. 'Somebody's been here tonight.'

She was right. The snow lay only thinly across the child's corpse. It could not have been long since it was left here.

Involuntarily he shivered, his eyes moving to the impenetrable darkness around them. Someone could still be out there. Someone could be watching them.

He slipped his arm through hers again, unsure of his motives. 'Come on. Let's get you home.'

CHAPTER THIRTY-FIVE

'This is getting to be a habit.' Howard was wearing another of his large collection of dressing gowns, a characteristically startling collation of primary colours he had no doubt picked up somewhere overseas.

'It's this bloody weather.' Pyke was wheeling his motorbike slowly into the lee of Howard's cottage. He dragged a tarpaulin from the rear pannier of the bike and draped it carefully over the machine. 'I was heading back to town–'

'Of course you were, dear boy. But you know you're always welcome here.' There was no edge to Howard's voice, no sense that his words were anything other than entirely sincere.

'I don't want to disturb you.'

'What's to disturb, dear boy? What would I be doing on a night like this, apart from keeping well out of the way of the snow?' Howard peered past Pyke into the frozen night. 'Speaking of which, you'd better come in. It's freezing out here.'

'I had noticed.' Pyke followed Howard through into the warmth of the hallway, shrugging off his overcoat, bending to unfasten his heavy boots. Howard had always kept the house slightly too warm. Like many of Howard's habits, it had vaguely offended Pyke's austere sensibilities, but he was glad of the welcoming heat.

'You'll be wanting a drink, of course,' Howard said over his shoulder. 'Gin or scotch?'

Pyke hesitated. This was a bloody bad idea. Another bloody bad idea. He didn't really even know why he was here, what had brought him back to this Godforsaken place. He had spent a hard lonely miserable day in the lab working on Fisher's body and then on that poor child's body, largely only either confirming the initial judgments he had made on the hoof or simply that there were no more solid judgments he could make.

Some time in the late afternoon, as the snow-coloured light thickened to dusk, he had grown thoroughly sick of the bleak sparse surroundings of the laboratory and decided to take a ride out on the bike. Even that had been madness. The threatened snow had held off all day and the main road had been cleared, but the temperature had stayed below freezing and the road surface was likely to be lethal.

But that was it, of course. There was something invigorating about the danger. No doubt that was why he rode the bike in the first place. No doubt that was why he did half the things he did.

Why he was here.

He could blame the weather, but he had chosen to put himself out in it. He had chosen to ride in this direction. His own choice.

'Drink?' Howard repeated. He was waving the gin bottle, which, Pyke thought, had already seen some use that evening.

'Thanks, Howard. And thanks for taking me in again. Can I have some tea first?'

Howard hesitated momentarily and then poured himself another large measure. 'Sit down. Get yourself warmed up. I'll bring you the tea.'

Pyke lowered himself onto the sofa and stretched out his stockinged feet towards the high-banked log fire. Not much sign of austerity Britain in this household.

'What brings you back out here so soon?' Howard called from the kitchen. 'Those bodies again?'

Pyke rose slowly and stepped over to the kitchen door. 'There were some details I needed to check for the report.'

Howard was busying himself warming the teapot, his head down. 'You're too conscientious, you know. That's your trouble. Anyone else would have waited till the weather improved.'

Pyke gazed at the top of Howard's balding head, wondering whether he was being mocked. 'I had to come out. If the snow melted, I wouldn't be able to check anything.'

Howard nodded slowly, as if acknowledging the truth of Pyke's assertion. 'You're the expert. Just didn't think you'd want to get caught in the snow twice.'

'I didn't. But I was stupid enough to do it, and here I am.'

'And, as I say, very welcome you are too, dear boy.' Howard smiled, sliding a cup of tea towards Pyke. 'Now let's make the most of it.'

CHAPTER THIRTY-SIX

The first pale light of dawn found Winterman trudging slowly through the snow back into the village. The previous night, he and Mary had arrived at her house just after eleven, the snow still falling heavily around them. The main road, cleared earlier in the day, was already covered, the drifts higher in the hedgerows.

As she had showed him to the spare bedroom, he had wondered whether it would be in order to show some gesture of – what? Affection? Concern? A kiss on the cheek, a touch on the hand? In the circumstances, nothing seemed appropriate.

He had no idea what she was thinking. Any emotion between them had been dulled and dissipated, first by his own narrative and then by the experience in the graveyard. She had gazed at him expressionlessly, and he wondered whether she was expecting some move on his part. Was she disappointed when he had murmured a polite goodnight and closed the bedroom door?

There was no way of knowing, he decided, as he stamped his way through the heavy banks of snow. Perhaps later he might discover whether his reticence had been the only appropriate response or an opportunity missed.

Despite their discovery in the churchyard, he had slept soundly enough, with no further dreams that he could recall.

He had woken at six thirty, dressed quickly and let himself silently out of the house. Everyone else – Mary, her mother, the children – were, as far as he could tell, still sleeping.

Outside it was dark, though there were signs of dawn in the east, the sky bruised and translucent. The last of the night was dense with stars, a sickle moon low over the horizon to the west.

It was colder than ever, far below freezing. He had borrowed an additional overcoat that had been hanging in Mary's hallway, wrapped up in layers of clothing like a human dirigible. He wanted to run, to expend some energy to get the warmth back into his limbs, but the treacherous ground made even that impossible.

By the time he reached the church he was cold to the bone. He stamped slowly across the churchyard, the snow clinging to his boots. The night before, he had barely registered the church itself. Now it loomed over him in the dim light, gothic and imposing, oddly threatening, too large for the village it supposedly served.

He had half-expected that the child's body would have been removed – spirited away as mysteriously as it had arrived, leaving him unsure what he had witnessed in the darkness. But it was still there – or something was – curling grotesquely in a snow-covered bundle on the top of the tomb.

The fresh fall of snow had rendered it less horrific, at least at first sight. Under the white coating, it might have been nothing more than a discarded bundle of rags, the detritus left by some passing tramp. Was it possible they had deluded themselves the previous night? Was he so spooked by this case that he was creating his own ghosts?

It took him only another step to see the answer. The twisted face – the dried mummified flesh, the sightless eye sockets – was twisted towards him, still uncovered by the drifts of snow. He could discern the angled bony arm, the white fingers reaching beseechingly towards him. Another child. No more than nine or ten years old, he guessed. But dead for a long time.

Even given what had already happened, the sight was shocking. Winterman had no idea how frequented the churchyard might be, particularly in weather like this, but someone would have found it quickly enough. Probably some aged widow or widower tending their late spouse's grave. It didn't bear thinking about. But none of it bore much thinking about.

He peered round the far side of the tomb. As he had expected the further fall of snow had concealed any footprints that might have been made around the gravestone. It was possible that the forensic people might be able to find some traces, but he had little real hope.

This was serious. Spooner had arranged for him to be posted to this desolate patch to be out of harm's way – or, at least, out of the chief constable's way. The first child's body, the body that Fisher had found, had been an intriguing mystery, but nobody at HQ had taken the case seriously. In such a rural environment, deaths, even children's deaths, were hardly unusual, particularly in recent years. The causes were mundane, even when heartbreaking – neglect, sickness, casual abuse, sometimes even starvation. Winterman had no illusions about the state of the country, the levels of poverty and deprivation out there. The '45 landslide hadn't come from nowhere.

But a third young corpse, alongside Fisher's murder, was not so easily dismissed. The locals would be getting concerned. If it hadn't been for the weather the local press would be sniffing round, the national press close behind them. Almost the only positive thing you could say about the bloody weather.

The available manpower was stretched thinly enough as it was, and the weather would put even more pressure on resources. All but the most major routes would be closed again, the trains running only sporadically if at all. Even if the weather improved, it was likely to be several days before any serious backup might arrive.

He pulled his layers of clothing more tightly around him and glanced at his watch. Seven fifteen. It wasn't likely that anyone would be about yet in this weather, but these country types tended to rise early. He glanced back at the ugly mound on the gravestone, shuddering at the thought that anyone else might stumble across it.

He couldn't move the body until forensics and Pyke had had a look at it. The only option was to get Brain to come and stand guard so they could keep people away. Time to be the bearer of bad news.

Winterman stamped his way slowly out of the churchyard. The village stretched out below him – the pub, a scattering of cottages and houses, the small village shop and post office, the snow-covered village green. Picturesque, under this blanket of white. At other times though, it wasn't the kind of rural township that found itself decorating the fronts of chocolate boxes. It was a working village, surrounded by bleak open fields, acres of farmland where landowners and tenants scraped a living growing beets and root vegetables. Rural poverty, battered by depression and six hard years of wartime, struggling with austerity. Wondering when the promised future was going to arrive.

The police station stood in the centre of the village, a few hundred yards beyond the pub. There was no sign of life. Even the shop was closed and silent, with an air of abandonment. The police house looked as uninhabited as anywhere else.

Winterman pulled hard on the bell, and was rewarded by the sound of a faint jangling from somewhere inside.

After a few moments, he heard another sound, a shuffling of footsteps, before the door was pulled open. Brain peered out, his eyes blinking and bloodshot against the morning light. 'Yes?'

'Morning, Bryan. Duty calls, I'm afraid.'

Brain blinked again. 'Morning, sir.' He appeared to regain his composure with impressive speed. 'You'd best come in. It's freezing out there.'

Winterman stepped in, removing his hat. 'Brass monkey weather,' he agreed, then added, with feeling, 'Too cold even for bloody brass monkeys, if you ask me. Unfortunately, we have work to do.'

'Work, sir?' Brain glanced pointedly at the replica grandfather clock that dominated one corner of the hallway. 'What sort of work?'

Winterman followed him through into the warmer sitting room. Hoxton was sitting by the fire, toasting his stockinged feet against the flames. There was no sign of Marsh. Winterman nodded to Hoxton. 'We've found another one.'

'Another what?'

'Another bloody body,' Winterman said. 'Another child. Just like the first two.'

Hoxton looked at him, clearly biting back some facetious comment he had prepared. 'Who found it?'

'Me and Mary. Last night. On the way back.'

'My God,' Hoxton said. 'You should have come to find us.'

'There was nothing we could have done. The snow was coming down. I just wanted to get her back home.'

'But the body–'

'It's still there,' Winterman said. 'That's why I'm here. There was nothing to be done last night, but we need to get the place cordoned off now. Keep out any sightseers. Protect the site until the lab boys can get here. And track down Pyke.'

'Elusive bugger, your Dr Pyke,' Hoxton observed. 'Never where he's supposed to be.'

'Probably just smarter than you and me then. Bryan, I'll need you to get up to the churchyard and keep on eye on the body. Not the most enjoyable task, even without this cold.'

'No problem, sir.' Brain stood upright, looking as if he was about to salute. 'What do you want me to say to people? If anyone comes along, I mean.'

'Is there just the one entrance to the churchyard?'

'There's no other way in unless you climb over the wall.'

'I'd suggest you position yourself at the gate then. If anyone comes, tell them there's a police investigation going on – which will be true, soon enough. Don't for goodness' sake mention the body. With a bit of luck, no one will be able to see it from outside the churchyard, so we should be able to keep it quiet for a bit. At least till we've had the scene examined properly.'

'I'll keep them out, sir.' Brain had the air of someone entrusted with a possibly lethal mission. He made his way hurriedly out of the room. Moments later, they heard the front door slam.

'I reckon you probably can rely on him,' Hoxton said. 'Bit more to that lad than meets the eye.'

'You're not wrong. We'll have to draft him over to our lot. Right, let's get to it. Where's Marsh?'

'Still sleeping it off, I imagine. I'll go and rouse him.'

'Be gentle with him. Probably still needs his beauty sleep. Not like you and me.'

'Beautiful enough, us.'

'Too right. Okay, I'll get phoning. See if I can round up some reinforcements.'

'Good luck with that,' Hoxton said sceptically. 'I'll see if I can round you up a nice cup of tea while you're waiting.'

CHAPTER THIRTY-SEVEN

Whatever his qualities, Brain ran a tight enough ship.

Winterman was standing in the middle of the business end of the police house. He had sat in there before, during the interview with William Callaghan, but hadn't really noticed the room. He looked around, taking in all the detail.

It was a small room, designed to accommodate all kinds of police business. And it was clear that Brain took that business seriously. The walls were lined with Government information posters, some of them dating back to the war but still relevant. *Food is a weapon – don't waste it. We can do it.*

There was a small table and three chairs. On the table was a tray with various forms stacked in neat rows. There were two olive-green metal filing cabinets and an imposing mahogany desk which didn't look like police issue. Above the desk, an Ordnance Survey map was pinned to the wall.

Winterman peered closer. A large-scale map of the local area with Framley just off-centre. Neatly labelled pins marked various local landmarks – the nearest fire station, two hospitals, various police stations. Three more pins, each adorned with a small black label, identified the sites where the bodies – Fisher's and the first two children's – had been found. Yes, Brain took the police business seriously.

Winterman picked up the phone and dialled the operator, asking to be put through to headquarters.

When the phone was finally answered at the switchboard, he asked for Superintendent Spooner.

'DI Winterman.' Spooner's voice boomed down the line. 'How are they treating you out there in the back of beyond?'

Spooner was a bluff figure, well liked if not particularly well respected by the majority of those who worked for him. Winterman's contact with him had been limited to date – Spooner had arrived after Winterman's departure to London – but he suspected that the rank and file might have got it wrong. Beyond the superficial bonhomie, he hadn't warmed to Spooner, but he'd already developed a wary respect for the senior officer's savvy and his survival instincts.

'They're treating me very well, sir,' he responded cautiously.

'Keeping you busy, are they, Winterman?'

'I'm certainly being kept busy, sir.'

'From what I hear, you've stumbled across a hotbed of crime. What is it so far? Three bodies?' Spooner could easily have been discussing the previous Saturday's football scores.

'Four, sir, actually.'

There was a momentary pause at the other end of the line. Winterman congratulated himself for having caught Spooner momentarily off guard.

'Does that mean another one?' The joviality had diminished, to be replaced by an obvious wariness. Winterman could imagine Spooner calculating the implications of this news.

'Another child. Just like the first two. We found it this morning, so we don't have any medical or forensic information yet, but it looks the same. The same age. Roughly the same period since death. Possibly even the same cause of death.'

There was another pause as Spooner absorbed what he was being told. 'Good God, man. What are they up to out there?'

'That's what I'm trying to find out, sir.' Winterman only just prevented himself from adding 'with respect.' 'But we need more resources.'

'So does everyone, Winterman. We're stretched as thin as a tart's negligee as it is.'

The metaphor was typical of Spooner. Trying that bit too hard. 'I appreciate that, sir. But this must be a priority. If we don't get some results, the local populace will start to panic.'

'Kiddie killer on the loose, you mean?'

'Something like that. It's only a matter of time till the press get hold of it. I'm sure they'd be here already if it wasn't for the snow.'

There was a pause at the other end of the line as Spooner weighed up the situation. 'Correct me if I'm wrong, Inspector,' he said finally, 'but these bodies have been dead for some time?'

'Apart from Fisher's.'

'So there's no reason to assume any killer is actually out there.'

'We don't know that there isn't. More to the point, neither do the local people. Someone killed these children. And someone's making sure we find the bodies.'

'And you've no idea why? Why the bodies are being revealed?'

'As yet we know very little. You'll appreciate that the investigation isn't easy in the current conditions.'

'Nothing's easy in the current conditions, Inspector. That's precisely why we're so short of resources.'

And touché, thought Winterman, cursing himself for allowing Spooner the opening. 'Yes, sir.'

'I do appreciate the situation. I'll see what I can do.'

'Thank you, sir.'

'Good luck, Inspector.'

I'll see what I can do, Winterman thought. *The mantra of unhelpful bureaucrats throughout the war. I'll see what I can do. Three-fifths of bugger all.* He placed the telephone handset back on its bracket, realising that Hoxton was standing at the door watching him.

'No luck then,' Hoxton said.

'He'll see what he can do.' He stopped as he registered the expression on Hoxton's face. 'What is it?'

'Something funny. Funny peculiar. Marshy.'

'What about him?'

'Not there.' Hoxton stood in the doorway, his hands thrust into his pockets, looking as if he were challenging Winterman to contradict him.

'What do you mean not there?'

'What I say. He's not there.'

Winterman frowned. 'He must have got up early. Gone out for a breather or a smoke.'

'Marshy don't smoke. I don't think he's slept in that bed either.'

'What?'

'Bed sheets have been tossed about. Made it looks as if someone's slept in 'em. But I'm not daft.'

'You mean Marsh has been out all night?'

'Looks that way. I'm pretty sure no one slept in that bed last night.'

'But he made it look as if he had?'

'Tried to.'

'Why would he do that?'

'No idea. Maybe got a ladyfriend hereabouts. But it's bloody odd. Not like the lad.'

'He's a big boy,' Winterman pointed out. 'He can look after himself.'

'Even so, I don't much like the thought of him being out all night in this weather.'

'Unless he's been with a ladyfriend, as you put it.'

Hoxton stared at him for a moment, his blank face revealing nothing. 'Who knows? But I've a bad feeling about it.'

CHAPTER THIRTY-EIGHT

Brain made his way across the churchyard, stepping cautiously through the heavy snow. It was full daylight, but the sky was still grey and lowering, threatening yet more snow.

He didn't think of himself as a cowardly man, on the whole. When duty called, he'd never been worried about squaring up to the drunks tumbling out of the pub on a Saturday night or the gypsies who needed moving on from someone's farmland. He'd even tackled a housebreaker once – a panicked young man who had threatened Brain with a non-existent knife.

But this case was beginning to unnerve him. He had found himself hesitating at the entrance to the churchyard, wondering what might be waiting among the ranks of snow-covered graves. He had glanced nervously at the looming church, conscious of the shadows in its angled walls and buttresses, shadows that might conceal… well, who knew what?

And there before him was the tomb Winterman had described. A long-gone local dignitary who had merited something slightly more ornate than the plain stones that adorned the majority of the graves.

Brain steeled himself for the sight of the child's body, unsure what to expect. He had not seen the first two infant bodies, and Fisher's prone corpse had carried little emotional impact. But the remains of a small child…

Though he felt mildly guilty to acknowledge it, the body proved an anticlimax. Even from a few feet away, it was simply a mound of snow, unrecognisable as something that had once been human.

Brain returned to stand by the gate. He shuffled backwards and forwards awkwardly, unsure what he was supposed to do. He was realising he had drawn the shortest of short straws. His only responsibility – albeit a critical one – was to keep people away. But at that time of day and in this weather, there was no one around anyway. It was, as everyone kept saying, bloody cold.

He stood for a moment contemplating the options. Just because this was a routine job, that didn't mean he shouldn't take it seriously. Attention to detail, that was what distinguished the best officers, especially those like Brain who had ambitions to progress into the CID. Unfortunate as this case might be, it was a once in a lifetime opportunity to make an impression on those who could help progress his career.

So he had to get this right, or at least avoid making a fool of himself. That meant, first of all, keeping away any unwelcome visitors which ought to be easy enough. Second, though Winterman had said nothing about it, it meant protecting the crime scene. Brain's knowledge of forensics was limited to the little he had picked up in basic training and the sensationalised details he gleaned from the crime novels he devoured so enthusiastically. But he knew the scene should not be disturbed.

In an effort to keep warm, he tramped along the stone path from the gate to the door of the church itself. He kept one eye fixed on the gate in case anyone should enter. The other eye he kept, much less assiduously, on the body itself, his mind speculating on the reasons why it had ended up in such a bleak spot.

It was on his fourth or fifth traverse of the path that he spotted something. He had walked a yard or two further than before, closer to the church, and, as he turned to walk back, he glanced towards the body and his eye was caught by something in the shadows.

Beside the gravestone, just a few feet from the body itself, was a darker patch, a stain showing faintly through the covering of freshly fallen snow.

Brain hesitated. He should fetch the inspector. But that would mean abandoning his post and he wouldn't be thanked if this turned out to be nothing.

He delayed a moment longer and then stepped out across the pristine snow towards the grave. He was right. There was something there. A darker patch, half-hidden beneath the overnight snow.

Blood.

He had no idea where the thought had come from, but he knew instantly that he was correct. He took another step forward and reached out with a finger to touch the soiled snow.

CHAPTER THIRTY-NINE

Pyke opened his eyes, already conscious that something was wrong. It was as if some lingering shred of a bad dream had lodged in his brain before waking. A nightmare in which he'd done something unforgiveable, committed some unspeakable crime. Incurred some unshakeable guilt.

Guilt.

He rolled over in the soft warm bed. Not his own bed. Not even Howard's guest bed.

Bloody hell. He was so bloody stupid. So bloody, bloody stupid.

He could smell Howard's distinctive cologne, another of those affectations that Howard maintained in the face of rationing and austerity. He could smell – this was the truth of it – Howard himself.

How much had he drunk last night?

Not that much. A few Scotches. A couple of Howard's patent cocktails.

He should have had more bloody sense. He had known what Howard wanted, he had known – he had always known – that Howard cared nothing for any consequences.

Pyke knew that, in his heart, he wanted the same. He had always wanted it. That was why he had become involved with Howard in the first place. But his head knew it was insane. He was gambling everything – his career, his livelihood, his friends. It was different for Howard. Howard was an actor, for God's sake. In that world, it was almost compulsory.

He sat up and pulled on a dressing gown that, presumably, Howard had left for him. It was like coming home. This bedroom.

The scent of Howard. The simultaneous sense of comfort and despair.

The bedroom was as immaculate as ever, Howard somehow managing to convey the sense that he had simply passed through, making a few tasteful adjustments, but leaving no corporeal traces.

Pyke glanced at his watch. Already nine thirty. He had been due at work an hour ago, though he had negotiated a flexible enough routine with the university over the years. They paid him peanuts, and allowed him to come and go more or less as he pleased. He eked out his income with the police work. At some point, that neat arrangement was going to come unstuck. Another risk.

He moved towards the bedroom door, mentally rehearsing the impending conversation with Howard. Then he stopped as it occurred to him that it would be politic to get dressed before he went downstairs.

So where had Howard put his bloody clothes? He couldn't imagine that, the night before, he had done anything other than dump them on the chair beside the bed. So Howard had presumably tidied them that morning, part of his familiar drive to ensure that nothing in the house appeared to have been touched by a human hand.

Pyke pulled open the doors of Howard's rococo wardrobe and peered inside. Howard's own handmade suits, expertly pressed shirts, a neat rack of typically gaudy ties. And a pair of boots.

Pyke leaned forward and peered at the boots. They were Howard's, sure enough – a pair that Pyke had bought as a present at a point when he could scarcely afford it. Howard had worn them two or three times before growing bored with them.

But he had worn them again, very recently. The boots were dark around the soles, still wet from a walk in the snow.

Pyke picked up one of the boots and stared at it thoughtfully. It was sodden, the sole and heel thick with mud, the uppers stained from the moisture. Howard had been out recently – certainly since the previous night.

Howard had never been one for moonlit walks. Or any other form of walks, come to that. If Howard had braved the overnight snow and mud, something odd was going on.

Pyke replaced the boot and closed the wardrobe door. Stepping quietly across the carpet, he opened the bedroom door. From somewhere below, he could hear the burbling of the wireless – a piece of light classical music typical of Howard's taste. Pyke paused for a moment, listening, before crossing to the bathroom.

The bathroom was another of Howard's affectations. He had eschewed the functionality that still characterised most people's sanitary arrangements. The overall design, Pyke supposed, was intended to suggest Chinese inspiration – swirling patterns of dark greens and golds. Pyke found it vaguely disorientating, like stepping unexpectedly into the depths of a jungle.

The bathroom was as immaculate as the rest of the cottage. But it was where Howard kept the large wicker basket into which he disposed of his dirty – or, more accurately, briefly worn – clothing, pending its twice-weekly washing.

Pyke bolted the bathroom door behind him. The wicker basket stood, as always, between the bath and the airing cupboard. He raised the lid.

On top were the clothes that, as far as Pyke could recall, Howard had been wearing the previous evening. Pyke could not quite remember – in truth, did not want to remember – what had happened to those clothes at the end of the alcohol-fuelled night. But, however and whenever the clothes had been removed, they had subsequently been put back on again. Another unprecedented action on Howard's part. Because the clothes, like the boots in the bedroom, had apparently been worn for an excursion into the snow. The expensive-looking trousers were damp and muddy. Even Howard's white silk shirt was speckled with dirt.

So Howard had been somewhere during the night. And Howard would not have left the house, in the small hours, in the snow, without some significant purpose. Some significant purpose likely to benefit Howard.

What the bloody hell had he been up to?

Pyke replaced the lid of the laundry basket, unlocked the door, and stepped silently back out on to the landing.

It was all another risk. That was the thing with Howard. There was always something else. Always another bloody risk.

CHAPTER FORTY

'Yes, it is urgent,' Winterman said. 'When are you expecting him?' He paused, listening. 'But he *does* work for you? I mean, he's still employed by the university?' Another pause, then Winterman gave a wry smile. 'Quite right. And, no, we don't know where he is either. Just tell him it's urgent, as soon as you speak to him. Tell him it's Framley again. He'll understand.'

Hoxton was sipping on his tea, staring out of the window at the snowdrifts outside. He turned as Winterman replaced the receiver. 'No luck with Pyke then?'

'Not been into the office yet. They assume he's stuck in the snow. '

'And the lass pointed out that he works as much for us as he does for them. Put you in your place.'

'Young people,' Winterman agreed. 'No respect. Anyway, he only freelances for us.'

'We probably pay him more than the university. And we both let him come and go as he pleases.'

'No point in trying to tame an academic. They always find their way back out into the wild.'

'Just as well,' Hoxton said, 'given how difficult it is to house-train the buggers.'

'No word on Marsh?'

'Not a dicky.'

'What do you reckon? Do we go and look for him?'

'Where would we look? We can't go scouring the streets. We'll just have to wait.' It wasn't clear what potential outcome Hoxton had in mind.

Winterman's response was pre-empted by the shrill ringing of the telephone. He snatched up the receiver, expecting news of Pyke. 'Police. Can I help you?' There was a lengthy pause, as Winterman took in what was being said. 'Where are you now? Okay, hang on, we'll be there in a few minutes. You're sure now?' Another pause. 'I believe you. We'll see you there.' He replaced the receiver.

'Don't tell me,' Hoxton said. 'Brain.'

'He's a smart lad. Reckons he's found something.'

'Thought he was doing crowd control at the churchyard?'

'He is. That's where he found it.'

'Found what?' Hoxton was already pulling on his large boots.

'Blood,' Winterman said. 'A bloody big pool of bloody blood. Right next to that poor child's body.'

'But not the child's?'

'No, not the child's. Been dead far too long for that.'

'Who then?'

The same thought had clearly entered both their minds. 'How the hell should I know?' Winterman said. 'I don't even know if it really is blood. Maybe Brain's got it wrong this time. Let's go and find out, shall we?'

Outside, the morning chill hit them like a blow across the face. 'My Christ,' Hoxton exclaimed. 'You'd have thought if they could invent an atomic bomb, they could do something about this bloody weather.'

They trudged up the high street, making slow progress on the frozen snow. Ahead, the church tower was dark against the heavy grey of the sky. As they rounded the corner past the pub, they saw Brain standing, his body hunched against the cold, with another man by the churchyard gate.

'Who the hell's that?' Winterman said. 'The bloody publican?'

Hoxton squinted. 'Looks like it. You might have guessed he'd be first on the scene. Gossip mongering's part of the job.'

'Hope Brain's not told him any more than he needs to.'

'Young Brain will have told him everything, and won't even know he's said anything. I always reckoned the army should have employed Norman, for all his dicky heart. He'd have been a whiz at interrogating enemy personal. Ten minutes with him and they'd have spilled everything. No bloody thumbscrews. Just Norman's silvery tongue.'

'You know how to cheer a person up, Hoxton. Anyone ever tell you that?'

'Not so's I recall.' Hoxton looked up, replacing his familiar morose demeanour with an unexpected smile. 'Morning, young Bryan. Morning, old Norman. What brings you out here on a day like this?'

Norman gestured towards Brain. 'Young Bryan here brought me out. Needed my telephone.'

Brain looked appropriately embarrassed. 'Didn't think I should abandon my post any more than I could help. Pub's the nearest place with a telephone.'

'Very good, lad,' Winterman said. 'And very public spirited of you, sir,' he added to the publican. 'Thank you. We'd better not keep you out in this weather. '

'In other words, bugger off, Norman,' Hoxton said. 'Let us get on with it. I'm sure this lad's already told you all you need to know. And I'm sure it'll be halfway round the village before you get back inside.'

'I don't know what–'

'This is George Hoxton you're talking to, Norman. Not newborn Brain here. Get back to watering your beer.'

Norman opened his mouth once more, then turned and trudged back towards the pub.

'You know how to win friends,' Winterman commented.

'It's the only language he understands.'

Winterman turned to Brain. 'Okay, lad, what do you think you've found?'

'It's over there.' Brain pointed through the gate towards the tomb. 'Just the other side of the grave. I'm pretty sure it's blood.'

'Okay, let's go see.' Winterman led the way back down the path, sticking to the same route that Brain had already taken, conscious of the need to disturb as little as possible.

As they drew level with the grave, Brain gestured towards the ground in its shadow. 'There. That dark patch.'

Winterman motioned the other two to stay back and stepped forward, again walking as closely as he could in Brain's footsteps. Something was seeping through the top covering of snow. Winterman crouched down, as Brain had done, and reached out to touch the surface.

He pressed a finger into the snow and raised it back to his face. Something dark and sticky. He held his finger under his nose for a second, then pressed it delicately against his tongue. Slowly, he rose to his feet.

'You didn't really have any doubt, did you?' he said to Brain.

'Not really, sir. But I wanted you to check.'

'It's blood, all right. A whole lot of it. Must have been spilled before the last fall of snow in the night.'

'It was snowing when you and Mary found the body?' Hoxton asked.

'It had just started. Which means the blood was spilt after we were here.'

'Looks that way, doesn't it?'

'So who?' Winterman walked slowly around the grave, keeping well back from the half-concealed pool of blood. Now that he knew where to look, he could see that it covered a substantial area – a darker patch spreading out towards the adjoining grave. 'Something's been moved across there.'

Hoxton moved closer behind him. 'Aye. I see what you mean. The new snow's covered it, but the ground's been disturbed. Something heavy's been dragged over it.'

'It's been dragged to the gate. It stops there.'

'Go on then, Sherlock. How does that happen then?'

'Elementary, my dear Hoxton. They dumped the body in a car.'

'Body? Don't pull any punches, will you?'

'It's either that or a sack of bloody coal,' Winterman said. 'And coal doesn't usually bleed, even these days.' He peered down the street. 'If there was a car, in the middle of the night, in a place like this, someone might have seen it.'

'Assuming anyone was around.'

'Assuming anyone was around.' Winterman glanced at Brain. 'Not so easy, this police stuff, eh, Brain?'

'No, sir.'

'Thing is, Brain, I haven't a clue what's going on here. We need to get more resources from headquarters. We need to track down bloody Pyke to tell us whatever he can about that blood, and about that poor wee bugger's body.' Winterman shook his head. 'This is just chaos.'

'And we still don't know where Marshy is.' Hoxton looked back towards the grave.

'No,' Winterman said. 'We still don't know where Marsh is.'

CHAPTER FORTY-ONE

Pyke paused at the top of the stairs, wondering what to say to Howard. Howard was more than capable of denying anything, even in the face of the most concrete evidence. He would have some tall story about what had happened in the night.

From below, Pyke could hear the burbling of a light tenor on the wireless, the steady whistling of the kettle. It was cold, unusually cold for Howard's house. Even though he was dressed, the chill of the air struck him as he reached the foot of the stairs. There was something else, something that he couldn't put his finger on.

As he pushed open the kitchen door, another blast of cold air hit him. The wireless was still playing in the corner, a smooth-voiced newsreader talking about further falls of snow. The kettle sat on the gas-stove, a faint trail of steam leaking from its spout.

That was what had been wrong. Earlier, crossing the landing to the bathroom, he had heard the murmuring of the wireless and the steady low whistle of the kettle. The repeatedly boiling kettle was an intrinsic part of every morning as Howard made himself cup after cup of weak tea, and Pyke had barely registered the sound.

Now he realised it had not ceased in the time he had taken to return to the bedroom and dress. It was still boiling, the whistle diminishing as the water evaporated.

Pyke picked up an oven glove and lifted the kettle from the gas ring. It was even lighter than he had expected, virtually empty. He switched off the ring and replaced the kettle, turning to look at the kitchen door.

It was open. That had been the source of the cold air. His mouth dry, Pyke peered out into the icy morning.

His first sensation was one of *déjà vu*. The body looked the same, spread out face down on the blank snow-covered lawn, a smudge of red visible to the left of its torso.

There was no question it was Howard. The pale blond hair, the garish dressing gown.

Pyke's immediate sense of horror was already wrestling with his professional instincts. He felt eerily calm, emotions stifled by routine. The truth would hit later, but for the moment he had a job to do.

He had no doubt Howard was dead. He needed to check, of course, but it would be nothing more than a token gesture. More to the point, Howard could not have been dead for long. How long would it take for a kettle to boil itself dry?

Pyke crouched as close as he could without disturbing the snow around the body. There was a mess of footprints, and a line of prints heading past the side of the house to the road outside.

Pyke lifted Howard's splayed arm. Although there was still some warmth to the body, there was no pulse. He rose and hurried across the garden and round the cottage to the main road.

There was no sign of anyone. But there were car tyre tracks in the snow on the far side of the road. It looked as if the car had arrived from the direction of Framley, then completed a U-turn before heading back in the same direction.

Pyke stopped, wondering whether he should try to follow. Then he saw the decision had already been made for him. His motorcycle still sat in the shade of the cottage where he had left it the previous evening. But the tyres had been shredded.

Somehow, the sight of his own disabled bike hit him more powerfully even than the sight of Howard's body. It was as if the bike was symbolic of something that had been lost. Not just Howard – that was devastating, but he had lost Howard already, even before his death. Something more. His own peace of mind. His own freedom. His own future.

He realised tears were running down his cheeks, uncontrollable. 'Oh, God, Howard. What are we going to do?'

CHAPTER FORTY-TWO

She rolled over in the bed, pulling the sheets and blankets around her, her body rebelling against the prospect of climbing out into the icy bleakness of the morning. These days, she felt a constant yearning for more rest, a resistance to the endless challenges the day would throw at her. The interminable penny pinching, the eking out of what few resources they had. The need to scrape together cash wherever she could find it.

The thought caught her in the stomach, like a clutch of fear. She didn't want to live like this, hand to mouth, doing things she despised.

Suddenly, perversely, she wanted to be up and active. She threw back the heavy weight of bedclothes, feeling the bedroom's chill even through her thick nightdress. It was only then she recalled the night before.

The walk back through the snow with the inspector – she still couldn't quite bring herself to think of him as Ivan, for all her apparent self-assurance in his presence. All the things he'd told her – his wife, his child. The sense that he had opened up, that something might have been starting between them.

Then the eerie gloom of the churchyard. That poor wee child's body.

She shuffled into her slippers, glancing at the alarm clock. Nearly quarter to eight, already. Her mother would have been up for an hour or more, building a fire in the parlour, making her staple porridge, waking the children. There had been no school so far that week as the snow had tightened its grip. Although for Mary's children the school was only a short walk, its catchment area – for pupils and teachers alike – was widespread, and no buses or trains had been running. But each morning, her mother had dutifully woken the two children, dressed them, and walked them to the school gates, just in case it should be open. The children hadn't complained. They had taken for granted that the school would be closed and had welcomed the time to play in the snow. It would be a shock for them when the snow eventually disappeared.

She stepped out on to the landing. The door of the spare bedroom was standing ajar, and she saw, with a pang of what she recognised as regret, that the room was deserted, the bed neatly made. There was no sign Winterman had even slept there.

Her mind was telling her to take care. There had been a moment, as they were saying goodnight, when she might have responded positively if Winterman had made a move. She had wanted him to – to do something or at least to say something. But that was just vanity. She wanted to be reassured she could still be attractive to a man like Winterman.

Another part of her was relieved that nothing had happened. She still didn't know quite what to make of Winterman. He was attractive, there was no doubt about that – what some people might call a 'catch'. He was good company. Not exactly charming – in Mary's mind, that implied a self-conscious, even slightly superficial, desire to engage with others. Winterman wasn't like that. He had said relatively little the previous evening, yet somehow had seemed the central presence. That was the word, she supposed. Presence. He had dominated the company without even trying. When he was silent, they all unconsciously sought his approval, waiting for him to laugh at their jokes, nod at their comments – which he did with alacrity all evening. When he spoke, they had hung on his words.

Presence. Mary had never encountered it before, not in that form. She had met plenty of men – local gentry, army officers, petty officials – who believed they possessed it but offered little beyond rank and pomposity. Winterman's effortless dominance was something else.

Whether it was an admirable quality was another question. There had to be a selfishness there. The situation with his poor wife and child – it was a tragedy, but it was a tragedy partly of his own making. And, for all his sociability, there was a reserve to Winterman she hadn't begun to fathom.

She descended the stairs, chiding herself for a lack of charity. Winterman's position was awful, even worse than her own. Her husband's death had been a dreadful shock, not least for the pointless manner of his dying. After his call-up, she had tormented herself with imaginings about what might happen, but had assumed that, if the worst happened, it would at least be in the field of battle. An accidental shooting in a training exercise had seemed the cruellest joke of all.

But it was over and done with. She couldn't forget it, but she could try to put it behind her. Winterman didn't even have that luxury. He was trapped in the past, unable to move on.

It was a little warmer downstairs. Her mother had lit a fire in the parlour and the coal-fired boiler heated the kitchen. Even so, Mary could see her breath as she walked through the hallway, and she could feel the draft of cold air from beneath the ill-fitting front door.

In the kitchen the two children were sitting at the table, eating bowls of porridge. Her mother was in front of the sink washing some crockery, staring blankly out of the window.

Mary smiled at the children. 'Morning, Mam. Think I overslept.'

Mrs Griffiths turned. 'Don't worry, love. You must have been up quite late.'

There was an edge to her voice. Not exactly disapproval. Anxiety perhaps. Mary had already decided to say nothing about the discovery in the churchyard. 'Not really. Must have been about eleven when we got back here.'

'The inspector was awake early. I heard him leaving before I was up this morning.'

'I don't know.' Mary wondered whether her mother was harbouring doubts – or perhaps even hopes – about what might have happened between her daughter and Winterman the previous night. 'There's a lot going on, Mam, what with these children and Fisher's death. I imagine he's working out of the local station till the road gets cleared.'

'I don't envy the poor man, having all this on his plate. New into the job as well. '

'I'm sure he knows what he's doing, Mam.'

'I'm sure he does. He struck me as a very capable young man.'

There was a definite undertone. Her mother's usual unsubtle attempts at matchmaking would soon be unleashed. Mary couldn't blame her mother. She'd spent most of her own life wanting to escape from this bleak back of beyond, and she didn't want her daughter to suffer the same fate. Mary had thought she'd made the break once, only to find herself back here.

She turned to the two children. 'You two off to school soon?'

'I think school's going to be closed again,' Graham said.

'You're probably right,' Mrs Griffiths said. 'But we need to check. The headmaster said they'd reopen as soon as they could get enough staff in.'

Mary glanced out of the window at the snow, the sky threatening yet more. 'I can't see that being today. But yes, you need to check. Can't have these two missing more school than they can help.'

Graham looked as if he was about to dispute this view, but Mrs Griffiths was already bundling the children from the table. 'Come on. Coats and gloves on. Let's go.' She turned back to Mary. 'What about your work? You're due in today.' There was no reproach in her voice, just anxiety about the prospect of a lost day's pay.

'I can't see how I can get into town. But I'll go down to Bryan's. If they're working out of there, I'll see what I can do to help.'

'That's good. That's the most they can expect, isn't it?'

'I think it's more than they expect. They've got their minds on other things, to be honest, Mam.'

'I suppose you're right.' Mrs Griffiths moved out into the hallway, supervising the children as they donned their heavy duffle coats. 'Come on, you two. We haven't got all day.'

Mary watched as her mother skilfully shepherded the youngsters out of the house, and then stood by the front door, briefly braving the biting wind, as the three figures made their way down the icy road.

But that's just it, she thought, gazing after them. *You do have all day. You have your whole lives, stretching out ahead of you. And you don't yet know quite how terrifying a prospect that turns out to be.*

CHAPTER FORTY-THREE

'Believes in security then, young Brain?' Winterman was fumbling with Brain's large key ring, trying to remember which key fitted the upper of the two deadlocks in the police station door. Brain himself had been left in the churchyard with the unenviable task of keeping watch over what had become a full crime scene. From somewhere inside, Winterman could hear the shrill ringing of the station telephone.

'Better safe than sorry,' Hoxton said.

Winterman cursed under his breath as yet another key jammed in the lock. 'Do you think every key on here has a use, or does he just collect them for fun?'

Hoxton peered past Winterman's elbow and pointed. 'Try that one.'

Winterman gazed at the older man for a second, as though doubting his sanity. Then he placed the key in the upper lock. It turned smoothly. 'Did your mother never tell you that nobody likes a smart aleck? Now which?'

Hoxton glanced briefly at the dangling bunch of keys, then touched one with his finger tip. 'That one.'

Winterman inserted the key into the lower deadlock. Again, it turned smoothly. He twisted the handle and pushed open the door. Inside, the telephone gave a final jangling ring and fell silent. 'Inevitable.'

Hoxton shrugged. 'The operator will have transferred it across to HQ. That's the usual arrangement. They'll take a message for Brain or try to deal with it if it's an emergency.'

'I'm not sure that's very reassuring. The way things are going round here, there could be all kinds of chaos breaking loose. I'd rather know about it directly than get told by HQ.'

As Winterman stepped into Brain's office, the phone rang again. He quickened his pace and snatched up the receiver. 'Police.'

'Where the bloody hell have you been? I thought that was supposed to be a police station?'

Winterman looked quizzically at the receiver. 'Pyke?'

There was a pause at the other end of the line. 'Is that Winterman?'

'Spot on. And "where the bloody hell are you?" is a very pertinent question. We've been looking for you all morning.'

'You've found me,' Pyke said. There was another momentary pause. 'Why were you looking for me?'

There was something about Pyke's tone. Winterman didn't know the man well. Their paths had crossed professionally on numerous occasions over the years, and they had developed a mutual respect for each other's abilities. Their usual mode of interaction was a joshing, very male banter, underpinned by a typical English unease with anything that might be interpreted as emotion. But Pyke did not sound in the mood for banter. He sounded like someone who was having great difficulty keeping his emotions in check.

'Is everything all right?'

Winterman heard an intake of breath, and for a second he thought Pyke might terminate the call. Then Pyke said, 'No, it isn't. It isn't at all, actually. Actually, it's pretty damned bad–' His voice cracked suddenly. He had obviously lowered or dropped the receiver, because Winterman could hear his voice as if from a distance. 'Oh, Christ.'

'What is it, man? Where are you?'

There was a clatter. Finally, Pyke spoke again, clearer this time. 'Sorry, Winterman. I'm in a bit of a state. It's a friend of mine.' He stopped again, struggling to retain control of his voice. 'Look, Winterman, he's dead. He's been murdered.'

Winterman looked up at Hoxton, who had been watching the exchange with undisguised curiosity. 'Murdered?'

'Yes, murdered. I can be pretty sure of that. It is my field, you know.' There was a touch of the familiar Pyke in the words, but the effort was half-hearted. 'He's been stabbed.'

'I'm sorry,' Winterman said sincerely, wondering what sort of friend this was. 'Where are you?'

Pyke gave brief directions to Howard's cottage. 'I don't know how easy it'll be to get here. The roads still look pretty treacherous, but the cottage is only just off the main road.'

'We'll be there as quickly as we can,' Winterman said. 'You'll be okay till we arrive?'

'I'll be as okay as I am now,' Pyke said. 'But no, I'll be fine. It's a shock, that's all.'

'Hold tight till we get there.'

'I'm not going to disturb the bloody evidence, if that's what you mean,' Pyke said, again showing a trace of his usual personality. 'I'm not a bloody amateur.' The line went dead, although Winterman assumed, with some relief, that Pyke had put the phone down in irritation rather than despair.

'Murder?' Hoxton said. 'You mean, *another* murder?'

Winterman replaced the silent receiver, only now beginning to take in what Pyke had been saying. 'Apparently.'

Hoxton was staring at him. 'What the bloody hell is happening to this place? It's a bloody little village. Now it's going to hell in a handcart.'

CHAPTER FORTY-FOUR

Winterman spent the next fifteen minutes on the phone to HQ, finally succeeding in dragging DS Spooner out of some supposedly critical meeting.

'This better be bloody good, Winterman,' Spooner boomed down the phone. 'You've just dragged me out of a meeting with the chief.' He spoke the last word with undisguised relish.

'I'm sorry about that.' Winterman's tone was studiedly neutral. 'But I think you'll find it's justified. We've another murder on our hands.'

Winterman could almost hear the turning cogs of Spooner's brain. 'Another kiddie?'

'Apparently not. We've just had the call. It's outside the village. But it sounds like the real thing.'

'Christ, what's going on in that place? You're a bad bloody influence, Winterman.'

'I'm doing my best, sir,' Winterman said ambiguously.

He had been wondering whether to advise Spooner about Marsh's unexplained absence, but as soon as he heard Spooner's voice he decided to keep that piece of information to himself. It was a risk. If something really had happened to Marsh, any delay might be fatal. But Winterman couldn't imagine that Spooner would give their case more credence if he heard some half-baked story about a junior officer going missing.

'So you're back again asking for reinforcements, no doubt.'

'We're really up against it here. There are only three of us – four with the local chap. We've got at least two crime scenes which we need to keep secure till we can get forensics done. That's before we actually start any investigations–'

'Yes, yes. You're sure this latest murder's kosher? I mean, it really is murder?'

'We're on our way there now. But we've good reasons for assuming that it's genuine.' Winterman was hoping Spooner wouldn't enquire too deeply into these reasons. He didn't want to bring Pyke's name into this until he had an idea what was going on.

'Think it's linked to – whathisname's – the vicar's murder then?' Finesse had never been one of Spooner's strong points.

'Fisher, sir. We don't know as yet.'

'Seems a bloody coincidence if not. Godforsaken spot like that. These must be the first killings in living memory.'

'The first unlawful killings,' Winterman amended gently. 'I imagine you're right. Which, as you say, would make it an extraordinary coincidence. Then we have the children's bodies too–'

'Good of you to remind me, Winterman. I was overlooking the dead kiddies. Quite a party you've got on your hands.'

'That's why we need backup, sir.'

'Okay, Winterman. I understand what you're saying.' Spooner was clearly calculating the risk to his own reputation if, as seemed increasingly likely, whatever was happening in Framley should turn into a major incident. 'I'll give this priority. We'll get a team out there as quickly as we can. It might take us some time to deploy people in these conditions though.'

'I understand that, sir. But the sooner you can get some resources here, the better.'

'Don't worry, lad. I understand the urgency.' Spooner's voice had taken on an avuncular tone which was already making Winterman feel uneasy. 'I'll take personal charge of this one now.'

'That's excellent, sir.' Winterman was struggling to keep any note of irony out of his voice. 'I knew we could count on you.'

'Oh, aye, lad,' Spooner responded jovially. 'You can always count on me.'

CHAPTER FORTY-FIVE

The house felt eerily silent once Mary's mother and the children had departed. Mary had washed and dressed, pulling on a second shapeless sweater against the cold of the day. She had hoped to make herself some toast, but they were already out of bread. Most of the available ration went to the children. Instead she refreshed the tea in the pot with boiling water, and drank a cup standing by the kitchen window, gazing out at the garden. Her mother had been standing in the same position earlier. Probably she had been thinking about that poor child's body, found in the dyke outside the back gate.

What was happening? In the middle of this frozen winter, the country on its knees, it was as if the earth was literally giving up its dead. Mary shivered suddenly, feeling exposed. It was as if all her own secrets – all the thoughts and memories she had buried over the years – were being dragged to the surface, exposed to the unforgiving light.

She glanced at the old clock that her mother kept, dutifully wound, on the kitchen dresser. It was already nearly nine. She should be moving, get herself down to the police station.

She pulled on her coat, carefully checking that all the lights in the house were turned off. She had heard talk on the wireless of severe power shortages, the impact of the war and the economy made worse by the current difficulties in transporting coal around the country. There were already power cuts in the day to conserve energy. The message was the familiar one. Eke out what you had. Make the best of things.

Outside, it was even colder than she had imagined. The temperature had dropped again after the previous night's snow.

She and her mother had made an attempt to clear the snow from the front path, but the ground remained treacherous. Mary made her way cautiously to the gate and out into the road.

It was probably only half a mile from the house to the centre of the village, but it felt much further on the icy ground, her feet constantly threatening to slip from under her. She was aware she hardly cut an elegant figure, bundled in layers of thick sweaters, a pair of worsted slacks and a heavy khaki trenchcoat she had inherited from her late husband. All that and a pair of scuffed walking boots, another legacy of her early marriage, when they had taken regular Sunday walks into the wilderness of the Fens.

That seemed a lifetime away, as did the elegant dresses and suits she had worn during their courting days. She still had a couple of reasonably smart suits she wore to work, but increasingly she found herself dressing for warmth and practicality. That was all there was. Keeping going.

She was growing accustomed to the quiet of the snow-bound world. There were no signs of life, no birds singing. Even her own footsteps were deadened by the cushioning of the snow. As she reached the turn in the lane she could see the churchyard gate.

'Mary?'

The unexpected voice almost made her heart stop, and her first thought was simply to run. Instead, she forced herself to stop.

'Mary. It's only me.'

'Bryan.' He had been concealed from her, hunched behind one of the stone gateposts, smoking a cigarette, seeking shelter from the bitter wind. 'You must be frozen.'

'A bit.' He pulled his heavy-duty police overcoat around him. 'I thought I'd be warm enough in this, but I can't stand still for long.'

'Are you…?' She gestured towards the far end of the churchyard, the gravestone that was, thankfully, lost in the shadows of the overhanging yew trees.

'Sentry duty. I'm supposed to keep people away.'

'It's still there then.' She didn't even know whether the body was male or female.

'For the moment. The inspector's trying to get some help from HQ.'

'That won't be easy. Everyone's stretched at the moment.'

'Yes,' Brain said. 'Though with finding the blood–' He stopped, clearly realising that he had said too much.

'What blood?'

He stood helplessly for a second, glancing over his shoulder as though hoping that some assistance would appear. 'I shouldn't really have said anything, Mary. I–'

She looked past him to where the shadows crowded the tombstone. 'Bryan, I found the body last night. You've got to tell me. This is all unreal enough without being driven mad worrying about what I don't know.'

Brain looked as if he might be about to burst into tears. 'You won't tell the inspector, will you? He told me not to say anything to anyone.'

'I don't imagine he meant me, Bryan. After all, I work for the police, don't I? I'm not just a member of the public.'

A look of relief crossed his face. 'You're right. I wasn't thinking about that. You're not just a member of the public.' He paused. 'But you won't tell the inspector?'

'No, Bryan, not if you don't want me to. So what's this about blood?'

Brain turned and pointed. 'Just the other side of the grave where you found the… well, you know. When I first got here this morning, I spotted something. There was a dark patch on the ground, under the snow. So I went to fetch the inspector.'

'You mean it was blood? But the body – I mean, the child–'

Brain looked momentarily nonplussed at having his explanation usurped. 'Yes, that's right. We haven't had the body checked by forensics yet, but it's obvious it's been dead for years. The blood was fresh.'

'So whose blood was it?'

'We don't know. But the inspector thought that something heavy had fallen on the ground there and had been dragged away.' Brain paused, clearly savouring the drama of the moment. 'A body.'

She stared at him. 'A body? Are you sure? I mean, is he sure?'

'I don't think he can be sure, yet. Not till we've had the forensics. But the inspector knows what he's talking about.'

'I'm sure he does,' Mary agreed. 'But whose body? It doesn't make sense.'

'None of it makes sense. But there's one other thing. I don't know if it means anything.'

'What?'

'Paul,' Brain said. 'I mean, DC Marsh.'

She turned back towards him, a tingle of unease running down her spine. 'What about Paul?'

'He's gone missing. I'm sure it's nothing. George thought he might have, you know, a lady friend…' Brain stumbled to a halt.

'What do you mean, he's gone missing?' As she spoke, Mary realised something was clicking into place in her mind, some unacknowledged thoughts sliding together like well-oiled cogs. 'How can he be missing? He went back with you last night.'

'Yes, I know. He was fine. We'd all had a bit too much to drink. When we got back we had a nightcap – I'd still got some Scotch that someone gave me. I let him have my room and gave George the spare. I slept in the cell. I knew I'd be up early anyway. We just thought he'd overslept this morning. Then when George went to get him he wasn't there. The bed was disturbed so it looked as if it had been slept in. George thought it had been thrown about to make it look as if it had been used, but really–'

'You're saying he hadn't slept in it at all?'

'I don't know. But that's what George seems to think.'

'You mean he left the house last night? After you'd all gone to bed?'

Brain once again looked as if he might burst into tears. 'I don't know. It's just what George said. But they don't know where he is.'

Without responding, Mary pushed past Brain and strode into the churchyard, walking down the path towards the tombstone. The white drifts of snow now fully concealed the grotesque shape laid out on its surface. Behind her, she heard Brain calling her name, shouting that she shouldn't disturb the evidence.

She ignored him and moved to the rear of the stone, her eyes scouring the ground till she spotted the darker patch Brain had described. When she found it, she dropped to her knees, touching the earth with her fingers as Winterman had done.

She raised her hand and stared at the sticky residue on her fingertips. Despite the cold, it was beginning to discolour, but there was no mistaking what it was.

She looked up at Brain, her face twisted with anxiety. 'Idiot!' she called. 'Bloody, *bloody* idiot!'

It took Brain a moment to realise her words were not directed at him.

CHAPTER FORTY-SIX

'Whose idea was this?' Hoxton dragged himself upright, his trouser knees and turn-ups soaking from the snow, and watched as Winterman carefully fastened the chains in place. Winterman's clothes seemed as pristine as ever, though his hands were oily. Hoxton crouched down again and turned the handle on the jack, lowering the tyre back to the road.

'Yours, I think,' Winterman said. 'Bloody good one too, if you ask me.'

'That's just what I was thinking. Suddenly seems a much better idea now we've finished it.'

Hoxton had spotted the snow-chains lying, slightly rusted, in the rear porch as they were locking up to leave. 'Why the hell would he have snow-chains? He doesn't even have a car.'

'Police issue,' Winterman had responded with confidence. 'One of those little gifts from HQ to make the policeman's lot a little happier.'

'But he doesn't even have a car,' Hoxton had persisted.

'Since when did that count for anything with HQ? If he'd had a car, they'd have sent him a bicycle pump. But we do have a car, so we might as well appropriate them. They might give us half a chance of getting out to this place of Pyke's.'

Twenty minutes later, they were on the road. Following Pyke's instructions, they headed west from the village, the tall spire of the church disappearing behind them.

'Can't be much further,' Winterman said. 'Keep your speed down. I don't have your faith in those rusty chains.'

'So who is this? The deceased. Some mate of Pyke's?'

'Your sensitivity does you proud. I don't know. Pyke didn't say much. Must have been a shock.'

'Especially if he was the one doing the murdering.'

Winterman turned to look at Hoxton. The older man was hunched over the steering wheel, his attention apparently fixed firmly on the road. 'Let's keep an open mind, shall we? At least till we've seen what's what.'

'Never opener.'

'Reckon this must be the turning.' Winterman gestured towards a narrower lane leading off to the right. 'There.'

The cottage was only a few hundred yards from the main road, tucked under the shade of a large oak tree. It was an elegant looking place. The building itself looked old – possibly a couple of centuries at least – but it had been renovated in the recent past. Pyke's motorbike, still with its shredded tyres, was parked by the front door.

Hoxton pulled to a halt outside the front door. It opened immediately, and Pyke stood framed inside. His pale shirt looked far too thin for the icy weather, but he seemed untroubled by the cold.

'Thank Christ you're here. I've been going crazy in there.'

Winterman glanced momentarily at Hoxton. 'Don't worry, man. We're here now. Let's see what's happened.'

He followed Pyke into the cottage, noticing that, despite the open front door, the temperature inside was warmer than anywhere else he had been recently. The elegance of the interior matched the external appearance of the cottage. Someone had spent money on the place. The paintings and ornaments that lined the walls and shelves were, to Winterman's untutored eye, equally costly.

He followed Pyke into the kitchen. More expensively understated décor, though the temperature was a few degrees lower.

The reason for that became evident immediately. The rear door into the garden was ajar. As Pyke pulled it open, the chill air swept into the room. Pyke gestured outside, but his own eyes were fixed elsewhere.

There was no mistaking the parallel with Fisher's corpse. This body too lay prone in the middle of what, beneath the snow, was presumably the cottage's rear lawn. The murder weapon appeared to be a knife or dagger, the blade of which was protruding an inch or two from the victim's back. A pool of blood had seeped out into the snow from under the torso.

'I'm sorry,' Winterman said. 'He was a friend?'

Pyke hesitated, as though questioning the terminology. 'Yes. A friend.'

'Who is he?'

'Was,' Pyke corrected gently. 'Howard Merriman. That was his real name.'

'Real name?'

'His stage name was Howard Martin. He was an actor.'

The name rang a vague bell, though Winterman couldn't immediately place it. Possibly he had heard it on the wireless or in some stage production.

'This was his house?' Winterman made no effort to soften the tense this time.

'Lived here since before the war. It was a wreck when he bought it. Spent a fortune on the place.' Pyke sounded like someone making small talk at a party.

Winterman eased the back door further open, conscious of the need not to disturb any fingerprints, and peered into the garden. There were footprints in the snow around the body, but it was unclear whether these belonged to one individual or more. There was at least one line of scuffed footprints heading towards the side of the house.

He contemplated taking a closer look, but decided to wait until Spooner's reinforcements arrived so they could ensure the crime scene was properly examined.

Winterman turned back to Pyke. 'Spooner's promised to send us some backup, urgently, so we can get things sorted properly. I also asked Spooner to organise us a pathologist.'

'Well, you couldn't let me anywhere near him, could you?'

Winterman held the other man's gaze. 'Obviously not, Pyke. Even if you wanted to be involved. Which I don't seriously imagine you do.'

'Part of me does. Part of me wants to do my bit to nail the bastard who did this. But I can see that's exactly why I shouldn't be involved.'

'Not just that,' Winterman said gently.

'No, not just that. But also because I'm a bloody suspect. That right, Winterman?'

'I don't think anything. Not yet. But you know I can't discount the possibility.'

'Don't soft-soap me, Winterman. I'm top of the bloody list. If only because I'm here, while the bastard who really did it is out there somewhere in the snow. Bastard shredded my bloody tyres, or I might have caught him for you. But you'll say I did that as well, I suppose.'

'It's not about what I think. We have to treat you as a prime suspect until there's good evidence to the contrary.'

'Christ, it's a bloody mess. There's no way out of this. Not the killing. Whatever you might think, I didn't do that. But the whole bloody thing.' Pyke turned and strode out of the kitchen.

Winterman gestured to Hoxton to follow. 'Keep an eye on him.'

Hoxton followed Pyke out of the room. Winterman stood gazing round the kitchen. The quality and style of the fittings matched the rest of the house, elegant and minimal, soothing pastel colours. Just the place to eat your boiled egg. Merriman had been a man of taste and discernment. And, it appeared, money.

Did actors earn enough to live in this style? Some did, obviously. But Winterman assumed it was largely confined to those who had made it big in Hollywood. As far as he knew, Merriman had been no Leslie Howard or David Niven.

Could you make this kind of living in British film or even on the British stage? Winterman had no idea. This was a nice house – many steps up from everyday life in Austerity Britain – but it was hardly a palace in Beverly Hills or a villa in Monte Carlo.

Winterman made his way out of the kitchen. From down the hallway, he could hear Hoxton speaking and some sort of responding grunt from Pyke. Winterman climbed the stairs. He wanted to get a decent look around before Spooner and his team arrived.

There wasn't much to see. Two bedrooms, one with a king-sized luxurious bed and a view over the empty fenland. The other, smaller with a double bed – presumably a guest room. Winterman noted that only the king-sized bed appeared to have been slept in.

He moved quickly around the guest room, opening the doors of the wardrobe and the bedside cupboards, pulling out the drawers of the dressing table. Most were empty, or contained odd items of no evident significance. There was an old cufflink box, a tightly rolled scarf – presumably discarded as no longer fashionable – a disappointingly empty notebook. The wardrobe contained a couple of suits – good quality, Winterman thought. He quickly searched through the pockets, unsure what he might be looking for, but again finding nothing.

He moved into the main bedroom. Here, the cupboard and drawers were fuller, though again none of the contents appeared significant. The only conclusion Winterman could initially draw was that Merriman owned an awful lot of clothes – most of them stylish, if more ostentatious than anything Winterman might have considered wearable, and all of them well made.

Having worked systematically through two cupboards and the dressing table, Winterman pulled open the doors of the wardrobe. Almost immediately, he pulled back the doors to their fullest extent.

In the centre of the wardrobe was a pair of boots – brown, heavy, well polished. Walking boots designed, unlike the other clothing Winterman had so far examined, for practicality rather than style. The boots were damp and covered in fresh mud. They had been worn recently, probably overnight or that morning.

Winterman rummaged through the remaining clothing, feeling into the suit pockets, but there was nothing else of interest.

He moved his attention to the shelves that lined the left-hand side of the wardrobe interior, most of which were stacked with neatly folded sweaters and shirts. He flicked through each one, and then reached into the back of the shelf and felt carefully around.

On the second shelf, his hand closed on a roughly wrapped paper package. He drew it out carefully and peeled back the top layer of brown paper. Inside was a substance which Winterman recognised as marijuana. Perhaps not surprising. Artistic types. He shrugged and slipped the package back into the shelf, replacing it as closely as he could to its original position. Let Spooner's men find that, if they could. Winterman had no desire to get Pyke into any more difficulties than he needed to.

But the boots were a different, more intriguing matter. He had little doubt they were Merriman's rather than Pyke's, although he could more easily imagine Pyke wearing boots of that kind. But the boots were small – too small for Pyke's hulking feet.

If Merriman had worn the boots the previous evening, perhaps before locking up for the night, the mud would have dried out, given the warmth of the cottage. Which suggested that Merriman had been outside either that morning or sometime during the night.

Winterman made his way into the bathroom. Just inside the door, there was a basket, presumably intended for soiled laundry. Winterman lifted the lid and peered inside. The basket was empty except for a shirt and a pair of trousers. He lifted out the trousers, holding them very carefully between his forefinger and thumb, and examined them. As he had expected, the bottoms of the trouser legs were damp and lined with mud.

He dropped the trousers back in the basket and, after a cursory examination of the cupboards below and above the washbasin, he walked slowly down the stairs. He could hear the voices of Hoxton and Pyke from the sitting room. Winterman glanced at his watch. One thing was certain. Once Spooner arrived, the show would be his. From everything that Winterman had seen, Spooner was not a man to be unduly troubled by the niceties of procedure, let alone considerations of guilt or innocence. What Spooner wanted was the case neatly tied up – a result obtained with minimum effort. If Pyke was innocent – and Winterman had to acknowledge that this was still a substantial if – Spooner's arrival would not be good news.

There was no way of knowing how long it would take for Spooner to marshal the necessary resources. Once he had done so, it would take him another forty-five minutes or so to get there, perhaps a little longer, given the snow. Worst case, Winterman had around an hour or so.

He stepped hurriedly down the hallway and pushed open the door of the living room. Pyke looked up in surprise, though Hoxton seemed as unfazed as ever.

'Okay, Pyke,' Winterman said. 'We need to talk.'

CHAPTER FORTY-SEVEN

'Mary?' Brain stood frozen, as though he thought Mary might have lost her senses.

She was crouching, her slacks wet from the snow, her fingertips stained red. She looked up at him, and for a moment it really did look as if reason might have deserted her. Then her gaze cleared and she pushed herself to her feet.

'I need to find Ivan.'

Brain looked at her blankly for a moment. 'The inspector?'

'Yes,' she said impatiently. 'The inspector. Is he at the station?' She was already walking past him, trudging through the snow towards the main road.

'I think so. Look, Mary, what is it? Is there anything I can do?'

'I'm probably just being stupid, Bryan. Making a mountain out of a molehill. It's just an idea I've had. But I want to discuss it with the inspector.'

Brain scuttled along beside her. 'If there's anything I can do–'

'I know. And it's sweet of you. I know you'd do anything you could to help. But it's a bit complicated. I think it's best if I discuss it with DI Winterman first.' She smiled. 'Anyway, you don't want to see me making an idiot of myself.'

Brain nodded, clearly doing his best to appear professional. 'I understand. You do what you think's best. Do you want me to walk you back to the station?'

'Of course I'll be okay, Bryan.' She had been about to add that this was Framley, for goodness' sake, what could possibly happen to her? Then she recalled everything that had happened lately. Suddenly she wanted more than anything for Brain to accompany her. 'It's only a five minute walk,' she added, steeling herself.

In the event, it was closer to fifteen, as she trudged ponderously through the dense snow, and it felt more like an eternity. The quiet unnerved her. She glanced repeatedly back over her shoulder, fancying she saw some movement in the shadows of the churchyard wall, the hedgerows, the blank windows of the apparently deserted cottages. The village seemed empty, as if its inhabitants had fled with the falling snow or locked themselves away for the duration.

Just once, as she approached the silent pub, she heard a noise, something betokening life. From somewhere on the other side of the village, beyond the tight-knit cluster of houses, she heard the sudden muffled roar of a car engine. She half-expected the car to appear around the corner, but instead the sound, already deadened by the snow, faded and the silence returned. She was left feeling even more alone.

The police station stood on the next corner, its blue sign hanging out over the road. It was a relatively new building – probably just pre-war – and its squat functionality seemed out of place among the old cottages that comprised the heart of the village.

She pressed the bell and heard an answering ring from somewhere in the depths of building, but there was no response. She pressed again and peered in through one of the windows. The interior was unlit, and there was no sign of anyone inside.

She straightened and looked around. Deep tyre marks led from the kerbside outside the station building. Was that what she had heard? The sound of Winterman and Hoxton driving away?

Perhaps that was why she had been left feeling so alone.

CHAPTER FORTY-EIGHT

'I don't even know your name,' Winterman said.

'Everyone calls me Pyke.' Pyke was sitting at the far end of an unexpectedly garish red chaise longue. Hoxton was in an armchair, looking as if he were trying physically to dissociate himself from the room's furnishings. Winterman could see why. The rest of the house had been relatively tasteful, dim lights and pastel shades. But Merriman had allowed his imagination to run riot in this room, which was adorned with crimson drapes, a crystal chandelier and a set of abstract paintings which were probably best ignored. It was presumably some sort of private den, perhaps the place where Merriman retreated when alone or – Winterman found himself mentally adding – in intimate company. The room would have made a more appropriate murder scene than the frozen garden.

Winterman lowered himself cautiously down on to the opposite end of the chaise longue. 'How long have we worked together, Pyke?'

'I wouldn't say we did work together, strictly speaking. I'm not a policeman.'

'Fair enough,' Winterman went on patiently. 'So how long have we – what would you say? – worked alongside one another?'

'I don't know. Ten years, off and on, I suppose. More off than on during the war.'

'And I don't even know your Christian name.'

'Everyone calls me Pyke.'

'Even your family?'

'Not much family left. Are we going anywhere with this?'

'Just building rapport. It's what they recommend before you start interviewing someone.'

'I thought they recommended leather gloves and a bright light. So this is an interview then?'

Winterman eased himself back against the chaise longue. 'Let me put it this way. About half an hour or so ago, I spoke to Superintendent Spooner to seek some additional resources. You know Spooner?'

'I've come across him. I can't say we – what was your phrase? – built any rapport.'

'I imagine not. Anyway, Spooner agreed to provide the resources, but only on the basis that he would oversee the case personally. He's on his way as we speak. Or, at least, as soon as he can be bothered to brave the snow.'

'All the time in the world then, I imagine.'

'You could be right. On the other hand, it could be that Spooner's remarkable instinct for self-preservation has already kicked in. I think he'll see this as a case with potential to career out of his control.'

'With the emphasis on career.' Pyke finally gave a faint smile. 'You think he'll want to take over.'

'Not formally, I imagine. That would be too close to taking accountability. But I imagine he'll want to supervise. If it goes well, he can take the credit. If it goes badly, I'm still here to carry the can.'

'The policeman's lot,' Pyke said. 'So what does this have to do with me?'

'Everything. Spooner hasn't risen through the ranks by not getting results. But he may not be choosy how he gets them.'

'Meaning.'

'Meaning he's not that bothered by concepts such as truth or justice. What he wants is an easy result he can stand up in court.'

'Which would put me firmly in the frame. Frame being the operative word,' Pyke added, with a touch of bitterness.

'So you say.' Winterman rose and pushed the living room door closed. There was no one else in the house, but he still felt a need for caution. He sat back down on the chaise longue, closer to Pyke. 'Look, I don't know what's going on. For all I know, you might have had every reason to kill Merriman–' Pyke opened his mouth to interject, but Winterman raised his hand. 'The difference between me and Spooner is that I'm not just interested in getting a result. I'm interested in the truth. It strikes me that, whoever was responsible for Merriman's death, you're in a bloody awkward spot.'

'You might say that.'

'Perhaps you'll be able to persuade Spooner to listen to what you have to say – though I wouldn't put any money on it. But even by speaking openly, you're likely to incriminate yourself – in other ways.'

'Very delicately expressed.'

'So my proposition is this,' Winterman said. 'That you tell me everything. The truth, the whole truth and nothing but the bloody truth, so help you God. I'll treat it all as off the record. When Spooner gets here, I'll tell him I've held off interviewing you until he arrived.'

'And what about your little friend there?' Pyke gestured towards Hoxton, who had been watching the exchange in silence.

'DC Hoxton has a choice. He can stay here and be part of this breach in protocol. Or he can go and sit in the other room and leave us to it. He could, if he wanted, report my actions to DS Spooner on his arrival. That would be the sensible thing to do, especially if you persist in patronising him.'

'I've been patronised by experts,' Hoxton said. 'Don't think this one's going to worry me. And I wouldn't miss this for the world.'

'There's your answer,' Winterman said to Pyke. 'So what's yours?'

'How do I know I can trust you?'

'You can't, unless you judge me on what you've seen over the last ten years. Frankly, it doesn't seem to me you've got many options.'

Pyke gazed at him in silence for a moment. 'Don't take up a career in sales. But okay. As you say, what have I got to lose? Where do you want me to start?'

'You and Merriman,' Winterman said. 'I think we've made our assumptions, but let's make sure we've got it straight.'

'"Straight" not being exactly the *mot juste*,' Pyke said. 'As I imagine you'd worked out, your being a detective.'

'How did you meet?'

'Home Guard, would you believe?'

'You weren't called up?'

'I was classed as a scientist. Reserved occupation, like you coppers. I'd like to say I felt guilty about it, but I just felt relieved. I've no problem in dealing with death, but I'd prefer it wasn't my own.'

'So what role did a forensic pathologist play in the war?' Winterman had no difficulty keeping a note of irony out of his voice, given his own ambivalent position.

'You'd be surprised. There were a couple of fairly hush-hush projects I was involved in. If you're an expert on the cause and effects of death, they assume you know how to help prevent people being killed. Or make it easier to kill them.'

'And you joined the Home Guard?'

'Felt I should do something. Not many air raids round here, except sometimes when they dumped a load on the way home. But we're close enough to the German coast for invasion to seem a possibility.'

'Merriman avoided the call up as well?' As far as Winterman was aware, acting had never been a reserved occupation.

'Medical grounds, supposedly. He never let on exactly what. I imagine they worked out that he was queer. It didn't take a lot of working out in Howard's case.'

Winterman was struggling to imagine Pyke and Merriman clad in the dull green serge of the Home Guard. 'Why did Merriman join the Home Guard?'

'Why did Howard do anything? Probably to meet men.'

'In the Home Guard?' This was Hoxton from the far side of the room. 'Optimistic sort then?'

'He met me,' Pyke pointed out. 'I think we both knew as soon as we saw each other. You get an instinct if you're... this way inclined. Part of the survival process.'

'And you formed a relationship?'

'We formed a relationship,' Pyke said. 'Would you like details?'

Winterman shook his head. 'I'm sorry. I know this must be painful. I just want to be clear.'

'We more or less lived together for about four years, towards the end of the war. People seemed to turn a blind eye at the time, even out here in the sticks. Gather ye rosebuds while ye may, and all that. I kept my house in town – for appearance sake, mainly – but spent most of my time out here.'

'But you're not still living here?'

'No, we split up. Over a year ago now.'

'Can I ask why?'

'Christ, why does any relationship end? We're not that different from you lot, you know. We'd just had enough, I suppose. No, that's not right. I'd had enough. Howard was more than happy to continue. In fact, I don't think he ever really acknowledged we'd split.'

There was something Pyke wasn't quite saying.

'But you'd had enough?'

'Of it all. Of having to pretend. Of leading a double life. Of the risks involved. Particularly in my line of business. Working with you lot. A lot of people don't care anymore, but plenty do. So I thought it was time I tried to go straight. Well, not straight exactly, but not bent either.'

'So the split wasn't about Merriman specifically?'

There was a moment's hesitation. 'It was, in part. Howard wasn't the easiest person to get on with. Don't get me wrong. He could be charm personified when he wanted. He could make you feel you were the only person who mattered in the world. But he was a selfish bugger. Or rather a self-centred bugger. Half the time, it didn't occur to him anyone else existed. The other half, he thought they were all there to cater to his needs.'

'Including you?'

'Especially me. I didn't mind most of the time. But he could be wearing. And over the last couple of years, he became more difficult.'

'Go on.'

'It was his career. He'd been fairly successful before the war. I mean, nothing spectacular. But he'd built up a solid stage career, begun to get himself noticed. Had one or two lead roles. Even a couple of minor roles in films.'

'I thought I recognised the name,' Winterman said.

'You might, if you're one of those people who reads the whole cast list for a film or goes to the theatre regularly. Or did pre-war anyway. If I'm cynical, I think one reason Howard was glad not to be called up was that he thought it might reduce the competition. There weren't so many plays being staged or films being made, but all that business continued throughout the war. With some of the more successful figures in the forces, Howard expected to move a few rungs up the ladder. But it didn't work like that.'

'It rarely does,' Winterman observed.

'I suppose not. But Howard resented it. He was getting older. He wasn't going to get the leading man parts he wanted. Another few years and there'd have just been character parts open to him…' Pyke paused.

For the first time, Winterman could see the stirrings of emotion in the other man's expression, as if the reality of Merriman's death had only now struck him.

'That made him harder to live with?'

'He was angry. Drank too much. He wouldn't say so, but he was finding it harder and harder to get decent work of any kind. Ironically, a lot of those who were called up made a name for themselves, came back bigger than ever. Howard had always lived beyond his means. Had a rather grandiose idea of the life he ought to be leading.'

'Like this house?' Winterman gestured vaguely around at the ornate decor.

'You'd spotted that? Yes, like this house. He bought this place for a song, but he spent a fortune on it. Not just the rebuilding. Everything in the place. He had to have the very best.'

'Where did he get it? Some of this stuff doesn't look as if it would have been easy to come by even before the war.'

'That was Howard. He knew people who knew people. If it was out there, he'd find a way to get it.'

'Illegally in some cases, I'd guess, looking at some of this stuff.'

'It's not for me to say. I honestly don't know. I never wanted to know. But I imagine you're right. Howard mixed with some people… well, let's just say that that was another reason to end it.'

'What sort of people?'

'Bad company. Rough trade. That gives the wrong impression though. Suggests Howard had a troop of gangsters in and out of this place. It wasn't like that.'

'No?'

'No. This was all a legacy of Howard's time in London before the war. He knew a few unsavoury characters. Real gangsters, some of them. It's amazing how many of them were queer, you know. Though most wouldn't have admitted it for anything.'

'Merriman brought some of that back here with him, did he?'

'He knew who to contact if he wanted something. That something might have been anything from a piece of furniture to illicit drugs.'

Winterman nodded impassively. 'Would he have made any enemies among these people?'

Pyke laughed unexpectedly. 'It's very likely. Howard generally wanted to be loved, but he was quite happy to be hated. Just so long as he wasn't ignored. He was definitely living beyond his means. Even before we split, the work seemed to have dried up. He wasn't helping himself, with the drink and his general attitude. I know he missed some auditions. He was rude to producers. Dismissive when he felt something was beneath his talents. He picked up one or two jobs, but nothing like enough to keep him in the style to which he wanted to be accustomed.'

'He was in debt?'

'I imagine so.' Pyke rubbed his eyes, staring down at the floor. 'But that's not all I'm saying.'

Silence fell across the room. Winterman glanced across at Hoxton, who had been sitting, blank-faced, listening to the dialogue. 'What else?'

'I've no evidence for this. Nothing that would stand up in a court of law. But he was getting money from other sources. A lot of money.'

'What other sources?'

Pyke closed his eyes and then slowly reopened them, his gaze fixed on Winterman's face. 'Blackmail.'

'Blackmail?'

'I think so.'

'You didn't report it?'

'Christ, man, I've no evidence. I didn't even want to think it. There were signs when I was living with Howard, but I blanked them out.'

'What sort of signs?'

'Fag ends of telephone calls. Odd behaviour. Howard had many qualities but discretion wasn't one of them. I found an envelope full of money once. He had some story about how an impresario had insisted on paying him in cash to avoid tax.'

'Who was he blackmailing?'

'This is all speculation. But I know what Howard was capable of. When it suited him – when it was to his benefit, I mean – he could be incredibly organised. If he wanted to do something like this, he'd do it properly. He'd protect himself. He'd make money out of it. He'd have picked his victims very carefully. People with something to hide and good reasons to keep it hidden.'

Winterman looked sceptical. 'He had at least one secret of his own. Risky, if you're engaging in blackmail.'

'Hardly, really. An actor turns out to be homosexual? Whatever the Sunday papers might say, that's not going to cause too many ripples, is it? Howard didn't exactly go out of his way to conceal it anyway.'

'If Merriman was involved in blackmail, I imagine we'll find evidence somewhere in the house.' Winterman didn't say he'd already made an examination – admittedly fairly cursory – of the upstairs rooms.

'Howard would have been careful. If there was stuff he was using, he'd probably keep it somewhere safer than here.'

'Is this suggestion something you're likely to want to share with DS Spooner?'

'Yes, of course. I mean, it is just speculation on my part–'

'But it would provide Spooner with an alternative explanation for Merriman's murder?'

'Alternative? You mean to the convenient lover's tiff theory? I suppose it would.'

'Don't misunderstand me, Pyke. It's not that I'm doubting what you're saying. But it's only speculation and pretty far-fetched speculation at that. I wouldn't be surprised if Spooner just saw it as an attempt to deflect attention from you.'

'So you're saying I should lie, or withhold information, from your senior officer?'

'I'm saying nothing, Pyke. This conversation isn't taking place. Isn't that right, DC Hoxton?'

'I've heard nothing,' Hoxton grunted.

'You've got to tell Spooner whatever you think is right. For all I know, you did murder Merriman. It's the most obvious explanation, and I couldn't blame Spooner for jumping to it. Speaking personally, I don't see you as the type. But I've been wrong about that kind of thing before.'

'Thanks for the overwhelming vote of confidence. For what it's worth, I didn't kill him.'

'For what it's worth,' Winterman said, 'I'm prepared to believe you. But that still leaves the question of why you're here at all. I thought you'd split up.'

Pyke's expression suggested he had no real answer to this question himself. 'That's the big one, isn't it? The answer is that I came back to Framley for reasons you know. That, in turn, brought me back here.'

'You couldn't keep away?'

'Something like that. I hadn't intended to come back. When you first dragged me out to this place to see that poor wee body–' He stopped, and for a moment Winterman thought Pyke might finally begin to show some real emotion. 'It was that night. I was on the way back on the bike when there was another fall of snow. I skidded and it didn't seem safe to go on. There was nowhere else locally I could go, and it seemed madness to try to carry on just for reasons of pride or embarrassment.'

'You just turned up on the doorstep?'

'More or less.'

'How did Merriman take that?'

'In his stride, as always. It was as if we'd never split up. As if I'd just been away for a few days. But that was Howard.'

'You've been here since then?'

'Christ, no. I just stayed the night. And I made it clear I was there only because of the snow. We had a few drinks, a pleasant enough evening. But nothing else.'

'But you came back again?'

'I did, didn't I? Explain that one. I suppose I wasn't really finished with Howard.'

'I'm sorry,' Winterman said. 'I really am.' He paused, inwardly cursing the policeman's instincts that would make him ask the next question, pitched just when Pyke seemed most vulnerable. 'Why did he go out last night?'

Pyke looked uncomprehending for a moment. 'Howard? You've seen the clothes?'

'I had a quick look round upstairs. Thought I'd better check the lay of the land before Spooner's lads got their mitts on it. I found the clothes and the boots. It looked as if he'd been out sometime late last night.'

'Or early this morning. I know. I don't know why though.'

'You weren't aware he'd gone out?'

'Not till this morning. I found the clothes, the way you did. I'll spare you the details, but I slept in Howard's room last night. I'm a heavy sleeper though. I didn't hear a thing. Either he got up sometime in the night or early and then had changed out of the damp clothing, back into his dressing gown.'

'Whichever it was, it suggests he'd been out before. Before he went out and encountered whoever murdered him.'

'Howard wasn't usually the sort for midnight assignations. Preferred his creature comforts. You were more likely to find him in that dressing gown than those boots. That's why I was so surprised to see them in the wardrobe this morning. Howard wore them more as a fashion item than anything else. Made him look rugged. Leading man stuff.' Pyke paused, clearly thinking. 'If you want my opinion, he must have gone out sometime in the night. It wasn't like Howard to leave anything uncleaned – certainly not just to stick them back in the cupboard like that. If he'd been out after he got up this morning, he'd have cleaned and polished them downstairs. He must have been out in the night sometime then just slipped them back in the wardrobe on the assumption I wouldn't spot them.'

'That would imply he didn't want you to know that he'd been out.'

'It would, wouldn't it? It's easy to see why you're the detective here.'

'You've no idea why?'

'Not at all. But if Howard was involved in blackmail, it wouldn't surprise me if one of his victims was local. He never liked putting himself out any more than he could avoid.'

'You're suggesting some sort of assignation last night? Linked to his death?'

'I'm suggesting nothing, old chap. You asked for my opinion.' Pyke rose and walked over to the window, which overlooked the rear of the house, out of sight of Merriman's prone body. 'Christ, I don't know, Winterman. All I can tell you is I didn't do it. There's no particular reason why you should believe me. But I didn't. And I'm not telling you this stuff about blackmail just to throw up a smokescreen.' He shook his head. 'Christ, what a mess.'

Winterman glanced across at Hoxton. 'For what it's worth, which frankly isn't much, I don't think you killed him. Partly because, if this was a crime of passion, it's a hell of a coincidence, given Fisher's death. If you'd cold-bloodedly copied Fisher's murder, you're smart and knowledgeable enough to have removed any trace of your presence and made yourself scarce rather than just telephoning us.' Winterman shrugged. 'But that's my sort of logic. I wouldn't kid yourself that Spooner will be of the same mind.'

'I've no illusions about Spooner,' Pyke said. 'There are a few innocent men behind bars because he was more interested in closing the case than in finding out the truth. And not just behind bars.'

Winterman watched him in silence. Pyke's unspoken thought was obvious. If he were found guilty of murder, the outcome could well be more than mere imprisonment.

'I'll do whatever I can, Pyke.' Winterman glanced at his watch. 'Is there anything else you can tell us?'

'I don't think so. Most of what I've told you is speculation. It's just brought home to me how little I knew about Howard. I don't know who he mixed with in London. I don't know who else might have been in his life. If he was involved in blackmail, I've no idea who the victims might have been.'

'If one of the victims was someone local if would have to be someone with a reputation to lose. And money. That narrows the field.'

'That's your territory, old chum,' Pyke said morosely. 'But it's still just speculation.'

'At least it gives me something to speculate about. Which is more than I've had so far.' Winterman looked again at his watch. 'I don't want to be caught with you when Spooner turns up. I'm going to leave you in the good hands of DC Hoxton, who's been sitting too far away to hear any of this conversation.'

'Not a word, sir,' Hoxton said.

'I'll do what I can,' Winterman said again. 'I'll try to persuade Spooner to keep an open mind. Failing that, I'll make sure I keep an open mind myself. You need to start thinking about precisely what you're going to tell Spooner when he gets here.'

Pyke nodded somberly. 'Thanks. It's Joshua, by the way.'

Winterman blinked. 'What is?'

'My Christian name. Some people call me Josh. The ones who don't call me Pyke.'

'Crikey.' Winterman gazed at him for a moment, then held out his right hand. 'Ivan.'

Pyke took the hand and shook it solemnly. 'Ivan. Bloody hell. If I'd known, I wouldn't have been so embarrassed about mine.'

CHAPTER FORTY-NINE

Mary had intended to walk quickly past the graveyard to avoid another conversation with Bryan. But as she turned the corner she saw a large black Humber police car parked across the gateway. Not their own Wolseley, which meant that other officers had arrived from HQ.

She slowed briefly as she reached the gate. Brain was just inside, morosely smoking a cigarette. He was looking lost, his limited role usurped by the arrival of the HQ team.

'Have they found anything, Bryan?' Mary asked. 'About the blood, I mean.'

'If they have, they're not telling me. But they're not telling me anything. Put me firmly in my place, they have.' A look of faint hope crossed his face. 'Did you find the inspector down at the station?'

'No, I'd missed him. It looked as if they'd headed off in the car.'

'They didn't say they were going anywhere. I thought they'd be back up here to examine the site.'

'Is this a friend of yours, Constable?' a voice said from behind him. 'Can I help you, madam?'

Mary had watched the plain-clothes officer approaching. 'I don't think so. What exactly did you have in mind?' To her left, she sensed Brain stifling a laugh.

'I'm afraid I'm going to have to ask you to leave, madam. The churchyard isn't open today.'

She smiled pleasantly. 'Are you the new sexton? I don't think we've met.'

'I'm a police officer, madam. This is police business.' The man hesitated, clearly recognising there was no reason why she should accept this statement at face value. He reached into his overcoat and produced his warrant card.

Mary registered that, despite his overbearing manner, he was nothing more than a DC. 'Thank you, Constable. I take it this is about the child's body?'

'What would you know about that, madam?' The superciliousness was slipping slightly.

'I was one of the people who discovered it. Along with DI Winterman.' Her smile widened. 'I imagine you'll want me to make a statement about it.'

'You know DI Winterman?'

'I work with him.' Taking pity, she added, 'On the civilian side, you understand. I'm trying to track him down. Do you know where he is?'

'I'm not sure that I should–'

'It's just that I've some information he asked me to collect for him. I'd understood he needed it urgently.'

'If you pass it to me, I'll make sure he gets it. As far as I know, he's over attending to the other murder enquiry with DS Spooner.'

The reference to another murder enquiry meant nothing to Mary, unless it was a reference to the Fisher case. She decided it wasn't the time to express her ignorance. 'That's very kind of you. Perhaps that would be okay.' She pretended to hesitate. 'But it's all rather complicated and he was adamant I should give it directly to him. DI Winterman can be a little crotchety if he thinks his instructions aren't being followed to the letter.' She was doing her best to avoid Brain's eye as she spoke.

The officer looked back over his shoulder. 'We're nearly done here so we'll be heading over there ourselves shortly. We're just waiting for the ambulance team to collect the body.'

Brain leaned forward eagerly. 'If it helps, I'm happy to keep an eye on things till they turn up. No sense in wasting your time.'

The officer had the grace to know when he was beaten. 'Okay, give us a few minutes and we'll head on over there.' He tuned and stamped across the snow-covered ground.

'Thanks, Bryan,' Mary said. 'I owe you a favour.'

Brain coloured slightly. 'Just doing my job. Anyway, it's nice to remind that bunch that I exist. What do you think he meant by another murder enquiry?'

'The Reverend Fisher's death, I imagine. Probably the inspector's having to brief them or something.' Even as she spoke the words, she realised she didn't believe them. Her thoughts were ill formed and unsubstantiated but the sequence of events – Marsh's disappearance, the spilled blood – had left her fearing the worst.

CHAPTER FIFTY

After finishing with Pyke, Winterman donned a pair of the clean cotton gloves he always carried and made a careful examination of the other downstairs rooms in the cottage. He proceeded cautiously, mindful of the risk of disturbing fingerprints and other possible evidence, but was able to examine the drawers and cupboards in the kitchen and hallway with reasonable thoroughness.

A cupboard in the hall contained a substantial pile of paperwork, but a brief examination of the contents revealed nothing of interest – electricity and gas bills, water-rates, some contracts for acting work, a couple of battered scripts. The kitchen drawers contained more paperwork, again mostly trivial – an unused 1946 diary, some handwritten copies of recipes. Tucked into a drawer near the cooker, he found a manila envelope containing four five-pound notes. Conceivably, this might be the remnants of a blackmail payout. More likely, it was simply money put aside for some domestic purpose. They could have the bank notes checked, but Winterman had little hope of a positive result.

The other kitchen cupboards were full of standard domestic detritus – brushes, a dustpan, a galvanised mop bucket. Nothing likely to be significant, though it would all need to be examined in due course.

He was disturbed from his half-hearted task by an imperious hammering at the front door. It took him a moment to unlock the door, and before he had it fully open, Spooner was already pushing past him into the hallway.

'Bloody hell, Winterman, hurry up. It's brass monkeys out here.'

Outside, Winterman could see a long black police car – rather larger than their own Wolseley. A Jaguar saloon. That, he supposed, was a measure of Spooner's style. Two plain-clothed officers were huddled by the car, clearly feeling the cold but showing no sign of following Spooner into the cottage. Spooner was going to make sure his back was fully covered before he allowed any witnesses to be present.

'Good to see you, sir,' Winterman said. 'You've made good time.'

'I'm not one to dawdle with something as serious as this, Winterman. Mind you, this bloody snow's a nightmare. They've got some of the main roads cleared, but it's all treacherous. Still, change on the way, or so they reckon.' He stopped and looked around him at the impressively decorated hallway and let out a low whistle. 'Nice looking place. This belong to the victim?'

'One Howard Merriman. Alias Howard Martin.'

'Alias?'

'An actor. Martin was his stage name.'

'Oh, I see.' Spooner's tone suggested actors were barely worthy of police attention. 'Okay, fill me in.' With his squat figure and brindled hair, Spooner resembled an overgrown badger.

'There's one thing you ought to know first of all, sir.' Winterman paused for a moment, savouring Spooner's expression of baffled anxiety. 'The individual who found the body is known to us.'

'Predictable enough,' Spooner snorted. 'Bloody actors.'

'I meant someone we've worked with. Doctor Pyke, actually.'

Spooner gazed back at Winterman in blank bafflement. 'Pyke? The quack?'

'The pathologist, yes, sir.'

'He found the body?' Winterman knew from previous dealings with Spooner that his favoured tactic was to repeat his interlocutor's words until there was no possible room for ambiguity.

'The body's out in the garden. Doctor Pyke found it this morning.'

Spooner blinked, still not quite absorbing what Winterman was saying. 'Pyke found the body? What the bloody hell was Pyke doing here?'

'He was staying here, apparently. He was a friend of the deceased.'

'So that's why we couldn't find the bugger, eh? Anyone remind him that he's paid to do a job? Still, convenient that he's here. Presumably he can give us the gen on the body.'

'With respect, sir, I'm not sure that would be entirely appropriate.'

Spooner blinked again and the badger resemblance grew even more pronounced. 'You mean–?'

'I'm afraid so. We have to treat him as a suspect. At least for the moment.' Winterman felt a little guilty at immediately leading Spooner in this direction, particularly after his promises to Pyke. But Spooner would have reached the same conclusion himself soon enough. 'He was the only other person in the house. His story is that he stayed overnight and that he came down this morning to find Merriman's body out in the garden. There's no particular reason to doubt that but–'

Spooner was catching on rapidly now. 'But if we don't it means that Merriman was killed by person or persons unknown.'

'As you say.' Winterman was settling into the flow of this new relationship with Spooner. 'Of course, it's quite possible that that was the case.'

'But for the moment we should stick with the obvious.'

'Or at least not discount it. Quite so. Occam's razor and all that.' As he spoke the latter words, it occurred to Winterman that Spooner might take that as a reference to the murder weapon. 'Probably best if I show you the body first, and then we can decide what to do with Pyke.'

'You've not interviewed him yet?'

'I thought that best left for your arrival, sir. Given the sensitivities. DC Hoxton is looking after him through there.' Winterman gestured towards the sitting room at the end of the hall. 'The body's this way.' He led Spooner into the kitchen. The back door had been left ajar and, by contrast with the rest of the house, the room was now chilly. Winterman pointed out into the garden. Spooner followed with more elephantine steps, apparently careless of the impact on any evidence.

Spooner's eyes followed the pointing finger to where Merriman's body lay prone in the snow. 'Bloody hell. Stabbed?'

'Stabbed. It may be only coincidence but the positioning of the body is almost identical to that of Reverend Fisher's.' Winterman thought there was no harm in bringing this point to Spooner's attention at the earliest opportunity.

'Reverend…? Oh, the murdered sky pilot. Just the same, eh? That's interesting.'

'It may be. Two almost identical stabbings in an area like this in a few days does seem unlikely.'

'Any reason for Pyke to be in the frame for Fisher's murder?'

'Not that I'm aware of. But obviously it's not an angle we've pursued. Pyke actually did the examination of Fisher's body, but there's no other connection I know of.'

'That doesn't mean there isn't one,' Spooner pointed out. 'Or that Pyke didn't decide to copy what had been done to Fisher. Throw us off the scent.'

Spooner moved to stand close to the door. He showed no inclination to venture out into the garden, though it was unclear whether this was the result of squeamishness or aversion to the cold.

'What about motive?'

'Difficult to say, until we've interviewed Pyke. We don't know the nature of his relationship with Merriman.'

Winterman had tried to keep his voice neutral but it was clear that Spooner's investigatory antennae were functioning.

'Relationship? They had a relationship?'

'I presume so. Of some sort. Doctor Pyke stayed here last night.'

'Just good friends, eh? Or are you suggesting something more?'

'Just giving you the facts, sir.'

'What you'd expect though, isn't it? Bloody actors. Nancy boys.'

'A little outside my experience, I'm afraid,' Winterman said. 'And I don't really know about pathologists.'

Spooner stared at him for a moment, as though suspecting irony. 'Is that what this is then? A lover's tiff?'

'Rather serious for a tiff. But I suppose that's one possibility.'

'How did Pyke seem?'

'Shaken, as you'd expect. But no more than anyone would be who'd just found a friend murdered, I'd say. Any kind of friend.' Winterman was conscious he was drifting away from the tone of neutrality he'd been striving to maintain. 'He didn't seem like someone who had just committed a murder, but the ones who have usually don't.'

'That's true enough.' Spooner gestured out towards the garden. 'What about those footprints in the snow? Whose are they?'

'We need to get them looked at properly, see if there's anything that can be sketched. I've not gone too close because I didn't want to risk disturbing the site till the doc had looked at the body. They're fairly jumbled but my impression is that there are two sets leading from the body. Pyke said one of them was his.'

Spooner raised an eyebrow. 'Pyke's?'

'Yes, he says he went out to examine the body and saw a trail of footprints leading round to the front of the house. Also reckons there are some tyre marks in the snow on the road.'

'All very convenient. We can follow the tyre tracks all the way back to the murderer's house, no doubt.'

'Not if the main road's been cleared. Pity.' Winterman smiled to show Spooner he was sharing the other man's irony.

'Okay,' Spooner said, 'let's get the show on the road. 'The quack's on his way. We called Carson because we couldn't run Pyke to ground, but I sent him out to the kiddie's body first with a couple of my team. From what you said, we needed to get that one sorted before some old biddy stumbled across it. But I've got a couple of trained crime scene officers here. I'll get them started on the ground around the body till Carson turns up.' He paused. 'So what about the kiddies' bodies, Winterman? What's that all about?'

'I haven't the foggiest, sir. It's like nothing I've ever seen. Three children's bodies. Dead for years. Noone reported missing. Makes no sense at all.'

'Christ, Winterman, I'll say one thing for you. You know how to make things happen. We send you out to the back of beyond, and not only do the locals drop like flies, but you even manage to conjure corpses out of nowhere. Must be some sort of gift.'

'Not one I'd recommend acquiring, sir.'

'You don't think there's any link with this? Or with the sky pilot's murder?'

'Who knows? Fisher found one of the children's bodies, but that could have just been coincidence. There's nothing so far to link Merriman with them.'

'Except that he's a nancy boy.'

'I don't think that implies any link in itself, sir,' Winterman said smoothly. 'Even if Merriman was a homosexual, my understanding is that that just means he was sexually attracted to men. Nothing else.'

'A deviant's a deviant in my book.'

And a very enlightening book that must be, Winterman thought. 'I suppose we have to keep an open mind.'

'That's the spirit, Winterman. Let's see what Pyke's got to say for himself.' He smiled. 'Should make quite an entertaining exchange. Last time I saw our Doctor Pyke, he was on his high horse because I'd supposedly messed up some of his precious evidence. I'm going to enjoy taking him down a peg or two.'

CHAPTER FIFTY-ONE

With one final glance at the prone body, Spooner strode back out into the hallway. In the process, Winterman noticed, his heavy boots managed to stamp very effectively on any lingering evidence that might have been left on the kitchen floor. Still, Pyke was in no position to complain.

Spooner was halfway across the hallway when there was a further knock at the door. He looked back quizzically at Winterman, who took his cue and moved past Spooner to open it. He was greeted by the long morose face of Carson, the pathologist. 'DI Winterman,' he intoned, solemnly then, glancing over Winterman's shoulder, he added, 'And Superintendent Spooner. I believe we have another body?'

By contrast with Pyke, who had always maintained a degree of gallows humour, Carson seemed singularly well fitted to his job. He exuded a deathly air, and any lingering lightness of spirit tended to evaporate in his presence. But – and this was his only similarity to Pyke – he knew his job inside out.

'We do indeed,' Spooner said. 'Give him the guided tour, Winterman.'

Winterman led Carson into the kitchen and pointed to the French windows. 'The body's out there in the garden. You can't miss it.'

A faint smile played across Carson's lugubrious face. 'If I have any difficulty, I'll come back for more detailed directions. By the way, there's someone outside waiting to see you.' He spoke the last words in a slightly clandestine tone, as though it were some secret between the two of them.

Winterman nodded his thanks and stepped back into the hall, intrigued. Spooner was standing near the door of the living room, clearly eager to begin his interview with Pyke. Winterman gestured to the front door. 'Someone wants me, apparently. You go on, sir. If you want someone to take notes, DC Hoxton's very experienced. I'll be with you shortly.'

Spooner looked irritated, presumably because Winterman was exercising some independence of thought. 'I'll wait. You know the background.'

'I'll be as quick as I can.'

Winterman peered out the front door, half expecting to find Marsh standing outside. Instead, Mary was waiting a few yards away, close by a newly arrived Humber police car. Winterman glanced back over his shoulder. Spooner had moved so that he could follow Winterman's gaze out of the front door. His expression of irritation was mingled with one of undisguised curiosity.

'Inspector, I've brought the information you asked for,' Mary called.

Winterman was fazed for only a second or two, glad that his back was to Spooner. 'Thanks, Mary. Well done for tracking me down.' He looked back at Spooner, who had moved down the hall to witness the exchange at close hand. 'Mary Ford,' he explained. 'Works in the office. Asked her to track down some names and addresses for me. Villagers to be interviewed.' He stepped out into the cold air. 'Better stay out there, Mary. Crime scene and all that.'

She greeted him by the car, fumbling in her handbag for a small leather-covered book. 'It's just my diary, but I've got to give you something.'

'I'll give it you back later,' he murmured, 'and I won't peep.'

'You won't find much of interest if you do. I need to talk to you.'

'I gathered that.' He glanced back to where Spooner was watching them, framed in the cottage doorway. 'Why so secretive?'

She hesitated, her eyes following Winterman's gaze. 'Who's that?'

'Superintendent Spooner. From HQ. He's overseeing the investigation.'

She nodded, absorbing this information. 'It's about Paul.'

'DC Marsh?'

'Bryan told me you didn't know where he was.'

It was Winterman's turn to hesitate. He lowered his voice still further. 'It looks as if he went out last night sometime. Hoxton thinks his bed wasn't slept in. I don't know whether to be concerned or not.' He paused. 'I haven't broken the news to DS Spooner yet.'

'Bryan said you found some blood.'

'There was some blood by the gravestone, yes. Where we found the child's body.'

'Do you think it was Paul's?'

Again, Winterman found himself wondering about the relationship between Marsh and the young woman in front of him. 'We don't know. Carson will have collected a sample, but until it's analysed we don't know anything.'

'Do you think it might be?'

'Mary, we really don't know. There's no reason to think it is. There's no real reason to worry about Paul yet. He can look after himself.' Winterman glanced over his shoulder again, conscious Spooner's patience was likely to be limited.

'Ivan, there are some things I need to tell you.'

Here it comes, he thought. The truth about her relationship with Marsh. It was probably best to have it confirmed sooner rather than later.

'Paul's my cousin. We try not to make a big thing of it now we're working together, but we're pretty close. Like brother and sister.'

Like brother and sister, Winterman found himself mentally repeating. 'I thought Paul wasn't local?'

'He's not. Not originally. His mother was Mam's sister. She moved to Nottingham after she married. Paul was sent out here at the start of the war with his younger brother.'

Winterman was working out the ages. Marsh was in his early twenties – maybe twenty-two, twenty-three. At the start of the war, he'd have been a teenager. 'They were evacuees?'

'Not part of the official programme, though we had plenty of those around here. But they were living in the centre of Nottingham. His dad worked in the Players factory. When the war broke out, their mam and dad thought it best to send them to stay with us.' Winterman noticed that there were tears in the corner of her eyes. 'We got on well. Paul's a couple of years younger than me. His brother was a few years younger still–' She stopped, as if she didn't know how to go on. 'I'm sorry,' she said, registering his backward glance. 'You're busy.'

'It's not that. It's just I'm conscious Spooner's likely to interrupt us before very long.'

'I'll tell you properly later. But what you need to know is that Paul's little brother vanished.'

'Vanished?'

'In the first summer of the war. The hot summer. We used to go out to try to see the fighters going over, the three of us. One day, while out with some other friends, we managed to lose Gary, Paul's brother.'

Winterman had registered that Spooner had detached himself from the doorway and was heading in their direction. 'What happened?'

'We never knew exactly. Gary dawdled behind. We were chatting, hadn't realised he wasn't there. Then we couldn't find him. Paul never forgave himself.'

'What's this got to with Paul's disappearance?' Winterman nodded to draw her attention to Spooner's approach.

'I don't know. Maybe nothing. Paul had a thing about this for a long time. It's what drew him to the police force. But he's not talked about it for years. But then I thought – these bodies. Paul might have seen a chance to find out something. To find out what happened to Gary.'

'Anybody mind if I break up this jolly social occasion?' It was Spooner, standing watching them from some feet away.

'Sorry, sir. Mary was just explaining the list of addresses she's brought.' He waved the diary vaguely towards Spooner, his palm concealing its real nature.

'I hope it's useful bloody information,' Spooner said. 'Pardon my French, madam.' He bowed slightly towards Mary.

Winterman glanced at Mary. 'I'm sure it will be. You can give me the rest of the detail later, Mary. I'm sorry. There's a lot to do.'

'I hope we've not brought you out of your way,' Spooner said to Mary.

'I live in Framley. I couldn't get into the office today. That's why I thought I'd make myself useful and bring this up to the inspector.'

'Very commendable,' Spooner said. 'Researched it at home, did you?'

Mary said nothing, and Winterman made a mental note that there was a danger of underestimating DS Spooner.

'Come on, Winterman,' Spooner went on. 'Time to see what Pyke's got to say for himself.' He peered up at the leaden sky. 'All very well for you youngsters, but I'm sick of this bloody snow.' He turned and furnished them both with a broad but mirthless smile. 'Still, change is on its way, eh, so they say?'

Part Two

March, 1947

CHAPTER FIFTY-TWO

The sound of the rain woke him again.

He lay for a long time, his eyes open, staring into the darkness, listening to the sound. The rhythmic beating on the roof, the clattering of the spray against the window, the roar of the water along the gutters, spewing into the down spouts.

Endless noise. His body held as if in chains.

It was the dream again. The recurrent dream that seemed to lead him a little further forward each time. The dream that ended with him chasing Sam through the sodden undergrowth, trying to reach his little boy before–

It took him a moment to realise he was awake, that he had been awake for some time. He rolled over, expecting the cushioned silence of the snow-covered world.

It was raining.

He could still hear it. The pounding on the roof, the spray on the window, the echo of the water in the guttering.

Winterman dragged himself from under the bedclothes and stood upright, the lino cold under his feet. It took him a moment to locate the paler grey of the window, and he stumbled towards it, banging his shoulder against the unexpected solidity of a wardrobe.

He stopped and blinked, trying to regain his bearings. Everything seemed skewed, a world shifted on its axis.

He wasn't home. He was in the guest bedroom at Mary's house. The room was smaller, more cluttered, differently laid out.

But it was still raining.

Baffled, he made his way cautiously across the room and pulled back the curtains. The room looked out on to the Fenlands at the rear of the house, across the narrow road and the dyke where the child's body had been discovered. Gradually his eyes grew accustomed to the dark and he discerned the shapes that comprised this flat landscape.

And it was raining.

The snow still lay thick across the fields, but there were already bare patches where the shallower snow had begun to thaw. If the downpour continued, the snow would not survive for long, perhaps not even till morning.

It was hard to believe. The snow had been there for weeks and had seemed as if it might stay forever. It was vanishing though almost as rapidly as it had first arrived. On that, at least, Spooner had been right.

The interview with Pyke had been a tiresome business as Spooner tried to trick, cajole and finally threaten Pyke into admitting his guilt. Pyke, for his part, stuck to a relatively straightforward exposition of the facts. He refused to acknowledge his homosexuality on the grounds that, first, it was nobody else's business and, second, there was no reason to incriminate himself. For the moment, he was simply a witness doing his best to help the police with their enquiries. If they wanted to arrest him, they should go ahead and do so. But the core of his narrative – he had come downstairs and found Merriman's body out in the garden – remain unchanged.

Eventually, after close on two hours, Spooner had called it a day. He knew his threats to arrest Pyke lacked credibility. They might in due course be able to gather sufficient evidence to arrest and charge him, but all they had was circumstantial. The examination of the body and the crime scene had revealed little. The weapon was an undistinguished hunting knife. Carson had shrugged. 'The kind of thing most farmers would have around here. Just a practical tool.' There were no fingerprints on the knife, and Pyke claimed never to have seen it before.

'We ought to check whether it matches the weapon used to kill Fisher,' Winterman said. It occurred to him that they could ask Pyke, but that hardly seemed appropriate. They could check the files back at the office.

'It'll be difficult to be certain,' Carson pointed out. 'A lot of damage was done to the wound there. It may not be possible to draw any firm conclusions about the exact nature of the weapon, though I could exclude plenty of options. I'll set out all the detail in the report. Don't know if it'll help you much though.'

The footprints had been checked. There was another set, mingled with Pyke's, leading from the body to the front of the cottage, potentially supporting Pyke's version of events.

'Maybe he had an accomplice,' Spooner had suggested doggedly.

Few of the footprints were clear and none was firm enough to take an imprint, but they had attempted to sketch the design of the sole. There were, as Pyke had reported, car tyre marks leading from opposite the cottage back to the main road.

'Something fairly large,' Winterman said. 'With tyre chains.' The tread was unclear though, and it was impossible to draw any meaningful conclusions.

'Nothing that gets us very far then,' Spooner had confirmed, morosely. 'Tomorrow we start all the usual stuff – interviewing the neighbours, such as they are. Try to track down whatever car this was. In this weather, someone ought to have spotted it.'

'Assuming anyone was out to spot it,' Winterman said.

'And in the meantime we have to let Pyke go, but we keep close tabs on him.'

That had been largely it. Spooner had detailed a uniformed officer to keep an eye on Pyke's flat, but even he had little expectation that it would lead to anything. Spooner and his team had headed back to town, with a schedule of interviews arranged for the next day.

Winterman and Hoxton had been left standing at the front of the cottage. It was the mid-afternoon, early March, but the sky was leaden and it felt as if evening was already falling.

'With all due respect,' Hoxton said, 'I suspect that DS Spooner has no more idea than we have.'

'With all due respect, I think you're right.'

'And what about Marshy?' Hoxton raised the question that was on both of their minds.

'I don't know. I've been telling myself that there must be some simple explanation, but I don't know how long I can keep believing that.'

'Marshy's always been a bit of a law unto himself, shall we say?'

They were walking back through the heavy snow towards the car. 'How do you mean?'

'Not exactly a loose cannon. He's always been good at the job. Dependable and all that. But he gets bees in his bonnet.'

'What sort of bees?' Winterman thought back to his brief conversation with Mary.

'All kinds of things. Takes the job too seriously if you ask me. Never been one of my problems.'

'You think he could have gone off on some frolic of his own?'

'It's possible. That's all I'm saying. He forgets that this is a job like any other. You do it as well as you can but you don't let it take over your life.'

Winterman was fumbling for the car keys. 'How do you mean?'

'It's like this.' Hoxton was standing on the far side of the car, peering over the high roof. 'In the job, you do your best to catch villains. You do your best to prevent crime or to solve crime when it's happened.'

'Hard to argue, George.'

'But you don't let it get to you, do you? If some villain gets away, that's life. You win some, you lose some. I put it behind me, and make damned sure I do my best to catch the bugger next time around.'

'That's the only way,' Winterman agreed. 'Anything more and you drive yourself bananas.'

'Have a word with young Marshy about that. He lets it get to him. It eats away at him. As if he's got some divine mission to put these villains behind bars. When it doesn't happen, he gets more and more frustrated. Won't let it lie.'

'Doesn't sound particularly healthy.'

'I don't want to overstate it. But he's conscientious. Where most of us would give up, he carries on. We had a case a few months back – petty breaking and entering. We'd fingered a couple of youths we thought were behind it but couldn't get the evidence to convict. I'd more or less thrown in the towel. It was hardly worth the effort for what they'd stolen. But Marshy kept at it. Went round all the pawn shops and second-hand outfits tracking down every last useless ornament, getting witness statements about who'd sold what. In the end, he got together enough of a case to get them convicted.'

'Sounds impressive.'

'Oh, it was. It's just a bit – disproportionate.'

'But that's the nature of the job. Most of what we do's a waste of time. But you never know in advance the parts that aren't.'

'I know that. But when Marshy gets the bit between his teeth, he tends not to let go.'

Winterman unlocked the car door and climbed into the driver's seat, leaning over to unlock the passenger door. He had been making light of Hoxton's comments, but the echo of Mary's words was enough to give Winterman concern.

'So what do we do about Marsh then?' he asked, as Hoxton flopped down into the seat beside him.

'What can we do? I mean, short of a fully-fledged search party. We haven't got any clue where he might have gone. All we can do is wait. Either till he reappears or till we're really sure he's missing.'

Expressed in those terms, it sounded a cold-blooded strategy, but there was no obvious alternative. 'I take it we want to stay close to home though?'

'Up to you, guv. But I'm staying here, if that's all right with you. Brain'll put us up at the station for another night, I'm sure.'

'I was thinking I'd see whether Mary can put me up again.' Before Hoxton could start jumping to any conclusions, he added, 'She said she wanted to talk to me. When she came across this afternoon. She said that she and Marsh are close. Grew up together.'

'Aye, that's right. Didn't you know? Cousins. That's one reason we wangled her the job in the office after her husband died.' He paused. 'What's she been told?'

'Not much. Brain told her we didn't know where Marsh was.'

'Brain by name and Brain by nature. But he weren't to know, I suppose.'

'Tell me about Mary.' Something in Hoxton's tone had attracted Winterman's attention.

'We're a bit protective of her, I suppose. She's been through a lot. It hit her hard when her husband was killed. Hardly surprising. Struggling to make ends meet. Two little kiddies. Then that happens. And, like I said, it wasn't even what you might call a heroic death. You couldn't even tell yourself he'd died for a purpose. She took it bad.'

'Bad in what way?'

Hoxton gazed at him for a moment, as though contemplating Winterman's motives. 'I don't exactly know what you'd call it. Delusional, I suppose. Convinced herself the death wasn't an accident. Reckoned someone had killed him deliberately.'

Winterman was slowly manoeuvring the car back on to the road. 'Why would anyone do that?'

'Because he was on to something she reckoned. Something he was looking into.'

'What sort of something?'

'She didn't know or wouldn't say. The whole thing was supposedly pieced together in her mind from bits and pieces Jim had said after he got back from Dunkirk. She reckoned he'd got some idea he wouldn't talk about. And that was why he was killed.'

'You didn't think there was anything in it?'

'What do you think? I mean, we took her seriously enough. But the truth was she had nothing to go on. When we asked her what it was that Jim had said to her, even she couldn't say for sure. It was all chat that her fevered imagination had pieced together into something more.' He eased himself back in the leather seat, warming to the story. 'I'm no trick cyclist, guv, but it's not difficult to see how she might have wanted it to be true.'

'Then at least he wouldn't have died for no reason?'

'Something like that. But she wouldn't let it rest. Kept banging away at it. Wrote letters to anyone she could think of. Chief Constable. Her MP.'

'Hamshaw?'

'Hamshaw. Very polite, I recall.'

'Every vote counts.'

'Aye, and the poor bugger needed every one he could lay his hands on in '45. Though I bet Mary's wasn't one of them. She got completely wound up in it. Had a decent office job in town but she gave that up. Her mam was tearing her hair out.'

'But Mary came through it?'

'Thanks to her mam, mainly. That and the kiddies. I think she realised that if she carried on, it was the kiddies who were going to suffer. That got through to her in the end.'

They could see the sparse lights of Framley ahead, pale in the overcast afternoon. 'You think she's still vulnerable?'

'She's been through a hell of a lot.'

'Marsh's brother?'

'You know about that then?'

'Mary told me this afternoon.'

Hoxton leaned forward, frowning. 'This afternoon? When she came across to see you. That's what she wanted to talk about?'

'Yes, that and Marsh's disappearance.'

Hoxton was staring out of the window, watching the flat fields, featureless under the snow. 'I don't feel good about this. I don't feel good at all.'

'In what way?' Winterman could see ahead the row of cottages that included Mary's house. Beyond that, the squat overgrown church tower was black against the lowering sky.

'It sounds like how she was before. Making a big deal about nothing. Making connections where none exist.'

'But Marsh's brother did die.'

'So I understand. But there was nothing mysterious about it. He drowned.'

They pulled into the roadside next to Mary's house. 'Drowned how?'

'This is all second hand. I didn't know either of them in those days, but these stories carry fast in these parts. It was that hot summer of 1940. Mary must have been about fifteen, Marshy a year younger. All the kids used to go out to try to see the aircraft going over. They cycled up to some gravel pits up north of the town to go swimming. Always dangerous, them places – a lot deeper than they look. There was a bunch of them. Gary was eight or nine. By all accounts a bit of a tearaway. They'd been swimming, were cycling back when someone noticed Gary was missing. He'd not come out with the rest of them or he'd gone back in, no one was quite sure. But they reckoned it was just like Gary to go off on his own, taking some stupid risk. Drowned in the gravel pit.'

'They found his body?'

'No. But them things are bloody deep. They tried to dredge it, but found nothing. Mind you, they hadn't got the manpower then to do things properly.'

'So no one knows for sure he drowned?'

'What else? If he hadn't, they'd have found the body. Got cramp or something and got pulled under. Wouldn't be the first. Marshy never forgave himself, and Mary took it hard as well. But it weren't no one's fault, other than Gary himself. I don't like the idea that Mary's harping on about that again. She was just a girl. Mind you, she's grown up quickly. It was only two or three years after that she met Jimmy, home on leave. Not much longer after that before she was married and widowed. That takes your childhood away pretty smartish.'

Winterman had the sense Hoxton was trying to move the subject on. 'What about Marsh? What did he think?'

'Blamed himself, as I say. But didn't want to admit Gary had just drowned. Kept saying there was more to it, that Gary had been snatched somehow. Like Mary with Jimmy, persuaded himself it wasn't just a stupid pointless accident. But life's full of stupid pointless accidents.'

Winterman sat for a moment, staring through the windscreen at the empty road. 'Mary has a point though, doesn't she?'

'How'd you mean?'

'Whatever the truth about Gary's death, if Marsh still believes there was more to it, then finding these bodies might have triggered something. You said yourself he's not one to let things lie.'

'So where does that leave us then? In terms of Marshy, I mean.'

'I haven't a clue. Unless Gary's disappearance gives us some lead.'

'Can't see it. Gary went missing miles from here. Can't imagine Marshy's gone traipsing up there.'

'All I can do is talk to Mary then. See if she says anything that sheds any light.' Winterman pushed open the door. 'You take the car down to the station. I'll see you down there first thing. Or tonight if I'm denied hospitality here.'

'Don't think you'll be denied hospitality here. Take care though, won't you?'

'Take care?'

'With Mary. She's more vulnerable that she looks.' He laughed. 'I've just thought. That's two of you had breakdowns. The halt and the bloody lame.'

Winterman paused in extracting himself from the car and glanced back at Hoxton. For all his gregariousness, Hoxton was impossible to read. 'That's not bloody funny, George. That's not bloody funny at all.'

'I know, guv,' Hoxton said quietly, a new note to his voice. 'I wasn't joking.'

That had been only hours before, and yet it felt as if it had taken place in another world. Winterman stood at the window, dressed only in his vest and underpants, staring out at the dim landscape. He should be cold, he realised. He had grown accustomed to the below-freezing temperatures, the biting winds across the flat fields.

Suddenly, it was mild. Still far from warm, but after the last few months it felt almost tropical. Outside the rain was still falling, heavily, steadily, as incessant as the falling snow had been only days before. Already the pristine landscape looked frayed, soiled, the pure white giving way to the sodden earth beneath.

He thought back to the conversation with Hoxton in the car, the sense then that there was some undercurrent to their dialogue, something Hoxton was not saying. Then he recalled his later whispered conversation with Mary, sitting hunched against the smoking coal fire, her mother playing with the children in the next room.

And he wondered what tomorrow would bring.

CHAPTER FIFTY-THREE

Mary had greeted him warmly, apparently unsurprised that he was seeking to stay another night.

'No news of Paul?' She closed the front door and ushered him into the relative warmth of the hallway.

'Afraid not. Hoxton's heading back down to the station in case Brain's heard anything.'

'He'd have come up here if he had anything to tell me.' She helped Winterman take off his heavy overcoat. 'Come through into the front room. Mam's in the kitchen with the children. Are you hungry?'

'No, I'm fine,' he said, not quite truthfully. He was conscious of the extent to which he was imposing on these people, literally eating into their limited rations.

'I've put some stew on for later.' She spoke as if reading his mind. 'Not much to write home about. But Mam's good at sweet-talking the butcher.'

'I'll bring you some of my ration. I never use it all anyway. Pay you back for putting me up. Or putting up with me.'

'Don't be daft. It's hardly a hardship. Nice for us to get some company.'

He followed her into the front room. A coal fire was burning in the hearth, smoke rising from the scrappy piles of fuel. She gestured towards it apologetically. 'We're getting low. We've been eking it out but I can't remember when the coal man last came.'

'It's the same everywhere. They're getting coal to the factories and power stations by sea, apparently. But it's still not reaching the likes of us.'

'This wasn't how it was supposed to be. We thought it would be all right once the war ended.'

'Not quite paradise yet.'

He motioned for her to sit at the end of the sofa closest to the fire. For a moment, he thought politeness would cause her to demur, but finally she lowered herself on to the worn cushions. He took a seat beside her, feeling absurdly like a young man courting his first girl.

'You were going to tell me about Paul.' The Christian name still felt awkward in his mouth. 'This afternoon, before Spooner interrupted us.'

'I'm worried about him. He gets things into his head. His brother–'

'Tell me about his brother.' Winterman wondered whether to mention what Hoxton had said, but told himself that Hoxton's version of events was nothing more than hearsay.

'Gary idolised Paul. It was partly the usual big brother thing. But also, Gary was pretty lonely out here. It was a shock to find himself shipped out here from the big city, away from his family and his friends.'

'Must have been a shock for Paul too.'

'Paul was that bit older. And he's a personable sort. It didn't take him long to make new friends.'

'Including you?'

'Including me. I was a year or so older. Normally, that might have been enough to keep us apart. You know what youngsters are like. A year's a lifetime at that age. But there weren't that many young folk around here. You couldn't afford to be picky.' Her expression suggested she was recalling some particular incident. Winterman felt a momentary pang of jealousy that he hadn't known her then.

'But there were a few of us around that age. Enough to make a little gang, if you know what I mean. We went to the pictures or the odd dance. Not that there was a lot going on. But it was a glorious summer. Most of us had left school and it wasn't difficult to find work, what with all the men being called up. There were plenty of jobs going on the farms and the local factories. It didn't feel real, somehow. It felt – I don't know – temporary, as if we were all waiting to see what would happen next.'

'I remember it.' Winterman thought back to his own experiences in the early years of the war. 'I don't know what we expected.'

He recalled the months of phoney war, and then the reports of German victories on the wireless, the sense of threat expanding across Europe, gradually closing in on his own tiny world. The feeling, in that first summer after the fall of France and the Dunkirk evacuation, that it was only a matter of time before the Nazi forces were trampling the country underfoot. It had felt as if they were in suspension, unable to get on with their lives but with no means of planning for the future.

The hot summer had seemed to mock their fears, long scorching days that held endless untapped potential. There'd been Sunday afternoon walks with Gwyneth and the baby, returning as the vast translucent sky darkened to mauve after sunset. After the air conflict had begun, the occasional sighting of aircraft, the glint of sunlight on a distant Spitfire or Hurricane. And, later, the ominous night-time sound of the bombers. Every boy claimed to know the difference from the steady drone of the Allied aircraft and the limping note of the incoming Germans.

'On Sundays,' she went on, 'we used to cycle up to some old gravel pits that had been flooded for swimming. We'd take a picnic and make a day of it. Paul wanted to stay on at school but didn't know if his parents could afford it, and he'd found some summer work in one of the local factories. I'd started in the offices of the local bus company – basic clerking stuff. Most of us had a bit of money to spend. Not that there was much to spend it on. But the pits were a popular haunt that summer, though not particularly with me.'

'Why not?'

'The place gave me the creeps. It was a bleak spot, even in summer, in the middle of woodland. And you got some dubious characters hanging around. Probably hoping to get a glimpse of teenagers in their swimsuits. I don't know. The lake was icy and much deeper than you expected. We weren't really supposed to swim there – there'd been a couple of drownings or near drownings. But that just made it more attractive.'

Her eyes were glazed, as if fixed on some point in the far distance. 'So what happened with Paul's brother?'

'We'd been up there for the afternoon, four or five of us. Taken some sandwiches. Done a bit of swimming, a bit of sunbathing. Sitting around chatting, the way you do at that age. Talking about the war. What else was there to talk about? That awful Mr Hitler and what was going to happen next. The boys all pretended to have some inside knowledge. But they worried about how long it would go on, whether they'd be called up. Anyway, it got to five o'clock and we thought we should head back. It's a good half-hour's cycle ride – probably more, when I think about it. We'd gone about half a mile or so, and I was chatting away to Paul as we rode, and then somebody noticed Gary wasn't there.'

'He'd been with you all afternoon?'

'Gary was a bit of a monkey. There was no harm in him, but he was always messing around, trying to impress his big brother. He'd been pulling stupid stunts all afternoon. Dive-bombing people in the water, that kind of thing. Paul had got fed up with him. When it was time to leave, Gary had played up. Didn't want to go, kept jumping back in the water. You know how kids are.'

'What happened when you realised he wasn't with you?'

'Paul was livid. He told us to carry on while he went to find him. But in the end I went with him.' Her expression suggested she was willing herself back to that day. 'There was no sign of him. We didn't even know whether he'd started off with us and peeled off, or whether he'd not been with us at all. We hunted around, but there was no sign. Paul was tearing his hair out. He didn't know whether to be furious because Gary was playing some joke, or worried he wasn't there. We went around shouting and then debated whether we should just set off home anyway and leave him to catch us up. Paul was getting really worried by this time.' There were tears in her eyes.

'What did you think?'

'I thought at first Paul was making a mountain out of a molehill. I was sure Gary would just jump out from somewhere. Then I thought he might have gone back in the water. Had some accident there.'

'What about his clothes? Did you find them?'

'They were never found. But we did finally find his bike and his bag. They'd just been left there, a little way from the pits. That was when Paul decided he was going to contact the police. There was no station nearby, so we ended up cycling into town.' She stood up suddenly, as if she could no longer go on with the story. 'I'll make us a cup of tea.'

'Finish the story first.'

'I don't know if any of this matters.'

'Neither do I, but we don't know where Paul is, and we don't have any other ideas about where to start looking for him.'

She lowered herself back down on to the sofa. 'Okay, I'll keep it short. We went to the police. At first, they didn't take us seriously. They thought Gary would be playing games. But when they realised that Paul was genuinely concerned, they came out. They got a car to take me and Paul home – which meant we broke the news to Mam, and then she had to try to get a message to Paul and Gary's parents. Well, you can imagine…' She slowed and took a breath. 'They got a proper search going that night, brought in volunteers to help. A day or two later they got divers in to search the lake.'

'But found nothing?'

'Not a trace, apart from the bicycle and the bag. Paul felt they were less thorough than they should have been. He thought they'd decided early on that Gary was at the bottom of that lake, and they were just going through the motions.'

'If you've got limited resources, you have to play the odds. They might have been right.'

'I've told myself that a thousand times. In the end, they decided that Gary had managed to slip and fall in, still fully clothed. It was plausible enough. I could imagine him falling out a tree or something like that.'

'But Paul thought differently.'

'At first he persuaded himself the police were probably right. He blamed himself dreadfully. I don't know what his parents said when they came rushing over, but it didn't help. I think they blamed him as well.'

'Easier than blaming themselves. They were the ones responsible for sending Paul and Gary over here.'

'Maybe. But Paul was all too ready to blame himself anyway, without anyone helping him along. I felt guilty as well. I felt we should have kept a better eye on Gary.'

'From what you've said, that was never easy.'

'He was just a child. We knew how reckless he could be.'

'What happened with Paul?'

'He became obsessed. He'd told the police about some man he thought he'd seen hanging about earlier in the day, but they didn't take much notice. There'd been people coming and going all day – other youngsters like us, a couple of hikers, someone walking a dog. Even if there was someone, there was no reason to assume it was anyone sinister.'

'But it's possible?'

'Oh, it's possible, all right. It's that sort of spot. We all thought the area attracted more than its fair share of dubious characters. But there was no real evidence.'

'There's no real evidence Gary drowned either.'

'That's the trouble. If they'd ever found Gary's body…' She swallowed, again choking back emotion. 'But it drove Paul mad. Almost literally. He became fixated on it. He used to cycle up there, over and over again, searching the area. He'd stop passers-by and ask them if they'd been there that Sunday and if they'd seen anything. He visited the neighbouring houses. In the end, he gave up his job to spend more time there.'

'How long did this go on?'

'All that summer. Two or three months, I suppose. Eventually, the police had a quiet word with him because they'd had complaints. But everyone was sympathetic. He was wearing himself out. He was behaving – well, not normally. He had no other life, did nothing else. His parents were getting worried. Mam was getting worried. He was still living over here with us. We got the doctor out to see him. Nervous exhaustion, he reckoned, whatever that meant. Recommended Paul should rest but of course he didn't. But then he collapsed. He was coming back from yet another trip to the lake on his pushbike. No one knew what happened. Paul couldn't remember afterwards. We think he just blacked out. Fell off the bike and it looked as if he was hit by a car though no one ever came forward. He was lucky someone found him. He was quite badly injured. Broke his leg and both wrists and he was very badly bruised. But it was a blessing in disguise. He was in hospital for two or three weeks, and spent months recuperating. He was champing at the bit but he just had to lie there. It gave him the time he needed to get over it.'

'Unlucky though, at one level.'

'How do you mean?'

'Being hit by a car. I mean round here the roads aren't so busy that you're generally in much danger as a cyclist. The car must have been very close to him.'

'We thought that. But there were no witnesses, and Paul couldn't remember anything, so it didn't seem worth pursuing. Paul was okay in the end, which was all we cared about.'

'But he never accepted that Gary had drowned?'

'Not entirely. He was a lot more balanced after the accident. But he still thought Gary had been snatched. He'd more or less accepted that Gary must be dead by now – he hadn't wanted to believe that at first – but he still believed his death hadn't been an accident.' She rose. 'I'm going to make that tea now, whether you like it or not.'

'I wouldn't dream of trying to stop you. But let me give you a hand.'

He followed her into the kitchen. Mrs Griffiths was sitting reading a library book. The two children were playing Ludo at the other end of the table.

'You don't mind if the inspector stays again tonight, do you, Mam?

'Not at all.' Mrs Griffiths smiled at him. 'I feel happier with a man about the place. Especially a policeman.'

'It's good of you to let me stay again. I said to Mary that I'll pass on some of my ration. I never get through it all anyway.'

Mrs Griffiths looked as if she was about to object, but then nodded. 'Every little helps these days. But only if you can spare it.'

'Mary was just telling me about DC Marsh,' Winterman said. Mary was looking at him from across the room as she busied herself with the kettle, but Winterman avoided her eye. 'I hadn't realised he was part of the family. I'd have made him stay here instead of me.'

'Don't be daft. Paul's welcome to stay anytime. Though we don't see as much of him as we used to.'

'I haven't seen much of him at work yet, but he seems to have the makings of an excellent detective.' It was largely flannel and no doubt Mary would see straight through it, but it was the kind of thing proud aunts liked to hear. And it was true enough, from the little that Winterman had seen.

'He works hard,' Mrs Griffiths said. 'And he never gives up.'

'That's certainly a major requirement in our line of work. A lot of it's about not giving up. He's a bright lad.'

'He is that. A bit too bright, sometimes. Always thinks he knows best.'

'He's in the right job then.' Winterman could feel Mary watching him, silently imploring him to leave her mother and follow her into the front room. 'We'll leave you to it, Mrs Griffiths. I'm just chatting to Mary about one or two work things.'

'You two go on.' She gazed back at Winterman, her face smiling but her eyes unrevealing.

He suddenly felt as if she could see right through him. Although quite what she could see, he had no idea.

CHAPTER FIFTY-FOUR

His own ghost story.

In the dark, the phrase drifted in and out of his mind, like a shred of a forgotten dream.

It could have been a ghost itself, the grey figure looming out of the swirling snow. He had been followed but that didn't really surprise him. His senses were dulled by the evening's drinking, and he was still unsure what had led him back up into the churchyard – perhaps, unconsciously, he had sensed someone else there. But he had seen the figure only in the moment before the blow had struck him, something black and heavy swinging out of the whirling darkness.

He had woken to a different darkness. Inside or at least under shelter. The ground under him was hard – rough flagstones, he thought. Somewhere he could hear an ominous scratching and scuffling – the sound of mice or rats.

He dragged himself to his feet. In the dark, his hand brushed against a wooden surface. A table or workbench. He grasped it, nearly falling as it rocked unsteadily under his weight, then fumbled his way along its length, bumping up against a rough stone wall. He shuffled further along the wall, his fingers traversing the coarsely hewn surface, once grazing themselves on an embedded metal hook. Finally, his hand reached a different surface – uneven planks of wood, several feet across, reaching high above him. A door, or at least a wooden covering where an entrance should be. He slid his hands across the surface, wood splinters stinging his skin, seeking a handle. There was nothing. He found the far edge and tried to dig his fingertips under the wood, but there was no give.

He continued his stumbling way past the doorway in the hope of finding an alternative exit. In a few minutes more, he had determined that he was in a small stone-built room with no apparent way out beyond the covered panel he had already discovered. He had bumped up against several objects – wooden crates, a broken stool, some piece of rusty machinery. An outbuilding or barn, then.

He stood still and listened. The scratching sounds had ceased, but he could hear something else. He moved back closer to the wooden door. It was the ceaseless drumming of rain, occasionally heightened as a buffeting wind blew it harder against the woodwork. Doubting his senses, he moved to the edge of the door and held his face to the narrow gap between wood and stone. There was no question. He could feel the stream of damp air against his skin, hear the pounding of the rain.

For a moment, he felt an odd sense of relief, as if, with the change in the weather, everything had changed, as if he were some fairy-tale character who had fallen asleep and woken into a different world.

The sensation vanished as quickly as it had arisen. He was lost, cold and trapped. And, though he knew nothing else, he knew he must have been brought there for a reason.

CHAPTER FIFTY-FIVE

Winterman was still at the window, transfixed by the falling rain, when he heard a soft knock at the bedroom door. He felt his way across the darkened room to find the tartan dressing gown Mary had left for him. It had, he assumed, belonged to her late husband. He pulled it on, unsure how he felt about that.

He opened the door to find Mary standing on the landing. She was wearing a dressing gown which looked disturbingly like the twin of the one she had loaned to him.

'I heard you moving about,' she said. 'I was woken by the rain.'

'Spooner was right about a change in the weather. I hadn't expected anything quite so sudden.'

She led Winterman back across the room to the window. 'I'd begun to feel as if the snow would be here forever. And now it feels as if this will never stop.'

'If it carries on, the snow'll be gone by morning. Though that might bring its own problems.'

'How do you mean?'

'Flooding. With all this rain and the melting snow. And the ground will still be frozen.' He moved to stand beside her. It was growing lighter outside. He glanced at his watch. Nearly five.

She turned slightly. 'It's strange. That dressing gown's been through the wash a dozen times, but it still smells faintly of Jimmy.'

Winterman could think of no immediate response. Finally, he said, 'You must miss him.'

'I suppose I do. I mean, I do. I was desolate when it first happened. For months. It just seemed so ridiculous. I was going to say unfair, but when was death ever fair? It's just that it seemed such a pointless way to die.'

'Tell me about him. You were going to say something earlier.' After they had eaten supper, while her mother had been putting the children to bed, Mary had started to talk about Jimmy. But Mrs Griffiths had returned and Mary had changed the subject.

'I was going to tell you about Jimmy and Paul,' she said. 'You know Jimmy was in the force?'

'Someone told me that.'

'Hoxton probably. More of a gossip than Mam, he is.'

'So I'd noticed. Where did you meet Jimmy?'

'I'm honestly not sure I can remember. Some dance or other, I expect. I'd been aware of him for years, while I was still a girl really. I used to see him around, a few years older than me. You'd notice him. You would if you were a girl anyway. Touch of the matinée idol about him.'

Winterman felt another irrational prick of jealousy, and had to remind himself the man in question was long deceased.

'We didn't start seeing each other till after he'd got back from Dunkirk. He was still stationed in England – he said while they decided what to do with him. I met him a couple of times when he was home on leave, and he made a play for me eventually. We went out a few times. Not exactly courting. Not at first anyway. But we got on. And… well, you know how these things go.'

Winterman wasn't sure he did. His own amorous conquests had generally been just that. Conquests. Not a gradual blooming, as Mary was describing.

'He'd joined the police before the war. He'd done a few things since leaving school – factory jobs, mainly. But he was wasting his abilities. He wasn't academically bright, but he'd got a decent head on his shoulders. He'd have made something of himself.' She stopped for a moment, and took a breath, as if she had only just registered the implications of her words. 'Anyway, he did well. Just a PC on the beat, you know. But making good progress. He wanted to try for the sergeants' exam. Then the war came along.'

'How did he come to join up? The police was a reserved occupation.'

'He was a military reservist. He was in the Territorials. He'd talked about joining the army before the war. I don't think he could ever have stuck being at home while other people were out doing their bit for King and Country. That wasn't the sort of person he was.'

Winterman said nothing. He had shared the same sentiments himself, back in '39, but for most police officers, joining up wasn't an option. Gwyneth had worked hard to persuade him, not just that he should think of her and the children, but that he could play just as useful a role in the police. He hadn't really believed it then and he didn't believe it now.

'He was at Dunkirk?' he said.

'He never really talked about it. People expected him to have the usual raft of stories, but he just kept mum.'

'Lots of people did. Those who made it.'

'He was different after Dunkirk. That's what people told me. I didn't know him before, not properly. But people said he'd been more carefree, content just to let life happen. When I met him, you sensed he wanted to get on with things. He was frustrated they kept him hanging about, as he saw it, for months on end in some camp.'

'You married quickly?'

'That was part of it. I met Jimmy at the end of that summer, the summer Gary went missing. I was seventeen by then. Jimmy had spent the months after Dunkirk on manoeuvres. There was a plan to send them off to Greece, supposedly, but nobody knew when it was going to happen. Jimmy had an extended leave and we started going out much more seriously. Before he went back, he'd proposed. Dad had died before the war, Mam didn't know what to think. It was a strange time. Everything had a sense of urgency about it. So I said yes. He went back to camp and came back again on leave after Christmas. We took the opportunity and tied the knot.' She smiled. 'It wasn't really the wedding I'd envisaged, but it was fine. Honeymoon was a night in Skegness.' She blushed slightly. 'And the result was the twins.'

'Did he go off to Greece?'

'It never happened. Not for Jimmy anyway. There was a change of plan. Wasn't clear what was scheduled for Jimmy's regiment after that. There were plenty of rumours, but they ended up kicking their heels on Salisbury Plain. It meant he got a few more spells of leave. He was able to see the twins.' She stopped, catching her breath again.

'What about Paul? He was still around? Was he never called up?'

'He wasn't eighteen till '43. Then they turned him down on health grounds, would you believe? The official line was that he suffered from asthma. He did, but I've never seen it affect him. I suspect they decided he wasn't mentally stable after what happened with Gary.'

'I don't know if that would be grounds for keeping him out of the services,' Winterman said. 'Some might see it as a qualification.'

'Anyway, they turned him down. But he was already keen on joining the police. They were taking cadets at sixteen because of the shortage of manpower. It was because he idolised Jimmy. Paul and Jimmy got on like a house on fire. I used to joke that Jimmy was only courting me so he could spend time talking to Paul about life in the force. I'm sure Jimmy would have gone back to the police after the war.' Her eyes were fixed on the rain-soaked landscape, but it wasn't clear what she was seeing.

'Had Paul got over what had happened to Gary?'

'Not entirely. He still believed that Gary hadn't drowned, that his death wasn't an accident. It was one of the things he talked to Jimmy about.'

'And Jimmy believed him?'

'Not exactly. But he took Paul seriously. He reckoned there'd been a few incidents up at the gravel pits – children being approached by strangers – before the war. There was even, going back a few years, a missing child.'

'Missing child?' In his mind's eye, Winterman could see the empty sockets of the children's skulls they had found.

'This was ages ago. I don't know – '36, '37, something like that. Somewhere up there. Jimmy reckoned they'd eventually found the child's body, dumped in a ditch, but they'd never solved the crime. Anyway, he was inclined to take Paul's ideas more seriously than most.'

'Including the police?'

'Including the police. But, as Jimmy said, the police were so short-handed they weren't looking for trouble. I'm not saying he thought Paul was right. But he thought it should have been investigated. That was why he started digging on his own.'

Winterman had assumed, since Mary had raised Jimmy's name, that her narrative was leading somewhere. 'What sort of digging?'

'Oh, not a lot. He was only home on leave for short periods. He called up some old colleagues. Spoke to a few of his local contacts.'

'Did he find anything?'

She hesitated. 'I'm not sure. Nothing concrete. But the last time he was here – I mean, the last time before...'

Winterman nodded. 'Go on.'

'A couple of nights before he went back, he met someone for a beer. One of his contacts. I don't know who. I got annoyed about it, because I wanted to be with him as much as possible before the end of his leave. He arrived home, a bit tipsy, to say he'd some information that would be of interest to Paul. He was being slightly secretive, which wasn't his style at all. Said he didn't want to say too much until he'd found out a bit more. Didn't want to get Paul's hopes up, I suppose.'

'Did he say anything to Paul?'

'I don't think so. Nothing of substance anyway. They spoke the next day and I remember Jimmy saying he was making some progress. But nothing else.'

'Do you think there was anything to it?'

'I do actually. Not necessarily that he'd found out anything important. But he'd got wind of something. I could tell when he came back from the pub. He was excited – no, that's not right. He'd got the bit between his teeth. That was the feeling I had.'

'But he gave no clue what it was?'

'No. He was a lot quieter the next day, once the beer had worn off. I asked him about it, and he said he'd put out a few feelers and was hoping to get some information back. That was the last he said about it. Then he went back.'

There was a moment's silence, disturbed only by the continuous washing of the rain against the window.

'I shouldn't have brought all this up,' Winterman said finally.

'No, it's fine. It's all behind me now. Sometimes I miss him dreadfully. But most of the time it's like another life. He left the next day, and three days later he was dead.'

'A training accident?'

'George must have told you. Did he tell you I went mad?'

'He said you took it badly.'

'I was devastated. It took me totally off guard. I don't really even know why. I mean, he was a soldier. We were at war. I knew that, sometime, I might have to face something like that.'

'It never makes it any easier.'

'No, and it wasn't just that. He'd come through Dunkirk pretty much unscathed. He'd had one or two other near misses. I thought he had a charmed life. If he'd been sent off to fight again, I imagine I'd have started worrying, but I was putting off thinking about that till it actually happened. This came out of the blue. A stupid accident. I just couldn't accept it. I started putting two and two together and making a lot more than four. I was the same as Paul after Gary disappeared. I convinced myself Jimmy's enquiries had ruffled some feathers. That it wasn't an accident.'

'It would take a lot to organise that,' Winterman pointed out. 'Do you know who actually fired the gun?'

'They hushed it up, which at the time made me even more certain that there was something fishy about it.'

'They kept the lid on countless training foul-ups during the war. To prevent damage to morale,' he added, in a fake BBC voice. 'To stop the top brass looking stupid, more likely. There's nothing particularly sinister in that.'

'Oh, I know. But at the time it all seemed very cloak and dagger. At first, they wouldn't tell me how he'd been killed. Then when I kept pressing them, they admitted he'd been shot, and finally they admitted it had been in training. But they insisted he'd been caught by a stray bullet, that they had no idea who'd fired it.'

'It's possible. Those exercises can be a melee. In fairness, they're trying to replicate the real thing. But they might have just been sparing the feelings of whoever was responsible.'

'It wouldn't have helped me to have known. But it didn't feel like that at the time. It felt like adding insult to injury. It just increased my suspicions.'

Winterman gazed at her for a moment, taking in for the first time the rich chocolate brown of her eyes, the flawless cream of her skin. 'Life's just a series of accidents. Mine is anyway.'

She nodded, her eyes fixed on his. 'All you can do is make the best of whatever's thrown at you.' Then she added, in little more than a whisper: 'Kiss me.'

For a moment, he thought he'd misheard her or that his own wishful thinking was leading him astray. Then she raised her lips and he realised that, for once in his romantic life, someone else was making the moves. *All you can do*, he echoed to himself, *is make the best of whatever's thrown at you.*

As he moved forward, he heard the rain redoubling its torrents, pounding on the windows and roof. But his body, finally, had cast off the chains.

CHAPTER FIFTY-SIX

Brain woke early, his head aching and his brain still befuddled by the whisky he and Hoxton had polished off the previous night. He had been secretly overjoyed when Hoxton had turned up in the early evening seeking accommodation for a second night. Brain's day had been pretty miserable, spent, for the most part, standing in the frozen church to no worthwhile purpose. The arrival of Carson and the HQ team had provided short-lived relief, but boredom had quickly been replaced by irritation at the supercilious disdain of the CID team. The sense of inclusion he had felt working with Winterman had melted away, and Brain was very firmly put in his place. Which, unsurprisingly, was back standing by the churchyard gate.

He had waited, as he had promised, until the ambulance arrived to collect the child's remains. Then, as evening fell, he had made his solitary way back to the station, reconciled to another evening alone. He assumed Marsh would have reappeared and Winterman and the rest would have returned to town.

Hoxton's arrival had therefore been both an unexpected pleasure and a source of concern, since it confirmed that Marsh had still not been traced.

'I thought he'd have turned up by now,' Brain said as he ushered Hoxton into the warmth of the station.

'So did we. Don't know what the bugger's done with himself.' It was difficult to know whether Hoxton's gruff exterior concealed any more tender response.

'You've not reported him missing?'

'Not yet. He's probably got his reasons for making himself scarce.' Hoxton made his way, blank-faced, through into the living room. 'But if he's not turned up by tomorrow, we'll have to do something.'

Whatever might have happened to Marsh, it was a pleasant enough evening for Brain. Hoxton, despite his surly demeanour, was good company, a fount of anecdotes about his career in the police service. They retired to the pub for a couple of pints and a plate of Norman's Spam sandwiches, and then, late in the evening, returned to the station with a bottle of whisky which Hoxton had somehow persuaded Norman to sell them. It was after midnight before they finally finished the Scotch and thought about turning in for the night.

Brain had been rising to begin locking up when Hoxton had held up his hand as if to silence the younger man. 'What's that noise?'

'I don't hear anything.' But even as Brain spoke, he realised there was something, though he couldn't immediately identify the sound.

'You got dodgy plumbing in this place? Or is it spooks? Sounds like someone running a bath upstairs.'

'Nothing wrong with the plumbing that I'm aware of. Wouldn't be surprised if this place was haunted, but I've seen no signs so far.'

Hoxton made no response, but climbed to his feet and stepped over to the front window. 'Good God. Come and look at this.'

It was the rain, of course. There had been no clue of its imminent arrival even when they had left the pub a couple of hours before. Brain moved past Hoxton, out into the hallway, and pulled open the front door.

The scent of the damp air hit him immediately. It was startlingly different from the icy cold that had been omnipresent for weeks – warmer, more welcoming. He was almost tempted to step out into it, despite the torrents of rain clattering down the street. In an upper window of the house opposite, another silhouetted figure was staring out into the night, marvelling at this extraordinary transformation.

'Would you ever have believed it?' Hoxton said from behind him.

'It's amazing. I've never seen weather like it.'

'It's been that sort of bloody year, hasn't it? Coldest winter on record, and now this. Christ knows what it'll do to the rivers.'

Flooding was a constant threat in these parts. A small rise in the levels of the local rivers was enough to send water washing across the endless flatlands. The fenlands the Dutch had helped reclaim in the seventeenth century were always under threat, but that was expected and, in general, under control. The bigger problems occurred when the levels rose still higher and the water encroached beyond the traditional flood plains into more inhabited areas. Brain had encountered several floods in his time in the police and the experience was never pleasant. He was always astonished that water could do so much damage, be quite so eerily threatening.

'Let's hope it lets up quickly,' he said.

Hoxton peered past him, staring up into the heavy night sky. 'Don't see much signs of it. Reckon this lot's in for the night at least.'

Hoxton's pessimistic prediction had proved accurate. Brain had woken two or three times in the night to hear the steady drumming of the rain on the slate roof. He was conscious Hoxton was also likely to be right about the risk of flooding. Unlikely as it might have seemed even twenty-four hours previously, they might soon come to regard the snow as a relatively minor inconvenience compared with what was coming.

Brain was always an early riser. His experience was that, especially in a farming community, the public's demands on its constabulary could begin well before dawn. This morning, the combination of anxiety and the previous night's whisky woke him even earlier than usual. His mouth was dry and his head aching, but it took him several seconds to work out that the real source of his worries lay elsewhere.

He had hoped he might wake to blue sky through the bedroom window. But his hopes had not been realised. It was not yet light, but that was partly because the sky remained as leaden as ever. The rain was pounding incessantly against the glass.

Brain rolled over in the single bed and looked at the alarm clock. Just after five. He contemplated another half-hour's sleep, but it hardly seemed worth it. He dragged himself from beneath the sheets and stooped to examine his reflection in the dressing table mirror. Not a picture of health. The combination of too much alcohol and too little sleep had left him looking sallow, dark-eyed, generally exhausted.

He pulled on some clothes and made his way downstairs. The large Victorian house was gloomy at the best of times. Even with the landing light on, he could barely see through the murk. Hoxton, he assumed, would still be sleeping. The older man had asked to be woken around seven, in time for a scheduled meeting with Winterman at eight. Their intention was to see where things stood with Marsh – in the hope that he might somehow reappear overnight – and then make a decision on whether to break the news to Spooner.

Brain was near the foot of the stairs, leading down into the hallway, when he heard a voice. He froze, his hand on the banister, for a moment thinking that he had imagined the sound, that it was some illusion created by the unaccustomed rumble of the falling rain. But there was no question. Someone was speaking below.

Without quite knowing why he did so, he remained silent, moving quietly towards the bottom of the stairs, straining his ears.

It was clear that the speaker was in the police office, talking on the phone. Brain hesitated, trying to identify the gruff half-whisper. Had Marsh returned after all?

It took Brain a second longer to recognise the voice as Hoxton's. Brain glanced back up the stairs to the bedroom where he had assumed Hoxton was still sleeping. The door was firmly closed, with no indication that the room was empty.

Still unsure why he had not made his presence known, Brain moved closer to the office doorway.

'I've done enough of your dirty work,' he heard Hoxton say. 'Years of it. I'm not getting involved in this one.'

There was a pause, while Hoxton listened to whatever was being said at the other end of the line. 'You want those courtesies,' he responded finally. 'You can do a bit bloody more to earn them. I'm not one for forelock tugging. I thought you'd have worked that out by now.'

Another pause, then: 'I don't care if he is missing. It would hardly be the first bloody time for that bloody boy. And, no, I don't care to modify my bloody language. Hardly the most important thing just at the moment, I'd have thought.'

Brain stood frozen, mesmerised by what he was hearing. Not so much by the words, as by the tone. This was a different Hoxton from the one he had drunk with the previous night. The gruff amiability and charm had melted away, replaced by a blunter form of plain speaking.

'Anyway,' Hoxton went on, 'he's not the only one gone missing. Bloody Marsh has gone AWOL as well. I don't know, but it seems like a bit of a bloody coincidence, don't you think? They're both loose bloody cannons, if you want my opinion.'

Brain was straining his ears, trying to make sense of what he was hearing. He'd assumed at first that Hoxton was talking about Marsh. So who else was missing? And who was Hoxton talking to? His words and tone didn't sound like those of someone addressing a superior officer.

Hoxton was silent again for a moment, and then he gave a theatrical sigh. 'Okay, you've made your point. As if I'd forgotten. What do you want me to do about it exactly?'

There was movement from inside the office, as if Hoxton was shifting something about – papers or files perhaps. Brain involuntarily took a step back, wondering whether to retreat into the living room or make Hoxton aware of his presence.

After a few seconds, Hoxton spoke again. 'Bloody hell. It's a wild bloody goose chase. He could be anywhere. You don't even know for sure that–' Another pause. 'You've seen the bloody weather, I take it. Cats and dogs. Not exactly the weather for pursuing some half-baked bloody– Okay, okay, I've told you. I've heard all that. You've got me exactly where you bloody want me. I know. There's nothing I can bloody do about it. You tell me to jump, I say how high. Won't stop me from expressing a bloody opinion though. Yes, and the same to you.' There was further silence. 'Okay, I'll go. If it is him, if he does know something, what do you want me to do about it? I don't imagine it's quite so simple when it's that close to home. I–'

There was another, longer silence. Then Brain heard Hoxton replace the receiver. The conversation, whatever it had been, was clearly at an end. Brain silently backed away into the living room and made his way to the kitchen at the rear of the house. He was preparing to turn on the tap and begin loudly filling the kettle, with the aim of suggesting to Hoxton that he had only that minute arrived downstairs.

But there was only silence behind him. After another minute, Brain heard the sound of the front door slamming. He stepped back through into the living room, whistling to alert Hoxton to his presence.

The living room was empty as were the hallway and the police office. Hoxton's overcoat, which had been hanging on the row of hooks by the front door, was gone. So, presumably, was Hoxton, out into the pouring rain. Following whatever instructions he had been given.

Brain opened the front door and peered into the street. The rain was falling harder than ever, an unbroken grey curtain across the village. Torrents of water swirled off the road into the dykes and ditches that lined the fields.

The snow had almost gone. The change from the previous day was startling. The curves of pure white replaced by bare earth and patches of grey slush. Remnants of the thicker drifts clung under the shelter of houses or trees, but even they were dissolving as Brain watched.

There was no sign of the police Wolseley. Hoxton had taken the car and driven – where? Grabbing his own overcoat, Brain hurried towards the edge of the village near the school, from where he could gain a view of the surrounding countryside.

The car was already further away than he had expected, travelling at a fast pace despite the weather, but he could see the flash of the headlights, bright in the gloomy early morning, as it turned along the main road up towards the next village.

There was no way of telling where or how far it was going. Brain looked at his watch. It was five thirty. Hoxton had been scheduled to meet with Winterman at eight. Assuming he was still intending to keep that appointment, he could nevertheless travel some distance and still return in time, particularly at the speed he'd been moving.

Brain could feel the trickle of rainwater down his neck, his soaking hair plastered across his head. He had stuffed his feet into a pair of light summer shoes that had been standing by the front door, and the dampness was already seeping through the thin canvas.

He made his way, at a slow trot, back to the station. He ducked back inside and dug out his cycling cape from the hall cupboard and swapped the canvas shoes for a pair of stout boots. Finally, he grabbed the notepad he kept on his office desk. He scribbled a rapid message and left it prominently on the table in the hallway. Winterman still had the spare keys to the station. If he turned up, he would at least learn immediately where Brain had gone.

Brain let himself out through the rear door. There had once been a garden there, but when the house had been converted into the police station the majority of the land had been sold off to a neighbour. All that remained was a small courtyard, with enough space to hold the rubbish bins and a small shed and coalhouse.

Brain hurried across the courtyard and unlocked the shed door. Inside, he found what he was looking for – the sturdy, police-issue bicycle. He rode it rarely in the winter – and it had not been taken out at all during the weeks of snow – but he kept it well maintained. With his head low against the pounding rain, he wheeled the bike round to the main road before climbing on.

Brain knew he was probably embarking on a wild goose chase. But there was no simple explanation for Hoxton's words and tone on the telephone. Brain was left with a sense that he needed to act urgently, even though he had no idea quite what to do.

He pedalled up the high street, gently at first and then gathering speed as he grew reaccustomed to the bike. In any case, he asked himself, as he pounded onwards, the rain beating against his exposed face, *what's the worst that can happen if I'm wrong?*

The worst that can happen, he thought, *is that I make a complete idiot of myself.* He pressed on, the water already seeping under the collar of his cycling cape.

Or, he added, *I get double pneumonia and die.*

CHAPTER FIFTY-SEVEN

Winterman was standing at the back door, smoking a cigarette, staring out at the steadily falling rain. He could feel the spray cool against his face, the freshness in the air.

'Still coming down?' Mary asked from behind him.

'It's still coming down. Thought you might be getting more sleep.'

'I thought about it. But I was wide awake.'

Winterman took another drag on his cigarette, then pulled out the packet to offer her one.

'Not yet. Cup of tea first, I think.'

'I feel I owe you an apology.'

She nodded, solemnly. 'You were very slow to offer that cigarette.'

'Very good. You know what I mean.'

'The kiss. Well, it takes two to kiss, generally.'

'It does to kiss like that anyway. I thought I was perhaps a bit forward.'

'You know, you're a sad disappointment, DI Winterman.'

'Is that so?'

'I'd heard you were a ruthless womaniser. Now you're worried about being a bit forward.'

He blew a cloud of smoke into the rainy air. 'It could all be part of my subtle seduction technique.'

'Too subtle for me then. To be honest, I was rather hoping we might go further than just a kiss.' Her eyes had moved away from his and were now focused on some point close to the horizon. 'In due course.'

'Is that so? I really must be out of practice.'

'You'll need to put the time in then.'

'Looks like it. If you're willing to help out.'

'That would be good.' She turned back to look at him, hers eyes fixed unblinking on his. 'Seriously, it would be good.'

'In the meantime, there's Paul to worry about.'

'Do you think he's all right?'

'He must be, surely. There've been some odd things going on, but a burly young policeman doesn't just disappear. My guess is he's out there following up some hunch of his own.'

'So where is he?'

'I haven't a clue. I'm going to have to come clean with Spooner today. If Paul is playing some game of his own, Spooner won't be pleased.'

'I assumed Paul was over it. But with these bodies…'

'He might have thought that, if these children's bodies could appear out of nowhere, perhaps Gary's could too?'

'Or at least that Gary's body might still be out there somewhere.'

'Poor bugger,' Winterman said. 'Both of them. Poor Gary and poor Paul.'

'It's the not knowing. After Gary disappeared Paul used to go from one extreme to the other. One day, buoyed up by the hope that Gary might be alive after all, the next day filled with the worst kinds of fears.'

Winterman's face was expressionless. 'At least with Sam, I've no illusions. I know exactly what happened to him.' He could see, in his mind's eye, the small beckoning figure that haunted his dreams.

'Oh, Ivan. I'm sorry. I wasn't thinking.'

'No. It's true. What happened was awful but it's better than not knowing. At least I can mourn properly.' He looked at his watch, keen to move the conversation on. 'I need to be off soon. I said I'd meet Hoxton at the station at eight. We'll decide what to do. Spooner and his people are meeting us at nine.' He gestured towards the pouring rain. 'This should make things easier, for the moment at least. We should be able to get things moving at last. Put the investigation on a proper footing.'

'You'll tell Spooner about Paul?'

'If Paul doesn't turn up this morning, I've no choice. I don't want to land Paul in it. But if he really is in some sort of trouble, I'd never forgive myself.'

'You'd better go. Maybe he's turned up at the station.'

He followed her back into the kitchen. 'You'll be okay?'

'Why wouldn't I be? You're the one braving the rain.' She looked up at the kitchen clock. 'Mind you, so will I. If the snow's gone and the buses are running again, I'll head into the office. It's not one of my days, but I've missed a lot of time lately.'

'I'd be surprised if the buses are running yet. It'll all be in chaos. With the risk of flooding, they'll probably keep them off the roads anyway. If it's not one of your days, I'd make the most of it. In fact, treat that as an instruction. I don't want you going out there today. Not with the weather like this.'

'I hope you're not letting personal feelings intrude on your official duties. Anyway, I'm not sure it's in your gift. Officially I report to Mrs Sheringham.'

'Mrs Sheringham's not here. I'll have to deputise. And, no, it's nothing personal. Just the boss's duty of pastoral care.'

'Fair enough. I'll stay here and walk the kids down to the school. We'll see whether there's any chance of that opening today.'

Winterman smiled, but there was a look of concern in his eyes. 'Take care.' Then he added, scarcely knowing what he was saying, 'I've lost enough already.'

She looked back at him, unspeaking. Finally she nodded. 'I'll take care.'

CHAPTER FIFTY-EIGHT

Somehow he had fallen asleep again. He opened his eyes, lying cramped and awkward on the stone floor. How was it possible for him to have slept?

In any case, the sleep had left him feeling no better. His body was aching, his limbs stiff, his mind fogged by confusion. He pushed himself to a sitting position, his fingers slipping unpleasantly on damp leaves and vegetation.

The darkness was less intense. As his mind cleared, he began to discern pale slender lines of light. Daylight creeping in through gaps in the structure. Along the edges of the door, past the shuttered window, between ill-fitting roof tiles.

Morning then. He clambered to his feet and stumbled towards the brightest strip of light – down one edge of the large doors he had identified in the darkness. He heard again the sound he had recognised in the night. Falling rain.

He pressed his eye to the narrow gap. He could make out little. But he could taste the dampness of the air, frustratingly enticing as he realised how thirsty he was.

The room was largely as he had imagined it. An outbuilding or barn, brick built, with solid looking walls broken only by a large door built of heavy wood. In lieu of an internal handle, a link of chain was screwed into the wood. He grabbed this and pulled. The door gave slightly, but it was fastened or padlocked on the outside.

There was little else in the room. The few discarded items of old furniture he had stumbled into in the dark, a scattering of rusty agricultural machinery. In the far corner, a loose heap of straw.

He was about to take a closer look at the door and window, when he heard the clattering of a chain being rattled, the squeak of the door beginning to move. He backed to the far wall, looking around for something he could use as a weapon. He stooped and grasped a broken piece of metal piping, feeling the satisfactory weight of it in his hand.

The door slowly opened, its bottom edge scraping noisily on the rough stone floor, and a shaft of grubby looking daylight penetrated the room.

CHAPTER FIFTY-NINE

Winterman raised the knocker a third time and slammed it down heavily, hearing the loud boom echoing through the interior of the station. He glanced at his watch. Five past eight.

Where the bloody hell was Hoxton? For that matter, where was Brain? Surely they hadn't both overslept. More likely, something had called them out already.

He gave the knocker a fourth, half-hearted slam, then fumbled inside his overcoat. He was already soaked. He had given up on his umbrella after it had been blown repeatedly inside out by the drenching wind. His police overcoat had offered little protection against the deluge. The rain was dripping off his hat, icy rivulets running down inside his collar.

He pulled out the keys. It took him several minutes, his fingers trembling with the damp cold, but he finally pushed the door open.

Inside, it was warmer and much drier. He dragged off his raincoat and hat, throwing them on to one of the coat hooks beside the door. He could sense already that the station was deserted, but he called Hoxton's and Brain's names in the vague hope that one of them might appear.

He was about to walk through into the police office when he caught sight of the note folded on the hall table, his own name scrawled across it. He opened it and read Brain's ill-formed writing: 'DC Hoxton's taken the car after odd telephone call. Have followed on bike. West out the village towards Welstone.'

Winterman shook his head. The note meant nothing to him. Where had Hoxton taken the car? What sort of odd telephone call? How was Brain proposing to follow a police car on a bicycle?

But something about the words made him feel uneasy. Some thought about Hoxton had begun to nag at his mind, though he couldn't pin down the source of his concern.

He presumed there had been no sign of Marsh, unless that was the explanation for Hoxton's "odd" call. In any case, there was nothing much Winterman could do until the others returned. Except think about how he was going to break it all to Spooner.

He made his way through to the office. He could at least call Mrs Sheringham and see if she had any news of Marsh. He was behind Brain's desk, his finger poised in the telephone dial, when he heard a voice from out in the hallway.

'Anybody home? Hope you buggers aren't still in bed.'

For a moment, Winterman thought it was Hoxton. Then he recognised the voice and rose to his feet, just as Spooner pushed open the door. Spooner's stocky body was bundled up in a heavy overcoat, a wide-brimmed hat pulled low over his forehead. He appeared relatively untouched by the rain.

'Sir.'

Spooner regarded him for a second, as if surprised by Winterman's presence. Then he pulled off the hat and unbuttoned the coat.

'Winterman. Didn't know if you'd be down here yet.'

'Just got here. I was calling the office.'

'Don't let me stop you.' Spooner strode across the room in a manner that suggested he had no serious expectation Winterman would go ahead with the call.

'No hurry, sir. Only picking up messages.'

Spooner nodded, gazing curiously around the room. 'Runs a tight ship, young Brain. Or a tidy one at any rate.'

'He seems well organised.' Winterman gestured towards the window. 'You were right about the weather.'

'Bit more dramatic than I'd imagined.' Spooner placed his coat across the back of the chair facing Brain's desk. He lowered himself into the chair and sat facing Winterman.

'You're earlier than we expected,' Winterman said.

'Early bird and all that. Truth is, I'd got up early to allow for the snow, then I realised the bugger had more or less gone. So I thought I might as well head down here anyway. See what was what.' He put an additional emphasis on the last four words, as if to imbue them with a particular significance. 'Where is everyone? Don't tell me I've got to go and rouse them.'

'I don't think so. PC Brain left a note. He and DC Hoxton have gone out on some business. Don't imagine they'll be long.'

'Up with the lark, eh? Country types. What sort of business would that be then?'

'Brain didn't really say.'

'You lot all stayed down here last night then? Cosy.'

'It seemed sensible. With the snow.'

Spooner nodded absently. 'What do you think of me, Winterman?' The question was abrupt, unexpected, a non sequitur.

'We haven't really worked together, sir. I'm not sure I can express an opinion.'

'No, I don't suppose you can. Which is probably just as well for both of us.' Spooner leaned forward across the desk, still smiling. 'But I could express an opinion for you, if you like.'

Winterman shrugged, but said nothing.

'The thing is, DI Winterman, you've got me lumped in with the rest of them.'

'I'm not sure I understand, sir.'

'You're not sure, are you? You're usually pretty sure about things, from what I hear, DI Winterman. Pretty sharp is what I hear.'

'If you say so, sir.'

'I've heard all about you, Winterman. High-flyer. Though not flying too high just at the moment.' He glanced round the office, his expression suggesting, perhaps, that a village police station was the appropriate level for Winterman.

'I don't think I'd ever have described myself in that way,' Winterman said.

'Plenty of others happy to do it for you. In the old days, at least.'

'With respect, sir, I'm not sure where this is leading.'

'You don't think much of me, Winterman, do you?'

Winterman could think of no response. He pushed back his chair, looking for a way to bring the dialogue to a close.

'You're not stupid,' Spooner went on, 'so I don't imagine you think I am either. But you think I'm unethical. Slapdash. More interested in furthering my own career and protecting my backside than in solving crimes. And you think I'm like the rest of them.'

Winterman remained silent. The conversation had reached the point where nothing he might say would make any difference to wherever Spooner was heading.

'I know what happened to you, Winterman. Word gets around. I know you ruffled feathers. I know your career got canned as a result. I suppose I almost admire you for it, even though you must have been a bloody idiot.'

Winterman looked up. There was a new tone to Spooner's voice, traces of a warmth that hadn't been evident before.

'I'm not like you, Winterman. You're right that my main objective is to look after number one. You wouldn't catch me doing what you did. Climbing out on a limb with a saw clutched firmly in my hand.'

'My motives weren't wholly altruistic, sir. As you're no doubt aware.'

'Aye. No doubt they weren't entirely altruistic,' Spooner echoed, a tinge of mockery colouring the last two words. 'But you did it. Most of us don't have… well, whatever it is. Courage. Recklessness. Stupidity. But just because we don't, it doesn't mean we're in the other camp. Most of us are just doing our jobs as best we can, while not buggering up our chances of taking home a pension at the end of it all.'

'I recognise that, sir.'

'Do you, Winterman? I hope so. Someone like you, you need to know who your friends are.'

'I didn't seem to have many friends. Not so's you notice anyway.'

'More than you think. If you'd give a few of the buggers the time of day.' Spooner pushed himself back in the chair, its legs creaking alarmingly. 'For a start, don't treat me like a bloody idiot.'

'I wasn't aware that I had been, sir.'

'Really? Let's start with your two mates here – Hoxton and Brain. You reckon they've gone out on some business, but you don't know what. For some reason, you and Hoxton decided to stay over here last night. I find you down here in the station at sparrow's fart. Now why do I think there might be something you're not telling me?'

'I don't know where they've gone, sir.' Winterman was beginning to recognise he might have misjudged Spooner. Or at least underestimated him. He pushed Brain's note slowly across the desk towards Spooner.

Spooner picked up the scrap of lined paper and scanned the words. Then he looked up quizzically at Winterman.

'Your guess is as good as mine, sir.'

Spooner frowned. 'What do you make of Hoxton?'

'Don't know, really.' Winterman gave the matter a moment's consideration. 'Salt of the earth copper, or that's the impression he'd like to give. Seems to know everyone in these parts. Bit of a gossip, but good at sucking up all the fag ends of information. Pretty smart. After a few weeks I couldn't say much more.'

'Do you trust him?'

'I've no reason not to trust him.'

'No, me neither. But I don't.' Spooner leaned back on the chair, tipping it so that it rested only on its rear legs. For a moment, Winterman was afraid the wooden frame would splinter under him. 'Maybe that bluff man of the people act's a bit too neat to be true.'

'I'm not sure I'm quite following this, sir.' Winterman pushed himself to his feet. 'Shall I make us some tea?' He felt that some kind of physical move might help him regain control of the dialogue.

'Why not? We can't do much till your chaps get back. I've suggested we meet up with my team here at around ten. Start to think about how we're actually going to tackle all this.' He dropped the chair back onto the ground and followed Winterman through into the kitchen. 'If that wouldn't be treading on your toes.'

Winterman was busying himself filling the kettle, tracking down Brain's teapot. He glanced back and surveyed Spooner's face for any trace of irony, but the other man was smiling benignly.

'We need all the help we can get, frankly.'

Spooner lowered himself on to an even more fragile chair than those in the police office and gazed at Winterman across the kitchen table. 'Aye. We all need to pull together on this one. Speaking of which, what's happened to your chap Marsh?'

Winterman was rummaging in the kitchen cupboard, searching for tea. The activity bought him a few seconds while he decided how to respond. His first thought was to play dumb, but there was something in Spooner's tone that warned him the question was not merely casual.

'That's a good question, actually, sir. Since you ask, I don't exactly know.'

Spooner was still smiling, apparently unsurprised. 'Losing your own men now, Winterman? That's not a good sign.'

'Not really.' Winterman had found the tea and was spooning it into the pot.

'Par for the bloody course in this place though. When exactly were you planning on breaking this news to me?'

'Just about now, to be honest. I'd been hoping that he might turn up this morning.'

'Bloody hell. How long's he been missing?'

'Thirty-six hours or so. He was staying here along with Hoxton. Seems to have gone out sometime overnight. We don't know why.'

'You've not been worried?'

'I'm getting worried now. He's an adult. Seems very capable, if a bit headstrong. I think he's off pursuing some line of his own.'

'Without telling you?'

'Apparently.'

'This about his brother?' Somehow, from everything he'd seen and heard over the last half hour, Winterman was unsurprised that Spooner should be aware of Marsh's history. 'Predictable enough, I suppose, with these kiddies' bodies turning up. You should have told me before.'

'I didn't want to start a full-scale panic. After all, how do we normally respond when someone reports an adult missing?'

'We assume they can look after themselves unless there's good reason to think otherwise. Fair enough. Mind you, I'd have been bloody livid if one of my people had gone AWOL like that.' There was an undertone of reproach in Spooner's voice, as if Winterman had failed some management test.

'These haven't been normal conditions. In any case, we've had a couple of other things to worry about over the last twenty-four hours.'

'Your Mrs Sheringham's heard nothing from him either,' Spooner said, gloomily. 'Just in case that's what you were about to check when I arrived.'

Winterman poured the tea. So that was another mystery solved. It was clear where Spooner obtained his information about Hoxton and Marsh. What was less clear was the nature of any relationship between Spooner and Mrs Sheringham. Something for another day.

'No milk, I'm afraid. Or sugar, as far as I can see.'

'The cup that cheers.' Spooner pulled a silver hip flask from his pocket and waved it vaguely in Winterman's direction. When Winterman shook his head, Spooner shrugged and poured a generous measure into his own cup.

'Seeing as there's no milk. So no theories on Marsh's whereabouts?'

'Not really. It's quite possible that the finding of these bodies had sent him off on some lead related to his brother.'

'Or sent him back over the edge. I understand he's got a bit of a history.'

'I don't know, sir. I heard he took his brother's disappearance hard at the time.'

'Hard enough to send him to the funny farm is what I hear.'

'Pity no one thought about that before deploying him on this case,' Winterman said pointedly.

'Aye, maybe not the cleverest of moves. I imagine they thought he'd be out of harm's way down here.'

Like me then, Winterman thought. A little quarantine ward, for those too dangerous to be allowed near the real action. Which, after Spooner's earlier words, made him wonder what Hoxton was doing among them.

'So what do we do about Marsh now then?' Spooner said. 'Treat him as a missing person?'

'I think we have to be concerned. Thirty-six hours, in the weather we've been having. And there's the blood that was found in the churchyard. That's being checked. Just in case. The question is whether we can afford to deflect resources away from the murder enquiry.'

'Of course we bloody can't. We've hardly made a start because of this bloody weather. But we can't just ignore the bugger either. Do we have the foggiest notion of where to start looking for him?'

'Not the foggiest, sir.'

'What about family?'

'No close family locally. I understand his parents live in Nottingham. The closest relative he's got around here is Mary Ford.'

'From your office? That would be the lass you were canoodling with yesterday?'

'She brought over some information, yes, sir.'

'Information, was it? I hope she's keeping you well informed. She's a relative of Marsh's?'

'Cousins, I understand. He was evacuated over here. Lived with Mary and her mother.'

'That would be Mrs Griffiths who found one of the kiddies' bodies?'

Once again, Winterman had cause to admire Spooner's memory and attention to detail. 'That's her.'

'You'll have asked young Mary where her cousin might be?'

'She's no idea. The spot where his brother went missing is miles away. It's unlikely he's gone up there.'

'What about her mother? She have any ideas?'

'She doesn't know Marsh is missing yet. But it's a route we have to explore.'

'I'll leave that one to you,' Spooner said. 'Seeing as how you've made the lady's acquaintance.' He made this sound slightly salacious. He looked at his watch. 'But later. We need to get down to business first. Think about these bloody murders. What are we going–?'

His words were interrupted by the sound of the front door being thrown open. A moment later, Brain appeared at the kitchen door. His oilskin cape was pouring water on to the linoleum floor, and, peering from beneath the hood, Brain himself bore a close resemblance to a semi-drowned rodent. He bent forward, struggling to regain his breath.

Winterman took Brain's arm, guiding him to one of the chairs. He was soaked through, shivering from the wet and cold. He looked up at Winterman, as though unsure of his identity.

'Try him with this.' Spooner thrust forward a cup filled with hot black tea. 'I gave it a shot from the flask.'

Brain's hand appeared too shaky to hold the cup, so Winterman held the rim carefully to the young man's lips. He coughed at the unexpected bite of the whisky, and then gratefully took a deeper swallow.

'Thanks. Bloody wet out there,' he added unnecessarily.

'Where've you been?' Winterman asked. 'I found your note but I can't pretend I understood it.'

Brain glanced nervously at Spooner then, still breathless, recounted his overhearing of Hoxton's telephone conversation and his subsequent pursuit.

'You went after him on a *bike*?' Spooner said.

Brain nodded, looking slightly embarrassed. 'I didn't know what else to do. Anyway, it worked, more or less.'

'You caught up with him?' Spooner asked sceptically. 'I knew those bloody Wolseleys were no good.'

'Not exactly. But I could see where he went. It's so flat around here you can see a car for miles. It was the only one on the road this morning.'

'Not bloody surprised,' Spooner said.

'I could see which way he was heading, north out of town. He went towards Welstone but turned off before that, towards the river. I saw the car go off the main road, then I lost it behind some farm buildings until it reappeared further along the riverbank. It looked as if he was stopping so I cycled after him.'

'Did you catch him?'

'More or less. I got to the river and the road that runs alongside it.' He paused. 'The river's already very high, spreading into the fields.'

Winterman could envisage it. The river was no more than a tributary of the Welland but at this point it seemed broad enough to be a major river in its own right. Like many of the fenland rivers, it was lined with washes, low-lying pastures designed to accommodate any surplus water as the level rose.

'Won't take long to flood those fields in weather like this.'

'I didn't like the look of it,' Brain said. 'You could almost see it spreading across the washes. The road's raised above the fens, but it'll get covered before long. That's one reason I came back but–' He stopped. 'I don't know what's going on up there.'

'How do you mean?' Spooner held out the flask, but Brain shook his head.

'I saw the Wolseley parked – I don't know, perhaps a quarter of a mile off the main road. There are some farm buildings along there – a barn and a couple of stone sheds. It's a natural island. Sticks up above the fens, and it's been built up further to accommodate the buildings. The car was parked just off the road.'

'Any sign of Hoxton?' Spooner asked.

'He was in the front of the car, just watching one of the buildings. I wasn't expecting that. I thought he'd have got out and be somewhere inside. Nearly caught me out. I didn't want him to think I was following him–'

'But you were,' Winterman pointed out.

'I know. But I was a bit embarrassed. I'd gone there with the best intentions. I wasn't trying to catch DC Hoxton out. I was worried. It all sounded so strange.'

Winterman nodded. 'You've been very conscientious. You did the right thing.'

Brain was clearly not entirely convinced himself. 'At first, I thought he must have seen me. But with all the rain – and he had the car engine off so the wipers weren't going – I don't think he could see much. I dropped the bike and moved round till I was at the side of the car.' He gestured down at the grey oilskins. 'This stuff gave me decent camouflage. I couldn't see much myself with all the rain, but I could see DC Hoxton in the car. He was watching the farm buildings.'

'You didn't see anyone else?' Winterman asked.

'Not at first. I moved round until I was at the back of the car. Then I could see more clearly where DC Hoxton was looking. There was something between the barn and the other building. Off the road. I was a bit confused at first, with all the rain still coming down, then I realised it was another car. But it was on its side – I don't know how long it had been there, but it must have skidded off the road and turned over.'

'Was there anyone in the vehicle?' Winterman asked, wondering whether, after all, Hoxton had simply been called out to some traffic accident.

'There was no sign of anyone. But the car hadn't been there long – I mean, hours rather than days. You could see the marks in the wet ground where it had ploughed off the road.'

'DC Hoxton wasn't doing anything?'

'He was just sitting in the car. Watching. As if he was waiting for something.'

Winterman glanced back at Spooner, whose expression suggested that this was no more than the kind of insanity he would expect to find in a place like this.

'What about the car? Did you get any details?'

'I didn't need to.' For the first time Brain looked pleased with himself. 'I recognised it.'

'It was a local car then?'

'Oh, yes, sir, definitely. It was the professor's.'

'The professor's? You mean Callaghan?'

'Yes. It was his all right. It's a big old thing. Like a hearse, I always think.'

'But there was no sign of Callaghan?'

'No sign of anyone, except for DC Hoxton.'

'Probably crashed it last night,' Spooner volunteered. 'Not surprising, if he took it out in that snow. He'll get one of the local garages to come and sort it out now the weather's warmed up.'

'You're probably right, sir,' Brain said. 'I imagine it'll be something like that. But he'll have to be quick, I reckon.'

'Why do you say that?'

'The water,' Brain said. 'It was rising all the time I was there. I've seen floods round these parts. But not like that. I've never seen it rise so quickly.' He looked up at the window of the police office. The rain continued to lash against the panes. 'If it carries on like this, that car'll be under water within an hour or so. The buildings as well, come to that.'

CHAPTER SIXTY

The door opened slowly, its lower edge grinding across the stone floor. He blinked as the light grew brighter, and thrust himself further back against the rear wall. His hand grasped the cold metal pipe, half-concealed behind his back.

The large door opened fully, and he blinked at the silhouetted figure framed against the grey light. He was tense, his body poised to react to whatever might be about to happen.

'William?' The figure remained still in the doorway, perhaps to allow his eyes time to adjust to the relative dark.

William moved the pipe further behind his back, his eyes fixed on the figure. He said nothing, waiting for some further clue as to what was happening.

'William? You're awake?' The figure took a single step forward into the room, and William finally recognised him. The policeman, the detective. The younger one. Marsh. Well, that was no surprise. His voice sounded more tentative than William had expected. As if he was also unsure quite why they were here.

'What do you want?' William said. 'Where are we?'

Marsh took another step forward. 'You know where we are, William. You know this place.'

The piping was cold in William's hand. He did know this place. He had known it, subconsciously, even when he had first awoken, in the pitch dark with only the scrabbling of invisible rats for company. When the thin grey light had flooded through the opening door, he had known it for sure.

'What do you want? Who sent you?'

'No one sent me. Who sent you, William? This wasn't your doing. So who sent you?'

William's back was pressed hard against the chill stone wall. 'I don't know what you mean. I don't know what you want with me.'

'I just want to know, William, that's all. I want to know who's behind this. I want to know what games are being played.' His voice was coaxing. As if they were in this together, complicit.

William had been expecting this, or something like this. It could have been any one of them, or someone else entirely. When Winterman had come to interview him, William had thought he must be the one. He had the right background, the right style – unlikely in a policeman. One of the others – Hoxton or Marsh himself – had mentioned that Winterman had moved down here only recently. That would have made sense. Shipped down here to deal with this. Shut it down before there was too much furore. Before the press got hold of it.

Perhaps it still was Winterman. Perhaps Marsh was just an agent, doing the dirty work while Winterman pulled the strings. That wouldn't have been surprising either. That was how the whole thing worked. Those at the top were protected while the minions did what needed to be done.

It didn't matter much now. William had done his best to muddy the waters. To stir up a stink that would bring everything to the light. But they had always been ahead. Fisher's death should have proved that if he'd had any doubts. Fisher's death and the way it had been handled. The removal of the one remaining witness, and William himself apparently implicated in the killing.

He should have realised he was out of his depth. But he had pressed on, one last attempt. Praying the snow would clear and that there would be a chance to expose all this before they closed everything down again.

But if Winterman was one of them and Marsh was one of them, there was no way of knowing how far it all went. It would all just be buried, one more time.

Marsh had moved forward another step, his expression benign. 'I just want you to tell me, that's all. Just tell me who it is.'

William tried to move away, edging along the wall. Marsh's words made no sense to him, but probably they weren't meant to. The tone reminded William of someone enticing a nervous animal. Warm, soothing, seductive. All the time, Marsh was moving closer and closer.

There was no option. William couldn't let himself be caught like this. This wasn't just a matter of self-preservation. Everything depended on him.

He waited till Marsh was within a few feet of him. Marsh's left hand, he noticed, was wedged firmly into his overcoat pocket clutching – what? A revolver? A knife, like that used on Fisher?

As Marsh stepped forward, he slowly withdrew the hand from his pocket. *This was it*, William thought. *I have to do it now.*

William jumped forward, swinging the pipe as fiercely as he could at Marsh's head. Marsh moved his upper body back, trying to dodge, the end of the pipe catching him on the temple. He staggered forward, dazed by the impact, as William swung again. This time his aim was truer, and the piping hit the side of Marsh's head. Marsh's body twisted, his eyes registering shock, as William hit him again, harder this time across the back of his neck.

Marsh fell forward, his forehead striking the hard stone floor. His body contorted for a moment and then lay motionless.

William stared with horror at the prone figure, a crumpled black heap on the floor. Marsh's hands, he noticed, both remained empty.

Bile rising in his throat, William dropped to his knees and frantically reached for Marsh's wrist, searching for a pulse. He knew he needed to check properly, calmly, apply his medical training, but all he felt was a growing panic and a certainty Marsh was already dead. As he fumbled with the heavy outer clothes, he realised that the overcoat pocket, the pocket into which Marsh had thrust his hand, was empty also. There had been no weapon.

He looked up and saw that a second figure was standing at the door, calmly watching.

'Oh, dear,' Hoxton said. 'It looks as if you've well and truly buggered things up now, doesn't it, young William?'

CHAPTER SIXTY-ONE

Mary was standing at the front door watching the rain. 'It's raining stair-rods. We're going to get soaked.'

'I can take them instead, if you like,' Mrs Griffiths said.

'Don't be daft, Mam. I'm quite capable of walking half a mile even in this weather. Probably a waste of time anyway. Bet they're still not open. Teachers won't want to venture out in this weather.'

'It's not as cold as it was though.' Mrs Griffiths had come to stand behind Mary, peering over her shoulder.

'Doesn't feel much warmer to me. And that school's as draughty as an old barn.' She looked back into the house. 'Come on, you two. Time to go.'

The children were loitering in the hallway, engaged in some complex private game. Graham looked up as she called, gazing curiously past her out into the daylight. 'It's raining.'

'I had noticed,' Mary said. 'Doesn't stop you going to school though, does it?'

Graham groaned but fastened his duffle coat, fumbling with the toggles. Ann watched him for a moment and then copied him. Finally, the children were ready and Mary led them out into the rain.

She had considered bringing an umbrella, but the bitter east wind would render it useless. Instead, she had donned an old oilskin coat that had belonged to her husband. She pulled up the hood and, clutching Ann firmly by the hand, began the slow walk down towards the village. Graham trotted a yard or two behind, as fascinated by the pounding rain he had previously been by the snow.

The change in the weather was a relief, she supposed. After weeks of snow and below freezing temperatures, the wet air was refreshing. But the surrounding fields were already waterlogged, the network of dykes rapidly filling. Flooding was an everyday hazard in a landscape like this, but she couldn't remember seeing the water-levels rise so swiftly. That would be all they needed.

Graham had stopped, kicking water from a puddle. His trouser legs were already sodden, but he seemed undeterred. The rain was just another new adventure. Ann, by contrast, seemed cowed by the ferocity of the downpour.

'Come on, Graham,' Mary said. 'We haven't got all day.'

Graham looked up at her with an expression which suggested that, as far as he was concerned, that was exactly what they had. Finally, he grimaced and trotted after her. She watched for a moment, and then turned and continued down the lane.

She passed the church, glancing through the closed gates with an involuntary shudder. The churchyard was deserted. As in the rest of the landscape, the snow lingered only where the greying drifts were sheltered from the rain. It was a desolate scene, even without the associations it now held for her.

Suddenly nervous, she clutched Ann's hand more tightly and turned to watch Graham. He was still behind her but had slowed down again, distracted by a rapidly thawing pile of snow. A torrent of rain swept across the road, driven by the rising east wind. As the downpour grew even heavier, she had the momentary illusion that Graham's body was fading, becoming less substantial.

'Graham!' Her voice sounded sharper than she had intended. 'We're going to be late.'

After a moment, the boy responded, at first reluctantly dawdling in her wake. Then another thought seemed to strike him and he ran past his mother and sister, splashing hard in the puddles with his wellington boots, down the deserted road towards the village.

CHAPTER SIXTY-TWO

'So what the bloody hell is Hoxton up to?' Spooner was pacing up and down the hallway. 'For God's sake, Winterman, can't you keep any of your men under control?'

Winterman looked at Brain. 'What time was the call this morning? The call you overheard.'

'I didn't notice exactly,' Brain said. 'Early. About five, I suppose.'

'Let's see what we can find out. Do you think it was an incoming or an outgoing call?'

Brain looked momentarily bewildered. 'I don't know. I suppose I got the impression – I don't know – that DC Hoxton was reporting in. Does that make sense?'

'None of it makes sense,' Winterman said. 'But it's worth a try. Hang on.' He disappeared back into the police office, and they heard him speaking to someone on the phone.

A moment later, he stuck his head round the office door. 'We're in luck. The call was made from here and fortunately for us it was just outside the local area, so it was connected by the operator. She took a bit of persuading to give me any information. Particularly given the recipient of the call.'

Spooner looked up, frowning. 'Oh, yes?'

'You're probably not going to like this. Lord Hamshaw.'

'Oh, bloody hell. Not Tommy bloody Hamshaw. You've got a death wish.'

'We don't know that he was talking to Hamshaw himself. Man like that must have staff.'

'Not so's you'd notice, from what I hear. Even Hamshaw's having to tighten his belt these days.'

Winterman recalled his mild surprise that Hamshaw had answered his own front door. 'Hoxton reckoned he'd made some bad investments.'

Spooner snorted. 'Too right. Most of them came in last.'

'It's not been easy for anyone over the last couple of decades,' Winterman pointed out.

'It's been bloody easy for the Hamshaws for most of that time. Living the life of bloody Riley. Don't get me wrong, Hamshaw's not short of a bob or two even now. He's just having to be a bit more careful how he spends it. If you believe the rumours, he allowed himself to become a little over extended with the wrong types.'

'Wrong types?'

'East End boys. Supplied Hamshaw with some of the wine and women, and other stuff besides, I shouldn't wonder. But they weren't so happy when the money began to run out. Hamshaw had to sell off some land to make ends meet, by all accounts, and now he's keeping his head down. Mind you, Hamshaw's ruthless enough when it suits him. He's screwed enough folk round here over the years.'

'That wasn't quite how I'd heard it.'

'And who'd you hear it from?' Spooner said. 'Hoxton? It wouldn't surprise me if Hoxton had his nose up Hamshaw's backside.'

Winterman frowned. 'When we interviewed Hamshaw, they didn't show much sign of knowing each other. A nodding acquaintance was my impression.'

'Aye, and Hoxton would have been doing the nodding. And the forelock tugging.'

Winterman realised what had been troubling him. 'Interesting, though, that Hamshaw already assumed that the latest body we'd found was another girl. Even though he pretended not to know we'd found it. Someone had been talking.' He turned to Brain. 'You said it sounded like DC Hoxton was – what was your phrase? – reporting in?'

'Something like that, sir. The tone was… well, it sounded like the kind of call you might make to a senior officer. Not that he was backwards at coming forward, if you get my drift, sir.'

'I don't imagine Hoxton was ever that,' Winterman said. 'He's always seemed to express his views pretty forthrightly to me.'

'He did that all right, but it still sounded as if he was receiving orders. Being told to sort it out.'

Winterman glanced at Spooner. 'We could give Hamshaw a call ourselves. See if we can winkle something out of him.'

'You want to antagonise Tommy Hamshaw, be my guest. Just don't mention my name. He's still got plenty of high-placed friends. On the other hand, you're not on the chief's Christmas card list anyway, are you?'

'Not for a year or two,' Winterman agreed.

The others followed him back into the office, where he dialled the operator and asked to be connected to Hamshaw's number.

The call was answered almost immediately. As if Hamshaw had been awaiting a call. 'Hamshaw.'

'Lord Hamshaw. It's DI Winterman. I visited you with my colleague, DC Hoxton, about Reverend Fisher's death.'

There was a momentary pause. When Hamshaw spoke again, he sounded more tentative. 'Of course. DI Winterman. How can I help you?'

'I'm very sorry to trouble you again. And it's a slightly odd question, I'm afraid. I believe you had a call early this morning from my colleague, DC Hoxton. He called from the station here so I'm assuming it was police business. We're trying to contact DC Hoxton urgently, and we wondered whether he might be with you.'

There was another brief pause. 'I'm afraid not, Inspector. Will that be all?'

'We wondered whether his conversation with you might have any bearings on his whereabouts, sir.'

'Well…' Hamshaw hesitated again. Winterman could almost hear the workings of the other man's mind. 'I really can't help you, Inspector. If you say DC Hoxton called this number, then that is no doubt the case. But I didn't take the call. Perhaps he spoke to one of my staff. I can make some enquiries, if you think it's important.'

'That would be very helpful, sir.'

'If I discover anything that's likely to assist you in locating DC Hoxton, I will of course call you back immediately.'

'Thank you, sir.'

'Good day, Inspector.'

Winterman replaced the receiver and looked up at Spooner and Brain. 'He claims he didn't take the call. Suggests that perhaps Hoxton spoke to one of his staff.'

'As far as I know, Hamshaw's staff these days comprises a housekeeper and a part-time gardener.' Spooner turned to Brain. 'Did it sound as if Hoxton was talking to Hamshaw's housekeeper?'

'No, sir. As I said–'

'So Hamshaw's lying through his teeth,' Spooner said.

'It would appear so,' Winterman said. 'I think we need to find out what Hoxton's up to, don't you?'

'You can take my car,' Spooner said. 'I'm not liking the sound of this, whatever it is.'

'You're not coming with us, sir?'

'My team is due to turn up any minute. We were all supposed to be meeting to kick things off, in case you've forgotten.'

'I'd not forgotten,' Winterman said. 'We'll try not to keep you waiting,'

'You do that, Winterman. And, yes, I know what you're thinking and you're right. I'll do what I can, but I'm going no further out on a limb than I can help. I don't know what Hamshaw's involved in, but he's still a big fish in these parts. I'm keeping him at arm's length.' His smile grew broader. 'Whereas your career's buggered anyway. So good luck.'

'Thank you, sir.' Winterman's face was blank. 'Good to know you're behind us.'

'A long way behind you, Winterman,' Spooner said. 'But still behind you. And you might eventually be glad of that.'

CHAPTER SIXTY-THREE

'Stand up slowly,' Hoxton said. 'And throw that bloody pipe over here. Gently.' He was holding a revolver which he waved calmly towards William. 'Don't try to be smart. My old pal here's loaded and eager to see some action.'

William showed no inclination to resist. His face was white and aghast, and he was staring down at Marsh's body as if scarcely able to believe what he had done. Still silent, he tossed the metal piping softly towards Hoxton's feet.

'Good boy. Now get over there by the wall.'

As William obeyed, Hoxton moved round, the gun trained steadily on the younger man, and crouched down by Marsh's prone body. Keeping one eye on William, he lifted Marsh's arm and felt for a pulse.

'You're a lucky lad. Not dead yet. You might escape the gallows after all. Nobody takes kindly to people who kill coppers.'

William's mouth opened, but no sound emerged.

Hoxton allowed Marsh's hand to drop. 'On the other hand, he's not in a good state. Not in a good state at all. I don't know if he'll survive till help gets here. And there might be brain damage.' Keeping the gun trained steadily on William, Hoxton grabbed Marsh's hair and pulled back his unconscious head, lifting the forehead from the rough stone floor.

It took William a moment to realise what Hoxton was preparing to do. 'You can't–'

Hoxton looked up, smiling, at William's baffled anguished face. 'Bit too late to start developing a conscience, boy. You're the one who put him down here.'

'He was… I mean, I thought–'

'He was going to kill you?' Hoxton's smile was unwavering. 'Not young Marshy. He's a gentle soul. Bit obsessive, but wouldn't hurt a fly. You'd no reason to start laying into young Marshy.'

William had backed up against the wall. 'I don't understand. I thought he… I mean, you and he–'

'A bit of a misunderstanding there, I'm afraid, boy. You thought Marshy and me were working together. But that's where you got it arse about face, if you'll pardon my French. Put it bluntly, you got the wrong man.'

'I don't–'

'As I say, a bit of an obsessive, our Marshy. But then so are you, aren't you, young William? You're another one who won't let things lie. In more ways than one. Pity really. From your point of view. You and Marsh should have got together. You'd have stood a bit more chance then. As it is, the only question is how best to tie up the loose ends.' He waved the pistol towards William. 'It's all worked out quite nicely for me, boy. Marshy here's not likely to live to tell any tales. You'll be neatly fingered as the cop-killer. Which should put you even more in the frame for Fisher's murder. I imagine Spooner will be only too happy for you to take the fall for Merriman's killing as well. Neat and tidy.'

It wasn't clear whether William was actually following any of this. He was pressed back into the corner of the barn, his eyes jumping from Hoxton's gun to the prone figure of Marsh spread on the floor.

'Of course,' Hoxton went on, 'it wouldn't pay for you to be too talkative. I don't imagine anyone's going to give too much credence to anything you might say. But it might encourage awkward questions, and all that's probably best avoided.' He peered at William, squinting with the air of an artist sizing up his subject. 'You know, young William, I reckon the best thing would be if you was to rush me. Attack me with that piping, just like you did Marshy. Because then, you see, I'd have no option but to shoot you. There'd probably still be a few sticky questions. Like what I was doing with my old pal here.' He gestured with the revolver.

'But I can be surprisingly plausible when I try. And I don't imagine anyone's going to make too much fuss about a cop-killer, do you?' His smile seemed genuinely humorous. 'So how's about it, boy? You going to give it a go?'

William seemed in no state to move at all. He was watching Hoxton with a mix of horror and bafflement, his body twitching.

'Think that would be the best thing all round, don't you, boy?' Hoxton said. 'Of course, doesn't matter if you don't rush me. No one's going to know how or where you tried to attack me, so I can just shoot you where you stand. But it would add a little realism if you were over here.' He paused, as if searching for the goads that would provoke William into action. 'Those bodies, boy. Smart of you to find them. How did you stumble across them? Must have been Fisher, I suppose. That was his ghost story, was it? He knew about all this, of course. Another one paid and blackmailed to keep quiet. Would have driven the poor bugger to drink if he hadn't been there already. But he knew. He really knew where the bodies were buried and talked to you in his cups. Did he tell you about your old man then?' He looked up, looking for William to react.

William gazed back, dead-eyed. 'I already know about my father. All about him.'

'You're no fool then, William Callaghan, are you? You poor bugger. You're worse than him.' He gestured towards Marsh. 'Chasing your own little ghosts. Out of your depth. I know you contacted the police about them bodies. I know because I made damn sure nothing happened, me and one or two others with more clout. Weren't difficult though. Some anonymous nutter rings up with a story like that, who's going to listen? I can see how that would have driven you loopy.'

William shook his head. It was clear he was beyond provocation.

'Time enough then, lad. Way that rain's coming down, this place'll be knee-deep before long. You don't want to play ball. I'll have to do it my way.' He grasped Marsh's hair, as he had before, and once again raised the head off the rough ground, preparing to smash it down hard on to the stone.

Unexpectedly, Marsh let out a groan, his eyes fluttering. His body twisted in pain and, still no more than semi-conscious, he pulled himself to one side. Hoxton, crouching on his haunches, momentarily lost balance and tumbled over onto Marsh's body.

William, operating more on instinct than reason, took his opportunity and threw himself forward to grab the piping. He grasped it in one hand and swung it hard at Hoxton's head.

Hoxton pulled back and the metal pipe caught him on the shoulder. 'You little bastard–' He fell back into a sitting position, his hand struggling to level the gun at William, finger tightening on the trigger.

As he fired, Marsh, still only half-awake, reached up and grabbed Hoxton's wrist, pulling the gun barrel down towards his own chest.

In the small room the shot was deafening. Hoxton looked down in confusion, and it took him a moment to register that Marsh had been shot, a neat brown-ringed bullet-hole in the centre of his white shirt. A pool of blood was already spreading across the floor from the larger exit-wound in his back.

Hoxton looked at the smoking gun in his own hand, then raised it up towards where William had been standing. But William was already moving towards the doorway. Hoxton fired but the bullet went wide, ricocheting into the roof of the outbuilding.

William stumbled out into the pounding rain, his feet splashing through the deepening pools of water. The surrounding fields were awash, he realised, reflecting the leaden grey of the skies.

Coming towards them, wheels streaming spray, its headlights blazing in the dark afternoon, was a long black car.

CHAPTER SIXTY-FOUR

'My god,' Winterman said. 'Look at the state of those fields.'

There were, in fact, no fields visible – only acre after acre of flat grey water. Even in the short time since Brain had returned to the station, the water level had risen to the point where the river had overflowed its notional banks. The water had spread, filling the empty reaches, turning the landscape into an expanding lake.

In itself, that was not a cause for concern. The reaches had been built for precisely that purpose. The low-lying land would accommodate the excess water as the river rose. But the rain was still coming down and the melting snow further up-stream would add to the volume. Already the water was lapping close to the raised edge of the road.

Winterman drove Spooner's police Jaguar with exaggerated caution. Conditions were easier than in the snow, but the roads were awash with surface water. Spooner had made it clear that the low-slung Jaguar, one of the first acquired for police duties, was his personal pride and joy.

'That the place?' Winterman pointed ahead of them through the streaming windscreen. The wipers could barely cope with the wind-driven rain.

'Yes, those buildings,' Brain said.

Winterman turned off the main road. The road surface was still above the water, and he could see where the narrow strip of road angled off towards the higher ground. But, as the afternoon drew on, the route would become increasingly treacherous. Already the buildings themselves were stranded on a narrow peninsula, circled by endless water.

Winterman slowed the car, peering through the windscreen for any signs of life. The buildings were away from the road, an opportunistic use of a patch of higher ground. There was a large barn, apparently long abandoned, its roof sagging, alongside two smaller outbuildings. The black Wolseley was parked at the edge of the road, facing the buildings. The driving seat was empty.

Winterman stopped a few yards from the Wolseley. As Brain had described, a second car was turned on to its side, close to the wall of the barn. There was a long skid mark leading from the road to the rear wheels. As far as Winterman could tell in the dim light, the skid-marks were fresh.

'This as you left it?'

Brain nodded. 'Except that Hoxton was in the car. And the water's risen a bit.'

'Come on then. Let's find out what's going on.' Winterman made a move to open the car door. Then his fingers froze on the door handle as a figure lurched out of the shadows, stumbling in a peculiar zig-zag towards them.

At first it was nothing more than a black shape. Then the stark white face was caught in the glare, wild-eyed and terrified. The face of someone running with the devil on his heels.

Winterman climbed out, his boots sinking into the sodden ground. 'William! It's me. DI Winterman.'

He had expected Callaghan to respond with relief, but his pale face showed only confusion. He paused momentarily, then looked back fearfully over his shoulder.

'William!'

For a moment, he thought Callaghan would ignore the call. But Brain was already out of the car and closing in on the young man from the other side. With no options left, Callaghan stopped and moved towards Winterman.

'Come here, man,' Winterman called. 'We're not going to hurt you.'

He intended the comment only as reassurance, but William's expression suggested he took the words seriously. 'You're not with him?'

'With who? We're not with anyone. Get in the car, man, you're soaked to the skin.' Winterman thrust William, barely resisting, into the back seat. Winterman clambered into the driver's seat. Brain fell into the car a moment later.

'They're in there,' William said. 'He's got a gun. I think he's killed him. But I…' The words were barely coherent. William was shivering from the cold and fear, his body convulsing.

'Who's in there? Who's got a gun?'

'Police,' William choked. 'Your man–'

'Hoxton? Is it Hoxton who's got a gun?'

William nodded frantically. 'He shot… he shot the other one.'

'The other one?'

'The other one. Your man.'

It was Brain who said it. 'You mean DC Marsh?'

'Yes. Marsh. He shot him. I think he's dead.'

Winterman felt a cold chill in his stomach. 'Hoxton shot Marsh?'

'Yes…but I–'

'Never mind. You can tell us the detail later.' They needed backup. Winterman had no idea what was going on, but it would be madness to face an armed man without support. But if Marsh was in there, possibly still alive, they had to do something.

He looked at Brain. 'I'm going in. You stay here with Callaghan. See if you can use that thing to get some backup.' He gestured down at the dashboard. Spooner's new car was fitted with a prototype police radio linked back to headquarters, an innovation due to be rolled out to the whole fleet in due course. From his experience of police technology, Winterman had limited confidence in its efficacy.

He pushed open the door and peered through the murky daylight for some sign of life. Seeing nothing, he cautiously climbed out and walked forward a few paces, his eyes fixed on the nearest outbuilding. As he drew closer, he finally saw Hoxton's figure, framed in the doorway.

'Hoxton?'

'Guv.' Hoxton was motionless, his expression impossible to read in the dim light.

'What's going on, Hoxton?' Winterman took another few steps forward.

He had left his hat back in the car, and the rain was dripping from his hair, cold water running down his back, inside his coat.

'We got him, guv. Callaghan. He's the one behind everything. He attacked Marshy. He's the one.'

'Marsh in there?'

Hoxton glanced behind him as if unsure of the answer. 'Aye, guv. He's not in a good way.'

'Who shot him, Hoxton?' Winterman had moved forward again. 'Was that you?'

Hoxton looked almost surprised at the question. He hesitated a second before responding, perhaps considering whether the forensic evidence would expose any lie. 'It was an accident, guv. I was trying to stop Callaghan.'

'Whose gun was it?'

'It was mine. Old service revolver. Long story. Shouldn't have brought it but… you know, self-protection.'

'What about Marsh? How is he?'

'Think he's bought it. He was already in a bad way after Callaghan attacked him.'

'What are you doing up here, Hoxton? What made you come out here?'

'I was looking for Marshy, guv.'

'But why here?'

'Just a hunch. You know how it is.'

Winterman was within a few yards of Hoxton. 'Thought Hamshaw might have told you.'

'Hamshaw? Told me what? Is Callaghan safe in the car, guv? Who's with him? Brain?'

'What did Hamshaw say to you, Hoxton?'

'Don't know what you mean. We should get Callaghan back.' Marsh gestured at the rising floodwaters. 'We haven't got a lot of time.'

'What did Hamshaw say when you called him this morning?'

'Not much. Just routine.'

'You didn't speak to the housekeeper then?'

'Guv?'

'Never mind. What sort of routine?'

'With respect, sir, this isn't the time. We need to deal with Callaghan. Ought to get Marshy moved as well before this lot gets any higher.'

'Brain overheard you.'

'Brain? Don't know what he heard. To be honest, not sure what you're going on about, guv. You feeling all right?'

'I'm fine, Hoxton. Just wet and cold. I want to know what's going on. What brought you up here. Why you shot Marsh. Where that gun came from.' Winterman paused. 'Why Hamshaw lied about your call.'

'Can't speak for Hamshaw. Anyway, who says he lied? This all young Brain's say-so. Nice enough lad, but I wouldn't rely on his judgment.'

'I'm just trying to understand what's going on. You've shot and killed one of your colleagues with what I assume is an illegal gun.'

'Accident, guv. The gun was for self-defence. I know I overstepped the mark there. But Callaghan's a killer.'

'And you knew Callaghan was here? Why did you come up here on your own? Why not get backup?'

'Long story, guv. I'll explain it all later.'

'I hope you will. I'm going to have to take you in, Hoxton, you realise that.'

'You've got to go through the formalities.'

'Not a question of formalities, Hoxton. You're responsible for the death of another officer. You've an illegal firearm. There are other questions that need answering. You and Hamshaw. And the others.'

'Others, boss?'

'The others that Hamshaw spoke to you about. Who are they?'

There was another longer hesitation. Finally, Hoxton moved forward, stepping out into the rain. The revolver was in his hand. 'You know, guv, now I think about it, I'm really not so keen about coming with you. I just want you to let me leave.'

CHAPTER SIXTY-FIVE

'Where are you planning to go, Hoxton?' Winterman said.

'I'll just disappear. Won't be the first time. In everyone's best interest.'

'People don't just disappear, Hoxton.'

'You'd be surprised,' Hoxton said. 'Takes a while but people forget. New people get to know you. Think they know you. Think you've been around forever.' He was smiling. 'Bit of money's all it takes. I've got that stashed away. Last resort. Not surprised it's come to it. Thought I'd have a bit more discretion in the timing, that's all.'

'What if I try to stop you?'

'Then I shoot you, sir. But I'd rather not.' He stepped forward, very slowly, the rain bouncing off his balding temples.

'I can't just let you go. You know that, don't you, Hoxton?'

'Your choice, guv. But I can't see you're going to achieve much, given my old pal here.' He raised the gun and pointed it steadily towards Winterman. 'Just let me get to the Wolseley. No skin off your nose, sir, if I might say so.'

'Except I'm a policeman, Hoxton. We don't do that.'

'That's another thing you might be surprised about, with all due respect. What policemen do, I mean.'

'Give me the gun, Hoxton.' Winterman gestured towards the open door behind Hoxton. 'If that was an accident–'

'It's not really about what happened in there. But you know that.'

'Who are you protecting, Hoxton?'

Hoxton took another step or two forward, the rain pounding on his hat and shoulders. 'Don't know what you mean, guv.'

'You were ready to come and face the music till I mentioned the others. Who are they?'

Hoxton continued to move slowly forward, keeping the revolver pointing directly at Winterman.

'Hoxton–'

The opportunity came unexpectedly. Hoxton, keeping the gun poised, one eye on Winterman, the other on the two police vehicles, stumbled on the frozen rain-soaked grass, momentarily losing his footing.

Winterman jumped forward, trying to force Hoxton back on to the ground. His left hand clutched Hoxton's right wrist, pushing the gun barrel away, wrestling to loosen the other man's grip on the weapon.

It was a desperate attempt, but there was no other chance of stopping Hoxton. For a moment it worked. Hoxton, still unbalanced, toppled backwards, his left hand clawing at Winterman's face.

Then the revolver went off, the sound shockingly loud even over the pounding of the rain, Winterman briefly relaxed his grip, convinced that one or other of them must have been hit.

Hoxton was scrabbling away from beneath him, apparently uninjured, and Winterman realised that he too was untouched. He made a frantic lunge, grabbing the back of Hoxton's raincoat and then the arm that still held the gun. Hoxton struggled forward on his hands and knees, mud smearing his hands and his suit. Winterman hung on behind, half-crawling, slipping on the still-icy earth.

Hoxton gave another heave and stumbled to his feet, leaving Winterman clawing at the air. Hoxton staggered forward, and then was up and away towards the road.

Brain had clambered out of the Jaguar, William close behind. Winterman was scrambling to his feet, unsure whether to be relieved or irritated that Brain had disregarded his instructions to seek help.

Hoxton was heading for the Wolseley. Brain stared at him for a second, unsure how to respond, and then moved to head him off, placing his stocky body between Hoxton and the car. Winterman tried to shout out a warning but the words were swallowed by the rain and wind.

Hoxton slowed, then swerved and changed tack.

Winterman realised what was happening and called out again, still unable to make himself heard. William had also guessed Hoxton's intent and had moved forward but was in no state to intervene. Hoxton pushed him easily out of the way and dragged open the Jaguar driver's door.

Brain had left the engine running, the headlights blazing in the grey, rain-sodden morning. He was running back but it was already too late. Hoxton was in the car, gunning the engine. As Brain reached the vehicle, it spun violently around on the frozen ground, throwing a deluge of spray into Brain's face. Then the car was back on the road and heading towards the village, its red tail lights vanishing into the sweeping gusts of rain.

Winterman reached the road just as the car was pulling away. 'Damn! Spooner's not going to like this at all.'

CHAPTER SIXTY-SIX

In the end, they had abandoned the walk to the school after only a few hundred yards. Until Mary reached the corner by the churchyard, she had not fully appreciated the impact of the night's rain. The fields around the village were already under water, a smooth steel surface broken only by the lines of roads and raised dykes, a few patches of higher ground, the occasional knot of trees. South of the village, where the land rose slightly, was still untouched, but the water continued to rise.

It was an eerie threat, silent but implacable. She had never seen the water rise so fast. Even if the rain were to lessen, gallons of water would still be pouring into the local rivers from upstream. And, for the present, the rain showed no sign of abating.

In the reclaimed land, serious floods came quite literally in waves. As the water rose, it would breach one defence after another, penetrating new areas with unexpected speed and ferocity. At those moments, the slow silent threat would turn into something very different.

She knew that taking the children outside had been the sheerest folly. She had been trying to maintain a semblance of normality. But Winterman was right. She should stay home, keep the children protected.

She hustled them back to the house, explaining the situation to her mother. In the distance, the road heading north was already partly under water, potentially cutting off the village from the neighbouring towns. As they hurried back, she had seen other villagers, clearly of the same mind, urgently taking steps to protect themselves from the rising water. Many local residents, conscious of the risks, kept sandbags ready for such an eventuality, although most had remained unused for years. During the war, there had been a fear that the German bombers, discarding unused bombs on their way back to the coast, might breach a significant dyke, but she was not aware it had ever happened.

Now the threat was real. Her husband had stockpiled his own hoard of sandbags in the coalhole at the rear of the house. She had little expectation that they would provide much protection – the rising waters would assail the house on all sides – but she felt the need to take some action to protect herself and her family.

'Come on, Graham. We need to build a fortress. Keep the water out.'

Graham was gazing at the flooded fields in fascination. 'Are we going to be flooded?'

'Not if we build the walls properly. We need to make this into a castle.'

He was still wearing his wellingtons and his large duffle coat, now sodden with rain. She tightened the belt on her own raincoat and led him back out of the front door. The rain was still pouring down.

'Help me carry out the sandbags,' she said.

He followed to the rear of the house and she found the bags, black with coal-dust. They were heavier than she expected, but she dragged one forward with difficulty towards the door. She started as a large spider scuttled back into shelter.

With some half-hearted help from Graham, she pulled the sandbag slowly around the house, placing it carefully against the front door. She calculated that even two or three bags placed against the exterior doors might help to keep the waters at bay. Beyond that there was little she could do.

They slowly dragged a second bag into position alongside the first, and Mary straightened up, wondering whether she had the energy to bring out a third. Graham offered little real help but she wanted to keep him distracted. She knew from experience that he was much more likely than his sister to worry. Ann would already be playing floods with her dolls, whereas Graham was worrying that they would all be washed out to sea.

She was about to begin on the third bag when she heard a car. Peering over the fence, she saw the pale headlights approaching from the village. Moments later, a large black car passed the gate at speed. She couldn't see who was driving and couldn't imagine where they might be heading. She wondered whether the road to the north was still passable.

The answer to the last question came quickly. After a minute or two, she heard the car returning, pulling to a halt outside her own gate. She looked out, expecting that the driver would be seeking directions.

Instead, she found herself looking through the open driver's window at Hoxton. 'George?'

'How do, lass.' Hoxton jerked a thumb behind him. 'You know anything about that road?'

She peered where he was pointing. The road looked to be under water. She shook her head. 'I've not heard anything, but I can't see that you'll get through there.'

'That's what I thought. Bit of a bugger, really, 'scuse my French. Got some urgent business for Spooner. This is his fancy motor. Need to get back to the office.'

'It looked better to the south. You might be able to get round.'

Hoxton nodded. 'Not sure I've got much choice. Don't want to get stranded though.' He paused, and then beckoned her gently. 'Can I just get your opinion, lass? Just something I'd like you to see. Bring the lad over as well.' He gestured towards Graham, who was huddling against his mother's coat. 'Won't keep you more than a second.'

Obediently, she led Graham into the road. 'What is it, George?'

Hoxton had the door half-open and was leaning out, the revolver in his hand. 'I'm sorry, lass. I'd rather this was anyone but you. But there you are. We don't always get what we want.' He gestured with the gun. 'You and the lad get in the back. If I can't get out this way, I'm going to need you and the lad as an insurance policy.'

CHAPTER SIXTY-SEVEN

Winterman dragged the other two back into the Wolseley. For a second, he feared they were stranded, but Hoxton had left the keys in the ignition. Winterman looked back at the cluster of buildings, already nearly cut off by the floods.

'We'll have to leave Marsh there. Get a team out to pick him up when this clears.'

It sounded callous, but he had already spent precious seconds checking that Marsh really was dead. There was little to be gained now from trying to collect his remains. But he felt a chill when he considered how long it might be before these floods subsided or what state the body might be in by then.

He still had no idea what had brought the three men to this desolate spot. William was in no state to be questioned, and their priority was to apprehend Hoxton. Whatever this was all about, Hoxton was a dangerous man.

Winterman started the engine and pulled back on to the road. The water was lapping up to the road surface, and would soon begin to wash over it. Before long the road would be impassable. He stamped on the accelerator and headed towards the main road.

'Did you get through to HQ on that radio gubbins?'

'Yes,' Brain said, in a tone of mild wonder. 'She was a bit confused as to who I was. I asked for backup but all the roads north of here are flooded. I suggested she contact DS Spooner at the station.'

Winterman glanced across at the young man. 'So he'll come out just in time to see his own car speeding past him?'

'I suppose so, sir. It was all I could think of.'

'It was the right thing to do. Not your fault Hoxton grabbed the other car.'

'Thanks, sir. I hope Superintendent Spooner sees it that way.'

'So do I, Bryan, so do I.'

They were back on the main road, higher above the endless floods. Even here, the respite felt only temporary. It would not take much longer before the floods reached this level.

'If the roads to the north are flooded,' Winterman said, half to himself, 'how's Hoxton going to get away?'

Brain shook his head. 'It won't be easy. If you want to get away from here, you have to go north. Otherwise, it's a long way round to anywhere.'

'So he'll try going through the village first?'

'I should think so. That would normally be the quickest route.'

'We'll go with that then. If he's forced back, we might cut him off. Worth a try anyway. We've no other options.'

They were approaching the outskirts of the village, the school ahead of them to the right.

'There!' Brain shouted, pointing through the windscreen. There was a flicker of lights through the cluster of buildings. Car headlights heading towards them. 'He must have turned round.'

'You know the village. Can we cut him off?'

'Once we get to the church, there's no other way out if the road north's closed. But you need to make sure he doesn't get to the centre of the village. There are a couple of other roads he could take from there.'

Winterman slammed his foot harder on the accelerator, heedless of the road conditions. Seconds later, they passed the police station on their left. There were no signs of any other vehicles – presumably the rest of Spooner's team hadn't been able to get through. He had a brief impression that the station's front door was open. Perhaps Spooner was inside, watching the passing cars with bemusement.

They passed the crossroad by the pub, heading towards the church. Any exit routes were behind them and Hoxton was effectively cut off.

As they rounded the corner, they saw the blazing lights of the approaching car. Winterman picked the point where the road was narrowest, bounded on one side by a wide water-filled dyke and on the other by the churchyard wall. He braked and spun the wheel tightly, pulling the car across the road so that it blocked the thoroughfare.

At first it seemed that the approaching car wasn't going to stop, either because Hoxton had seen the blockage too late or because he was trying to crash through the barrier. At the last moment the car screamed to a halt, skidding for several yards across the wet road surface.

Winterman could see Hoxton's white face staring blankly at them through the windscreen. Behind him, in the rear seats, were two more figures. Through the glass and the streaming rain, it took Winterman a moment to recognise them.

'Christ,' he breathed. 'He's got Mary and her boy in there.'

Even as he muttered the words, Hoxton was slamming the car into reverse and spinning it round.

'Where's he going?' Brain was peering through the passenger window. 'He can't get through that way.'

'Might not stop him trying.' Winterman pulled the Wolseley round into the road again and accelerated after Hoxton. He stuck to the centre of the narrow road, watchful in case Hoxton should attempt another turn. Hoxton was accelerating away, the reflections of his crimson tail lights streaming across the wet road. 'He doesn't know how deep it is. Might decide to give it a go.'

'He's crazy,' Brain said. 'He won't get a car through that.'

'Perhaps he doesn't think he's got a choice.' Winterman was thinking rapidly, wondering how desperate Hoxton might be. The thought of Mary and Graham in the car was horrifying.

The Jaguar had reached the water's edge. To Winterman's relief, Hoxton slowed the car as its front wheels touched the surface. The car moved forward another three, four yards, but it was already clear the water was too deep.

Winterman stopped some yards from the water's edge, angling the car across the road to prevent Hoxton from passing. He was half-expecting that, in desperation, Hoxton might try to ram his way past them to freedom. Winterman was growing fearful for the two passengers in the car, but recognised that, if Hoxton were allowed to escape with them still as hostages, their fate would be equally uncertain.

Finally, with the water lapping halfway up its tyres, the Jaguar came to an abrupt halt. The driver's door opened, and Hoxton clambered out, the revolver in his hand. He splashed into the water, the surface up beyond his knees.

Winterman cautiously eased himself out of the Wolseley, sheltering behind the car-door. 'Hoxton!' he shouted. 'You're not going anywhere. Give it up.'

The rain was still pouring down, sweeping across the surface of the water as the wind gusted from the east.

Hoxton peered at Winterman from under the brim of his hat, and gestured towards the car. 'I've got a little collateral in here. Just let me pass. Half an hour. That's all I'm asking.'

'And you'll release Mary and Graham?'

'Eventually, yes. When you've delivered on your side of the deal.'

'That's not good enough, Hoxton. Let them go now, and you've got a deal.'

Hoxton smiled. 'Really, guv? I thought policemen didn't do things like that.'

'Policemen don't risk innocent lives.'

'Fair enough. But if you let me go without these two, you'll be on the blower in five minutes and every policeman in the county will be alerted.'

Winterman looked at the heavy sky. 'You know as well as I do, Hoxton, it'll be the devil's own job mobilising any support in weather like this. You can see what this road's like. I don't know if the others are any better.'

'Neither do I,' Hoxton said. 'I don't know which roads are open and which aren't. That's why I need to buy some time. I've got more chance of doing that with these two as an insurance policy.'

'You know I can't let you get away with hostages. If I deliver my side of the deal, what's the incentive for you to keep them safe? They'll just be a burden to you.'

'I don't know what you think I am, guv. You think that's my style?'

'I don't know what you are, Hoxton. I don't know what you're capable of. Those children's bodies. Where did they come from?'

'Another long story, guv. I just do a job. A practical type, that's me. Prepared to get my hands dirty when others aren't.' He shrugged. 'But I just do the job and get out. Nothing less, but nothing more neither.'

'And Marsh? Was that necessary?'

'Told you, guv. It was an accident, believe it or not. That's all it was. But that's when things go to buggery. When you're careless. Ought to know that by now.'

'I can't let you go, Hoxton. Not unless you hand over Mary and Graham. If you do that, I'm prepared to do a deal. Give you time to get away.'

'You're a gent, guv. But I think it might not be in your hands anymore.' Hoxton gestured with the pistol.

Winterman glanced behind him and cursed inwardly. Walking steadily up the road towards him, clad in a black oilskin jacket he had presumably found in the station, was DS Spooner.

'It doesn't make any difference, Hoxton. Just hand over Mary and Graham.'

Behind him, Winterman could hear Spooner calling his name. But he had become aware, almost at the same time, of another sound, something almost imperceptible against the endless washing of the rain.

At first, Winterman couldn't understand what was happening. He had thought that, while the rain continued to fall here and upstream, the waters would rise at the same steady rate. But the flood defences added another level of complexity, and another critical point had been reached. As the waters rose still higher, the riverbanks were beginning to crumble under the relentless onslaught. Winterman learned later that adverse tides and winds, as if in a grand meteorological conspiracy, had even hindered the river's usual passage to the sea, further raising the level of the bottled-up waters.

Whatever the causes, the pace of the flooding had suddenly increased dramatically. The waters were already lapping around the Jaguar's doors, a much stronger current sweeping in from the river. Hoxton was thigh deep in the icy water.

Winterman heard Spooner's footsteps behind him, but kept his eyes fixed on Hoxton.

'What the bloody hell's going on, Winterman?' Spooner said.

'Hoxton's got Mary and her son in the car,' Winterman said briefly. 'He wants them as hostages to secure his getaway.'

'Like hell,' Spooner said.

'I think we're of one mind on that, sir. The question is how we stop him.'

'And how we stop my bloody car from getting wrecked,' Spooner growled.

It was clear, in any case, that Hoxton was taking matters into his own hands. He was wrestling with the door of the Jaguar, fighting the pressure of the rising waters. He struggled briefly, then banged heavily on the window with the pistol. Mary wound down the window and peered out, her face white and terrified. Hoxton grabbed her arm, indicating that she should climb through the window.

For a moment, her face showed relief. She paused, gesturing that he should help Graham from the car first. Then she realised that the gun remained pointed steadily at her head.

With the pistol against her neck, she clambered onto the car seat and squeezed through the narrow window, Hoxton taking her weight as she dropped into the thigh-deep water.

Winterman could see no way to approach Hoxton without putting Mary further at risk. He took a tentative few steps forward, the water around his ankles, his mind working furiously to find some practical means of engaging with Hoxton.

Then the decision was taken out of his hands. As Hoxton struggled with the weight of Mary's body, she twisted, bracing herself against the car roof, and kicked out furiously. She was still wearing the heavy walking boots she had donned for her aborted walk to the school, and solid leather struck Hoxton brutally on the forehead. She kicked out again, this time catching him on the side of his face, and then she dropped agilely into the water, clutching at the car to regain her balance.

Hoxton stumbled backwards, toppling at the edge of the road as the earth below crumbled under the flooding. He fell back into the deeper water, his voice choked as he tipped backwards. A moment later, he was paddling frantically, unable to swim, caught by some unexpected undertow.

Even in the last few minutes, the floods had risen noticeably higher. The waters were lapping around Winterman's calves. The Jaguar was shifting, buoyed by the flood, buffeted by the powerful current. Mary was clutching at the door, calling for Graham to climb out after her.

Winterman waded forward into the water. He was soaked from the rain and the chill of the river was barely discernible.

Mary looked over her shoulder, registering for the first time that Winterman was there. 'Graham's in here. I've got to get him out.'

The waters were halfway up the car's bodywork, and the vehicle had moved noticeably, the bonnet swinging round at an angle to the road. Beyond the car, in the grey haze, Hoxton floundered in the water.

Winterman forced his way forward, waist-deep by the time he reached Mary's side. 'Are you okay?'

'Don't worry about me. Just get Graham out of the car.'

'You get on to solid ground. Head for Spooner. I'll look after Graham.'

She hesitated for a moment, reluctant to leave her son. 'Just get him out.' She forced her way back to where Spooner was already wading out to meet her.

Winterman peered through the car window. Graham was cowering in the far corner of the back seat, terrified. 'Hello, Graham.' Winterman spoke as calmly as he could manage. 'We need to get you out of the car and back onto dry land. It's a smart motor, this one, but it wasn't designed to be a boat.'

Graham managed a weak smile in return. As Winterman held out his hands, the boy crawled slowly across the seat towards the open window.

Winterman was reaching for the boy's small hands when an arm suddenly folded around his own neck, choking off his breath and dragging him back from the car. He reacted a second too slowly, his fingers scrabbling vainly for a grip on the car bodywork.

'Sorry, guv,' Hoxton gasped. 'You don't get rid of me that easily.' His arm was hard against Winterman's throat.

Winterman was caught off balance, his fingers tugging at Hoxton's arm. Just as he was despairing of freeing himself, his feet found some purchase on the submerged ground. He pulled forward and jabbed his elbow hard into Hoxton's stomach. As he stumbled back, the older man momentarily loosened his grip on Winterman's throat.

Winterman twisted himself from Hoxton's circling arm and pulled away. They were close to the edge of the road. His arm hindered by the damp weight of clothing, Winterman swung his fist hard against Hoxton's face.

Hoxton crumpled backwards, landing with a gentle splash in the grey water. Winterman watched him for a moment, trying to work out whether Hoxton was still conscious, until his attention was caught by Mary's cry from the road.

The Jaguar had moved further and was tipping into the rising flood. Winterman pushed through the water, reaching for the door handle as the car shifted again. Its rear wheels were already slipping down into the deeper water.

Winterman could hear Mary calling from behind him. As the car moved once more, he caught site of Graham's white face, framed in the window.

The pale face of a child, staring.

'Sam!' he called out before he could stop himself. And then he wondered why, what that name had meant to him. It was as if the name belonged to a story that he had once heard, somewhere in another life, but which he had long forgotten.

The pale face of a child, staring.

He had assumed, without questioning, that the face in the recurrent dream was Sam's, the boy reproaching him for his failure to protect his young life. But it was the same face in front of him now.

The car moved again and, gaining momentum, it disappeared from sight, sliding off the road into the depths of the water.

Behind, he heard Mary scream. Not looking back, he flung himself into the frozen water, thrusting himself down into the murky depths.

At first, he could see nothing. Then, as his eyes adjusted, he made out the long black shape of the Jaguar, a yard or two below. He pushed further down, feeling the roof and the doors and the open window. Water had flooded into the car and, with the pressure equalised, Winterman pulled open the door. He thrust himself inside and saw Graham, curled into a corner of the interior. There was a pocket of air trapped inside the car, but it was impossible to see whether the boy remained conscious. Winterman took the boy in his hands, manoeuvring him carefully through the door. Kicking hard against the sodden earth, he thrust the two of them up towards the light and air.

It took longer than he expected to reach the surface, long seconds that felt like hours. Then his head exploded from the water, and, gasping, he raised Graham's limp body into the air.

The boy stiffened, taken aback by the sudden shock of air, and began to cry. Winterman had no breath left to offer comfort, but, grasping Graham beneath his arms, he kicked powerfully towards the higher ground where Mary and Spooner were waiting.

He stumbled as he felt the hard road surface beneath his feet, then staggered upright, lifting Graham towards Mary who wrapped the boy tightly in her arms.

Spooner put a hand on Winterman's shoulder, steadying him. Winterman doubled up, gasping for breath, his strength suddenly gone. Still half choking, he scanned the expanse of grey water, its surface pitted with the endlessly falling rain. There was no sign of Hoxton.

Mary was clutching Graham, the boy staring over her shoulder at the man who had saved his life.

The pale face of a child, staring.

'Good work, lad,' Spooner was saying. 'Now, if you fancy one more trip down there, you could go and rescue my bloody car.'

CHAPTER SIXTY-EIGHT

The sound of the rain woke him again.

He lay for a long time, his eyes open, staring up into the darkness, listening.

Then he twisted over in the large double bed, limbs tangled in the heavy blankets and eiderdown, the chill of the bedroom striking his exposed face and hands.

There was silence. No sound of rain. No sound out there at all.

Just the nearby sound of breathing. Mary, breathing softly, fast asleep on the other side of the bed.

He rose silently and crossed the room, picking his way in the darkness, careful to avoid any noise that might wake Mary. He pulled back the curtains and stared out into the star-filled night.

The waters had receded, though the riverside fields were still flooded. There had been severe flooding even in town, the waters reaching unprecedented levels. His own house had escaped unscathed, apart from some flooding at the far end of the garden.

He had half expected that the dreams would cease. And perhaps they had. They had, at least, changed in character. He no longer had the sense of chasing through the rain, plunging after the same lost child. Perhaps Sam was at rest. Or perhaps at least one lost child had been saved.

But the rain was still there. Still haunting his dreams. Perhaps it always would be.

Because the rain was still falling. And, though he had found some shelter with Mary, Winterman wondered whether it would ever really stop.

CHAPTER SIXTY-NINE

There were no answers.

Days earlier, when the floods had subsided sufficiently to allow normal life to resume, Winterman and Spooner had interviewed William Callaghan. It was a formal interview, but William was being treated only as a witness, no longer as a suspect in Fisher's murder. Hoxton's body had been swept away in the flood and had not yet been found, but the working assumption – for Spooner at least – was that Hoxton had killed both Fisher and Merriman. It was a convenient assumption, and Winterman hadn't pressed Spooner to provide a motive.

After the events in the flood, they had discovered William, still hunched in the back of the Wolseley, apparently in a state of physical and mental collapse, scarcely able to respond to their questions. When assistance had finally arrived, he had been shipped to a hospital on the outskirts of Cambridge, his father assuming responsibility.

Two weeks later, his physical health apparently improved, he had been moved to a convalescent home in the north of the country. It was a converted country house, another legacy of the families whose circumstances had declined in the course of the century. It was surrounded by an imposing tree-lined estate, but its interior was given over to shoddy plasterboard walls and endless beige and khaki corridors. Like all such places, it gave Winterman the creeps.

William's father was waiting to greet them as he had promised. 'I'm not sure I should agree to this,' he had said on the telephone. 'William's in a very delicate condition. He needs time to recover.'

'With respect, sir,' Winterman had responded, 'the decision isn't yours. This is still a murder investigation. His doctor has confirmed that his physical condition is satisfactory.'

'It's not his physical condition I'm concerned about,' Callaghan said. 'His nerves took a battering. I don't know that he's ready to be interrogated yet.'

'Just a few questions, sir. At this stage.'

As he met them in the entrance hall, Callaghan made one further attempt to dissuade them. 'William's not well. He's really very highly strung. You can't put this off for a few more days?'

'There are a lot of unanswered questions,' Spooner said. 'We're hoping that William will fill in a few of the gaps. We'll be very gentle.'

'You made it clear that this isn't a formal interview, Superintendent. He won't need a solicitor present?'

Spooner gazed at him for a moment, as if considering possible responses. 'No, sir. Not at this stage. We just need him to answer some questions. Your son has behaved oddly, but we've no reason to believe he's guilty of any criminal acts.'

There was another pause, and Winterman had the sense of some unspoken communication between the two men.

'Very well, Superintendent. Though I should warn you that my son is not necessarily a reliable witness.'

'Is that so, sir? And why do you say that?' Spooner's tone sounded genuinely curious.

'I've told you, Superintendent, William's not himself. He hasn't been for a while. He's a touch obsessive.'

'There seems to be a lot of it about in these parts,' Winterman observed. 'Must be something in the water.'

'All I'm saying, Superintendent,' Callaghan went on, with a barely perceptible stress on Spooner's senior rank, 'is that you shouldn't give undue credence to anything my son might say.'

'You're saying he's delusional?'

'Just prone to exaggeration. And the medication leaves him a little confused.'

'We'll bear that in mind, sir.'

In the event, Callaghan's advice was both merited and hardly necessary. There was no easy way to judge the veracity of William's account, but it was clear that he would not cut a credible witness if any of it ever went to trial. Although that consideration, Winterman suspected, was largely academic.

They found William, following his father's directions, in a private room on the second floor of the building. The room, with a polished floor and oak furniture, looked a cut or two above the austere utilitarianism of the building's public areas. Presumably the professor was paying for his son's care.

William was hunched in a high-backed chair facing the window. He was dressed in pyjamas and slippers, a thick plaid blanket tucked around his knees. He looked a pale emaciated shadow of the figure Winterman had interviewed only weeks before.

William blinked as they entered, seemingly bewildered by their presence. The professor had sought to join the meeting, ostensibly to protect his son's interests. Spooner had politely but firmly resisted, on the assumption that the father's presence would prove inhibiting. Looking at the young man's blank visage, Winterman wondered whether the presence of a familiar figure, even his father, might have provided some reassurance.

'William, it's me, DI Winterman. This is my colleague, Superintendent Spooner. We just want to ask you a few questions. Is that all right?'

William stared at him for a second, as if he had barely understood the question, and then nodded slowly. 'My father thinks I'm incapable. He's no doubt told you.' His voice had a slight tremble, but sounded coherent enough.

'He said you'd been unwell.'

William laughed, with no obvious sign of mirth. Then he looked from Winterman to Spooner. 'And how much do I trust you two?'

It was a reasonable question, Winterman told himself, after William's experiences with Marsh and Hoxton. He had no cause to trust the police. 'I don't know. How much do you trust us?'

'I trust you, I think, DI Winterman. I don't know why, but I do. As you for, DS Spooner, I don't know you enough to say. But it probably doesn't matter much anyway. You'll either listen to me or you won't. There's not much more I can do either way.' His voice was still uncertain, but he sounded calmer. It was as if he'd reached the end of some quest, though it was impossible to tell whether his objective had been achieved or simply abandoned.

'Tell us about the bodies,' Winterman said quietly.

William was silent for a moment. Again, it was as if he had barely taken in the question. 'I found them, the children's bodies.'

'Where did you find them?'

'They were buried. Just shallow graves. In the marshland behind those buildings. Where you found me.'

'The three bodies?'

There was another, longer silence. 'No, more. At least one more. I don't know.'

'How did you come to find them?' Winterman thought back to the marshy fenland.

It was relatively close to the road and the village, but not an area anyone would have reason to search. It was unused ground, too marshy to cultivate. At that moment, it remained under several feet of water and impossible to investigate.

'It was the reverend. His ghost story.'

CHAPTER SEVENTY

Winterman glanced at Spooner, who had lowered himself onto a sofa in the far corner of the room, clearly content for Winterman to take the lead.

'You were heard in the pub asking Fisher something about a ghost story.'

William blinked, as though this was news to him. 'Was I? I was drunk, I suppose. But then the reverend was drunk when he told me about it the first time. He was often drunk. I'm not surprised. We were both in the pub one night. Both three sheets to the wind. The rev kept himself to himself. Would tell you to bugger off if you tried to approach him. But that night, for some reason, we started talking. Or he did. I don't know what sparked it – something about his wife and daughter. You know they died.'

'I heard the story,' Winterman said, recalling now that it was Hoxton who'd told it. 'How his wife left him–'

'For my father?'

'So I understand. Your father's a widower?'

'He's divorced. He's what they call a ladies' man. Insatiable.' William almost spat out the word. 'He picked up Fisher's wife and, I imagine, threw her out when he'd had enough. One among many. It was the story of my childhood.' There was an edge to the final words that Winterman couldn't interpret.

'But Fisher wouldn't take them back?'

'The rev was deep into his cups by that stage. Not responsible for his actions. He was daggers drawn with my old man. They'd been that way for a year or two, and my father had made sure that Fisher was well and truly ostracised from village life. By the time she came back, Fisher knew where she'd been. He wasn't going to let her back in.'

'And the ghost story?'

'He was talking about his wife and child. Then he said that sometimes he saw his daughter, out there in the fens.' William stopped. 'It sounds ridiculous, but I believed him. Or I felt he was speaking some kind of truth. He told me he'd seen his daughter. Her figure, hazy in the distance, skipping across the marshland. That she wasn't alone. There were other children. Lost children. That's what he said. Lost children trying to find their way home.'

'He was talking about the spot where you found the bodies?' Perhaps, Winterman thought, Callaghan had been right about his son's mental state.

'Yes. I didn't take it seriously. But the idea haunted me. It made me think.'

'About what?'

'About things that no one round here talks about.'

'Tell me.'

William paused and looked at Spooner. 'You can ask him. He should know. He's been around long enough.'

'Go on, son,' Spooner said gently. 'Don't keep us in suspense.'

'When I was a child,' William said, 'even before the war, there were rumours about children going missing. I never knew for sure. It was the stuff kids tell each other. Someone four villages away who didn't come home from school. Someone's second cousin who'd gone off on his bike and never came back. You know.'

'You said yourself,' Winterman said. 'Stuff that kids tell each other.'

'Just before the war, a local child did go missing. Little girl called Morton. Vanished on her way to school. No one ever found her.'

'I remember that one, anyway,' Spooner said from across the room. 'Little monster, by all accounts. Always getting into scrapes. We reckoned in the end that she'd got herself into one scrape too many. Got herself trapped somewhere. '

'But you never found a body,' William said.

'That's the way it is sometimes,' Spooner said. 'She'll turn up when we least expect it. Sometime when they demolish a building or dig out a ditch. They'll find her poor little bones underneath. Wouldn't be the first.'

'In any case,' Winterman said, 'that's one child. It doesn't mean there was anything in the other rumours.' He looked over to Spooner. 'Do you recall any similar cases before the war, sir?'

Spooner shrugged. 'Not that I remember. There are always missing persons reports and some of them were probably children. They usually turned up safe and sound after a few hours.'

'Doesn't sound like much,' Winterman said to William.

'Then the war came,' William said. 'The evacuees. That all happened so quickly, within weeks of war being declared. There were dozens round here, mainly sent up from London. I was just a child myself, and suddenly – within a matter of two or three weeks – all these other youngsters had arrived.'

'Are you saying that some of the evacuees went missing?'

William glanced across at Spooner, then back to Winterman. 'I think so. There were kids I saw in the first few days – when they were all arriving together – that I never saw again. Just one or two.'

'How could you know?' There was something about William's earnest tone that set a chill down Winterman's spine. 'If there were dozens arriving. Surely you can't know who you saw and who you didn't?'

'No, I can't be sure,' William admitted. 'But I think I know. What do you think, DS Spooner? Do you think some of the evacuees went missing?' There was an odd undertone to his words.

Spooner gazed back at him impassively. 'Nationally, I've little doubt that they did. Do you know that we moved nearly a quarter of the population during September '39?' He paused, as if himself contemplating the magnitude of this undertaking. 'But some of it was chaos. Brothers and sisters got split up. Some got put on the wrong trains or sent to the wrong places. Almost every time it was sorted out in the end. But a few cases ended up in tragedy. Parents who never tracked down their children. It's not even necessarily that the children came to a bad end. It might just have been that, if they lost their ID and they didn't know where they'd come from, perhaps they never got back again.'

Winterman felt the nagging of a familiar horror, the images that had dominated his dreams. 'But you're saying more than that, William. You're suggesting that something might have happened to these children.'

'You've seen the bodies,' William said quietly. 'Where did they come from? Who are those children?'

It was an unarguable point. That was the greatest mystery. Who were these children? No one had reported them missing. Even in an insular community like this, surely the loss of a child – of several children – would be noted. But not, perhaps, if no one had known they were here in the first place.'

'You think it's possible?' Winterman asked Spooner.

'Of course it's possible. I was involved in sorting out some of the messes that were made in shipping those kids around. There were all kinds of problems. Kids who weren't on the lists. Kids who were on the list but not there. Usually it was just an admin foul up. But, if it was something more, we wouldn't have known. The question is though, son, just who are you accusing?'

William gazed up at Spooner as though this question hadn't occurred to him. 'What?'

'If you're saying that kiddies went missing, it stands to reason that someone took them. Someone killed them. Who round here would do a thing like that?'

William's expression was blank. 'That's the question, isn't it?'

'I'd say so,' Spooner said. 'Frankly, lad, these are serious allegations to be throwing about. Doesn't seem to me you've got much to support them.'

'Except for the bodies,' Winterman said quietly. 'Three bodies. Three children who came from somewhere.' He leaned forward, ignoring Spooner's expression. 'Tell us about the bodies, William. You dug them up.'

'I went exploring up there one afternoon. Before the snow came. I'd been in the pub at lunchtime. Had a few too many. I wouldn't have dared do it otherwise. And I wouldn't have fancied doing it at night. I'm a bloody medical student as well. Should take this stuff in my stride.'

'So what made you go?'

'I don't know.' He paused, his gaze fixed on Spooner. 'Curiosity, I suppose. It was a miserable afternoon, drizzling rain, cold. If I'd not been half-cut, I'd have given up straightaway. As it was, I wouldn't have persevered for long. But I didn't need to. It was soggy wet ground. Not quite marsh, but nearly. And it looked like someone had been digging there relatively recently–'

'But the bodies weren't recent?'

'I don't know. There was an area, six or seven feet wide, where someone seemed to have been digging. I prodded about a bit around there. Didn't need to go very far down before I found something. Cleared away the earth, and there was the first body. A poor little girl. The flesh was all preserved. Like leather. I dug a bit more, off to one side, and found two more. I think there were other bodies as well. But I can't be sure.'

Winterman was watching William carefully. There was a light buried deep in his eyes, very close to the spark of madness. If he hadn't seen the evidence himself, he wouldn't have believed the story for a moment. 'You dug them out?'

'It was horrible but I'm a medical student. They weren't the first bodies I'd had to deal with.'

'You should have left them. Called the police.'

'I wasn't thinking clearly. It didn't seem right that they should just be left out there in the elements. I cleared the earth from them, and dragged them up to the barn. I left the bodies there covered with some old straw in case anyone should come in – though I don't think anyone's been in there for years. Then I walked back home and called the police.'

'What happened?'

'I was drunk. They thought it was some kind of prank, I suppose. They didn't believe me anyway.'

'But you called again when you were sober.'

'That evening. I was put through to someone – I don't know, someone senior. He listened to what I had to say. Said they'd investigate and that someone would come out to talk to me. But they never did.'

Spooner leaned forward. 'Who did you speak to, son?'

'I don't know. I don't know if he even gave me his name. I went back the next day. I thought someone else had been digging there. After I'd gone. Someone had been digging in a wider area. It was hard to be sure, because I couldn't really remember exactly where I'd been before. But I prodded about with my spade. There was no sign of any more bodies.'

'But you said before–'

'The previous day, I thought there were other bodies. When I came back, there weren't. That's all I can say.'

'But the bodies you'd found?'

'They were still there, still buried under the straw. If someone had been there, they hadn't found them.'

'Did you go back to the police?'

William shook his head. 'You don't understand, do you?'

'We don't know what you're talking about, son,' Spooner said.

William gazed back at him. 'Maybe you don't. But I think it's too late anyway now. They've got their scapegoat. Hoxton did their dirty work for them, and now he can conveniently take the blame. For killing the children, for doing… whatever was done to them. For getting rid of the evidence. He can take the blame for everything.'

'You're saying it was someone else?' Winterman said.

'I grew up with it, though I didn't realise,' William said. 'I don't know who's involved. It wasn't just Hoxton who made sure that my calls were ignored.' William looked back at Spooner. 'Maybe you know better than me.'

'I don't think so, lad. I don't think so.' Spooner pushed himself to his feet. 'Thanks for talking to us. I think we've got all we can.' He gestured to Winterman. 'Shall we go?'

Winterman hesitated momentarily, still trying to fathom the light he could distantly see in William's eyes. 'Thanks, William,' he said finally. Then he rose and followed Spooner out of the room.

CHAPTER SEVENTY-ONE

There were no answers.

Pyke was waiting for Winterman in the snug of a down-at-heel pub in one of the backstreets behind the market square. He sat morosely at the bar, two pints of bitter set up in front of him. As Winterman perched himself on a neighbouring stool, Pyke slid one of the beers across.

'Cheers.'

'Cheers.' Winterman looked around the shabby room, catching sight of his own reflection in an age-spotted mirror emblazoned with the name of the brewery. 'Nice place.'

Pyke gave one of his characteristic snorts and followed Winterman's gaze as it passed over the stained and scratched table tops, the cracked leather of the seats, the chipped ashtrays. 'Queer hangout, believe it or not.' He glanced over at the overweight barman who was ostentatiously polishing glasses with a not-noticeably clean rag. 'Or used to be anyway. I've lost touch these days.'

'Going straight?' Winterman asked, sipping at the beer. The quality of the bitter was, predictably, on a par with the rest of the establishment.

'Not going anywhere very much, old chum, truth be told.'

'How are things?'

'Pretty bloody, overall. But could be a lot worse. At least I'm not in the frame for Howard's murder.'

'Our friend Hoxton seems to be taking the posthumous fall for all that.'

'I imagine that suits everyone.'

'Less paperwork all round. Speaking of which, what about work?'

'Again, could be worse. In the circumstances, Spooner decided to turn a blind eye to the other issue. So no stain on my character and all that. University know nothing about it, and Spooner's said there'll still be police work for me. As long as I keep my nose clean in the future. Not that it's my nose he's worried about, if you get my drift.'

'Decent of him, all told.'

'Aye. Decent of him,' Pyke agreed. 'Again, suits everyone, I imagine.'

'You think? I was afraid that Spooner would see you as an easy addition to his arrest tally.'

Pyke shrugged. 'Maybe. But, as you say, less paperwork. And this way he's got me exactly where he wants me.'

'Which is where?'

'Firmly by the balls, if you'll pardon the expression.'

'Why would Spooner want that?'

Pyke took a long pull on his beer. Finally, as if changing the subject, he said, 'Christ, it's all bollocks, isn't it?'

'What is?'

'All this. Why would Hoxton kill Howard?'

'Because Howard was blackmailing him? It was your suggestion.' To date, they had found no hard evidence to support Pyke's suspicions.

'Why would Howard blackmail a policeman without two pennies to rub together? If Howard really was into that game, he'd have had bigger fish to fry.'

'If he could find bigger fish. Maybe Hoxton was just one among many. We'll probably never find out.'

'No,' Pyke agreed. 'We probably never will. And I'm not going to rock the boat, not now. But it's all bollocks.'

'If you say so.'

'I say so.' Pyke raised his glass. 'Cheers, old chum. Let's all raise a glass to George Hoxton.'

CHAPTER SEVENTY-TWO

Mary, breathing softly on the far side of the bed.

He didn't know, even now, whether this was the right thing to be doing. Things had moved more quickly than he could have imagined, and he still didn't know whether he was taking advantage of Mary.

Her house had, mercifully, been spared the worst impact of the flood, although the waters had been literally lapping at the back door. Mary herself, once she had been dried and warmed, showed no physical ill effect. Graham had treated the whole thing as a terrific adventure.

Even so, Winterman suspected that it had all affected Mary more than she wanted to acknowledge. She seemed desperate to move on, to be active, as if the experience had again brought home to her the sense of mortality that hung over her life. On the face of it, her apparent energy seemed a positive development, but to Winterman it seemed brittle.

As a result, Winterman, the supposed ladies' man, had made no attempt to move things forward in their relationship, afraid he might be taking advantage of her vulnerability. A week or so later, when normal working life had more or less resumed and they were alone together in the office at the end of a day of paper-pushing, she had unexpectedly taken the initiative and invited him out for a drink. Feeling that his gallantry was being challenged, he had reciprocated almost immediately by asking her out for dinner.

In ration-bound Britain, the only options for an even half-decent meal were in town. With her mother acting as babysitter, Winterman had offered to put Mary up for the night, assuring her that there was a spare room and that his intentions were honourable. In the event, the meal had been worse than mediocre, both had somehow managed to laugh themselves silly on nothing more than a half-pint of mild and a sweet sherry, and at some point – Winterman was unsure exactly how or when – the honourable intentions had gone out of the window.

Mary, breathing softly, on the far side of the bed.

It was what he had wanted since he had met her. And the warmth, the companionship, was something he had needed for much longer. Something he had denied himself, with his son dead and his wife lost. It felt as if Mary was the one, but Winterman was wise enough to know that in the circumstances he might have felt the same about any attractive personable young woman. It would take much longer before he could be certain.

As for Mary herself, what was she doing here? Was she just making a grasp for life – any life – in the middle of a world that had for so long seemed dominated by death and denial? Did she want him, or would any mildly attractive, personable young man have done? He had no idea, but it seemed worth taking the time to find out.

That one night, that first night, he felt real contentment. It had taken some time for him to recognise the emotion as he lay silently in the dark. In that moment, he had had no notion of what the future might hold, where he was going or what he was doing. But, just briefly, he had managed to relinquish the past, to free himself from the dreams and ghosts that had haunted his waking and sleeping hours. For a second, all that mattered was now.

There had been other nights since then, and their relationship had developed and blossomed. Even Mrs Griffiths seemed to have approved, turning a blind eye to her daughter's nights away. It wasn't the time to begrudge anyone a little happiness.

Winterman was happy. He was happy with Mary, he was happy with what their future seemed to hold.

But he was no longer content. After that one restful night, the dreams had gradually returned, infiltrating his sleep with their images of the rain, the sense of dread.

They were not the same dreams. Something had been resolved. Sam was no longer out there, no longer reaching out his hands for salvation from the rising waters. Sam, Winterman thought, had finally been saved.

But there was still something out there, in the endless teeming rain. Some voices calling. Other lost children, still trying to find their way back home.

There were no answers.

CHAPTER SEVENTY-THREE

There were no answers.

'What do you think?' Winterman had asked Spooner, a few days later, as they sat together in Winterman's sparsely furnished office. 'About young Callaghan, I mean?'

'I think he's as mad as a hatter. Out of his tree.'

'He found the bodies.'

'Probably that's what drove him out of his tree then. That and the booze. It wasn't exactly a rational response, was it. Dragging out the bodies and planting them around the vicinity to… what, attract our attention?'

'Because the police took no notice.'

'Because whoever took the call thought, probably accurately, that he was a drunk talking rubbish. It sounds as if we fouled up, but I don't think anyone can be blamed for that.'

'What about his conspiracy theories?'

Spooner turned to face Winterman. 'Oh, for God's sake. I hope you're just playing devil's advocate here. We know what happened. We've even managed to trace Hoxton's convoluted history before he changed his name and moved here. Christ knows how he managed to get a job in the force with that big black hole in his past.'

Winterman had asked himself the same question. They had obtained a warrant to search Hoxton's terraced house and had torn the place apart trying to find some hard evidence. They had found nothing immediately incriminating, other than two hundred pounds in used fivers, carefully wrapped and stashed beneath the floorboards. But they had found a wealth of revelatory documents. Hoxton's birth certificate indicated he had been born in Lincoln and that his real name was Gerald Horton. That had provided enough information to enable them to trace some details of his early life. He had been just old enough to serve in the last few months of the First War. Unlike many, he had lived to tell the tale, but had been diagnosed with severe shell shock at the time of his demobilisation.

They had so far been unable to trace his movements in any detail after leaving the army, but had tracked him as far as Leicester in 1920. Three years later, a Gerald Horton of Leicester had been convicted of indecent assault on an underage girl. After that, they had discovered no reference to Horton until the arrival of Hoxton in Ely in the late 1920s. He had held various clerical jobs before joining the police, as a uniformed officer, in 1933. He had transferred to CID three years later, and his record since then was unexceptional but unblemished. Just before the war, for reasons that remained unexplained, he had transferred out of headquarters to the sub-station where Winterman had encountered him.

'You think Hoxton's squarely in the frame for everything?'

'What do you think?' Spooner said. 'He's got a conviction as a kiddie fiddler.'

'That doesn't make him a killer.'

'He killed Marsh.'

'Supposedly by accident.'

'Useful accident. Marsh wanted whoever was responsible for the kiddies. Thought his own brother was one of victims. That's why he dragged off young Callaghan when he caught him shifting that body into the graveyard. Thought he was abetting someone. If Hoxton thought Marsh was on to him… well, a convenient accident.'

'What about Fisher and Merriman? That was Hoxton too?'

'Why not? Hoxton got the jitters when the bodies started turning up, which I suppose, in his half-brained way is what Callaghan intended. Probably thought Fisher knew something. As for Merriman, your mate Pyke reckons he was blackmailing someone. If it was Hoxton, then Bob's your uncle.'

'All very neat.'

'Bloody hell, Winterman. Don't start chasing shadows. You're too good for that.'

'Get me back up to headquarters then,' Winterman said. 'And out of this godforsaken dump, sir.' The office was empty and bleak now that Hoxton's and Marsh's debris had been cleared out of the place. 'Just me and Mrs bloody Sheringham.' He had lowered his voice for the last few words, and now he smiled across at the blonde secretary sitting behind her typewriter, apparently unoccupied, regarding him with a steely uninterest. He thought her manner had become frostier, as if she held him personally responsible for everything that had happened.

'Don't cross Mrs Sheringham,' Spooner advised. 'Though I agree she's not the best company. What about your Mary?'

'She's only part-time.' As he spoke, some thought nagged briefly at Winterman's mind. 'And she's hardly my Mary.'

'Not what I hear. But you're right. We need to make a decision about this office. Either move some more officers out here or shut it down.'

'Your decision. But I know what I'd recommend.' Winterman regarded the older man who was sitting opposite him. He still didn't know whether to trust Spooner. He'd underestimated him, that was for certain. But his initial instinct had been right. A few years off retirement, Spooner wasn't going to stick his neck out. 'You didn't answer my question about Callaghan's conspiracy theory.'

Spooner's expression was unchanging. 'I thought I had.'

'What if there's something behind what he says? What if Hoxton was just a footsoldier, doing someone else's dirty work? It would make more sense of Merriman's murder. Why would Merriman blackmail Hoxton? He hadn't got two farthings to rub together. Whereas if Merriman was blackmailing someone with some money and a reputation…'

'Like Hamshaw?'

'For example.'

For the first time, Spooner looked genuinely angry. 'Look, Winterman. Just leave it. Hamshaw can be a ruthless bastard. It'll be worse for you if you go stirring things up.'

And even worse for you, Winterman thought. 'I'm only suggesting we–'

'We do nothing,' Spooner said. 'If I find you've even spoken to Hamshaw without my say-so, I'll have you on a charge so quick your feet won't touch the ground. Is that clear?'

Clear enough, Winterman thought.

He had spent the day mulling over Spooner's words. He still felt uneasy. It wasn't that he necessarily gave any credence to what William had said. It was more that he felt an unease, a sense that stones were being left unturned. That was the world they were in. Resources were short. No one could waste time on half-baked fancies. Even ignoring Spooner's warning, there was nothing to be gained from prising open that particular can of worms. And a lot to be lost.

By the time he arrived home that evening, Winterman had decided to follow Spooner's orders. He knew himself well enough to recognise that, in part, his reluctance to do so stemmed from nothing more noble than simple stubbornness. He didn't like being told to back off. But stubbornness wasn't a good motive for anything. Whatever Spooner's own motives, he was right.

Winterman pushed open his front door, his mind already moving on to the prospect of an evening with Mary. Probably just a visit to the pub, some fish and chips, and then back here. She hadn't been in the office for a couple of days, and Winterman realised he had been missing her.

As he stepped into the hallway, he stooped to pick up a buff foolscap envelope from the doormat, glancing at it with curiosity. The envelope was blank and had been hand delivered. He tore it open and tipped out the contents.

It was a set of half a dozen photographs. Winterman stared at the top one for a moment in bafflement. It showed a squalid-looking backstreet, probably somewhere in the town. In the centre of the picture, there was the door to some kind of sleazy private members' club. From his time on the beat, Winterman knew exactly what sort of club it was likely to be.

There was a figure caught entering the club. A woman, her back to the camera, a scarf wrapped tightly around her head. No features were visible, and the figure's body was little more than a grey silhouette. But Winterman knew at once it was Mary.

He flicked rapidly through the remaining photographs. The rest were interior shots, poorly lit as though the photographer had been reluctant to use a flash. All of them showed Mary. In the first, she was standing behind a tawdry-looking bar, serving bottled beer to an overweight man. In another, she was sitting next to the man, clearly trying to look attentive. Others showed her in the same position, her expression one of forced joviality.

The penultimate photograph showed the man pawing ineffectively at Mary's blouse, a clutch of white fivers in his hand. And the final photograph showed Mary holding open a door, presumably in the same dismal clubroom, for the man. At the bottom, someone had typed, neatly: 'More where these came from.'

Winterman stared at the photographs. He recognised something that had briefly nagged at his brain earlier in the day, when he had talked about Mary working part-time. It was a trivial detail from right at the start. When Mary's mother had found the child's body in the dyke, she had telephoned for Mary at the office. It had been one of Mary's days off, but she had not been at home. She had had a job – some kind of job – that her mother knew nothing about. Perhaps she still did.

It was not so surprising. They paid her as much they could afford in the office, but it was little more than charity. She had to support her mother and her children, and there was little work to be had. These were hard times.

The message of the photographs was clear, he supposed. It was a warning. If you stir things up, we'll do the same. Perhaps it had come from Spooner, perhaps not. Winterman had already voiced his unease to others at headquarters. But the warning was effective enough. He couldn't begin to imagine what the impact might be if he were to respond – on Mary, on her mother, on the children.

It was all so unnecessary, he thought bitterly. He had already decided to do nothing. It was almost as if they – whoever they might be – wanted to provoke him, prove how impotent he really was. Just to show that they were in control.

He took the photographs between his finger and thumb, carried them though into the parlour and dropped them into the fire grate. He found some matches and set fire to the prints, watching until the last fragments had been consumed. The gesture was little more than symbolic. No doubt more copies could be made. But it made him, momentarily, feel a little better.

CHAPTER SEVENTY-FOUR

Mary, breathing softly on the far side of the bed.

Winterman lay awake, the last dregs of the familiar dream still fogging his mind. He had spent most of the night awake and, when sleep had finally come, he had found himself once again out in that endless rain, sensing the floodwaters rising. He had woken with a start, his mind filled with a terrible, unfocused sense of dread.

Then he remembered the photographs. The stilted evening they had spent together, Mary knowing that something was wrong, he barely able to speak. Winterman knew she thought that the relationship was fizzling out almost before it had begun, and he didn't even know whether she was wrong.

Lying there, he thought that she was. It was too important to let go. The truth was he loved Mary.

Tomorrow he would speak to her. Tomorrow he would find out the truth. And, tomorrow, together, they would decide what to do next.

He rolled over in the bed, tangled in the sheets and blankets, knowing that he would not sleep again that night. Finally, he made his way across the darkened room and, as so often before, pulled back the curtains to stare out across the night-shrouded fens.

He could see the first deep crimson signs of dawn in the east. It was a fine night, the sky full of stars. Before long, it would be the start of summer.

But in his own mind the winter was barely over. The rain was still coming down, heavy and relentless. Somewhere out there, there were the children, still lost, still reaching out. Still trying to find their way back home.

And there were no answers.

Part Three

March, 1947

CHAPTER SEVENTY-FIVE

Even the ticking of the carriage clock swept Winterman straight back to his childhood. It was a sonorous tick, redolent of solidity and fine craftsmanship. It had always been there, so familiar as to be almost unnoticeable. One evening, a few days after returning, he had neglected to wind it. In the morning, the silence had been unexpected, disconcerting, as if something had been sucked from the air.

He had wondered, from time to time, about the clock's history. Was it a family heirloom of some sort? Or had his parents bought it sometime in the early days of their marriage? It had been there as long as he could remember. He had never thought to ask while they were alive. The clock had been just one more item on the inventory he had compiled as executor of his father's will. Whatever its history might have been, it was an heirloom, part of his own inheritance, along with the house and everything else in it.

Seven o'clock. Time to wake Mary. Make her a cup of tea in bed. He had been up since just after four, watching through the uncurtained windows as the sky slowly lightened. The weather had picked up. It looked set to be a fine spring day, the low sun picking out every burgeoning leaf in gold.

He had realised, as the first sliver of the rising sun had emerged from behind the distant horizon, that today Mary was not due to work at the office. One of her non-working days.

Mary had previously stayed over only on the days when she was due to come in to the office. It had made sense. They had observed the proprieties, supposedly to spare Mary's mother any embarrassment. Winterman rarely stayed over at Mary's house, and when he did he slept in the spare room. Mary's nights at his had been justified on the basis of convenience. It would be pointless to ferry her back to Framley at the end of the evening. Mrs Griffiths undertook the occasional babysitting duties, and in return they all maintained the fiction that Mary also used Winterman's spare bedroom.

But it meant that Winterman had never witnessed Mary's movements on the days she was not due to work with him. Until now.

After a visit to the pictures – they had seen some odd romantic film about nuns in the Himalayas Mary had been keen on – they had finished the evening with a quiet drink in one of the more salubrious town centre pubs. Winterman, his mind running endlessly over the past day's events, knew he had been lousy company. He could sense Mary's discomfort. He had assumed he would drive her back at the end of the evening, and had been surprised when she told him that she had arranged for her mother to babysit.

He had been unclear about Mary's motivations for staying over. Perhaps each of them had been expecting the other to announce the end of their relationship. In the event there was nothing more momentous than a late night cup of tea and a tacit acknowledgement they were both too tired or too tense for any romantic conclusion to the night.

But here she was. Asleep, upstairs. While Winterman sat turning the same thoughts endlessly over and over in his mind.

He was rising, preparing to put the kettle on, when the living room door opened. Mary was standing, wrapped in his old tartan dressing gown, looking as if she had been deliberately posed in the doorway.

'You've been up a while,' she said.

'Sorry. I tried not to disturb you. Couldn't sleep.'

'More nightmares?' He had told her, half-embarrassed, about his recurrent dreams – the rain, the lost child.

'Some dreams. But I was thinking.'

She moved to sit on the sofa, a cautious foot or two away from him, tucking the dressing gown decorously across her knees. 'Yes, that was pretty evident. Last night as well.'

'I was awful company.'

'We both were. Both thinking.'

'It's always a bad habit. So what were you thinking about?'

There was a moment's silence. Then she said, 'You want to get this place aired properly. It doesn't feel lived in.'

'Is that what you were thinking about?'

'No. But I like this house. I could imagine living here.' Another moment's hesitation. 'I need to talk to you.'

'About your other job?' He had tried hard to keep any note of bitterness out of his voice and thought he had just about managed it.

'Somebody's been talking then. This bloody place.'

'Not exactly talking. Someone sent me some photographs.'

'The bastards.' She shook her head, tears in her eyes. 'That's what I wanted to talk to you about.'

Winterman instinctively reached out a hand and touched her arm. A moment later, he was holding her hand, feeling her fingers trembling between his. 'You knew about the photographs?'

'Not until yesterday. Someone sent me a set too. Photographs taken in the bar–' She gulped, as if scarcely able to speak. 'They made me look–'

Winterman gripped her hand more tightly. 'It doesn't matter.' He didn't know whether or not he was lying.

She pulled her hand from his and jumped up from the sofa. 'Of course it bloody matters. Those photographs, they made it look as if I…' She was clearly unable or unwilling to find the right words. 'They sent you the photographs? The same photographs? What did you think?'

Winterman pushed himself to his feet. 'I don't know. I couldn't make any sense of it. So tell me.'

'There's nothing to tell, not really. I had another job. Do you know how little money I've got? How much we struggle to make ends meet? And, no, it's not the most salubrious job in the world. Barmaid in some sleazy bar where every other customer's trying to pick you up. But he pays better than any pub round here and I'm just a bloody barmaid. That's all. Nothing else. I get a few quid extra because I'm prepared to dress up a bit and let some of those sad sacks lech over me. Nothing else.'

Winterman opened his mouth to offer some platitude, then realised he had nothing to say. He had doubted her. Just for a short time and reluctantly, almost disbelievingly. But he had doubted her.

'So why didn't you say something before?' He was aware that even now he sounded accusatory.

'Because it's cash in hand. Because it's a sleazy dive which is probably home to half the spivs and crooks in the county. Because you're a policeman. Why do you bloody think?'

It was a fair response. He wasn't sure how he'd have reacted, and he didn't yet know her well enough to make any demands on her. 'But you would have told me eventually, I suppose.' Now, he thought, he just sounded petulant.

'I suppose so. I wasn't planning on staying there much longer anyway. It just a way of making ends meet. It wasn't exactly something I did for fun.'

'I'm sorry. Tell me about the photographs.'

She looked at him as if about to say something else then pushed herself up from the sofa. 'I've got them in my handbag. We can compare them, see if they really are the same.'

'I can tell you if they are. But we can't compare them.' He paused, stalled by her quizzical expression. 'I burned them.'

She smiled, then suddenly laughed. 'And you're supposed to be the brilliant detective. Good job I kept the evidence, isn't it?'

CHAPTER SEVENTY-SIX

Five minutes later, they were sitting at the kitchen table, sipping tea, staring at the photographs Winterman had spread out across the varnished table. There was no doubt they were identical to those he had destroyed.

'I was set up,' she said.

Winterman flicked again through the various prints, noticing quite how striking Mary looked even in these dimly lit shots. He had to admit, seeing them again, that there was nothing incriminating here. The sequence of shots had been selected to create that impression. 'How did it happen?'

'Easily. The first few shots are genuine enough. That's what he expects us to do–'

'Who expects you to?'

'Charlie. Charlie Driscoll. He owns the place. I've been told he's the Honourable Charles Driscoll, but I don't believe a word of it. I've met few people who are less honourable.'

'Doesn't mean he doesn't have the title. I've met a fair few dishonourable Honourables. Anyway, go on.'

'Charlie wants us to… oh, you know, flirt a bit with the customers. It's harmless enough, I suppose. We're there to look decorative.'

Winterman didn't doubt it though he was less convinced of the harmlessness. 'Who is this chap? The customer.'

'Haven't a clue. He wasn't someone I'd seen before. One of Charlie's business associates, I assumed. It's a member's club, so I suppose he's a member.'

'Though I don't imagine Charlie's too scrupulous about checking people's *bona fides*.'

'I imagine not. And if you ask him, he'll just deny all knowledge. Very discreet is Charlie.'

'So what about the last few shots? What's going on there?'

She looked up at him. 'Not what you think.'

'I–'

'I'm joking. Be quiet before you incriminate yourself any further.' She picked up one of the photographs. 'I can remember it quite clearly. That chap had had one or two drinks – couple of large scotches, if I remember correctly. Gave the impression he might have had a few somewhere else beforehand. Bit shaky on his pins. Anyway, he'd just knocked back one of the scotches when he said he didn't feel well. Said he felt a bit queasy, and did we have a gents he could use. We don't really, because there's a public convenience outside and Charlie's too mean to provide anything else. But he's got his own place in the office behind the bar and I didn't think he'd want this chap throwing up in public. So I offered to take him through to the back and…' She gestured to the photograph. 'Bob's your uncle.'

'So who took the photographs? These have been lit. Not well, but enough that you can work out what's happening. You must have seen the flash?'

'There was a bunch of actors at the far end of the bar – we get a lot of them from the theatre – and someone was taking photographs. Maybe more than one person. I imagine that's how they worked it.'

'Anything written on your prints?'

She flicked through them and shook her head. 'Nothing. What about yours?'

'"More where this came from."' He smiled ruefully. 'Another reason I shouldn't have destroyed them.'

'I'm flattered that you did. But what's it all about?'

'I think it was about keeping me quiet.' He briefly recounted his conversation with Spooner.

'You think Spooner sent them?'

'No. I'm still prepared to believe Spooner's not one of them. He's just looking not to rock the boat. I don't think he'd try to scare me off.'

'That might be what he wants you to think.'

'Of course. I've no particular reason to trust him. But I've no particular reason not to, just yet, and I'd rather keep all the friends I can. The truth is I blabbed my mouth off about Hoxton to others at HQ. Anyone could have sent these.'

'So why send them to me as well?'

'The same reason, I suppose. Keep you quiet. Perhaps to drive a wedge between us. They'd expect you to keep quiet about it, and probably expect me to do the same.'

'It nearly worked. Last night, I thought we were through, even though I didn't quite know why. That's why I decided to say something. Whatever was going to come between us, I didn't want it to be my secrets.'

He took her hand. 'I think I love you.' He paused. 'Did I just say that?'

'I rather think you did. And I rather think I feel the same.' She took a sip of her tea, grimacing at the lukewarm liquid. 'But why me?'

'Why do I love *you*?' he asked, mock serious.

'No, idiot. I mean, why do they – whoever they are – think it's worth warning me to keep quiet?'

'Just because you know me, I suppose. But you're right. It seems excessive. There's no reason for them to think you're likely to cause any trouble. You're not a troublemaker like me. Maybe they think you know something. Perhaps they thought I'd already discussed it all with you.'

'Or perhaps they thought I knew something myself.'

'It's possible. But what?'

'Perhaps whatever it was Jimmy thought he knew. Maybe something that Paul found out. Perhaps something about Gary.'

'It's possible. That's the trouble. Anything's possible, but we don't have anything definite.'

'We have one thing.'

'What's that?'

'The fact that this didn't work.' She gestured towards the photographs. 'They thought it would drive us apart. It hasn't. It's done the opposite.'

'It's done more than that.'

'How do you mean?'

'Yesterday afternoon, after I'd spoken to Spooner, I was ready to give this up. I let him persuade me I was overreacting, that I was conjuring conspiracies out of thin air. I was going to let it drop, probably against all my instincts, if not my better judgment. Whereas now…'

'Now?'

He picked up one of the photographs and looked again at the image of Mary standing behind the tawdry bar. 'Now I know it's real. Now I know someone's trying to warn me off. I don't much like being warned off. All in all, it's a pretty spectacular own goal, I'd say.'

'If you say so. But be careful.'

'My career's halfway down the drain anyway. What have I got to lose?'

'You've got your life,' she said. 'And you've got me.'

CHAPTER SEVENTY-SEVEN

'It's not what I expected,' Winterman said.

'What did you expect?' Pyke asked. 'Long mahogany benches? Intricate sculptures of test tubes and retorts? Electrical boxes with valves and flashing lights?'

'Something like that. And I expected it to be a proper building.'

Pyke glanced up at the discoloured ceiling of the pre-fabricated construction that housed the laboratory and nodded. 'I think we'd all have expected that. As a minimum. Instead, as you've correctly observed, we have to work in a glorified bloody shed. Not that I work here much these days. I'm seconded to the Home Office for the forensic stuff. But I'll always think of this as home. Let's go and get a pint.'

Winterman followed him back out into the sunshine. The shabby functionality of the laboratory building was thrown into even sharper contrast by the old university buildings surrounding it.

'Supposedly just a temporary measure. But that was in 1942 and I don't see much sign of them rushing to replace it.'

'No money, I imagine. That seems to be the story everywhere.' Winterman hopped across the street behind Pyke, who had only narrowly avoided being run over by a greengrocer's van. Pyke ducked into the narrow doorway of a pub, gesturing for Winterman to follow.

By the time Winterman had made his way into the shade of the public bar, Pyke was already ordering the beers. He looked over his shoulder at Winterman. 'Inside or out? There's a beer garden at the back. Though it's not much to write home about.'

'Let's go out. First decent day we've had this year.'

'They're forecasting a hot summer. Believe it when I see it. But the weather's gone crazy. I blame those A-bombs.'

The beer garden was, as Pyke had suggested, an unimpressive affair, little more than a tiny courtyard surrounded by high brick walls. The landlord had made an effort with a stone trough filled with plants which, in the first warmth of spring, were beginning to bud. There were three tables and an assortment of chairs apparently scavenged from any available source. But the yard at least served as a suntrap, catching the full glare of the midday sun. Winterman lowered himself cautiously on to one of the wooden chairs and took a sip of his beer, enjoying the unfamiliar glow of the sun on his face.

'Cheers.'

'Cheers.' Pyke raised his glass in return. 'So, to what do I owe this unexpected visit? Not that I'm complaining. Any excuse to get out of that place and into the pub.'

'Just a social call. More or less.'

'Oh, yes?' Pyke raised a sceptical eyebrow. 'I'm honoured. So why are you really here?'

'Nothing official. If Spooner knew I was pestering you, I'd be out on my ear. I just want to pick your brains a little. You don't think Hoxton acted alone, do you?'

Pyke regarded him for a moment. 'I've told you. It's all bollocks. But I'm not going to muddy the waters.'

'Not even for Howard's sake?'

Pyke had already finished most of the beer, Winterman noticed. 'There's nothing I can do for Howard now. All I can do is keep my own life on the straight and narrow.'

'Fair enough. I can't blame you for that. I'm treading a risky path here myself. I've been told to keep well away from it.'

'By Spooner?'

'Spooner made it very clear I should back off.'

'You think Spooner's bent?'

'I'd say not. But he wants a quiet life. Doesn't want anything that might deflect him from the smooth path to retirement.'

'Just like me then. Okay, I'm not going to help you officially, but feel free to pick away at my brains off the record. What can I tell you?'

'I'm clutching at straws really. What about the forensics on the children's bodies? Is there anything there I should know?'

'Nothing that didn't go in the official reports. All killed at roughly the same time – probably within a few months in 1940, but difficult to be precise. All relatively well-preserved, consistent with them being buried in the fenland. Cause of death difficult to determine, but no obvious signs of any trauma on what's left of the bodies. I'd go for asphyxiation in some form, but that's mainly because there's no sign of any other cause. '

'No clue as to their identities?'

'Not to speak of. There's not much left of the clothes to draw any conclusions from. A couple were wearing what looked like homemade garments. One had fragments of what might have been a school uniform.'

Winterman nodded. All the detail was familiar to him. The apparent presence of the school uniform had excited them briefly, raising the possibility that the remains might be those of the young schoolgirl who had vanished before the war. But to date they had been unable to trace the girl's mother, who had supposedly moved to Lincoln, or any other medical or other records that might help confirm the child's identity. It remained a lead but an increasingly tenuous one. 'Nothing else?'

'Not that I can think of. Perhaps you'll find some other evidence once they get round to excavating the area where the bodies were found.' There was a wry edge to Pyke's voice.

Although the flooding had now largely receded, Winterman had detected no obvious enthusiasm among senior officers for further investigation of the area, even though there might be scope for finding additional evidence. Or for that matter more bodies.

'What about Fisher's body?' For the moment, Winterman left the question of Merriman's body, conscious he was still unsure about Pyke's emotional state. In any case, Pyke had not been involved in the autopsy though Winterman had little doubt that he would have examined the report.

'Nothing you don't know. It's the same as Howard's,' Pyke said, answering the unspoken question. 'Stabbed. In both cases, the murder weapon was apparently obtained at the scene and then left there. Nothing inconsistent with the suggestion that Hoxton was the murderer, though nothing much to confirm it either. No useful forensic evidence. No fingerprints on the murder weapon or around the crime scenes, other than the victims. And young Callaghan's, in Fisher's case. Plenty of Hoxton's around both houses, of course, but nothing inconsistent with his being part of the investigating team.'

'Overall then, not a bean?'

'You've pretty much got the size of it. Incidentally, I'm dying of thirst, hot day like this.'

Winterman took the hint and fetched two more pints of bitter. When he returned, he found Pyke aimlessly doodling on a notepad, his pencil inscribing endless concentric circles. Pyke looked up as Winterman placed the brimming glasses on the rough surface of the table. 'So what is it you're looking for exactly?'

'I told you, I'm clutching at straws. But I'm looking for something concrete. Like you, I don't believe this was all about Hoxton. He was a nasty piece of work, but he was just–'

'A fixer?'

'Something like that. He was there to do the dirty work and perhaps he satisfied his own… inclinations along the way. But there's more behind this.'

'A grand conspiracy?'

'Anything but grand, I'd say. But something.'

Pyke had begun to draw radial lines across the circles, creating something that resembled a target. 'I don't doubt you're right, old chum, but you were warned off, just as I was. Even if that was just Spooner protecting his backside, it suggests this goes some way up the line. You can't go tilting at windmills on your own. Not unless you've got something pretty solid.'

'That's why I need evidence. What about Howard's effects? Is there likely to be anything there?'

'In my capacity as executor,' Pyke said, with mock pomposity, 'I've been through everything. All the papers, all the documents. If Howard really was involved in blackmail, he kept it well concealed. Mind you–'

Winterman looked up from his beer. 'Yes?'

'Your chaps did a thorough job of searching his house themselves, long before I got hold of the paperwork. Looking for evidence.'

'Our chaps? You mean Spooner's people?'

'I assumed so. This was after it all blew up. I had the call from Howard's solicitors to say I'd inherited the bulk of the estate, and his will had appointed me as executor. But I was also told I couldn't get access to the house for a few days as the police were checking it for evidence.'

Winterman frowned. 'We had the crime scene people in there, and then a couple of Spooner's people checked the rest of the house. But that was immediately after you reported the murder. It would have been a fairly thorough search in case there was anything that shed light on the killing. But it wouldn't have taken days.'

'This was after that. The next week probably. It was four or five days before I got the green light to go in.'

'What state was the house in? Did it look as if it had been searched?'

'It was immaculate. Howard was a tidy soul, but this would have done him proud. But I had the impression it had been searched very thoroughly. Some of the furniture had been moved and I could see some signs that they'd prised up floorboards.'

'More thorough than anything we'd have needed, I'd have thought. Any sign of anything missing?'

'Not obviously. I knew the place pretty well so I'd have spotted if anything major had been taken. But that doesn't mean a lot.'

'Not if they found something that Howard had been concealing.'

'Exactly.'

'Could Howard have hidden anything anywhere else? A safe deposit box?'

'Of course it's possible. But there's no reference in the will to any safe deposit. I can't think of anywhere else. My guess is that, if there was anything, it was in the house. And that, if there was, it's not there anymore.'

Winterman sat in silence for a moment then, waiting till both he and Pyke had their glasses in their hands, he banged his fist hard down on the table. The wooden frame shook, but no drinks were spilled.

Pyke smiled. 'I'm always impressed at how you keep your anger under control. The question is why you're so angry. Why does this matter to you so much?'

'Smart question, doc. I could give you all the obvious answers. That we're talking about children and, yes, I'm still mourning the death of my own child. There's a lot in that. But not everything. It's also because I came into this job to do something. To do something positive. I'm no saint, God knows. But I did have some vague ideals. That was what got me into trouble the first time. I naively thought other people might care about the same things I did. Turned out most of them didn't. Either they were on the other side or at best they just wanted to keep their noses clean.'

'Welcome to the real world, chum.' Pyke had already polished off the remainder of the second pint. 'Want another?'

'Better not. I've got work to do this afternoon.'

'Real work. Or more of this.'

'You don't think this is real work? I'm just beginning to realise this is all there is. I'd allowed myself to forget that. I was turning into Spooner, going with the current.'

'Whereas now you're swimming upstream? Your funeral, old son. Just don't expect many of us to be swimming alongside.'

'I think I'd worked that out.'

'Which doesn't mean I won't help you. As long as I can keep my own head below the parapet.' Pyke stared expectantly at his empty glass, as though willing it to refill. 'Not that I've helped you much so far. What about Callaghan?'

'Young William? He seems in no condition to contribute much. Some sort of breakdown. He gave us a pretty incoherent account which didn't contradict the official interpretation of events.'

'A breakdown, eh? Funny, I'd heard that's what you had.'

'Seems to be a lot of it about.' Winterman nodded thoughtfully. 'I wonder what medication William's on.'

'I wonder. And I wonder how actively his father's involved in his case.'

'Pretty actively was my impression. He was staying in some private place. I presume his father was paying. You know Callaghan senior?'

'Only by reputation.'

'What sort of reputation?'

'Controversial, let's say. Academically well regarded. Medical research, specialist in bacteriology. One of the pioneers, but a bit of a maverick. He doesn't exactly have a low opinion of himself.' Pyke paused, as though picking his words. 'I don't know the details but there was some sort of stink before the war. He was involved in some hush-hush stuff at Porton Down. Had a falling out with the powers-that-be down there.'

'Porton Down? Chemicals and stuff?'

'Chemicals and germs. Remember Gruinard?'

'The anthrax island? Not one of our more glorious wartime episodes.'

'Bloody cock up from beginning to end. Or, if you're more generous, it turned out anthrax was an even more effective weapon than they'd envisaged. The low point was them trying to burn off the heather to kill off the spores, only to release clouds of deadly bloody gas into the atmosphere. '

'Don't remember that being reported in the press.'

'There was a hell of a lot never made it into the press. And probably never will. Not in our lifetimes anyway.'

'This was what Callaghan was involved in? Germ warfare?'

'Your guess is as good as mine, old son. But he was a bacteriologist, so what was he doing at Porton Down?'

'They were researching germ warfare there before the war?'

'Not officially. It was one of those areas, like gas, we were all supposed to disapprove of. While in reality all the major powers were vying with each other to come up with the most lethal varieties. The way I've been told it, the Germans were a long way ahead of us on the nerve gas front – and thank Christ they didn't take advantage of that. But we held pride of place on the germ front. Not that anyone will ever tell you that officially.'

'What about Callaghan?'

'All I know is what I heard on the academic grapevine at the time. And academia's nearly as good as you lot at closing ranks. There was some big dust-up between him and the authorities at Porton Down. I suspect it was Paul Fildes – sorry, Sir Paul Fildes – the bigwig who led the biological weapon research there during the war. Also a microbiologist – and more eminent even than poor old Professor Callaghan. Don't know what the dust-up was about, but I imagine Fildes emerged victorious. Put Callaghan in his place. Which was back up here.'

'Back to being a big fish in a smaller pond. And you've no clue as to the nature of this dust-up?'

'It's not often that academics want to keep quiet, but when they do you won't get a word out of them. The Porton Down stuff's highly classified anyway. There's not much chance of catching them rinsing out any dirty laundry.'

'I don't suppose it's likely to help me much anyway. I seem to be just hitting dead ends.'

'That's the way it'll be, old chum. If there is some grand conspiracy here, no one's going to be leaving clues lying around for you to stumble across.'

'I'll just have to go digging for them then, won't I?'

'On your head and all that.' Pyke pushed himself slowly to his feet. 'But I'll tell you what. If you're serious, you'll definitely be needing another pint.'

CHAPTER SEVENTY-EIGHT

'We can't go on like this,' Winterman said.

Mrs Sheringham had been pounding away at her typewriter as though her life depended on it. Given the uncertain status of the office, Winterman reflected, it was quite possible that her job might anyway. For the same reasons, their current workload was almost non-existent. Winterman had a suspicion she was simply re-typing old reports but could find no way to ask the question.

She had barely acknowledged his presence in her office, but now she raised her head. 'Sir?'

Winterman pulled up one of the austere metal-framed chairs and sat down opposite her. 'For the moment, there's just you, me and Mary working out of here. Until the powers that be decide what to do, we've got to make the best of it.'

'As you say, Inspector.' She gestured vaguely towards the typewriter, indicating the need to get on with her work.

'I know you probably don't like me, Mrs Sheringham. And I'm sure you don't approve of my relationship with Mary–'

'It's none of my business, Inspector.'

'You probably blame me for everything that's happened here over the past few weeks.'

'On the contrary, Inspector. But it's been a great shock. Especially poor DC Marsh.' Even now, Winterman noticed, she couldn't bring herself to use the young man's Christian name. 'He would have gone a long way.' Her eyes were glistening with tears. Not for the first time, Winterman found himself wondering about the mysterious Mr Sheringham.

'It was a great loss–'

'As for that other one,' she went on, almost spitting out the last word, 'I can't pretend I ever really liked him. But he took us all in. I still can't quite believe it.'

'It's hard to credit.'

She looked at Winterman almost as if seeing him for the first time. 'You know, when we heard you were being posted here, we all assumed you were coming to keep an eye on us. Not just to head up the unit, but to spy on us. It was DC Hoxton who put that idea into our heads. Kept grumbling that HQ didn't trust us, thought we must be up to all kinds of fiddles. That was why they were sending another inspector to keep an eye on us.'

'You had an inspector here before.' Winterman remembered the outdated nameplate on his office door. 'DI Cross.'

'We were bigger in those days. Five or six constables, a couple of sergeants and the inspector. The place went into decline, and we expected they were going to shut us down, transfer us all up to HQ. So it was a surprise to hear they were sending another senior officer down here.'

'I think it was mostly to do with getting me out of their hair. You'll have heard the gossip, I don't doubt.'

She didn't take the trouble to disagree with him on the last point. 'That was what DC Marsh said. But DC Hoxton kept grumbling that there was more to it than that. He said that was why Superintendent Spooner kept sticking his nose in down here. Those were *his* words, you understand.'

'Superintendent Spooner?' Winterman recalled his own surprise at Spooner's informed knowledge about the office and his assumption that Spooner must be close to Mrs Sheringham. 'Did you see a lot of him?'

'Not a *lot*.' Winterman was interested to note that Mrs Sheringham's skin had taken on a colour which, in anyone else, he might have associated with a blush. 'But he had a habit of turning up unexpectedly. And he phones me regularly. Just for a chat and an update, he says. He always used to ask me a lot of questions about the other members of the team. Especially about DC

Hoxton. I suppose the superintendent did have suspicions about what was going on here. DC Hoxton did take a few liberties. With the car, for example. But perhaps the superintendent had some more serious suspicions about DC Hoxton. Perhaps that was why he had you posted down here.'

It was an interesting theory. It had seemed a remarkable coincidence – that it all should have blown up just when Winterman was sent down supposedly out of harm's way. Was it possible that he'd been sent down here for quite the opposite reason? Because Spooner wanted someone to find out what was going on?

Winterman would never know for sure. But it would be typical of Spooner to get someone else to do his dirty work for him, and it made sense of Spooner's odd little speech about who Winterman's friends really were. If it were true, it left Winterman feeling uncomfortably manipulated.

'There's no question Superintendent Spooner has his wits about him.' Looking to change the subject, Winterman gestured towards the typewriter. 'Do you have enough work to be getting on with?'

'Plenty. I was going to have a word with you about these reports.' She pointed to a thin sheaf of papers stacked neatly by the side of the typewriter. 'There are four now. Three from the local constabulary, and one passed down from HQ.'

'Reports?' Winterman reached out and picked up the uppermost typewritten sheet.

'Break-ins. There seem to have been several locally.'

Winterman skimmed quickly through the short report, drafted by one of Brain's counterparts. It was trivial stuff – a burglary in one of the local villages. The intruder had gained access to the rear of an isolated cottage while the owner was away for the night. No obvious damage had been done. The report speculated that the intruder had succeeded in picking an aged lock on the rear door. Only a few low value items had been stolen. The owner had noted a small amount of cash, a few trinkets and ornaments, and some tinned foodstuffs.

Winterman glanced through the remainder of the reports. Similar stories, each a few days and a few miles apart. The last report, prepared by Brain himself, described an apparently identical burglary in a house on the outskirts of Framley. This time, the mode of entry was slightly more puzzling in that there was again no evident damage to the property and the owner had recently fitted modern locks on the exterior doors. Winterman knew from experience, though, that the owners who protested most vocally about the quality of their domestic security were the ones most likely to have forgotten to lock up.

Again, the items stolen were of minimal value. A couple of items of jewellery – which Brain implied had been over-valued by the owner – an overcoat, and, as in the first case, some foodstuffs. Winterman looked up. 'Sounds like some down-and-out. Getting some food and a few bits and pieces he can sell.'

'Or gypsies.' Mrs Sheringham's tone was somewhere beyond disapproval, suggestive of utter bafflement at an alien way of life.

'Sounds more like someone acting alone,' Winterman said, neutrally. 'Have we picked up any reports of anyone unfamiliar in the areas concerned?' It was safe to assume Mrs Sheringham would already have explored these avenues.

'Not really. I spoke to some of the local PCs. There were one or two rumours of strangers but nothing substantive.'

'Do we tend to get many of these kinds of offences locally?' In the town, burglaries were relatively commonplace, but Winterman imagined that out here many people still felt able to leave their doors unlocked.

'Very few. We have a small spate of break-ins a year or so back, but that was a little different.'

Winterman vaguely remembered what Hoxton had told him about Marsh's over-enthusiastic pursuit of the perpetrators. That conversation felt as if it had taken place in another lifetime. 'A little more serious?'

'A little. There were several burglaries at some of the bigger houses in the area. Including Professor Callaghan's if I recall correctly.'

Winterman had little doubt about the efficacy of Mrs Sheringham's powers of recall. 'Professionals?'

'As it turned out, no. We'd assumed it would be. They were stealing some quite valuable items. Ornaments, painting, some jewellery. I remembered Professor Callaghan was particularly exercised because they'd been through his library and had taken one or two rare books. Seemed to know which houses to tackle, and had a good idea which items were most saleable. The experts told us they were likely to be professionals because most of the stolen items weren't things you could dispose of locally.'

'But the experts were wrong?'

Her expression indicated that particular outcome was far from unexpected. 'Apparently. We'd almost given up and handed the case back to HQ. If they were professionals, they weren't likely to be based locally. But DC Marsh had some sort of hunch it was a local matter after all. His view was that the selection of the victims suggested local knowledge. For the most part, they weren't particularly wealthy people. Better off that the average but not exactly rolling in money. DC Marsh thought that even if the burglars themselves were from outside the area, they were obtaining information from someone local. He kept pursuing it, even when we'd more or less given up officially.'

'And he was successful?'

'In the end. He was persistent, and finally he picked up a tip-off from one of his informants. It turned out to be two youths from one of the neighbouring villages. You know the type. They'd been in and out of trouble for petty crimes. I suppose they'd become a little too ambitious. Anyway, we raided their houses – their parents' houses, in fact – and found several of the stolen items hidden in one of them.'

'Did they admit the burglaries?'

'Denied all knowledge. Even claimed they had no idea how the stolen items had found their way into the house. Didn't even have the nous to come up with a plausible story.'

'They were found guilty?'

'One of them was – the one found with the stolen goods. He's still locked away. It was his third or fourth conviction for theft, and by far the most serious. The other one was acquitted in the end.' She spoke with some disdain. 'His accomplice refused to implicate him and the evidence of his involvement was only circumstantial.'

'That's very interesting. You know, Mrs Sheringham, I think we could make a very effective team.'

For a moment, Winterman thought she smiled in response. A second later, she had returned to her typing with a dismissive nod of her head, and he was left unsure whether it had been anything more than his imagination.

CHAPTER SEVENTY-NINE

'I can't believe it,' Mrs Griffiths said. 'After all that's happened–'

Brain shuffled awkwardly across the kitchen floor, struggling as always to find the right words. 'This is nothing, really, Mrs Griffiths. It could have been much worse.' He closed his mouth, recognising from her expression that his attempt at empathy had been typically clumsy. He had been only a word or two from telling her she had been lucky.

'I know I'm making a fuss about nothing, Bryan. But it feels like the final straw.'

'I didn't mean–' *Oh, shut up*, Brain told himself. *Just get on with the practicalities. That's what you're good at.* 'I just meant we can get this fixed very quickly. I'll get Bob Pritchard to come and look at it later if he's free. He does all the joinery down at the station.'

Mrs Griffiths peered at the bolt, which had been torn physically from the back door of the house. 'Is it likely to be expensive?'

'I've given Bob plenty of business over the years. This won't take him five minutes. He'll do it for free, I'm sure.' Brain wasn't at all sure but he had already decided that if necessary he would pay for the repair out of his own pocket. 'You didn't hear anything?'

'No. I'm surprised because I'm not a heavy sleeper. But my bedroom's at the front of the house.'

Brain examined the doorframe with what he hoped resembled an expert eye. 'From those scratches, it looks like it was done with a crowbar. If he did it slowly, it probably wouldn't make much noise.'

'What about the lock?'

It was a good question. The lock was old and didn't look particularly robust, but it had been opened rather than broken. 'I'd say he picked it.'

'Sounds like a professional then?'

'I wouldn't assume that,' Brain said confidently. He had already discussed the recent spate of break-ins with his colleagues in other areas, and they had concluded that the culprit was likely to be some itinerant down-and-out. 'If it was a professional, he'd probably have been more choosy about what he took.' Brain didn't add that a professional would probably also be more choosy about the houses he broke into. 'You'd have lost some valuables.'

Mrs Griffiths looked sceptical. It occurred to Brain – characteristically just a few seconds too late – that although the missing items weren't valuable, they had undoubtedly cost Mrs Griffiths money she could ill afford. 'I suppose you're right. Mind you, it's a large part of this week's ration down the drain.'

That was true enough as well, Brain thought. The intruder had helped himself to various foodstuffs – a loaf of bread, a piece of cheese, some home-baked biscuits, fruit. 'Have you noticed anything else missing?'

'Not really. I can't swear there's nothing gone because I haven't been through everything yet, but there's nothing obvious.'

'We think it's a vagrant. There've been several break-ins around the area recently, and it's been mainly foodstuffs and odds and ends stolen.'

'Poor soul. I don't approve of this, but you have to feel for someone like that, don't you?'

'I suppose so. There are a lot around. Ex-servicemen, some of them, as well.'

'Makes you ashamed, doesn't it, after everything they did for us. They shouldn't be reduced to this.'

'Times are hard. Though it doesn't justify criminality.' That was the kind of thing, Brain supposed, that a policeman ought to say, though he wasn't entirely sure he believed it. 'Is your Mary back here this evening?' He had understood that Mary had not been in the house the previous night when the break-in had occurred. He knew as well as Mrs Griffiths did where her daughter had spent the night, though he assumed it would be tactless to raise the matter.

'She'll be back soon. I'll feel a lot better when she's here. That's the worst thing about this. The thought that someone else was in the house with me and the kiddies. Even if it is just some poor soul down on his luck.'

'I'm sure that's all it is, Mrs Griffiths. But it's not a nice thought all the same. I imagine we'll catch up with him sooner or later. Either that, or he'll move on.'

Mrs Griffiths turned and looked again at the open back door. Outside, there was the small well-tended garden. Beyond that, the open fenland and the dyke where, weeks before, she had found the tiny child's body.

'Let's hope so, Bryan. Let's hope so.'

CHAPTER EIGHTY

Winterman pulled the Wolseley in to the side of road and gazed out at the large Victorian villa. He was still unsure about the wisdom of what he was doing. He told himself that technically he wasn't disobeying Spooner's orders. Spooner had told him not to bother Hamshaw, but hadn't said anything about Professor Callaghan. On the other hand, Winterman couldn't persuade himself that Spooner would be happy.

He climbed out of the car, adjusted his hat and reached back into the car to pull out his raincoat. It had been sunny earlier but the sky had clouded and was threatening rain.

As he made his way up the short front path to Callaghan's door, it opened to review Callaghan standing inside, wearing his hat and overcoat.

For a moment, Winterman felt he had succeeded in catching the older man off guard. Something in Callaghan's expression suggested Winterman's presence was more than merely unwelcome.

If this were the case, Callaghan recovered quickly enough. 'Inspector. What brings you here? I'm afraid it's not a good time, as you can see.' Winterman suspected the tone would have been much less amicable if Callaghan had not had a ready-made excuse to turn him away.

'I'm sorry, sir. I won't delay you more than a moment.'

'I'm afraid you won't delay me even for that, Inspector. I'm really in rather a hurry.' Callaghan was already moving past him.

'Of course, sir. I just wanted to speak to you about some break-ins that have been reported.'

It was a half-hearted attempt to delay Callaghan's progress – Winterman had concluded the chances of doing so were minimal

– but, to Winterman surprise, Callaghan stopped and turned, a frown on his face. 'Break-ins, Inspector?'

'Yes, sir. We've had several in the area over the last week or so.'

'Really, Inspector? What does this have to do with me?'

It was a good question. Winterman decided to follow his intuition. 'You haven't experienced any incidents of that kind yourself, sir?'

There was a pause before Callaghan responded. It was only momentary but long enough to give Winterman the true answer to his question. He could sense Callaghan weighing up precisely what information Winterman might have.

'Not in the last week, Inspector. I must say, much as I appreciate your concern, this does seem a highly individualistic approach to policing. Are you proposing to speak to every local citizen?'

Winterman smiled. He now knew two things. First, that Callaghan had indeed suffered a break-in. Second, and much more interesting, that he was prepared to lie about it.

'Am I correct in thinking you did suffer a burglary a year or so ago, sir?'

'I'm sure you've consulted your files, Inspector. I can't recall exactly when it was, but yes, I was burgled.'

'Just over a year ago.'

'I don't pretend to understand the significance of this, Inspector, though no doubt you have your motives for accosting me in this way. Are you suggesting this burglary a year ago is somehow connected with the current spate of break-ins?'

'I'm just checking up on some facts, sir.'

'What kind of facts, Inspector? You'll find that the perpetrator of my particular burglary is safely behind bars.'

'So I understand, sir. I also understand that there was a suggestion he might not have acted alone.'

Callaghan blinked, clearly disconcerted by Winterman's level of knowledge. 'As I'm sure you're aware, Inspector, an accomplice was charged but acquitted because of lack of evidence. That might have been avoided if your colleagues had prepared their case more effectively.'

Winterman recalled that the colleague in question had been Paul Marsh. Callaghan obviously had few qualms about speaking ill of the dead.

'Can I ask what was taken in the burglary, sir. I understand there were some books and papers?' When in doubt, Winterman thought, follow your gut. It may not always bring you to your preferred destination, but it gives you an interesting journey.

There was another, almost imperceptible hesitation. 'There was some disruption in my study, if that's what you mean, Inspector. But I fear the burglar – or, as you say, burglars – were rather out of their depth. Some old books were stolen, but only one or two rather ostentatiously bound affairs. Far from the most valuable items in my collection, I'm pleased to say.'

'And papers, sir?'

'Not as far as I could tell, Inspector. I don't recall reporting any missing. Of course, it's possible that something might have been removed from the files but if so it couldn't have been anything of significance or I would have noticed its absence.'

Almost a denial, but not quite. Enough space to allow Callaghan some quick footwork if, for example, it were to turn out that Winterman had tracked down some missing document.

'I'm sure that's right, sir. It would be an odd thing to steal in any case, wouldn't you say, sir?'

'Quite so, Inspector. Which is one reason why I fail to understand the purpose of this conversation. As I said, I am in rather a hurry, so if we've finished…?'

'I think so, sir. I'm very grateful for your assistance.'

'I'm gratified you've found our conversation useful, Inspector.' Callaghan was turning away when Winterman spoke again.

'I don't want to detain you any further, sir. I wonder if you'd mind if I had a look around the exterior of your house? I can walk round by myself.'

There was another longer pause, as Callaghan turned back towards Winterman. 'Whatever for, Inspector?'

'Just to check your security, sir. We'd always much rather help prevent crimes if we can. If I have a look at your doors and windows, I can advise you how to reduce the risk of any further break-ins.'

'I'm very grateful for the offer, Inspector. But I'm afraid that's not possible.'

'Sir?'

'The gates to the rear of the house are locked. I don't have time to fetch the keys.'

'That's a shame, sir. Another time perhaps?'

'Another time certainly, Inspector. But now I must be going.'

Before Winterman could say more, Callaghan walked briskly down the path. Winterman lingered briefly by the house, noting that Callaghan glanced back as he made his way to his parked car. Winterman smiled in return, and walked slowly over to the Wolseley.

He was tempted to wait until Callaghan had gone so he could check the rear of the house. He had little doubt he would find some evidence of a break-in. The question was why Callaghan preferred to keep that evidence to himself.

That, at least, was one of the questions. There were plenty of others. Such as why Callaghan had seemed so uncomfortable in discussing the earlier burglary. Or why he was prepared to lie, not just about the recent break-in but also about what had been stolen by the previous intruder.

But the biggest question of all, Winterman thought, was quite who or what it was that had made Callaghan so transparently, nakedly afraid.

CHAPTER EIGHTY-ONE

'That should do it,' Winterman said. 'For tonight at least. But I think your mother should get a better lock fitted.' He leaned back to inspect his handiwork. He had rescrewed the bolt onto Mrs Griffiths' rear door, further down the frame from where the screws had been ripped from the wood. 'Probably Brain's chap can do that for you if he could get here tomorrow.'

Despite Brain's promises, the joiner had been tied up finishing a job at the other end of the county. Mary had arrived back in the late morning to find her mother pacing up and down the kitchen, wondering how to deal with the broken door. Mary in her turn had walked down to the station to call Winterman.

'Can you come over after work? Mam's in a real state. I feel partly responsible, given I was away last night.'

'No problem. Do you want me to stay over?'

'That would be a help. We won't be able to get the door properly secured until tomorrow. It would reassure Mam if you were around.' She had paused, a faint smile on her face. 'Spare room though, love. What with Mam and the kids and everything.'

'I assumed so. One day it'll be different.'

'I'm holding you to that.'

On his arrival, he had examined the back door. The main lock was old and hardly of the finest quality, but to Winterman's limited knowledge it looked to have been picked with some expertise. There had been nothing the intruder could do about the interior bolt, so his solution had been to prise open the door with a crowbar, ripping the bolt from its fixings in the process.

But, Winterman asked himself, what sort of vagrant carries a crowbar?

'Do you keep any tools outside? In the coalhouse or anywhere?'

Mary looked at him curiously. 'Not that I'm aware of. We've got a toolbox with a few bits and pieces inside.'

'What about garden implements?' It was possible that the door had been levered open with a spade, although the marks on the doorframe suggested otherwise.

'We've got a few things, but Mam keeps them in the cupboard over there.' Mary gestured towards a cupboard in the pantry leading off the kitchen. 'She thinks they'll go rusty outside.'

Winterman peered out into the garden. The earlier sunshine was long gone, and the rain looked set in for the evening. It was a fine rain, different in quality from the torrential downpour that had brought floods weeks before, but sufficient to invoke a note of unease in Winterman's mind.

'I wonder why he picked on us,' Mary said from behind him.

She had moved to stand next to him, and they both let the cool damp air drift across their faces. Definitely spring rain, he thought. 'Just your bad luck, I imagine. Could have chosen any house.'

'He might have got richer pickings elsewhere.'

'Can't be much of a life, whoever he is. We've ended up with too many in that position. Wasn't quite what we expected from the great landslide victory, was it?'

'You're almost making me feel sorry for him.'

'I do, really. You can't condone him stealing, but no one should have to steal to live.' He placed an arm around her waist. 'Your mam doesn't have to worry. He won't come back. He'll be off to steal from someone else now.'

'I know. And it's not as if we've anything worth stealing in the first place. But you can't blame Mam. She was all alone here with the kids last night. Must have been an unnerving thought, someone rooting around in here.'

Winterman nodded then, as if in response to her words, led them back into the kitchen, slamming and bolting the door behind them. For all his reassuring words, his unease had not diminished. Something was still out there, and the rain was still coming down.

CHAPTER EIGHTY-TWO

There was a little whisky left in the bottle from the night before the flooding, so Brain treated himself to a nightcap. It had taken him a while to come to terms with the events of the past weeks. He was a straightforward individual. Far from stupid, as Winterman and others had come to recognise, but lacking in guile. People often said there was no side to him. What you saw was, to all intents and purposes, what you got.

He had therefore been even more shocked than most to discover the truth about Hoxton. It was odd to think he had entertained Hoxton in this very house, sharing his hospitality and this same bottle of whisky with no inkling of Hoxton's true character.

Then there was DC Marsh. He had respected Marsh – he was the kind of policeman Brain aspired to be – even if he hadn't fully warmed to him. A tad too serious, a little too obsessive about his work. Brain had never learned the full story, but he understood it had been precisely that compulsive desire to uncover the truth that had resulted in Marsh's death.

Brain longed to be a detective. He had thought Winterman had begun to respect him, and he had hoped he might draw on Winterman's patronage to move out of this uniformed rut into the investigative role he craved. But nothing had happened. Once the Hoxton case was put to bed, Brain had found himself back in the village, tramping his circumscribed beat, dealing with down and outs who stole nothing more exciting than a loaf of bread.

He looked at the clock. Nearly eleven. Well past his usual bedtime. He had been listening to a play on the wireless, and then, half asleep in his chair, had become caught up in his own reverie.

He dragged himself to his feet, contemplated the empty whisky bottle, and wondered about a cup of cocoa before bed.

It took him a moment to realise he had been roused from his semi-comatose state by the shrill ringing of the telephone. Rubbing his eyes, he stumbled, still not completely alert, into the police office. 'Yes? Police.'

'For God's sake, man, where've you been? Can you get out here?'

'What?' For a second Brain wondered whether he had somehow contrived to miss the opening of this dialogue. 'Who is this?'

'It's George Callaghan, man. I need you out here.'

'Professor Callaghan? What seems to be the trouble, sir?' He would never have recognised the old man. He had rarely heard him sounding anything other than urbane and rather superior.

'Oh, for God's sake, man. There's someone outside prowling around.'

'Who's outside, sir? We've had a few break-ins lately, but we've no reason to think the perpetrator is in any way dangerous–'

'He's in the garden. I know he's tried to break in already. Just get over here, Constable. Get some backup if you can.'

There was silence, and Brain realised the line had gone dead. He pressed down the contacts on the telephone and listened. There was nothing wrong with his own line. It was Callaghan's connection that had been cut.

Brain straightened up, still staring at the phone. He had no option, he realised. He had to go out to Callaghan's house. Most likely, it was all a fuss about nothing. But Callaghan was not someone to panic without a reason. It was difficult to imagine the old man being unnerved by some vagrant in his garden.

Brain pulled on his boots and his overcoat. He had half-hoped that the rain might have stopped, but it was coming down harder than ever. He had intended to cycle over to Callaghan's but the rain and his own increasing nervousness prompted another idea. Callaghan had advised him to get some backup. He knew from Mary's visit earlier that Winterman was staying over at Mrs Griffiths' house that night.

Past eleven. Was it too late to disturb Winterman? Brain told himself that he had to take Callaghan's call seriously. He was sure – he was almost sure – Winterman would feel the same.

CHAPTER EIGHTY-THREE

Like Brain, Winterman had also stayed up longer than he had intended. Mrs Griffiths had retired early, and he had spent the evening with Mary, discussing possibilities for their joint future, reaching no firm conclusions. Winterman felt pinioned by the past, desperate for another future to begin but unable to see how he could make it happen.

He was due for another trip to London the coming weekend, the first since he had moved back out here. He would make his usual dutiful visit to Gwyneth, to the hospital where she was being cared for, where, as always, she would fail to recognise him or know he had been. Then he would catch a bus up to the North London cemetery where Sam was buried. It somehow seemed a fitting place – overgrown, filled with decaying Victorian Gothic, a small enclave of calm and birdsong in the middle of the bustling city. He would sit there for a while. Finally he would get another bus back to Liverpool Street, and begin the long journey home.

After Mary had gone upstairs, he had sat for another hour or so in the cramped sitting room, feeling in need of a drink but knowing there would be nothing in the house. He told himself he was thinking, mulling over the options, but he knew his mind was blank. There were no options.

He was about to retire to bed himself, resigned to the spartan anonymity of the small spare room, where he heard the gentle knocking at the front door. Baffled as to who might be calling at that time, he made his way into the hallway to open the front door.

'Sir.' It was Brain, as enthusiastic and indefatigable as ever. 'I didn't want to knock too loudly in case you'd gone to bed.'

It took Winterman a moment to process the statement. 'So why knock at all?'

'I think I might need your help, sir. But I didn't want to wake you if you'd already gone to bed.'

'No, quite right.' Winterman was still not fully taking this in. 'Help with what?'

Brain quickly explained about the call from Callaghan. He had half-expected that Winterman would dismiss the matter, but in fact Winterman seemed to take it more seriously than Brain himself.

'The call was cut off? Callaghan put the phone down?'

'He might have done. But it was very sudden. I hadn't realised he'd gone at first.'

Winterman was pulling on his boots. He peered past Brain through the open door. 'Rain's not stopped?'

'Harder than ever.'

Moments later, they were in the Wolseley heading up towards the north end of the village, past the cottage where the first child's body had been found, past Fisher's empty cottage. They turned left, the road running alongside the railway line for half a mile past a row of railway cottages, then into the more salubrious area of Victorian and Edwardian villas.

Callaghan's house, tucked behind its garden walls and neatly trimmed hedges, showed no sign of disturbance. Lights were burning in several downstairs rooms.

'I hope it wasn't some kind of joke.' Brain followed Winterman up the path to the front door. The rain was coming down even harder. They were both bent double against the wind-swept downpour.

'Does Callaghan strike you as the type to make jokes?' Winterman reached the front door and, in one movement, pressed hard on the bell and, with his other hand, slammed the knocker down against the door.

There was no reply. Winterman pressed his ear to the door's panelling in the hope of detecting some movement within. He looked back at Brain and shook his head before pounding the knocker even harder against the wood. He tried the door handle, but the door was, as he had assumed, firmly locked.

'We'll never get this open. Looks like oak. Let's try round the back.'

Brain nodded, impressed at Winterman's decisiveness. He did not appear to be worrying, as Brain himself would have done, about the possibility that they might shortly be faced by an irate Professor Callaghan disturbed from his slumbers.

Winterman opened the wooden gate that led to the back garden. He noted, without surprise, that despite Callaghan's earlier claims there was no lock on the gate.

As soon as they entered the garden, Winterman knew something was wrong. Light spilled out on the neatly trimmed lawn through a pair of French windows standing wide open to the rainy night. He moved till he was standing directly opposite the open doors, keeping well back from the cone of light in case of any danger from within.

He could see an ornately decorated reception room. Not the room in which Winterman and Hoxton had first interviewed Callaghan, but similar in its style and anonymity. At first, Winterman thought the room was empty. Then, stepping forward, he saw a figure spread-eagled on the floor.

He moved cautiously towards the open windows, alert for any movement from within. There was nothing except for the ceaseless beating of the rain. Winterman gestured for Brain to join him and stepped carefully over the threshold.

The windows had been open for a while, and the carpet and parquet floor inside were soaked from the rain. The room itself was immaculately tidy and showed little sign of recent human habitation.

Except for the body.

Callaghan was spread face down across the carpet in front of the sofa. A pool of blood was expanding from beneath his head, staining the edge of the carpet deep red. There was a bullet wound in Callaghan's temple, a further splashing of blood across the base of the sofa. Winterman had little doubt he was dead.

'Try not to touch anything,' he said to Brain. 'You stay here.'

Brain looked apprehensively behind him at the dark garden. 'You think whoever killed him might be still be here?'

'That rather depends on who killed him.' He pointed towards Callaghan's right hand. A revolver lay on the wooden floor, its position suggesting it had slipped from his fingers.

'You think he killed himself? But what about the intruder?'

Winterman shrugged and stepped cautiously across the room, taking care to disturb nothing. He gestured for Brain to stay where he was.

Winterman slipped on one of his pairs of fine cotton gloves, and, taking care not to obscure any fingerprints that might be on the door handle, he eased open the door into the hallway beyond. The light was on in the hall, and Winterman could see that the front door at the far end was firmly bolted. It took him only a moment to check the other ground floor rooms – the reception room where he had previously met Callaghan, another drawing room, a study, a cloakroom and a kitchen. There was no sign of anyone else.

The telephone was on a table by the front door. He lifted the receiver and confirmed it was still connected. He had assumed Callaghan's call to Brain had been terminated by the line being cut but it appeared not. He dialled the operator and asked to be connected to Police HQ. It took him a few moments to explain the situation to the duty office.

'Get a team out here as quickly as you can. And make sure you inform DS Spooner,' he added, unsure even as he spoke quite why he felt it was so important for Spooner to be told straightaway. Not for the first time, his instincts were jumping ahead of his rational mind.

He replaced the receiver and ran up the stairs to check the bedrooms on the first floor. One was clearly Callaghan's own, another presumably used by the still-hospitalised William. Three more were apparently unused, alongside a bathroom and separate lavatory. All were empty.

It was only a cursory examination, and Winterman supposed that someone might conceivably still be concealed about the house. But he felt a strong conviction that, other than himself and Brain, there was no living soul there. If an intruder had indeed been in the house, he must have left through the window through which the two police officers had entered.

Winterman's unease was growing. He had a sense – which he realised had been there since Brain had first described the call from Callaghan – that they were being played. That this was some kind of endgame, even though he had no idea even what kind of match had been played.

'I've checked the house,' he told Brain. 'There's no one inside. And I've called HQ. They're sending support straightaway. You wait here till they get here.'

It took Brain a second to register the significance of what Winterman had said. 'You're not staying here, sir?' He glanced once again out at the garden, clearly contemplating the implications of staying in the house by himself.

'You'll be fine, Brain.' Winterman's mind was already elsewhere. 'The others will be here before you know it.'

'But where are you going, sir?'

'There's something I need to check.' Winterman was already moving towards the open window.

'Can't you wait till the others get here, sir?' There was a note of pleading in Brain's voice, though he was doing his best to conceal it.

Winterman looked back for a last time before stepping out into the wet night. 'I'm sorry. But I don't think I can take the risk.'

CHAPTER EIGHTY-FOUR

Winterman drove back into the village, conscious he was driving too fast on the wet roads, and pulled to a skidding halt outside Mrs Griffith's cottage. The only lights were those he had left burning in the hallway and front room. It occurred to him, initially with a touch of irritation, that he had not remembered to bring a door key out with him. He would have to wake Mary or her mother to get back into the house.

Then it struck him he also had no recollection of securing the back door of the house before leaving. That thought sucked the breath from his lungs.

He jumped out into the rain. It was coming down even harder, sweeping coldly in from the fens. He pulled his hat low over his forehead and hurried into the garden, heading for the rear of the house.

As he turned the final corner, he stopped. The back door was wide open to the night and the rain.

It had been closed when he left, he was sure. Perhaps Mary or her mother had come downstairs for some reason, had peered out into the rain. But the kitchen was in darkness.

Winterman stepped forward. He felt in his pocket for the small police torch he always kept in his overcoat. As he reached the door, he banged it wide open, flashing the torch beam around the kitchen, trying to ensure that anyone inside would be disadvantaged by the sudden light.

'Out here, guv.' The voice came from behind him, only just loud enough to be heard above the rain. 'You were quicker than I expected. Should never underestimate you, should I?'

Winterman turned, aiming the torch into the rain.

Hoxton was dressed in a filthy torn cycle cape, a flat cap pulled low over his eyes. He held out his hands to demonstrate that he wasn't armed.

'We best go in out of the rain,' Hoxton went on. 'I've a few things to tell you.'

For a moment, Winterman contemplated seizing Hoxton by force. But he knew he had to play out the scene, see where it would lead. He nodded and followed Hoxton into the kitchen. Hoxton was already closing the internal door into the hallway. Winterman switched on the light, momentarily dazzled by the glare. 'If you've touched–'

'Everyone's safe. For the moment. I just want to talk.' Hoxton lowered himself to sit at the kitchen table. There was a waterproof canvas bag on the table in front of him.

Winterman dragged out a chair and positioned himself opposite Hoxton. 'Everyone assumed you were dead.'

'I nearly was. I'm not a swimmer. While you were dealing with the boy, I was caught by some sort of undertow. Dragged me off downstream. I thought I was a goner, but I got thrown ashore half a mile or so outside the village. Even then, I should probably have died but I'm a tough old bugger.'

'Where've you been since then?'

'Living rough, round and about. Stole some clothes. Stole enough to live on. Came back here.'

'Why come back? You could have made the perfect escape.'

'I still will. But I had to finish things off first. Get what I was owed.'

'Who owes you anything, Hoxton?'

Hoxton seemed to be looking straight through him. 'I imagine I've become the scapegoat for all this? For everything?'

'You're a killer, Hoxton. Why wouldn't you be the scapegoat?'

'Don't be too hard, guv. I'm not a saint. But I'm just small fry. I was always going to take the fall if anything went wrong. But they should have paid me for it. That was the deal.'

'Who should?' Winterman was beginning to weigh up his options, wondering how he could detain Hoxton.

'All of them. Callaghan. Hamshaw. The rest.' Hoxton pushed forward the canvas bag across the table top as if it contained the explanation for his presence.

'You're making no sense, Hoxton. I'm placing you under arrest for the murders of–'

Hoxton held up his hand. 'Can if you like, guv. Won't make no difference. Better if you listen to what I've got to say first.'

'Five minutes. Then I'm taking you in.'

'They welshed on the deal. Callaghan and Hamshaw. They shouldn't have done that. I kept my side. Couldn't even get back to the little stash I'd tucked away at home. There was enough cash there to tide me over. But the floods had cut it off. You lot'll have claimed that by now.'

Winterman said nothing. As far as he could recall, there had been no mention of any cash being found at Hoxton's house. Someone's pocket had been lined, Winterman had no doubt.

'What is it you're saying? That this is all some grand conspiracy?'

'Not very grand. But yes, something of a conspiracy. You must have already worked that out, guv, smart bugger like you.'

'I thought it was just you. George Hoxton. Child molester.'

'That's how they've got me labelled, is it?'

'You've got a conviction. Or least Gerald Horton has. Sexual assault on an underage girl.'

'You have been busy. Don't suppose it mentioned she was a streetwalker. Could have been twenty-five, turned out to be fifteen. Wasn't that long ago it would have been legal.'

Winterman's expression showed his distaste. 'It was assault.'

'She tried to steal my wallet. I tried to stop her, and she cried rape. Then let on she was only fifteen. Serve me right for being wet behind the ears. It doesn't make me a kiddie fiddler.'

'What about these bodies then? You're saying that wasn't you?'

'Aye, that was me. Finished 'em off, any road. Some might have said it was a blessing by then.' Hoxton was speaking as if this was something he had to say, something he had to get off his chest. 'I'm not proud of it, any of it. But I was just doing a job. Just doing what I was paid for.'

It was a mantra Hoxton kept repeating, Winterman noticed. He wondered how much of Hoxton's mental state had its roots in the First War. Soldiers witnessing and perpetrating atrocities, telling themselves they were just doing a job. 'Tell me,' Winterman said.

'You called me a child molester. It wasn't me though. It was Hamshaw, he was the one who was that way inclined. Him and some of his odd mates. You go check. You'll see Hamshaw's history. Patron of children's homes. You know how some of them places were run. Nobody cared. Nobody cared what Hamshaw and others got up to.'

'Are you saying–?'

'You know what I'm saying, guv. I got into doing dubious errands for Hamshaw's cronies. Some of 'em in the force, as well. That was how it started. Someone found out my record wasn't quite as unblemished as it might have been. Turned the screw a bit, got me doing some of their dirty work. Didn't matter much to me if it brought me in a few extra quid.'

'What sort of errands?' Winterman had half an eye on the canvas bag, noting that Hoxton was keeping his hands firmly across it.

'This was before the war. Some of them in the force were a bit closer than they should have been to some of the big villains. Money changed hands to help keep the right noses clean. You know that, guv, more than most. I helped the money to change hands. In those last days before war broke out, there was all kinds of stuff. Dodgy contracts for supplies. Illegal imports. Black market. Christ knows what it cost the war effort.' He smiled. 'Though it was supposedly all in the name of patriotism. That's what Hamshaw always said.'

'What about Callaghan? Where does he fit into this?'

'I feel almost sorry for Callaghan, truth be told. He was probably the only half-decent one among them. At least he really believed all the patriotism guff.'

'I heard he was involved in germ warfare. Had some falling out with the bigwigs at Porton Down.'

'That smart brain of yours again, guv. It'll get you into trouble. You heard right. This was all hush-hush, the way it was told to me. But there were things going on even before the war that nobody'll ever talk about. Experiments with gases. Far worse than that bastard stuff we faced last time around. And experiments with germs. All kinds of stuff. Even the plague, I heard, if you can believe that.'

'Callaghan was involved in some of that?'

'That's what I heard. And what I heard was that Callaghan was less squeamish than most. That he'd started testing some of his products out on real people. That was what led to the bust-up. He'd gone further than some of his colleagues felt was quite proper. Usual bloody story. These bigwigs don't care what happens as long as they can keep their hands clean. Callaghan thought they were just being hypocrites.'

'You're saying that Callaghan continued his work up here? On human guinea pigs?'

'Callaghan wasn't one to take no for an answer. He wanted to be proved right. With Hamshaw's help, he could get hold of the right – material. At first, children from the homes. Then, after the war started, evacuees. Kids who were already lost in the system.' Hoxton paused for a moment, his eyes blank. 'You should ask your friend Dr Pyke what else was wrong with them poor little kiddies that turned up. But Pyke's another one who's been encouraged to turn a blind eye.'

'Pyke?'

'I don't know for sure, of course. I was just a humble servant. But I know what was wrong with some of those kids, and none of it showed up in Pyke's reports. Yes, the poor little buggers were suffocated in the end. I know that because I did some of them myself. But my job was to put an end to their suffering, not cause it.'

'You can't expect me to believe this.'

'Frankly, guv, I don't much mind what you believe. But it's in your interest to know who your friends are. Nothing much wrong with Pyke, apart from the obvious, but he's another one who's taken his pieces of silver.'

'What about Merriman? Who killed him?'

'You got me bang to rights on that one, guv. I wouldn't want you to think that Pyke was capable of the likes of that. All Pyke's done is kept his mouth shut when it mattered.'

'Pyke thought Merriman was blackmailing someone.'

'Aye, and Pyke had a good reason to think that. Because Pyke was the one who'd let slip what Callaghan had been up to.' He paused, and was smiling again. 'And I was the one who fed Merriman the evidence.'

'You did? Why?'

'I'm no fool, guv, as you've probably noticed. Playing both sides against the middle. When I found out Merriman was trying to put the squeeze on Callaghan, I did a deal with him. Fed him some more concrete evidence in return for half the takings. That's what funded my little personal stash.'

'So why kill him?'

'When things started going belly up, it was my job to get the lid back on. Anyway, I didn't want anyone finding out what I'd been up to with Merriman, did I?'

'And Fisher? He was yours as well?'

'All my own work. Nearly got caught with that one. I got him in the garden, had a cloth with some chloroform on it, nice and discreet. Thought I might even manage to make it look like natural causes. Then young Callaghan turns up, three sheets to the wind. Realises Fisher's dead, but collapses on the couch while I'm still lurking outside in the bloody cold. So I wiped Callaghan's prints all over that knife and stuck it in Fisher's body while he was still just about warm. It put Callaghan in the frame for a bit and help muddy the waters, though I didn't really think anyone would buy Callaghan as a killer. But the reverend was always a risk. I was never sure how much he really knew. I think his wife found out something about Hamshaw and Callaghan's little games when she was living with Callaghan. That was why she tried to go back to Fisher. Didn't want her own children to be anywhere near that world. I don't know how much she told Fisher before he threw her out. But she told him something. All that stuff about the ghosts of children.'

'Perhaps that was exactly what he saw.'

'One way or another, you might be right, guv. They paid him off with that cottage and a nice little pension but he was still a risk. After he found the child's body, he said a few things in his cups that got them worried. I was sent to find out what he knew. Never really did because he saw me in the garden, came at me with that bloody knife. I'd rather not have killed him, but it did the job.' He paused, as though reflecting on this last phrase. 'And I did my job, and those bastards welshed on the deal.'

'So you came back and killed Callaghan tonight?'

Hoxton's expression was impossible to read. 'Callaghan's dead, is he? I can't say I'm very sorry. However he died, I'd say he killed himself, wouldn't you?'

'Not if you pulled that trigger.'

'All a bit academic, anyhow. I'll soon be gone from here. You'll never find me.'

'We've had this discussion before,' Winterman said. 'I can't let you go.'

'Can't see as you've much choice.' Hoxton pushed the canvas bag across the table towards Winterman. 'But if I were you, I'd forget about me. I'm small fry. Concentrate on what's in there.'

Keeping his eyes fixed on Hoxton, Winterman slowly opened the bag. Inside where two large ring-bound files, each filled with typewritten papers.

'He was a meticulous man, Professor Callaghan,' Hoxton went on. 'Kept copies of everything. His own form of insurance policy. If he went down, he was going to make sure everyone else went with him. I stole one of his files when I broke into his house last year. I gave a few critical bits to Merriman to help him with his cause. But that was peanuts compared with what's in those files.'

Winterman pulled out one of the files and flicked through its pages. It was a mix of stuff – scientific papers, reports, letters, some yellowing photographs. None of it made any immediate sense to Winterman, but he recognised some of the names mentioned.

'Some interesting names, eh?' Hoxton said. 'One or two you came up against last time you went tilting at windmills. If you try again with that lot in your hands, you'll stand a much better job of knocking them down.'

It was true. Even his cursory glance had told him this was potential dynamite. All his suspicions about corruption had been true, had in fact been only a fraction of the truth.

'I've burned my bridges,' Winterman said. 'No one would believe me, whatever evidence I produced.'

'Go to Spooner. He might surprise you. But do it. You and me and him – we've got different reasons for wanting to bring them down. But we all want to do it. It's all yours.'

That was the issue. Hoxton was offering this as the price of his own freedom. The unspoken deal was that Winterman would take the evidence and turn a blind eye to the self-styled small fry. But Hoxton was a murderer. Whatever his state of mind, whatever his reasons, he was a killer of adults and children alike. Winterman had no right to let him go.

'I can't do it, you know. I can't let you walk free. You can't buy me off with this.'

'Never imagined I could, guv. Seen enough of your scruples to know how they work. That's why I had to make sure it was you got this. Spooner might have the clout to do something with it but he'd never have the balls to stick his head above the parapet alone.'

'So I'm placing you under arrest for–'

'Don't waste your time, guv. I'm going. You can't keep me here.' There was something in his tone Winterman found chilling. 'You got other things to worry about.'

'I told you, Hoxton, if you've touched–'

'I've done nothing. Everyone's safe. For the moment. But you might have been wondering where I was coming from when we found each other in the garden. Grand lad, that young Graham. I reckon he was bloody brave with his mam in that car. Even braver tonight.'

'What the bloody hell have you done with him?'

'He was very co-operative. Hardly awake when I took him from his bed. I brought him down here, got him to put on his wellingtons and took him over the road into the fields.'

'Tell me what you've done with him.'

'I took him across a couple of fields to one of the dykes. Spent a bit of time earlier reconnoitering and found one with some handy tree roots coming in to it. Would you believe I still had my police handcuffs? Meant I could cuff him to the roots at the bottom of the dyke – some water in there already so it's not the most comfortable place. I left him with his head well above water.' Hoxton glanced at the window behind him. 'But in this rain I don't know how long that'll last. Then there's the exposure to worry about. Poor kid was just in his pyjamas.'

'You bastard.' Winterman was already rising from the table.

'I think we already knew that,' Hoxton agreed. 'But always practical. I reckon you've half an hour or so, but I wouldn't waste any time.'

'Tell me where he is.'

'You'll find him,' Hoxton said calmly. 'Two fields out to the south. There's a large tree. He's perhaps ten feet west of the tree. You'll find it even in this weather. If you're quick.'

'You're coming with me.' Winterman reached out to grab Hoxton, but the older man slipped back adroitly.

'I don't think so, old chum. I'm on my way. You try to stop me, you'll just waste more time.' Hoxton rose and, with infuriating calmness, made his way to the kitchen door. 'Good luck.'

Winterman was already pushing past him out into the pouring rain. Hoxton followed him out. This time, wary of what else Hoxton might contemplate, Winterman had taken the key and locked the door from the outside. 'Okay, then,' he said, 'if you're not coming with me, just go. Now. Before I do something we'd both regret.'

'Very wise, guv. I knew you were a smart one.' Hoxton thrust his flat cap back on his head. 'But good luck. I mean that. Good luck with everything.'

CHAPTER EIGHTY-FIVE

It was the same dream. The same dream, yet again. Over and over again.

He could hear the child's voice echoing in his head. A strained voice, caught momentarily on the gusting wind. Calling out. A voice in need. Perhaps in pain. He stood in the back garden, the rain ripping through his clothes, straining his ears, peering into the darkness for some sign.

Then he was rushing out into the lane, jumping across the dyke – the same dyke where the second child's body had been left – stumbling across the uneven, mud-bound field. Peering into the dark for the tree that Hoxton had described. Listening for the voice he knew he must have imagined.

It was slow going on the sodden earth, but he finally reached the end of the first field and scrambled across another dyke, his feet dropping into the chill water. There was more mud, another field. At first he could see nothing. But at last he made out the angular branches of the tree, barely visible against the rain-filled sky. So early in spring the foliage was hardly grown. In the dark, the tree resembled a twisted skeleton, angled against the wind, buffeted by the rain.

After what seemed like an eternity of dragging his feet through the uneven mud-covered terrain, he reached it. The dyke was behind it, wider and deeper than the two he had crossed already. He stumbled along its edge, shining his torch down into the murky water.

The pale face of a child, staring.

'Sam!' He had called out before he could stop himself. Realising, he shouted again. 'Graham! It's me. You're safe now.'

He stumbled down the edge of the dyke, struggling to remain upright on the slippery ground. Then he was beside Graham, who was staring back at him, silent, with terrified eyes. It took Winterman a moment to see where Graham had been tethered to the root. Winterman had no keys to the handcuffs, so he grabbed the thick root in both hands and pulled as hard as he could. He had no knife or other implement to cut the thick strands and for an awful moment he was convinced it would prove too tough for him. But finally, to his relief, the root moved, twisted and then broke in his grip.

Just as he had done in the floods, he gathered Graham into his arms and dragged the child's body out of the dyke towards the rain-soaked ground. Both of them were caked in mud, and the ceaseless downpour rendered the slope back up to the field almost unclimbable. It seemed as if it would be impossible to reach solid ground, but then with a heave he succeeded in lifting Graham on to the bank and was able to scramble up beside him.

Pausing just a second to regain his breath, he lifted Graham again and stumbled slowly back towards the lights of the house. 'You're safe now.'

Graham looked to be unconscious, and he knew he was speaking only to himself. But also, perhaps, Winterman thought, he was speaking to another child who could no longer hear his voice.

CHAPTER EIGHTY-SIX

'The question,' Spooner said, 'is why do you think you can trust me?'

Winterman watched him from across the table. 'You came highly recommended.'

Spooner smiled as though they were sharing some private joke. 'You can, of course. Trust me, I mean. But there's no way you can be sure of it.'

'I'm not sure it much matters.' Winterman waved his hand towards the files on the table between them. 'There's nothing I can do with this on my own. No one would listen. If I can't trust you, there's nobody else. So I don't see I've got much to lose.'

'That's probably true.'

'And there were a couple of other things I began to think about. First, it was you who sent me out to the back of beyond, supposedly to keep me out of mischief. Yet there were some pretty odd things already happening out in Framley. Why send out someone who's got a reputation for stirring up trouble?'

'Just my lousy judgment, I suppose.'

'Must be. Then, after we'd got Hoxton in the frame for everything, you went to a lot of trouble to warn me off.'

'Much good it did me.' Spooner leaned back in his large leather chair. He was toying with an unlit, expensive looking cigar.

'Some might think it was rank bad tactics on your part, given my well-known dislike for being warned off. Counterproductive, even.'

'I take if you've some point other than criticism of my management style?' Spooner put the cigar to his lips, but showed no sign of lighting it.

'Then, just when I'd almost decided not to rock the boat, I receive a set of photographs implying a different kind of threat.'

Spooner raised an eyebrow. 'Really? Did you report this?'

'Not yet. But again, oddly enough, it proved counterproductive. Started me rocking the boat all over again.'

'Glad it's not just me showing bad judgment then. And your point is?'

'That perhaps you're rather good at delegation.'

'Important quality in a manager. Anyway, however it happened, you've uncovered quite a hornet's nest.' Winterman tapped the uppermost file gently. 'This is big stuff, you know. Goes right to the top.'

'Though much of it's unsubstantiated. It depends a lot on Callaghan's word.'

'Even the circumstantial stuff is pretty strong. Perhaps not something that would stand up in a court of law, but it'll never come to that. This is about credibility. There's enough there to force resignations.'

'Up to the chief?'

'Would that please you?'

Winterman considered the question for a moment. 'I don't think he should carry the can just because it happened on his watch. But if he was up to his neck in it as well, then yes.'

Spooner reached into his desk and pulled out an ornate desk lighter. He ritualistically prepared to light the cigar. 'You know, I've been waiting a long time for this. This place has been rotten for years. I've seen good people – people like you – come in and either get turned or crushed. I've seen the buddying that went on between the chief and the likes of Hamshaw. Even during the war, when we should have been pulling together, they were just lining their pockets.' He finally succeeded in lighting the cigar. 'The best you could hope for is that people like me would keep their heads down. I've spent twenty years keeping my head down.'

'What you going to do with the files?'

'I've already shown them to the local MP, the Labour man. He's fully behind it. The way things are going, the Government's only too keen to find any opportunity to rubbish the old lot. He'll get the Labour councillors on our side. It'll happen.'

'I hope so. What about Hoxton?'

'We've put out a nationwide alert. But I'm not hopeful. Hoxton will be pretty adept at disappearing. I suspect he managed to extract a sizeable sum of money from Callaghan. Probably encouraged Callaghan to think he could buy him off.'

'Before killing him.'

'We don't know that for sure. Everything was consistent with suicide. Callaghan's fingerprints on the gun. The angle of the impact.'

'That was Pyke's judgment, was it?'

Spooner blew a cloud of smoke across the room. 'Doctor Pyke didn't reach a definitive judgment. But yes, everything consistent with suicide.'

'And we're supposed to believe Hamshaw committed suicide the same evening? Some coincidence.'

'Perhaps not so much if they both thought the jig was up. It seems likely Hoxton visited both of them with the aim of extorting money. Perhaps they both realised they couldn't keep the lid on this forever.'

'So that's it? Two suicides, a few discreet resignations or early retirements. We're talking about medical experiments on children, child murders, child molestation.'

'It's the best way. It's the only way. The more this is forced out into the open, the more they'll close ranks.'

'And what about you?'

'What about me, old son?'

'This won't do your career any harm, will it. Clear out a few spaces above you. Make a few new friends in high places. All without sticking your head above the parapet.'

Spooner blew another cloud of smoke, this time closer to Winterman's head. He was unsmiling. 'It's an ill wind, lad. And maybe you're right. Maybe I am good at delegating.'

CHAPTER EIGHTY-SEVEN

Mary sleeping on the far side of the bed.

We need to think about the future, Winterman thought. *We need to decide what we're going to do. There must be options. If not divorce, then annulment.* Something that would allow him to get free. It wasn't that he wanted to shirk his responsibilities. He was resigned to caring for Gwyneth. But he wanted a future. A future with Mary.

He didn't even know what his own future held. His first thought after his conversation with Spooner had been to resign. Leave the force, try to breathe some cleaner, less-tainted air.

But where would that be? What else could he do? And whatever he might think of Spooner, one phrase from their conversation had lodged in his mind. Those good people – the good policemen – who had been turned or crushed by the force of the culture around them.

Those were officers like Paul Marsh. Perhaps even officers like Bryan Brain, doggedly doing their bit without thanks or recognition. And officers like Jimmy, Mary's late husband. Winterman had no idea whether Jimmy's death had indeed been an accident – yet another coincidence – or whether he was another who had come a little too close to the truth.

They would probably never know. Just as they'd probably never know whether Gary had really been one of Callaghan's victims, or just another senseless accidental death. But that was the point. All you could do was keep chasing the truth.

Winterman owed it to Jimmy and to Paul Marsh, and to all the others like them, to carry on. Do his bit. Ensure that, whatever else happened, he wasn't turned and he wasn't crushed.

Wide awake, he climbed out of bed and, as so many times before, made his way to the window. The dreams seemed to have stopped. He no longer saw the pale staring face, heard the thin strained voice. No longer endured the ceaseless pounding of the rain. No longer woke with the same empty sense of loss.

The sky outside was clear, reddening with the first signs of dawn over the flat expanse of the fens. Another fine day to come. Behind him, he could hear Mary's calm breathing, content in the depths of undisturbed sleep. Ahead, the landscape stretched out, featureless to the horizon. Winterman stood, his mind for once at rest, waiting patiently for the first bright rays of the sun.

Printed in Great Britain
by Amazon